SECRETS OF THE SEA

Nicholas Shakespeare was born in Worcester in 1957 and grew up in the Far East and Latin America. He is the author of *The Vision of Elena Silves*, winner of the Somerset Maugham and Betty Trask awards, *The High Flyer*, for which he was nominated as one of Granta's Best of Young British Novelists, and *The Dancer Upstairs*, selected by the American Libraries Association as the best novel of 1997 and adapted for the film of the same title directed by John Malkovich. His last book was *In Tasmania*, winner of the 2007 Tasmania Book Prize. He is also the author of an acclaimed biography of Bruce Chatwin.

ALSO BY NICHOLAS SHAKESPEARE

Fiction

The Vision of Elena Silves
The High Flyer
The Dancer Upstairs
Snowleg

Non-Fiction

Bruce Chatwin
In Tasmania

NICHOLAS SHAKESPEARE

Secrets of the Sea

VINTAGE BOOKS
London

Published by Vintage 2008

2 4 6 8 10 9 7 5 3 1

First published in Great Britain by Harvill Secker in 2007

Vintage
Random House, 20 Vauxhall Bridge Road,
London SW1V 2SA

www.vintage-books.co.uk

Addresses for companies within The Random House Group Limited
can be found at: www.randomhouse.co.uk/offices.htm

The Random House Group Limited Reg. No. 954009

A CIP catalogue record for this book
is available from the British Library

ISBN 9780099507772

Printed and bound in Australia by
Griffin Press

To Anne Rood, for introducing me to Dolphin Sands,
and in memory of her husband Trevor (1927–2004)

There is the land-locked valley and the river,
The Western Tiers make distance an emotion,
The gum trees roar in the gale, the poplars shiver
At twilight, the church pines imitate an ocean.

A.D.HOPE

A home is like the sea.

BULGARIAN PROVERB

CONTENTS

PART I

Wellington Point,
February–May 1988

CHAPTER ONE

THE WEEKEND ALEX MET Merridy he had driven to Wellington Point to look for ice-cream sticks in the school rubbish bins.

It was blowing hard when he came out of the playground and he could tell that it was about to rain. Across the narrow lane a movement caught his eye. Two girls helping each other over a high paling fence.

His heart sank.

He knew one of them – Tildy. She was younger than him, nineteen, with a tiny waist and cushiony buttocks and strong, almost manly shoulders. Her hair was dyed blonde, with a severe fringe. From certain angles she looked minx-like. On this afternoon, she wore a familiar tight-fitting green skirt.

It all rushed back – the warm honeysuckle smell of her young-woman's bedroom, the disarray of her bathroom cabinet, his regret. He held tighter to his plastic bag.

She put her bare foot onto the other girl's laced hands, and his attention jolted to the person preparing to lift her up. This one had thick dark hair cut short in a bob. Her lips shone with the same coral gloss as Tildy's, but she looked different.

Before he could slip back the way he had come, Tildy noticed him.

"Hey, Alex . . ." rising up to sit on the fence.

She hauled herself onto the top of it and sat, her legs splayed like a wish-bone, and looked down at him. A grin crept over her face, which under her make-up Alex knew to be freckled.

In the light drizzle that had begun to fall, Alex stood where he was, mortified. Feverish, congested, filthy, this is not how he would have chosen to be seen by anyone. He had spent the morning jetting the sheep for fly, and his coat and jeans were spattered with Pyrethrum.

"Hi, Tildy," in a voice hoarse with flu, and watched her squeeze a narrow foot into the shoe.

Because she was a "blow-in", like himself, Tildy was not one of the girls with whom he had played catch-and-kiss in this lane behind the school. She had grown up in the north of Tasmania, before her father bought the Freycinet Court Hotel two years back. She worked in the canteen at the school.

"Where have you *been*, stranger?"

"I've been crook," he said, concentrating on her foot, trying to keep the image of the little balls of pantyhose at bay, but they were there forever, tangled up with the skin-coloured bra, the Kleenex smudged with lipstick.

She gave him another chance: "Were you coming to see me?"

His joints ached. Even his knuckles hurt as he stifled a cough with the back of his hand. "There was something I needed to get from the school," and raised his head.

She nodded at his plastic bag. "Not stealing my tucker, were you?"

"Of course not."

"What's in your bag, Alex?"

"Just sticks."

"Sticks?"

"Yeah, ice-cream sticks."

"What in heaven's name for?"

The other girl walked a pace or two away.

Alex stepped onto the grass where she had stood. "Listen, Tildy," in a low voice, at once ashamed and contrite. "I'm sorry I haven't rung you."

Tildy flexed her foot, studied the drizzle drops accumulating on the toe of her shoe.

Bedridden, with a streaming cold of the sort that he had learned to catch when he was at school in England, Alex had been able to blot out the memory of their evening together, but now it returned in a cloud of heavy pollen.

"I mean it," he said, and coughed again. "I'm really sorry. I couldn't get out of bed for three days, and there were things I had to do on the farm."

She drummed her heel against the side of the fence. "So you *weren't* coming to see me?"

He shook his head unhappily. "Tildy, I'm sorry."

She looked at his pale face and the plastic bag he was hugging to his chest, and looked away.

On a rotary clothes-line over the fence, a damp shirt dipped in the wind. Her friend waited. Whom Tildy now remembered.

"Get your bum over here, Merridy. Meet this great guy," and to him: "Alex, this is Merridy. We grew up together." Then, possibly to boost her appeal, "She's at uni in Melbourne."

Still, the girl did not turn, but crouched as though she were pulling something from the ground. "Perhaps Ray will get the wrong idea," she said over her shoulder. "Maybe you ought to go on your own."

Her voice was almost a sigh, a coming to the surface of someone who was no longer a childhood friend doing something that children did.

It came to Alex where he had seen her. Pushing a wheelchair with a sick-looking man in it, and walking two steps behind had been a gaunt, middle-aged woman, probably

5

her mother. They were making their solemn procession up the main street.

Despite his fever he could still visibly see Mrs Grogan's expression as she backed out of the chemist's with her poodle in her arms, talking to someone, and tripped into the lap of the invalid.

Tildy glanced sharply down. "I told you, I'm not invited. Hey, Alex, give her a leg-up."

The young woman stood and turned.

About white-throated needletail swifts, his father had told him something that Alex had never forgotten: They spend a third of their life in the air before they nest. In the days and weeks ahead, Alex wondered if this did not define his own trajectory, feeding and sleeping on the wing, and alighting on solid earth on the evening he caught sight of Merridy standing against Ray Grogan's fence. For a long while afterwards he would cleave to the idea that his life, halted at the age of eleven by the accident, began humming again in that moment.

Rain making grey the washing. Tildy in her tight skirt manoeuvring her legs to the far side of the high fence. And the sea of sadness within the face that looked at him, and made Alex in that moment feel tall and alone and – in another remembered phrase of his father's – more useless than a second toe.

Her face grew simpler. "Hello, Alex."

Their glances touched, and now she was assessing him through blue eyes wide apart.

The way they stared. It was how wayward people recognised one another. Whereas on Tildy her lip gloss was part of a riot of colour which harked back to a period of adolescence that Alex would rather forget, this girl's lips had the tinge of the orange lichen on the rock where he went to sit and watch the sea. He turned his eyes from her with

6

huge reluctance, but not for long. He looked up at Tildy, her blonde hair, her gloss, and back to the girl's lips.

Her gaze swam into his and tickled through him and fluttered down.

"Hi, Merridy," he said, and his voice had an unfamiliar note.

She smiled, her expression enigmatic. Already her eyes were pulling away. They did not seek his approval or understanding. She was waiting for someone and it was not him.

"Help her up, Alex," came a tetchy voice from the sky.

The smoke of barbecuing tuna mingled with the aroma of rotting seaweed and the sound of male voices.

"*C'mon.*"

"Right," and cradled his fingers as he had seen Merridy do.

Merridy hesitated. Then slipped off her shoe.

He held his breath, looking away from her knees.

She bent her tanned leg, and rested her rough-textured, rather muddy heel in his knitted palms.

He left them, two girls perched on Ray Grogan's fence. Only when he turned into the main street did it occur to him to wonder why on earth they wanted to be up there.

A minute later Alex climbed into his ute and sat behind the wheel, looking through streaks of rain at the end of the road to the sea and – at the end of the sea – the deep blue line of the horizon. He could still feel the imprint of her heel.

CHAPTER TWO

AT A SMALL, ROUND window – a porthole, really – high above Talbot's store, two eyes observed Alex through a pair of long brass Zeiss binoculars. The brass still had vestiges of camouflage paint on it.

The general store was Wellington Point's largest building as well as the town's main employer, a fortress of brown brick and bluestone that commanded the north end of the street and the jetty. Its proprietor was Albert Talbot, who since his return half a century before from New Guinea, where he had spent nineteen months as a coast-watcher, tracking enemy troop movements day and night from the hills above Blanche Bay, was known to venture downstairs only occasionally, most often for funerals. Otherwise, he sat at the fourth-storey porthole in his eyrie, a tartan blanket across his knees and his mournful eyes presiding over the cricket pitch and golf course, over the waters of the bay beyond, even keeping half an eye on the bowling green.

Mr Talbot was patient for one so spare and strict. From force of habit he made notes of the vessels that arrived at the jetty, of the young men growing up, the girls coming of age. He had no children or wife himself. The few people he regularly spoke to were his manager (who would bring him the gossip and the rumbles); and less frequently his shop-girls, whom he allowed to enjoy the run of the ground floor, but would never invite into his private quarters. Lacking a family, he tended to regard those who shopped at his store as his dependents.

At a desk in what also served as a bedroom, he had a huge skylight above the bed, and watched over by the stars he compiled his weekly *Newsletter*, typing out each word letter by letter – as in the months when he had to send messages over his dry-cell radio set, ten words per minute in Morse code. Talbot's *Newsletter* was distributed free at the tills.

But mainly he looked out at the street – it reminded him of the old coast road through the plantations – and the townspeople, who in certain respects differed not one jot from the light-skinned Kukakuka headhunters, Pygmy tribes and cannibals amongst whom Mr Talbot had once lived.

There was one road into Wellington Point and one road out. On warm days, it smelled of blueberry muffin and chemist's scent and tractor exhaust. To the west a spine of hills stretched inland, coated in dense Crown forest: an avalanche of bluegums, wattle and sassafras that tumbled down the slopes and drew up at the outlying farms. On the east side lay Oyster Bay and the long rocky arm of the Freycinet Peninsula – a ridge of glittering quartzite that had risen from the ocean bed in the Permian era.

"Just how long ago is that, Alex?" Tildy had asked.

"About two hundred and ninety million years."

Wellington Point was one of the smaller towns on Tasmania's southern east coast and belonged to Australia's oldest rural municipality. That it should have come by a reputation as a retirement village was a source of irritation to those like Mr Talbot who remembered when it was a thriving community the same size as Swansea, across the bay. Now the place was virtually a backwater. In tourist promotions of the island, Wellington Point (pop. 327) was routinely omitted from the map while Swansea was unfailingly labelled "the jewel of the East Coast". In Swansea, they looked upon Wellington Point in the same way as mainland Australia looked on Tasmania. Which is to say, they affected not to notice it.

Like its more successful neighbour over the bay, the township of Wellington Point was a promontory of farmers, pensioners and convalescents drawn here – as was Tildy's mother, now dead – by the absence of winter fog and a high daily average sunshine. Fishermen came for the bream and honeymooners for the view of Oyster Bay, which had once been compared to the Bay of Naples. Among the honeymooners whom Mr Talbot had – years ago now – watched get out of their white Ford Zephyr, still hung about with paper streamers, were Alex's parents, Basil and Marjorie Dove.

Basil Dove had had a great-grandfather who fought under Wellington in the Peninsular Wars. This thread of a connection to the peninsula here may have clinched it for Basil in his decision to strike out with his new bride for the east coast on the morning after their marriage in Hobart. In a hotel lounge in Wellington Point, he would learn from a retired English journalist how veterans of the Napoleonic wars had settled this promontory, which was named by a Captain Greer who had survived the whole campaign in the Peninsula and even fought at Waterloo, and who organised his convicts to axe down the thickets of bluegums and native cherry that grew to the water's edge. Whether it was Basil Dove's grey eyes that he boasted could see "for ivver", like his fellow Cumbrian John Peel, or his romantic spirit, Alex's father was instantly able to picture Greer, surrounded by fallen trees and recalling the battlefield where he had forfeited an ear; the dead bodies of the 88th, his regiment of foot, stretching in all directions. The promontory was now a home to the Greer Golf Club.

The site cleared by Greer and its panorama were spectacularly lovely. The sun rose between the Hazards, sparkling across the bay onto Talbot's on clear days, and, at the south end, onto the Freycinet Court Hotel where Alex's parents had spent their honeymoon: yellowish, mock-Tudor, with narrow windows and a courtyard.

In between, on blocks of identical size, were the primary school where Alex had been schooled until the age of eleven, a charity shop, a newsagent-cum-baker, two bed & breakfasts, the chemist's, the Town Hall, the post office, a real-estate office, a nursing home – where Tildy's mother had died eleven months ago now – a bowls club, a Uniting Church and a Wesleyan chapel.

The chapel of Alex's boyhood was today the Bethel Teahouse, owned by Welsh sisters Rhiannon and Myfanwy from Hay-on-Wye. It was, like Talbot's, one of very few buildings in Wellington Point that did not sit with its back to the bay. There, from a counter at one of the Gothic-shaped windows, Alex could watch the jetty and listen to the log-trucks slapping on their brakes as they approached the school.

CHAPTER THREE

JAZZ SOCIAL
The Louisa Meredith Nursing Home invites you along to
a night of entertainment with the well-known Barney
Todman and his steel pedal guitar, playing jazz-style music
from the Thirties through to the Eighties.

Come along and dance the night away or sing along or
just come and listen to the music and have a fun night out
with friends.

Where: The Town Hall
When: Saturday 27 February
Tickets: $17 (includes pre-dinner drink and smorgas-
bord dinner)
Music will start at 7.00 p.m. See you there.

It was another five days before Alex saw Merridy again.
On Tuesday afternoon, he sat in the Bethel Teahouse,
Darjeeling on counter, and flicked through Talbot's
Newsletter. It was late summer and Wellington Point was
having a dance. He thought of who he might invite to the
Jazz Social. The image of Tildy's friend swam into his
mind – the flash of a goldfish under a flat still surface –
but Alex had no idea where she lived, and he could not
very well ask Tildy for her address.

He turned the page.

A warning not to drink the town water. A theft from
the bowls club: still no arrest. The local cricket league
scores. Sergeant Finter, the lumbering policeman in whose

team Alex used to play as a ten-year-old, had scored fifty-four against Swansea. And a poem by Agnes who ran the Op-Shop, a sterilised but nevertheless musty room where Alex had handed over all his parents' clothes.

A white shape went by. He looked up in time to see a van reversing a trailer with quite a nice-looking speedboat towards the jetty. On the side of the van italic letters spelled out *THE LONG HAUL*, and beneath: *Jos. Silkleigh removals*. The van stopped on the ramp and a man in a wetsuit climbed out to unhitch the floating boat, a twenty-foot runabout with a navy-blue hull and trim. He tied her expertly to the jetty. Alex was impressed. It was a cloudless day. The man was going snorkelling. Alex envied him.

He blew on his tea. Beneath Agnes's poem, the next meeting of the Wellington Point reading group: *Mavis Pidd will speak about her recently released autobiography: "A Self-Published Life"*. There was a column on the Summer Flower Show. Mrs Fysshe had taken second prize in the forced rhubarb category. Alex was reading how Harry Ford had won the Betsy Grogan Cup for his assorted chutneys when a face came up to the window.

It was – not immediately, but in lapping ripples – the young woman whom he had helped up onto the fence.

She peered inside. He hoped for a second it was at him, but whoever it was her blue eyes sought she did not see them, and then it became her own reflection that she needed to vet.

He sat very still as she stared at herself, the candid expression of someone who did not know that she was being watched. This afternoon she wore a tortoiseshell comb in her hair, but no lipstick.

Alex was aware of a surge in his chest. Then a voice whisked her round and she was adjusting to an athletic figure who crossed the road at a gallop. Ray Grogan in his brown suit and neat ginger moustache. And – on this particular afternoon – a gold stud in his right ear. Looking at her like a mink about to take a sea trout.

He felt himself rise to his feet as the two of them came inside.

"Hi, Alex," said Ray with a hint of animus, and piloted her to the most distant table.

Alex could not hear their conversation, but he saw that from time to time Merridy shook her head. Ray worked in Tamlyn & Peppiatt on the main street – selling and managing farms far and wide, organising home loans and dealing with holiday rentals – but it was easy to see him on a beach, cutting the throat of a bushranger for the reward while the kookaburras croaked their encouragement. Ray with his glib talk was the only man in town whom Alex categorically disliked.

Then Ray got up and swaggered across the room as if he were in Parliament and not in a teahouse on the east coast, and through the door that led to the toilet outside.

She was staring at the table.

"Hi," he said.

"Hi." Not looking up.

"Alex Dove. I met you the other day."

"I know," in that voice. "You live at Moulting Lagoon." She lifted her head.

"Anything wrong?" he asked.

"Not really."

"Ray doing a Ray?"

"What's a Ray?"

"If you don't know, you're in the middle of it."

She laughed.

"He's sure got the magic touch," Alex said.

She rocked back in her chair. "Oh, come on. Don't wind

me up. He caught me with my guard down. I should have told him to get lost."

"Why don't you?"

"I didn't want to offend him, but there's a certain type of pushy fellow who gets up my nose. I hate feeling passive like that."

"Hi, Mr Dove."

Alex looked around reluctantly.

A boy stood in the centre of the tearoom.

"Rob, if it's your mum you're after, she left ten minutes ago."

The boy went on standing there with a timid expression. "Hey, I just wanted to thank you for the other day. It was tops."

"Glad you had a good time," and explained to Merridy: "Rob came out with his school and watched the sheep being dipped."

"And how to mark them!" raising his leg. Scrawled on his jeans, a faded orange D.

Alex smiled. "You realise what that means, don't you? Now you'll have to work for me. Come again in shearing time and you can write it on a sheep."

When Rob had left, Alex told Merridy how just after Christmas the school's Deputy Head had telephoned him. There had been a falling-out with Jack Fysshe and they were looking for someone to take children in the holidays around a working farm.

Alex had given over a day to Rob's class. He had ridden them each on his tractor. He had lifted them all onto a horse and then shown them how to milk a cow.

She said: "That was kind of you."

"Not really. In England, that's what I was going to be, a teacher," and leaned forward. "What were we talking about?"

"Ray."

"Oh, God . . ." he groaned. "What did he want? What does Ray ever want?" Women somehow did not wish to be attracted to him, but were. By and large, men, of course, found him odious and shallow and vain, but women didn't see that – until it was too late. Merridy, being a little brassier, a little brittler and more consciously tough than most girls in this town, might prove an exception to Ray's motto that a cock could never have too many hens.

"He's invited me to the Jazz Social," Merridy said.

"But you won't go?"

She gazed at Alex and with a slow motion shook her head. But the exasperation might have been aimed at him.

His cheeks boiled. He glanced down at the plastic bag at his feet, containing three bottles retrieved from a bin behind the hotel.

"Would you come out for a meal one night?" he said.

"You mean with you?" Not unkindly, but surprised.

"Right. With me."

She went on sipping at him. It had surprised her less to discover that he had slept with Tildy. At the time when she removed her shoe, she knew nothing about him, but his hands were clearly pleased. "He seems nice," she had said, putting her shoe back on.

"He is. Thoroughly," Tildy had murmured, her interest already shifting to what was happening over the fence. "But it was never going to work out. Even I could see that. I just knew my mother would have really liked him."

Across the table, Alex was smiling. Enjoying her forthright stare.

She thought, looking at him: From the moment I arrived in this place, men have not stopped hitting on me. But Alex's smile inspired confidence. She felt a mysterious sense of relief to see him there. He was tentative and she liked that. And withdrawn. A self-sufficient man but kind, who grazed his cattle and was educated. So Tildy had led her to believe. "He was going on about this ruddy novel. The way he talked about that book, I reckon he'd have preferred to take *it* to bed rather than me!"

Merridy recalled Tildy's indignation and thought of a book she had herself been reading the night before – a reprint on sale in the hotel, written by a Victorian settler to this coast, Louisa Meredith. She had not bought it, but would read a few pages whenever she was not having to help Debbie with the dishes, and it made her tingle with wisdom and unspecified fine feelings. And gentility and uprightness. Everything, in fact, that she had hoped to experience at university.

Yes, I'll come for a meal, under the influence of her book. Is what she meant to say.

"Hey, leave my girl alone!"

She turned her head towards the handsome shouter in his shiny brown tailor's cloth.

"Not your girl, Mr Grogan," she said.

"You don't know what you're missing," replied Ray and glared at Alex. He resumed his place and squeezed her arm with a hand that was large and clean and scrubbed of the blue biro that Alex remembered from the classroom, covered with the correct spellings of English kings and queens and, on one occasion, English trees.

She lowered her head, but did not withdraw her arm.

"Bye, then," said Alex.

"Bye," ordered Ray, clicking his teeth.

Alex looked at them for a moment. He gathered up his bottles and left.

Unable to shake off the sight of Ray Grogan's ginger-freckled fist on Merridy's arm, Alex walked fast from the teahouse and along the footpath that seemed to sway under him like the suspension bridge in the school playground.

The wide shy street was quiet, and behind the hedges and the Norfolk Island pines the owners of the single-storey houses had one eye on the cricket and one on the thin drift of smoke from their barbies. In the early morning the street would stir with log-trucks heading out for Hobart, but at five in the afternoon Wellington Point contained the promise of the empty road and the faint sewerage smell of seaweed that presaged rain.

Doing his very best to think of anything, anything but the real-estate agent, Alex made his way past the school, along the esplanade, and towards the jetty and the street where he had parked his ute. The tide was out, the sun catching the white tips of the low waves and the mauve dorsal of the peninsula. However down at heart Alex might get to feel on the farm, he would never tire of this view – unlike certain of his schoolmates. He knew one or two who preferred nothing more than to sit slumped with their backs to the bay, their heads in the *Mercury* or peering through wreaths of home-grown marijuana at porn videos bootlegged from Canberra.

A branch creaked above him. The air had been still when he entered the teahouse, but a breeze had blown up. He opened the door of his ute and stopped. The noise of the wind in the pines. Grit in his face. An ice-cream wrapper sucked up into the sky. He closed the door and walked on. The thought of the snorkeller drawing him down the concrete boat ramp and onto the jetty.

It was a saw of Miss Pritchard's geography class that the next land mass south was the polar ice cap. As always when Alex walked out on the eighty-yard-long jetty, he was aware of being at the end of the line. With a keener pang than normal, it struck him – surveying the horizon

– that he really did live in one of the earth's more remote places. One of the more unvisited, too.

Until the road was finished in 1911, the town was reachable from Hobart only by horse and cart, or by sea: a journey taking up to three days, the steam packet sailing down the Derwent, round the Iron Pot lighthouse, past Betsy Island, Blackjack Reef and across Storm Bay to the canal at Dunalley, coming out north of Eaglehawk Neck, round Hellfire Bluff, through Mercury Passage to Swansea and Wellington Point.

Though this jetty was still here, where the scallop boats had unloaded, the bay had silted up. South-easterly breezes with sand-bearing waves had shallowed what was two fathoms of water at the time of the packet to a mere three feet, so that only shoal-draught boats could tie up alongside. At weekends, out-of-towners launched their tinnies from the ramp, anchoring off Dolphin Sands to catch flathead, but vessels with a keel avoided Oyster Bay. Talk of a marina every few years invariably petered out in agreement that whoever was going to build it would have to construct an overlapping groin on the other side of the promontory – and have mighty deep pockets. Wellington Point boasted no such entrepreneurs and probably would not have made one coming in from outside welcome. As Alex's father had soon discovered, this was not a Yorkshire village bobbing with life and fishing boats. It was a town on the sea without sea-life, affected by the same elements that affected the farm; and was vulnerable – even on the clearest, calmest day – to southerly busters from Antarctica. Fierce, sudden winds that gusted up without warning, driving the surface of the sea into the bay and giving rise to extreme tides and flooding.

Perhaps this explained Alex's sudden concern for the snorkeller. He had known too many occasions when a mainlander or tourist had misread the weather conditions and set out across a perfectly calm sea, expecting the calmness to last through the weekend.

He reached the end of the jetty – four corroded planks – and looked out, his eyes sweeping the bay for a solitary blue-and-white hull. Past Maria Island, the Hen and Chicks, Schouten . . . but it was no good. All he could see was a young woman sitting at a table. And Ray.

CHAPTER FOUR

SIMPLY TO TOUCH HER reluctant flesh gave Ray a jolt of comfort. He was desperate to seduce Merridy. She had come into his office two weeks ago, on a mild afternoon in early February, wheeling her invalid father.

Ray leaped up, in his enthusiasm to close the door almost slamming it against a foot. He peered around it to see a thin woman, dressed in loose-fitting nylon slacks with an onyx crucifix dangling from her throat.

"You must be Mrs Bowman," and flashed her an indulgent look. "Please, come in."

Still she stood there in her trance. Her face white and lined, with nostrils nipped in and eyes red-rimmed from weeping.

"Mum, this is Mr . . ."

With no effort he shifted his smile to the young woman. "Ray Grogan. But please call me Ray. As in sunshine."

"We've come to inspect one of your retirement units," Merridy continued flatly. "I believe Mr Framley has been in touch."

She wheeled her father up to the desk.

"Ah, yes, yes," Ray addressed the wheelchair. "We've been expecting you, Mr Bowman. Welcome to the heart of Tasmania's relaxed east coast!"

Mr Bowman looked rotten. On this afternoon, he was in pain with a bloodshot eye after he had tried to join his wife and daughter at breakfast and had fallen getting out of bed. His second accident in a week.

Ray asked cheerily: "Can you see me, sir?"

21

A slow shake of the head.

Ray turned his attention back to Merridy. "I think you'll be pleased with the unit. It's a pioneering scheme. I like to describe the philosophy behind it as 'independence with a sense of well-being'."

He fished in a drawer for a set of keys. "Shall we walk or shall I drive you?"

"Well, where is it? How far?"

"End of the street and across the cricket pitch."

"We'll walk," decided Merridy. "The air might do my father good."

In the eight hundred yards from the office to the retirement unit, Ray sought to engage Merridy in conversation.

Already from Keith Framley, her relative, Ray had learned a fair amount. Merridy's father – the man she propelled up the footpath – had been a mechanical engineer who was electrocuted in Zeehan while installing a lift in the tin mine there. The shock had brought on an aneurysm that slurred his speech. He couldn't complete the simplest sentence – humiliating for someone remembered by Tildy's father as a man who enjoyed nothing more than to recite poetry.

Because of his accident, Mr Bowman's wife, from whom he had been separated, had come back to look after him – as had his daughter, who had taken a year off from her studies at Melbourne University.

"It must be tough for you, leaving your course like that," glancing sideways with keen green eyes.

"I was only in my first year," she said crisply, all her concentration on the asphalt ahead.

"Keith speaks very highly of your dad."

"My father helped him early on."

"Keith says he remembers your dad always with a book of poetry in his hand."

"Then he's exaggerating."

"I like poetry myself, I used to read it aloud at school," Ray sailed on. "Did – does your dad like anyone in particular?"

Merridy twisted her head to look at Ray. "Well, a favourite is Edward Lear."

"Edward Lear?" his eyes boring into hers. He touched his moustache, a soulful expression on his face. "Now that does ring a definite bell."

The property to which Ray escorted the Bowmans was called "Otranto", a modern one-storey villa behind Louisa Meredith House. The nursing home had funded the building of three "independent self-care living units", according to Ray's description in the brochure, of which this one was still for sale. Keith, a second cousin of Merridy's father, was on the charity's board. As soon as he learned of her husband's accident he had telephoned Mrs Bowman and encouraged her to bring Leonard immediately to Wellington Point to convalesce, even as he had brought Mrs Framley. The Bowmans could stay at his hotel free of charge while they inspected the unit or until other appropriate accommodation was found. He defied them not to adore Wellington Point. Its recuperative air had performed minor but measurable miracles for his late wife, even if it could not in the end prevent the cancer from spreading to her brain. "It's heaven on a stick! Reminds a lot of people of the Bay of Naples."

"Naples," said Mrs Bowman.

From Zeehan, Merridy called to enquire if there was anything she could do to repay his kindness.

23

"Nothing!" said Keith, who had never forgotten how helpful her father had been when a bed & breakfast had come up for sale in the Bowmans' street in Ulverstone. "Nothing at all."

But a day later he telephoned to crave a favour. What he wondered was, would Merridy be willing to help out in his newly opened cocktail bar.

Ray drew back the melon-pink curtains and stepped aside for Mrs Bowman to take in the view of Oyster Bay that was only partially obscured by an ochre wall. Beyond the wall was a close-cropped lawn where two people squatted dressed in white.

"It's close to medical facilities. And while you're here you don't pay rates, Hydro, only your own phone bill. Plus, there's a nurse-call system for emergency," and indicated a button on the wall above the pneumatic hospital bed.

Mrs Bowman bent down – crucifix swinging – to her husband. "What do you think, Leonard? Would this suit?"

From the wheelchair came a whining noise incomprehensible to Ray. He paused to plump up a pillow and waited until Mr Bowman fell silent before tapping the door-frame. "The unit is constructed throughout in environmentally friendly materials to minimise energy usage, and there's an irrigated drip system in the landscaped garden. The whole idea is to make you feel very much at home."

"That's nice," said Mrs Bowman, a thin hand mashing the onyx Christ into her throat. She walked over to the window and stood in the alcove, her concentration on the neat lawn and the two white-haired women stooped there. She released her hand from her throat and spread it on the glass.

Ray noted that something in Mrs Bowman had mended. "As you can see, our town has a thriving bowling club. The green is a stone's throw away. And should you wish to join there, my mother is the president! You know, it's funny, but I always find myself telling newcomers to Wellington Point the same thing. Excellence, dignity and respect are the priorities of our little community. And companionship."

"It's perfect, I'm sure," Merridy broke in. "But what happens when we come to sell?"

Ray smiled at her. He could tell who made the decisions in this family! "Should you ever wish to sell," he ploughed on without missing a beat, "the unit reverts back to Louisa Meredith House, and half the profits go to the family." He positioned himself to catch her eye. "I hope that won't be for a long while."

Many years later, when his jaw lifted with pride at the *Mercury*'s description of him as "the David Boon of real estate", Ray would date the recovery in Tasmania's east coast property market to his sale of this retirement unit. Ray took the credit. It was his description of "Otranto", he advised Mr Tamlyn on his return to the office, that had swayed the Bowman family. "You should have seen the lady's expression when I told her about the bowlo."

Since joining the company office seven years before, Ray had discovered that one enjoyable aspect of his work consisted in writing short paragraphs to accompany the half-dozen photographs that Tamlyn & Peppiatt advertised each Friday in the *Mercury*'s property section. At primary school, his worst subject had been English: it was a standing joke in the class – in which Ray consistently hovered close to the bottom – that Ray Grogan had to cheat to spell his own name. But at his office desk, he developed a knack for describing the most ordinary-looking weatherboard shack in such a way that people would more often than not wish to view it.

It was very simple. Properties were like dogs: they took on the characteristics of their owners. As Ray bade farewell to the Bowman family outside the nursing home, he reflected that Mr Bowman was a ruin that no amount of renovation could restore. His wife, rewired, upgraded and tastefully refurbished, had potential, although her religion might be an obstacle to a quick sale. He perceived her in the same light as he had once viewed the Bethel Teahouse. Not for the faint-hearted, but offering great prospects for enterprising buyers looking to invest in a historical quarter. Renovate. Renovate. Renovate. This dame is just crying out for you to rescue her from her loneliness!

As for the daughter . . . His eyes lingered on Merridy as she wheeled her father around the boundary to the hotel. This gorgeous 1960s prestige home has long been coveted by many, but owned by few. Rarely on the market, an inspection will not disappoint. Do not miss this golden opportunity!

Nothing he could think of, though, quite captured the commanding, grave beauty of the young woman who passed in front of the score-keeper's hut and turned into the hotel courtyard.

Her impregnable and valiant look would have Catherine-wheeled the stumps of most men, but an unhappy woman appealed to Ray's vanity. The fact was that if she were a house, then he had never come up against anything so splendid, so grand, so classical – unless it was Talbot's (which Albert Talbot had made clear that he would never in any circumstance put up for sale, not while there was breath left in his body). No, she was more one of those Crusader castles that he was taught about in his history class. Walls eight metres thick that no amount of cannon-fire could broach, with buckets of boiling tar tipped onto the head of anyone rash enough to scale them.

But where properties were concerned, he had the patience of a snake.

Merridy could feel his eyes like marbles on her neck and shivered. She pushed the wheelchair quicker, her mother following in silent contemplation. Not until they reached the courtyard did her mother say: "What was your honest opinion of that young man?"

"Awful."

"And the place?"

"It will do."

"Couldn't we get a better deal if we rented? If your father . . ."

"Well, we've got to hope he doesn't. Anyway, I think Keith is keen to have his rooms back."

"I will write the cheque tomorrow."

They had arrived at a door with a brass "7" screwed into it. Keith had allocated them a suite in a ground-floor block next to the main building. Merridy opened the door and together the two women lifted Leonard's body out of the wheelchair and onto the bed. Her father's feet had shrunk and his shoes slipped off as they lay him down. A wheezing noise issued from the dry lips, the sound of air bubbling through the fluid on his lungs.

Merridy looked at the bloodshot eye that roved the ceiling, the cracked skin. The lines in his face were inscriptions that had weathered and were now unreadable. "We're making the right decision, Mum," in a quiet voice.

Her gaze remained on her father while her mother rinsed a glass and filled it with tap-water and gulped it down. The walk had tired Mrs Bowman.

Suddenly, she was spitting out.

The noise whipped Merridy around. "Mum! Keith said we're not to drink the tap-water."

Mrs Bowman grimaced, spitting again into the basin. "I forgot," wiping the taste from her lips.

"Over there – I put it over there."

Mrs Bowman drank two glasses of water from the bottle and lay down beside her husband. She licked the corners of her mouth. "I found the church, Merridy. There is a late service this evening."

"What time?"

Mrs Bowman checked her watch. "Nine o'clock." Then picked up the photograph that she had propped on the bedside table, a black-and-white photograph of a young boy racing barefoot along a narrow strand.

He would be with her forever. Her only regret was, every time she turned her eyes to him, that she had not told him how beautiful he had looked in his boots.

"I'll make sure I'm back in time," Merridy said, and sat on her Glory Box – a wooden steamer trunk at the foot of the bed – to take off her shoes. She crossed her arms and stared a moment at the orange lino. Then she stood up, put on a pair of dark tights and the navy-blue skirt and jacket which Keith insisted that she wear, kissed her mother on her forehead and her father on the cheek, and set off across the courtyard, her book under her arm.

There were two places to drink in Wellington Point. The Returned Servicemen's Club on Greer Street and the Freycinet Court Hotel. In a bid to excite more customers, and partly to distract himself in the hollow months after his wife's death, Keith Framley had the previous winter fitted out a cocktail bar at the suggestion of a mate in the hotel trade who overheard at a convention of travel agents in Bali that Tasmania was set to become a destination for the discerning European tourist. His mate had blundered. There *were* no tourists here in 1988, not in Wellington Point. Steady drinkers went to the pub in Swansea for their beer. The odd backpacker misdirected to Framley's cocktail bar at the extremity of the globe almost invariably preferred to join regulars in the public bar on the other side of the hotel.

The only person to disturb Merridy's reading that night, around seven o'clock, was Keith's despondent daughter.

"Hey, Tildy," said Merridy, and closed her book.

"Have you seen Dad?" her face drawn beneath the flawless fringe.

"In Hobart."

"What's he gone to Hobart for?" hunting around in a black handbag until she found her lip gloss.

"The cricket, could it be?"

"Oh, yes, the cricket," in a disappointed voice. She finished touching up her mouth. "Like some?"

"Not really."

"Go on, take it. If you want to get on in this place, you wear lip gloss. That's a fact."

"No, it's an opinion."

"No, no, believe me, it's a fact. Put this on and you'll see. You'll be a hit with it. Hey, what you reading?" She picked it up. "Louisa Meredith. *My Home in Tasmania*." It might have been some unpalatable medicine. "Part of your studies, is it?"

"I borrowed it from the front desk."

"Looks boring," Tildy yawned.

"It's interesting – if you're interested in history."

"I'm not interested in history. What sort of history, anyway?"

"I was learning how they got the feathers off the black swans at Moulting Lagoon."

"Really?" She climbed onto a stool and looked around the bar. "How did they? Someone I know, his family made their money from swan down."

Merridy found the place. She read aloud: "*The general custom was, to take the birds in large quantities in the moulting season, when they are most easily captured and extremely fat; they were then confined in pens*, without any food, *to linger miserably for a time, till ready to die of starvation, because, whilst they are fat, the down can neither be so well stripped off, nor so effectually prepared.*"

The sound of Tildy listening made her look up.

Tildy's lips were trembling. "That's me! That's me! Oh, Merridy, I'm no different. I know how those swans feel."

"Why, what's the matter?"

"I have a pain, it's right here," and squeezed under her breast. "Normally if I have a pain there's a good reason. But this pain is different. I can't make it go away. I can't breathe. I can't sleep."

Merridy put the book down. "Maybe it's indigestion."

"I've never felt so bad," said Tildy, and lunged over to a table to seize a paper napkin. She blew her nose and dabbed one eye and then the other.

"Maybe you're in love."

"Oh, Merridy. How can you be so cruel? Now I know how Mr Twelvetrees suffered."

Merridy straightened a brick that was on the counter.

"You haven't forgotten Randal Twelvetrees?" accusingly.

"Oh, no."

"He liked you. My God, he did."

"He was just ill, poor man."

"Obsessed more like," and blew her nose again.

"It was more my mother who affected Randal, Tildy. As I think you know."

"Whatever, whatever. Pointless, I know, to ask about *your* love life. Am I not right?"

Merridy had not taken her eyes from the brick. Baked by a convict and with its frog filled with Redhead matches to strike on the side, it was one of half a dozen that Tildy's father had bought from an antique shop in Battery Point and scattered on tables and counters around the hotel.

She began separating the matches. "My hands are pretty tied at the moment," in a tight voice. "For romance."

"Oh, Merridy, how selfish of me," and Tildy's eyes watered again. "I'm so sorry about your dad."

Merridy lay the back of her hand on Tildy's wrist. "Who is he?"

Tildy's disconsolate face looked up. "Have you a moment? I know you've got a lot on your plate, but I need someone to talk to."

With a nod of her head, Merridy indicated the empty room. "I'm all yours – until ten to nine."

"This is so embarrassing," and went behind the counter. "No, I can do it." She poured herself a double shot of the Captain Morgan – one of the rums that her father had stocked in the bar for discerning customers and which she much preferred to Bundaberg. "You wouldn't keep anything from me, Merridy? I couldn't stand that."

"I wouldn't keep anything from you."

"Well, it's Ray Grogan."

"Ray Grogan?"

"You met him this afternoon. He showed you the unit."

*

Ray, in case Merridy had not already heard, was a man renowned in the district for having bedded most women in Wellington Point – not including Tildy.

His reticence on this score was a source of frustration that Tildy had begun to mistake in herself for passion.

"Why not ignore him?" Merridy suggested.

"I've tried to. Believe me, I've tried to," looking up and down for tonic. "But it's no good," and sniffed.

Around about the time of Merridy's appearance in town, Tildy had decided that the handsome real-estate agent was all she ever wanted. Even though part of her could see clean through him to the other side.

"I was so furious the other night, I up-fronted him: 'You're nothing but a proper slut, Ray. That's all you are.'"

"And his reaction?"

"He told me that I couldn't be more mistaken. But I know Ray." She poured the tonic into her rum and swallowed. "He screws them in his clients' beds or wherever he's showing them around," grimacing. "He's got keys to every house in Wellington Point, I wouldn't be surprised. He even shags them in the score-keeper's hut! Oh, he's a shonk. You should hear his lines. They're the same for every woman."

"Must be good ones," observed Merridy, who had heard enough.

But the bit was between Tildy's teeth. "He was pashing on with Rose-Maree, promising that all he ever wanted was to give her pleasure. And telling Abbygail that she smelled like the Taj Mahal by moonlight. He's nothing but a root-rat. And don't think he minds how old they are! Teresa overheard him at the RSL saying that he knew Mrs Prosser found him attractive because when he put his hand down her pants it was like feeding a horse – and she must be over sixty. Oh, he's disgusting," and shivered.

32

"But you aren't just disgusted?" toying with the lip gloss that Tildy had left on the counter.

"I don't know. I can't tell you how many times I've said to myself: Right. That's it. Step back, Tildy."

"Have you told him how you feel?"

"No. He has enough tickets on himself." And shivered again. "Such a skite."

"He must have something good hidden away," Merridy said.

"Oh, Merridy, it's not that!" Her voice had risen to a wail at the injustice of it. Beyond the porkies that he told her, beyond his reputation for – in her father's words – "rooting like a leather-punch", Tildy discerned the outline of a different Ray; the Platonic version, as it were. "The truth is, there's a side of Ray which is actually quite sweet and generous."

Merridy was not convinced. "What's in it for you?"

"Well, I'm not alone," her eyes downcast. "And now he's having a birthday party on Saturday. He's invited Rose-Maree and Debbie and Abbygail and Teresa. He's even invited the girls from the Bethel Teahouse. But the bastard hasn't invited me."

She grappled with the upturned rum bottle. Empty.

Merridy plucked the bottle from its holder and dropped it into the bin. Above the counter the clock said 8.55.

"Listen, I've got to go. But if you want my opinion, I think you should have nothing whatever to do with him."

Next morning, first thing, Merridy walked into Tamlyn & Peppiatt and handed over her mother's cheque for the deposit on the unit.

Ray scrutinised Mrs Bowman's signature. He clipped

the cheque to the folder on his desk. "What are you doing this Saturday?" light as spray.

"I'm busy," Merridy said.

"Would you like to come to a party?"

"No."

He gave a pleasant laugh. "It would be a chance to meet some locals."

"Why haven't you invited Tildy?"

"Tildy? Do I know a Tildy?"

"Tildy Framley, my cousin."

"Oh, Tildy!" guarded, all of a sudden. "You're right. I haven't."

"Is there a reason?"

He hesitated. "Tildy and I . . . Listen, it's difficult—"

"Invite Tildy to your birthday party and I'll come."

He stared at her, weighing what she had said. "That's blackmail."

"So . . ." At the door, with her back to him, she paused. "Tell me, why don't you like her?" addressing the carpet, its fake Aboriginal design. "She likes you."

"I *do* like her," his voice high-pitched and apologetic. He twisted his moustache. "But . . . But . . ."

She turned, bristling. "But what?"

On that Saturday afternoon, Ray looked up from his tuna steaks – and there she was, head in the wet gum leaves, sitting on his fence right next to Tildy, and gazing down at his family and friends and the barbie that had started to hiss. Despite the damp, the sight of Merridy rekindled furtive hopes.

"Hey, girls, come on down."

"Both of us?"

"Both. Of. You."

After that, he was overly welcoming. He poured a Bloody

Mary for Tildy, saying how pleased he was to see her, and took her over to speak with Rhiannon; and a tomato juice for Merridy.

"Here you are." His eyes moved from her lip gloss that emphasised the whiteness of her skin. He had never seen a face so white – like milk to tempt a snake.

She accepted the glass. A pulse of colour darted into her cheeks, then was gone. "I suppose I should say Happy Birthday."

"Couldn't keep away, eh?" swilling the thought of her naked around the bedroom of his mind.

"Lord, I tried," she laughed. "Nothing else to do in this godforsaken village."

He was wearing blue shorts daggered in white slashes, and had a footballer's build, with ginger hairs on his chest, and was tall.

Something puzzled him. "Why the fence? Why not come round the front like everyone else?"

"Fences are for gatecrashers."

"But I invited you."

Her body moved inside her clothes, away from the wet clinging cotton. "Not without her," nodding at her cousin.

"You mean," it began to dawn on him, "you really are here only because of Tildy?"

"What other reason could there be?"

He pretended to study Tildy, who was pretending to talk to the Welsh sisters, although her body faced the wrong way.

"That's not kind," he murmured, hurt, and yet Merridy's annihilating laugh only intensified the appeal of her. He looked at her bust pushing against her damp blue dress. And gave one fiftieth of his concentration to her cousin across the yard and even less to the horizon that he decided to address.

"Merridy, look at the sea, it goes on and on to the South

35

Pole and makes me feel a grain of sand." He adopted a pensive expression and wished that it would stop drizzling. He was talking like a version of himself that he would like to be. It sounded OK. It felt good. He could not understand why she was still laughing. But he was not in her fantastical scheme.

Five days after his party, Ray was removing the details of "Otranto" from his office window when he caught sight of Merridy standing on her own outside the Bethel Teahouse. He seized the moment.

"Hey, Merridy!"

"Oh, Ray. Hi."

"What are you up to?"

"I'm looking for my mother, actually."

"Let me buy you a coffee. There's something I want to ask you."

"What?" standing her ground.

"Do you like jazz?" and pushed open the door.

"It depends. Why?"

"Come on in and I'll tell you."

He could have done, though, without Alex Dove sitting there to witness his humiliation.

"Who was that?" asked Merridy to break the silence after Alex had disappeared out of the Bethel with his clinking bag. She knew, but was curious to know more.

"That," Ray said, "is Piers Dove."

"Piers Dove?" At the same time thinking: But Tildy called him Alex.

"Oh, I can tell you about Piers Dove," too pleased at the sight of her attentive face to be alert to the reason.

"Then tell me."

"He's a Pom," said Ray philosophically. "Although we were at school together."

"He looks all right."

"Yeah, in his sleep," with a murky smile.

"And where does he sleep?"

"Over at Moulting Lagoon."

"With someone?"

"Lives on his own. TV reception's not good. Nor is the bore-water." He grinned, squeezing her arm. "He was crazy even before his parents had an accident," and with his free hand tapped the side of his temple.

She cocked her head. "What accident?" interested where before she had been merely curious.

CHAPTER FIVE

TALBOT'S STORE
We apologise for any inconvenience caused by the refur-
bishment of the food aisles. From March 3, Bread and
Cereals will be relocated to Toiletries.

Deadline for the March 9 Newsletter: *Tuesday, March*
1, 5 p.m. All notices and advertisements to Mr Talbot.
Donations to offset the cost of production are welcome. Ed.

The binoculars tracked Alex to the end of the jetty with the same attention as they had observed him reappear in Wellington Point after an absence of twelve years. The scuttlebutt was that young Mr Dove would be gone back to England by the end of the week, once he had sorted out his affairs. Mr Talbot had heard this from his manager, Fred Coggins.

That was four years ago.

Whatever Albert Talbot made of Alex's behaviour, he was unlikely to say. It was his inflexible habit never to make comments about what people did. Only to watch, listen, remember – as in his wartime watches.

"You have one instruction, Sergeant Talbot. And you will reissue it to yourself every morning until the war is over: Make yourself invisible. That way you won't get caught, and you certainly don't want to get caught, son, take it from me. My advice to you, furthermore, would be to keep your head well down vis-à-vis the natives, too. If you're going to live in the bush, you've got to have a very, very clean nose.

That means: Don't fraternise, don't take them to your hidey-holes, and – above all – don't borrow any of their women. Natives don't like that, Talbot. But tell you what I do want to see when you get back. I want to see bruises all over your head and body. That's where the wild animals have bumped into you because you'll be invisible."

These had been his orders from Lieutenant Black, a compact watchful type himself who had picked Sergeant Talbot to be the radio-op – "because," he said, "you get on with people." They had met when Albert was taking his St John's Ambulance certificate.

Dropped ashore in Jacquinot Bay, Albert had followed Black's orders to a tee. Safe as in church when sitting up there in the thick scrub, beneath a ceiling of sago palms and a red-and-blue silk parachute in which to catch the creepy-crawlies – or to cut clothes from. Living on swede and yams and dehydrated American rations as he crouched there – with no weapon, with nothing but his brass binoculars – behind a screen of vines and long grass, tracking the least movement of the Japanese. Where they ate, slept, the planes that flew over, the warships that stopped off in Rabaul, plus anything untoward. And twice a day reporting back what he saw on his ATR4 radio, in a code derived from sentences taken from a by-now damp copy of Agatha Christie's *The Secret Adversary*, the words coming back to him in stray and disembodied phrases upon which once upon a time hung the freedom of the Christian world and now no longer made the slightest sense . . . "Repulsive goes the Whole Hog."

Half a century on, Sergeant Talbot's radio was now his *Newsletter*. Together with the general store, it defined his life. Because, wisely or not – and he thought, on balance, not – he had obeyed Lieutenant Black's other stricture: about keeping away from women.

He had had opportunity and provocation galore. In the light of his first-aid training, he was expected to perform minor medical procedures on the natives. Alerted by drums, the women would walk for two days. They came down from the hills and lined up for him. Bent over, each carrying her child in a *bilum,* taking the weight of the string bag in a broad strap around her forehead. They were finely built women, with bold brown eyes that looked straight into his, and black hair that he wanted to touch. He conversed easily with these women – he knew them as *meri* – and spoke to them in proper pidgin taught by the missionaries. They were so immediately welcoming that he did not have to navigate a whole lot of prejudices, because they did not appear to have any. Many had been tortured to extract information about Australians. He dressed their spear cuts and bullet wounds. He drained their hands which sometimes blew up huge, like inflated rubber gloves. He injected them against fevers and yaws. And yet he had not known intimacy with a single *meri.* (There had been one never-to-be-forgotten occasion when, yes, he had known the desire, but the Japanese had put paid to that.) With the consequence that Sergeant Talbot's detachment had got to be a habit. Educated not to be an encumbrance, he had not been one. But as he grew older he had come bitterly to wonder if, all things considered, he mightn't have preferred to swap his very clean nose for the excitement and mess of an involved heart. The mess that he watched unfold below day by day, and now in Alex Dove.

At the end of the jetty, Alex could see no sign of the snorkeller's boat.

Meanwhile, the wind had toughened, hurling the waves

against the pylons and bringing the first pellets of rain. They stung his cheek in the same instant that he heard the whoosh of something rushing past – and a flock of tiny birds flew out of the sun from the direction of Schouten Island.

The end of February and the swifts had come back, their colours radiant as if polished by the breeze on the long journey south. He followed them, one curved wing beating faster than the other, as he had watched them with his father on the top of Barn Hill. Alex had not known his father well, but there were things he had said that Alex could never forget. "Main point in life is to experience life. Some of those swifts may have flown from as far afield as Mongolia to warn us." For they were storm-signal birds, heralds of a humid north-easterly. When you saw them circling high in a thermal and listened to their shrill twittering, it would be only minutes before you heard the first crack of summer thunder.

Immediately, black thoughts flurried in on the backs of the birds. A cramped apartment in a red-brick mansion block in south London. The gloomy, low-ceilinged room and the lift, a vertical coffin that shuddered up past metal grilles through which his eyes fell on tense faces.

He thought: No, I love this place.

Alex felt good. Better than felt. Less than an hour ago, when he had pushed open the door into the teahouse, he was on the point of believing in everything that Ray Grogan said about him. He was a misfit. He would never make a good farmer. He might as well chuck it in and go back to London to teach. But now he was happy. Happy at the sight of the swifts and also at the prospect of a little more rain to put a tinge back on the paddocks. Above all, happy to think of the black-haired young woman in the Bethel. Her smile returned to him over Ray Grogan's arm, a dim light flashing its enigmatic message across the darkening water.

He turned, walked back, crossed Greer Street – a short road with three parked cars and Sergeant Finter eating flat-head – and climbed into his ute and drove home. Twenty minutes on and he still could feel a strange flicker inside him, like the jet of blue flame in the shape of a human figure that in his boyhood Bill Molson, his parents' immediate neighbour, claimed to have observed hovering above the marshes behind Moulting Lagoon; at least, that was the story.

Nor had this feeling diminished when Alex woke. As the day wore on, the prospect of seeing Merridy Bowman pushed every other thought from his head.

Until he met Merridy, Alex had not pictured the kind of woman with whom he wished to share his life, how she might look. Now he discovered her traces everywhere; in the colour of the sand blown up from the beach; in the swallows under the eaves on the back deck; he even heard her voice in the iron windmill. When a helicopter tilted over the house towards Wellington Point he thought maybe she was looking up at it, too.

The next time he saw her in town, bustling out of Tamlyn & Peppiatt surprisingly early on a Thursday morning, she was the averted glance across the road. Walking a purposeful walk that he would have run eight miles to see.

"Hey, Merridy!" He started towards her with the exaggerated carelessness of someone on a vital mission, exhilarated.

She turned. Looking different in profile. Surprised

perhaps by his childish trick of opening his arms to attract attention.

"That meal," he said. His breaths came quick. It was absurd how nervous he was. He was seven or eight years older than her, dammit!

"What meal was that?"

He knew what he wanted to say, but it came out wrong. "The other day. I asked you out for a meal."

"Oh, yes," and gave a smile in which there was reticence and relief.

"I was wondering if you would take me up on it . . ." But his words did not fit. They had the looseness of a borrowed garment. He felt them drop about his ankles.

She rescued him. "When would you like?"

"Any time. Are you free Saturday?"

"Where?"

He faced the street for inspiration. "What about . . . what about . . . I know – the hotel?"

She looked at him with a curious expression and seemed on the verge of saying something.

"Or would you prefer somewhere else? Swansea perhaps?"

"No, no, I'll see you at the hotel."

The reason for Merridy's distractedness was the embarrassing night that she had spent with Ray Grogan, the culmination of his energetic campaign to lure her into an empty bedroom in a Tuscanised brick bungalow south of Wellington Point.

He had focused his attentions on her ever since she turned down his invitation to the Jazz Social, sauntering every lunchtime into the cocktail bar on no provocation and ordering a ten-ounce of Boag's that she had little alternative but to pour. And then, because there was never anyone other than himself to serve, engaging her in soft, beseeching talk.

It was perfectly, painfully obvious that Ray's flattery was habitual. It was his vernacular; he was not expressing his passion for her, but making the bed for its possibility, uttering ridiculous compliments in a steady flow until she no longer heard them. She beat him away, and still he came back. He was robust in the face of rejection, and that was somehow attractive.

Failing to interest her in the more recondite aspects of the local property market, Ray resorted to the dependable formulae that he employed for seduction. The lines tripped from his lips with the same ease as the phrases that came to him at his desk and that he taped to the windows of Tamlyn & Peppiatt.

"Confidentially," he said, "how would you like to go out with me?"

She gave him a disagreeable smile. "I don't think so, Mr Grogan. Ginger men always fall for me, but I can't stand them."

"I'll dye my hair for you," he proposed.

She looked at the stud in his ear. Debbie had told her that he had bought it to celebrate the sale of "Otranto": "Green, pink, purple, orange, I won't change my mind."

"Come on, Merridy, at least call me Ray," he pleaded. "I'll show you a wonderful time, really I will," he whispered in a humid, tropical breath, a root-rat with a gold stud. He sensed that this was the wrong tack to take with Merridy, but by force of habit found himself heading there. "Every passionate relationship I've had has begun passionately," he confessed. "But nothing to compare with this, Merridy. Nothing."

"Give me one reason why I should believe a word you say. One good reason."

"No, you're right, perhaps you shouldn't. Yet perhaps you want to. What's more, perhaps you need to."

She laughed. "I've never heard such bullshit." She had met his type in her first year at uni. Ray was an acupuncturist who knew nothing about women, but knew by dull rote the seven spots where to touch them so that in surprisingly more instances than not, and against every instinct, their cheeks dimpled and their skin tingled in a strange way up the insides of their legs.

"You're a clever girl, Merridy. All the same, I'd feel sorry to be your partner."

"Is that so?"

"You know what they say: *If you wish to be loved, love.*"

"'They say' is a big liar." Then: "Have you been reading a manual?"

"You mustn't, Merridy," with a grave face, "judge me by your past experiences."

And so uninsultably on he went. He had the resilience of the punching bag that he was rumoured to keep in his gym. It meant that Merridy could be rude to him and say what she really thought – without that penetrating either.

Until the moment came when she decided that the only way to tackle Ray Grogan was head on.

One Tuesday noon, he struck a match against the convict brick and studied the flame with an earnest expression.

"You're not going to smoke, are you?" she said. "I hate smoking."

"I do appreciate, Merridy, that we don't have much to offer you here."

"What do you mean?" at this new departure.

45

"Well, you're beautiful, you're intelligent," tuning his voice to a concerned note. "You should be at university, not stuck in Wellington Point."

"I have to be here. My father's dying."

"But one day, maybe sooner than you think, you'll have to think of yourself. And if you look at everyone in Wellington Point, which is a small place, and you take away the gays and the lesbians, of which there are an inappropriately large number, and then you take away the happily married men, of which there are quite a few by the way – that's all they know! – and then you take away the many no-hopers – the drunks, the drugged, the ditsy – then all you're left with is me. And though it hurts me to say this, I'm aware that I'm no catch for the likes of you. So of course, you'll go back to the university. Why wouldn't you?" He blew out the flame and gazed at her with an expression of plausible vulnerability.

It surprised her, what she felt. She expected to feel derision, but she was unexpectedly stirred. He was, after all, physically attractive and touching, and she made a deliberate effort to look at him as though the weight of his stare was a hairy caterpillar crawling over her. "Don't you have any homes to sell?"

"Market's off the boil. Not like me," with a solemn, beery chuckle. He slouched forward. "If you like, I could read you poetry." And tapped his nose.

She could tolerate it no longer. She put down her tray and faced him. "All right, Ray-as-in-sunshine," hand on hip. "Let's go."

The unexpectedness of it caught him by surprise. "Where?"

"Where do you think?" her cheeks dimpling.

A slow smile returned to his face until he was positively beaming. "Listen, there's a house out of town I've got to prepare for inspection. It so happens," and jangled his pocket, "I've got the keys right here. The bedroom has a terrific view of Schouten. A terrific view."

"No," she said so emphatically that he jerked his glass. "I'd like to see *your* house."

"*My* house?" Ray Grogan looked tense, uneasy, not at all prepared for this.

She went up to him where he sat at the bar, laid the back of her hand against his cheek, smelled his dog's breath between the glistening teeth.

"What, the old hunter doesn't want to kill?"

"What about Keith?" he stammered. "Won't he be missing you?"

"Not on my afternoon off," already putting her arms into a coat.

Less than ten minutes later, Merridy stepped into Ray Grogan's lair.

"Do you share this with your parents?" noticing three fibreglass fishing rods behind the door.

"No, I live on my own."

She paused to unbutton her coat in front of a poster of the Taj Mahal. Further along the wall was a poster of the Sphinx, pyramids in the background; and one more, of a glittering gold dome and minarets.

"I always wanted to go to Egypt," taking off his jacket. "Don't know why. It's probably a shit-hole."

Before laying his jacket over the back of a leatherette chair, he slipped a hand into one of its pockets and transferred whatever he found there to his trousers. "Well, what do you think?"

"About what?"

"My place. Here, give me that."

She let him take her coat and sat down on the sofa and looked around. "Oh, nice," she said. "Very nice."

"I bought it off a chemist who had to leave town in a hurry," he said, coming to sit beside her. "I turned the garage into a gym. Maybe you'd like to see?"

"I don't think so."

He edged nearer, stretching a practised arm along the backrest. "You know," he said, "it's wrong what they say about estate agents."

"What do they say?"

"Oh, stupid things," and looked sad and misunderstood. "That we're the least trustworthy profession – after car salesmen, mark you, and journalists and policemen."

"I never read those surveys." She leaned forward a little to ease off her shoe.

"Can I tell you something?" stroking her hair and inspecting a lock of it with fierce intent. "You smell like the Taj Mahal looks by moonlight."

"Oh, bull," she laughed and pulled up her jacket.

"Whoa there! What are you doing?"

"Getting ready for your paintbrush," she said merrily. "Isn't that what you want?" And unfastened her bra.

He stared at her breasts, the shadow of the lace curtain falling on them in the pattern of a hot snowflake. She was buxom for someone her height. Even so, he was alarmed by her pace. "Hey," licking his upper lip, "something to drink? When do you have to get back?"

"I don't know. When I've had a wonderful time maybe," and dropped her bra on the carpet and sat back.

He went on staring at her on the leatherette sofa, the bright afternoon light streaming through the front window onto her white arms and breasts, her face without make-up.

"What about some music? I could put on some music. What do you like?"

"Have you any choral hymns?"

He watched for a sign that she was teasing him. But she seemed deadly serious. His mouth parted in a lamentable smile. "I was thinking Leonard Cohen. I'm not actually sure I have any church music."

His arm snaked back along the top of the sofa and he studied her hair again. "You don't want a Campari or something? I've got a bottle somewhere."

"No, I just want you to shove your sash into my gash."

Merridy spoke the words in a clear, pleasant manner. She could have been trying them out for the first time. Or singing a familiar hymn.

An undisguisable fear crept over his face. He spoke in a dry, dazed voice.

"There's something I'd like to understand about you."

But Merridy did not want anyone else's understanding. Least of all Ray Grogan's.

She leaped up and walked fast, across the thick brown carpet, and slipped into the bedroom – the quick, discreet movement of a girl who might have been late for a lecture.

He came in and she was waiting like fate on the bed, shoes already off, eyes looking up at him and her body poised, ready to take notes.

She pointed down at her tights. "All you have to do is take these off and put your hand here."

When, the following morning, Ray did not appear at the usual hour at Tamlyn & Peppiatt, his boss grew worried. Ray was booked to show Mrs Prosser a shack on a three-acre block in Merthyr Drive.

On telephoning his home, Mr Tamlyn discovered that Ray was indisposed.

He asked Teresa: "Was Ray ill yesterday?"

"Not that I saw," she harrumphed.

"He says he's really under the weather. He says he has the flu." Mr Tamlyn cursed and reached for his jacket. "That means I'll have to go. What's Mrs Prosser's number?"

CHAPTER SIX

WELLINGTON POINT BOWLS CLUB
Results for Saturday.
Talbot Shield:
   Swansea 79 defeated Wellington Point 63
   M. Levings 20 – B. Grogan 17.
   Next Saturday will be President's Day/Appreciation Day combined. Old and new members will be made very welcome. Come and join the fun. B. Grogan (Pres. & Sec.).

Shortly before 7 p.m. the following Saturday, Alex drove into Wellington Point to have dinner with Merridy at the Freycinet Court Hotel. It was the night of the Jazz Social and cars were parked bumper to bumper along the main street. He found a space behind Nevin's garage and was locking up his ute when he saw a large woman coming up the alley towards him. Tildy in her war paint. Heading in the direction of the Town Hall.

He remembered that determined, excited walk. Across her bedroom. Both were trying to appease a hunger and fill a stinging blankness. "Why don't you put that down?" she had urged, indicating the novel in his hand. "Harry told me you went to Oxford. Well, I ought to warn you, I don't read much, not unless it's *New Idea*." He remembered the powdery vanilla smell of the room, like the hay-fever tang of wattle. Quickly, he took in the bottles with their tops off, the stray tampons and hairpins and creams, the magazines that she traded with the shop-girls at Talbot's. He had not had sisters and the exaggerated femininity unsettled him. Had he remained in Wellington Point at the age of eleven, he might have ended up in a thick-scented room like this, with a girl like this. She had dimmed the lights and turned on a tape-recorder and swayed her buttocks, mimicking the words so exactly that it might have been Nina Simone herself who gyrated towards him, her arms reaching out with a hopeful smile, until with a desperate little gasp, she said: "Fuck me, Alex." He had dropped his book to the floor and torn down his pants as if peeling the price off himself so that she would not have to see his cheapness. And remembered how she stood up afterwards, sighed, and went to the bathroom, stretching her lolly-green skirt down over her tights.

She was almost level when she noticed him. "Why . . . Alex," and batted her eyes. "You look like you're dressed for a funeral."

"Tildy . . ." He had changed clothes three times until he found the combination of shirt and trousers that seemed to him just right.

"Are you coming to the Social?"

"No."

"Hope it's not *your* funeral," she said brightly.

"Listen, I want to apologise."

"What for, sweetie?"

"I'm sorry I haven't been in touch."

"Don't worry about it. You were crook. Now I'd love a chat, but I have to meet someone."

He watched her hurry up the street towards the Town Hall, growing small as she climbed the steps, and felt something pop when the door closed behind her. She had come out from under his skin, an ant-sized thorn that no longer hurt or inflamed.

Ticking with anticipation, Alex waited in the empty restaurant. On the corner table where Debbie had placed him was a wine bottle with candle wax all spewed and a laminated menu from which pretty soon he could recite every dish.

He had suggested the Freycinet Court Hotel because there was nowhere else to eat in Wellington Point. But now as he sat there, he realised that there was a sentimental reason, too. His parents' honeymoon. When sorting out their belongings, Alex had come across a 1950s brochure stuck inside an album of wedding photographs. The hotel, ideally situated, in the consideration of the copywriter, boasted gardens and lawns, home cooking, hot and cold water. Plus electric light, wireless and sewerage arrangements, as well as access to a nine-hole golf links. The proprietor had even provided a quote: *No holidaymaker at Wellington Point need fear suffering from ennui.*

The rest Alex had learned from Harry Ford, the retired Fleet Street journalist who was one of his parents' few surviving friends. Towards the end of their honeymoon fortnight, according to Harry, Alex's parents walked along Dolphin Sands and made love in the dunes. On the same day they explored Moulting Lagoon.

Behind a small cemetery they came upon a track. There was a wooden gate with a padlock. Basil Dove knocked the dottle from his pipe and climbed over.

"At the end of the track was this farmhouse for sale. They decided there and then to buy it."

Quite why his father should have divulged these details to Harry – whose great regret was that ill-health had left him unable to advance in newspapers, and who had been in Wellington Point forty years expecting to die – Alex had no idea. Perhaps because he was the only other Englishman in town.

Alex looked again around at the unoccupied tables. The place had altered from his last visit, shortly after his return from England four years ago. Then he had asked the waitress for a mango. He might have asked her for a pre-phylloxeric Lafite from her expression. Two more proprietors and now the hotel was owned by Tildy's father, a blusterer with a grey handlebar moustache who – according to Harry – had been retired from the North Hobart Cricket Club because of his beer gut. Framley's taste was reflected in the green chintz pelmets that stretched over the windows and the chaffinch noise that issued from a concealed alarm when Alex had first come into the dining room, causing Debbie to come scurrying from the kitchen.

"Ah, yes, Mr Dove," smirking. "The discreet table for two." She led him to it. "You're the first," in tones that failed to conceal her curiosity about his guest, Alex Dove being considered quite a catch in her small circle.

Outside, it was still light. Alex listened to the street noises. Fred Coggins, whom he vaguely remembered from school, locking up the Talbot emporium; the skimpy figure of Rose-Maree yelling out to Joe Hollows, a boy who had briefly helped him put up fences; Tom Pidd hooting the horn of his ute as he drove slowly past Abbygail the chemist, a keen golfer who did not disguise her ambition to be elected to the council so that Wellington Point could have a sports complex; the sound of an electric guitar being tuned.

In a corner of the restaurant, the coffee-maker gargled.

Perhaps she had forgotten. At 7.15 he borrowed two coins from Debbie and, not wishing to be overheard, went into the street to the public phone. The mouthpiece stank of vomit, lipstick and fried flat-head. He dialled Louisa Meredith House and was put through to the Bowman unit, but the line was engaged. He waited five minutes before trying again. A couple in evening clothes walked by, laughing at something. He heard the engaged tone and returned to the restaurant.

Twenty minutes later, a voice was saying: "I'm sorry." Two lips shyly kissed his cheek. "The phone rang as I was leaving."

"I didn't mind waiting."

"Liar," and pulled in her chair. "My mother always told me that people count up the faults of those who keep them waiting. Do you lie about other things, too?"

He smiled, relieved to see her sitting there. "Only when I'm hungry," he said.

"That's good." She picked up a menu. "I suppose you've decided."

"I ought to warn you – the choice won't be what you're used to in Melbourne."

"Oh, I don't know."

It warmed him to watch the tanned arm with the unusually fair hairs as she fidgeted with the menu. Her blue dress had something animal about it. Under the thin cotton, her breasts swayed like censers, releasing the incense of her perfume.

"You know what I'd love more than anything?" She looked up. "A plate of oysters."

She saw his expression and immediately reached to touch his hand. "Don't worry," she laughed, but in a kind way. "I've learned never to expect oysters in Great Oyster Bay."

"They're recommending the wallaby."

55

She gave a quick look around. "I wouldn't," leaning forward. "It's been in the deep freeze six months."

"It says here 'freshly farmed'."

"Keith lies through his teeth and expects the girls to do the same. He tells customers that the ice cream is home-made when in fact it comes out of Peter's tubs which have their labels peeled off. And you mustn't believe that the scones are home-made and oven fresh. They're frozen and microwaved. 'Don't let them hear the ping,'" in Framley's voice.

"You have a spy in the kitchen?"

She studied the menu. "Now if I'm not having oysters, what shall I have?"

But he wanted to know. "How come you're so well informed?"

"Keith Framley is my father's cousin."

"Oh." And realised that he would have known this had he lived in Wellington Point instead of eight miles outside. Or spoken to Tildy. Everyone was related to each other in Tasmania.

"He let us stay in the hotel before we moved into the unit." She was reading the menu. "I also work here in the evenings. Part of the rent."

"So it's not exactly a treat," he said thickly, "bringing you here."

"Of course it is!"

They were interrupted by Debbie coming to take their orders.

"Ready?" arching a brow when she saw who it was. "Sorry, Merridy, didn't see you come in."

"I'll have the chicken satay," Merridy decided.

Unseeing, Alex turned the menu over. "I might have the steak."

"And to drink?" asked Debbie with a starched expression.

"Tea for me."

"You're not drinking?" said Alex.

"What's tea if it's not a drink?"

"And for you, Mr Dove?" said Debbie, making him feel that he had to pay for her disappointment.

"A glass of Coombend red."

When Debbie had left, Merridy put down the menu. She looked him in the eye. "Listen, I'm very happy to be here. And very sorry I'm late. It's a rule of my parents. Never keep anyone waiting. Ever."

Her face responded shinily to the overhead light. He still could not bear to examine it too closely. Her coral mouth. Her blue dress that was devoted to the contour of her breast.

Picking at the candle wax, he asked about her parents.

CHAPTER SEVEN

HOW MUCH MERRIDY TOLD him then became confused with how much he discovered afterwards.

She was twenty years old, born in Ulverstone on Tasmania's north-west coast. Her mother was a Sunday school teacher, the middle child of strict Methodist parents from Adelaide. The Proudlocks had come to where the most neglected souls on earth had called them and because of the wretchedness to be found in Tasmania. They knew that God was exacting. When informed of their daughter's decision to marry Leonard Bowman, a mechanical engineer from Melbourne, Merridy's grandmother gave a sorrowful headshake. "I have asked Him from the bottom of my heart to increase my suffering and He has obliged."

Merridy's father had trained at night school when he was sixteen. He started in workshops, building bus bodies, and then was put in the drawing office. He designed cases for cameras to go down to 10,000 feet, and water tanks and lifts for mine shafts. But there came a hideous moment when none of this engaged him.

As a student in Melbourne, and during the first eight years of his marriage, Leonard had a conviction amounting almost to a religion. He believed that the world was full of patterns and that even human behaviour could be determined by mathematical equations. The motion of the waves on a windy day was determined by an interplay of these equations. They might be immensely complex, but they could be resolved down to a neat truth – and if only the man or woman in the street learned to switch on a certain part of their brain they would not have to stumble along in the dark.

Leonard was two months short of his fortieth birthday when – overnight – he lost his faith. Up to this point, he had lived according to the precept: "Science requires the simple: it won't tolerate the unnecessary." From this time on, the unnecessary gave meaning to his life.

To conquer his grief, he began to write children's stories. He penned and illustrated more than thirty of these over the next decade. But he was keeping a conversation alive that nobody wanted to hear. The editors who returned his manuscripts were unanimous in their admiration of his drawings and also in their judgment that here was a poetry lover who had never progressed beyond doggerel, whose sure limit was Edward Lear. In the saddest period of Merridy's upbringing, he read to her every night from *A Book of Nonsense*, to the eventual consternation of her mother, who one night burst into Merridy's bedroom and screamed at the pair of them that she was fed up with runcible spoons and would live a contented life were she never to hear those detestable verses again.

But not at the beginning. Not at the beginning.

Leticia Proudlock was twenty-one, young, pretty and naïve when she tripped over Leonard on her way to the daffodil show at the Leven Theatre.

The man who restored her to her feet had arrived in Tasmania that week to take up a job in Burnie. The liking was mutual. He admired her purity and her legs. She saw in him a man of science who might give her practical knowledge of a world that so far she had experienced through the rigid filter of the scriptures. She would adore Leonard principally for everything that her parents were not. Plus he was more sophisticated and ten years older. In Melbourne, he had had European friends. He read poetry and loved foreign cuisine, but was not averse to expressing himself in the vernacular of the workshops. Best of all, he was blessed with a rolling laugh that scattered his sense of the ridiculous into the deepest crevices, and specifically the Methodist Hall in Ulverstone where Leticia had passed a hefty proportion of her adolescence.

Four days after their encounter, he arrived at her parents' house bearing gifts of smoked oysters, blue cheese and brown bread that he had had shipped across Bass Strait on the *Abel Tasman*.

On the formica table in the kitchen was a plastic colander. Leonard fitted it on his head.

> *For the Jumblies came in a Sieve, they did –*
> *Landing at eve near the Zemmery Fidd*
> *Where the Oblong Oysters grow . . .*

At 91 Water Street, Leonard's nonsense verse and gifts fell on rocky soil. "Get that vomit cheese out of the fridge!" ordered Leticia's father as soon as Leonard had departed the house. Luke Proudlock was a teetotaller who never failed to refer to the Bible and whose only passion – apart from his God and his briar pipe – was bowls. He refused to eat plum pudding in case it contained brandy, and used words like "yonder" to describe a country that his forefathers had sailed from in 1832 – "as free settlers". He was accustomed to his wife's stodgy cooking, her custard and coddled eggs. He shoved aside a plate of smoked oysters with the words: "It's like eating snot." Served up spaghetti a week later: "I'm not eating this foreign muck."

If Luke Proudlock felt intimidated by Leonard's spaghetti, he was angered by Leonard's atheism. He and his wife abominated this young man from Melbourne for corrupting their untarnished daughter. They had picked out that she would marry Randal Twelvetrees, the son of the local minister, not a Godless mechanical engineer from the mainland who knew *The Hunting of the Snark* by heart, who believed that religion was like alcohol – "It turns ordinary men into heroes, Mr Proudlock, and heroes into ordinary men" – and whose party trick was to read their futures in a Royal Worcester teacup. The marriage was doomed, even if it was the wish of Him who wept for Lazarus.

Their prophecies were not realised until Merridy was five.

"Do you have siblings?" Alex said.

"I had a brother," she said in a small, deliberate voice.

"Had?"

"He disappeared. But I don't want to talk about that."

Alex waited. Once again, he had a sense of the ocean of sadness within her. But she was not going to elucidate. Flatly, she went on: "The shock gave Mum a stroke."

Mrs Bowman was bedridden for a year, receiving her husband and daughter in a pale grey nightdress and holding them sobbing to her paralysed chest. Then, once they were safely out of the room, she returned her face to the wall. Another year before she could speak again or move her limbs. As soon as her muscles were restored, she took up bowls to exercise her arms. And spiritualism.

On the third anniversary of her son's disappearance she read an advertisement in the Burnie *Advocate*. "You may have lived on earth before! New places or people you pass may seem oddly familiar to you; have you known them in a previous life?" The notice cautioned that certain secrets of life and mental development could not be divulged indiscriminately. That afternoon, she sent off for a thirty-two-page booklet, *The Mastery of Life*, and a fortnight later was welcomed into the Rosicrucians, hoping through them to be reunited with her missing child, who would now be ten.

For the next four years, she kept in touch with a retired Welsh railway engineer who passed on a series of messages from her son. Then, when Merridy was twelve, Mrs Bowman abandoned Taffy Guest and the Rosicrucians and returned to the faith of her parents. She had come to an excruciating realisation. Her loss was her penalty for disobeying God. Her son had wandered off one Sunday morning when the family ought properly to have been at prayer – not visiting steam engines – and was never seen again. She copied out a passage from the Bible and showed it to Merridy's father: *He was the chosen one for the sacrifice that had to be made and in that fact we may find our guarantee that all is well with him.*

"For goodness' sake," Leonard exploded. "God no more exists than I am a purple giraffe." And quoted David Hume to the effect that the life of a boy, even the life of their precious son, was of no greater importance to the universe than that of an oyster.

> "*O was an oyster*
> "*Who lived in his shell*
> "*If you let him alone*
> "*He felt perfectly well.*"

But Mrs Bowman had been shaken by religious fear. Whatever her extravagant feelings for Leonard before their son's abrupt departure from their lives, she now viewed her husband in the clear and unforgiving light of a false shepherd, an idolater, a Satan who had counterfeited the image of Christ. And how was an idolater punished? This she did not show Leonard: *Thou shalt stone him with stones, that he shall die, because he hath sought to thrust thee away from the Lord thy God.*

When her parents argued, Merridy was put in mind of an old pump that had lost its bearings through sucking up so much air and mud.

"Mum used to scold Dad. He was hopelessly entangled in the categories of science. Technological progress had bred pride etc. etc. While Dad kept telling her that she was an idiot for believing in a myth. He hated what he called 'the Methodism in her madness'."

Upon returning to the embrace of her church, Mrs Bowman outdid even her parents in the intensity of her devotion. All the pent-up dicta of her childhood to which she had been pleased to block her ears returned in a furious salvo. Her horror of sexual contact became absolute. Until the evening arrived when Leonard came upon his wife in the hallway, dressed in her peppermint-green coat and zipping up an ancient leather holdall.

"What ho, Lettice?"

"I'm going to stay with Doss."

"When can I expect you back?"

"I'm leaving you, Leonard."

Forced to choose between parents, Merridy elected life with her father, but her mother, who went to lodge with her younger sister in a large, depressing house two streets away, had weekend rights, which invariably commenced with Mrs Bowman escorting Merridy to the Friday-night dance class at the Methodist Hall.

The rest of the weekend was not less grim. In her sister's house on Weybridge Drive, Mrs Bowman bobbed like a decoy duck on the roughened waters of her faith; her features set in an unalterable expression of piety to draw the fire from her Godless husband and wayward daughter.

Her son, on the other hand, was equal unto the angels. But he would be worthy of a part in the Resurrection only if she atoned. So she acknowledged her iniquity. She regretted in her daily prayers that she was a backslider who had gone away from God's ordinances. She had not trained up her child in the way he should have gone. And out of her husband's earshot never tired of reciting to Merridy her favourite verse from Thessalonians: *If we believe that Jesus died and rose again, even so them also which sleep in Jesus will God bring with Him.*

Merridy preferred her father's verses about the Dong with the Luminous Nose. She rejected her mother's petrified morality that nothing could dissipate.

The bitter truth was, once her brother disappeared there was no purpose to life that Merridy could think of. She, too, now inhabited a "yonder" which bore no relation to earth. She was unable to believe in a deity that had removed her favourite person from the face of it. A deity, furthermore, that had turned her mother into a passionless automaton.

Merridy's weekends were an agony for a girl who could recall her mother as a jubilant and loving woman, with a round carefree face. Settled in her new home, Mrs Bowman had the pared-down features of atonement. Once on Saturday, and twice on Sunday, she attended church, the services conducted by the minister whose son she had rejected. Merridy sat in the front row and watched Minister Twelvetrees when he was not looking, his finger pointed upward, his pious face, long and narrow and worn, like the sole of a shoe at the communion rail. What Merridy loved most had been taken from her, and now her mother by God and Minister Twelvetrees.

So she made a promise: she would not allow herself to love again.

Her father, meanwhile, stumbled about his wifeless house, neglecting to eat, refusing to take off his wedding ring. Even though she had deserted him, he treasured the woman he had loved and married, with whom he had fathered two children.

His response to her desertion was to dive back into the hard comforts of science. He threw away his mediocre children's stories, his fanciful drawings, his squeezed-out tubes of Winsor & Newton paint, and concentrated his energies on what he could build in solid three dimensions. God's designs for his servants were never so meticulous as Leonard's plans for the water tower at the paper mill in Burnie, or the mechanised cranes and bulldozers that he once had created for his infant son and now lavished on Merridy, and which she pretended to herself were ponies and dogs. From her father, Merridy adopted her chuckle, her weakness for strong language and her taste for red pasta sauces.

The nearest Leonard came to Christian piety was the respect he taught Merridy for immortal characters like the Dong, the Snark and the Pobble – part of the comforting menagerie of creatures whom she had learned to cherish in the months following her brother's disappearance. And for everything electrical.

Determined to rescue his daughter from her mother's orbit, he encouraged Merridy to apply to a university on the mainland, to move beyond the confines of the

Methodist Hall and Edward Lear. "I want you to have the chance of doing something miraculous with your life – even if it's only a tiny miracle."

"What about our sieve?" asked Merridy, half-joking.

"Our sieve?" He had forgotten. "Bloody hell – our sieve!" Colouring, he resumed: "If we're ever going to build it, all the more reason for you to go to university."

She was nineteen when she won a place at Melbourne to study civil engineering. She had completed almost a year when her father was electrocuted.

After attending a morning funeral in Zeehan, he came out of the pump house in level seven at the Renison Bell mine and was convulsed by spasms. A runaway trolley had trapped an exposed wire as it picked up speed and the live part of the wire flailed against the rail that he was following. The resistance of people to electricity varies, and Leonard might not have suffered so badly had he worn his normal shoes. But he was wearing dress shoes and the leather soles had become damp as he tramped up the passage. The 400-volt shock chucked him off the rail and his hand with its wedding ring on clutched at the side of the shaft and touched a metal support. The flashback burned his face and contracted his hand around the metal. His science taught him that he had four chances every second to pull away, but his body was in too violent a spasm at the electricity rushing in, and it was not until his assistant cracked him away with a wooden brush that he fell free. By then, Leonard was unconscious.

He was taken to hospital in Burnie. Two days later the skin hardened on his feet and his right foot started to go black. Burning from the inside out.

The shock that had blackened his foot might have killed

another man. Instead, Leonard had what Mrs Bowman liked to describe as a life-after-death experience that lasted six minutes. In a lucid interval he reported to his wife, who out of religious duty had returned to nurse him, that he saw a dark tunnel and light at the end of it and felt calm. He waited until he had Merridy on his own before giving a different version, in which he claimed to have observed a large hill with a one-legged man walking with a goose.

"He wondered if it could be my brother," said Merridy, staring at the dish that Debbie had brought and separating the three sticks of chicken satay.

Her father was a month in intensive care. In September, he returned to Zeehan. He had nowhere else to go – he had sold his property in Ulverstone once Merridy left for university. The mining company agreed that he could occupy the house until the end of the year. But a week after his homecoming Merridy heard a gasping sound.

"No air . . . need oxygen."

She took one look. "Dad, I have to call the ambulance. You realise once I call an ambulance you're out of my hands?"

Two further months in Burnie hospital. Another homecoming. But this time harder to follow the twists of his mind. The aneurysm, apart from slurring his speech, had planted on his face an expression that reminded his daughter of the toeless Pobble.

Leonard's accident was proof positive to Mrs Bowman of the workings of a divine providence. She lost no opportunity to tell him so when Merridy was not looking. He could only respond by thumping the table with his good fist and saying: "O, O, O, O." Once, when Merridy heard her father remonstrating, she raced to see what was up. Accused of upsetting her husband, Mrs Bowman defended herself: "I was only saying how much God loves him," at which he thumped the table again and exclaimed: "O, O, O, O," shaking his head with an agonised frown.

Meanwhile, December approached and with it the end of the lease. When, a week before Christmas, the mining company offered Leonard the house for as long as he wanted, Mrs Bowman declined.

So at the end of January, at Keith Framley's instigation, Merridy packed her father and mother into the family Peugeot and drove south to Wellington Point. Mrs Bowman was indifferent to her surroundings, as she had been in Zeehan and before that in Ulverstone. In her Bible-clouded imagination, Wellington Point was another filthy step on the Scala Santa. The three principal things that she had to ask God's forgiveness for in the year 1988 were her lack of warmth towards her estranged husband, her sensuality towards God, and her want of charity to her daughter.

Merridy had set aside her studies in Melbourne to help her mother look after him. When her father did not die immediately she stayed on against her mother's wishes.

CHAPTER EIGHT

To Merridy, her parents' unhappiness was a scandal that she proposed to avoid. She looked forward to the day when she could resume her degree, have her own room again – like Tildy.

"How long have you known Tildy?" Alex asked.

"I've known her since I was" – flattening her hand, Merridy could have been dowsing a flame – "this high."

They had grown up on the same street in Ulverstone. Tildy's father then ran a bed & breakfast three doors down from Merridy's house. The memory of her cousin was connected with Mandeville Gardens, a wide crescent planted with pear trees, where, on Friday evenings and chaperoned by her mother, Merridy walked to the Methodist Hall for Randal Twelvetrees' dance class. Merridy was the brighter of the two. Books, films, museums – she had seen the Francis Bacon exhibition in Melbourne. Tildy occupied herself, rather, with men.

"She hasn't changed. And now she's fallen for Ray Grogan," Merridy said, her laugh edged with disapproval. Or was it regret?

"Like every girl in Wellington Point," and felt a spark of envy for his old schoolmate.

"You don't like Ray, do you?"

"Oh, Ray's all right." It was just that nothing was interesting to Ray unless he could see it undress. When he contemplated Ray's ornate womanising, Alex wondered if the man was not in fact gay.

"I warned you. One more lie – and I'm leaving."

"No, he's fine," Alex hurried on. "He's done very well with his business. He can sell sand to the seals, can't he? Maybe it's his moustache I don't like. Who does he think he is?"

"Errol Flynn?" she ventured, amused.

"In his mother's dreams."

"Speaking of whom, I met Mrs Grogan last night."

"What, the president of our bowls club?" He thought of the owl-beak nose and asbestos face, soft and grey, and smiled.

"That would be her. She's invited my mother to become a member."

"Everyone suspects her of stealing from the kitty. It wouldn't surprise me." Nothing about the Grogans surprised Alex. "Was it Ray you were speaking to on the phone just now?" looking up.

She lowered her eyes, nodded.

He was unable to stem his thoughts: Merridy appeals to Ray because she's new. Every other girl here he's had, save for Tildy – and that's because they're two peas in a pod.

She said: "You haven't told me why you dislike him?"

"I sat beside him in class when we were kids."

"Is that a crime?"

"He cheated. He wrote the answers to exams on his hands." Afterwards, at school in Cumbria, Alex could never look at the English landscape without seeing interposed Ray's palm. The words written in blue biro in shambolic capitals. Sycamore, beech, elm.

She nodded. "Sounds like Ray. Anything else?" Cheating was not enough?

"Oh, I don't know," and tried to laugh. "Wasn't he bitten on the chin by a tiger-snake who died in agony? I don't think Ray ever lost that ugly look on his face."

"A lot of people find him attractive."

"I don't like the way he treats people, that's all."

"How does he treat them?"

"You'll find out if you let him."

"Maybe it's a local thing. Isn't that how you behaved with Tildy?" Her blue eyes returned a bold stare.

"It's not how I wanted . . . it's not how . . ." he repeated uselessly. At the same time, a need to speak of his lapse with Tildy seized him with the force of a cramp. "No, you're right, it was my fault. I could have said no. I should have said no." But they clinked like kidney stones in a jar, his words.

To the rescue bringing more tea came Debbie, with another glass of red wine for Alex.

Alone again with him, Merridy said: "So Ray cheated. Is that all?"

He did not want to tell. But his expression was crying out.

"Alex . . ."

He jutted his chin, not because he was brave but because other young men did when not wanting to dob.

She had decided. "If you don't tell, I'm going. This minute."

Merridy half-rose from the chair and waited there, suspended. The flesh between her breasts had the unnatural whiteness of the powder that his father laid in trails for ants.

Then to keep her from leaving he was blurting it. A revolting rite of passage devised by Ray for Alex to prove that he was an Aussie who belonged and not a Pommy bastard who had no place here. Even now, sixteen years on, Alex could hear ringing in his ears the voice of Ray Grogan bullying him across the playground, pushing him with all the authority of an eleven-year-old captain of cricket to assault the newest member of class as he set up a pyramid of marbles. And so Alex had strolled up to Jack Cheele – who smiled trustingly at him, "Hi, Piers, wanna go?" who had no idea what was about to occur – and kicked him, hard, in the balls. An action so out of character and committed from a wish to try and include himself in the local hoonery. At least that was his excuse. Ray Grogan had no excuse. He had kneed everyone in the balls all his life. But the astonishment in Cheele's face was something that Alex had carried with him ever since; a pinch of shame in his guts that preyed on his mind at inappropriate moments. "Piers . . ." gasping. Doubled up on the ground. Those anguished, accusing, ineradicable eyes. It was practically Alex's last memory of the school. He never told his parents and they never found out. A week later, they set off in their car for the auction room in Campbell Town.

"And what happened to Cheele?" Merridy was asking, still suspended. Something about the way that he lowered his voice a little, sounding grave, made her believe and forgive him. She saw Alex in that moment as a lion in a poor zoo, prey to teasing boys. Prodded and prodded, until he behaved like a hyena.

"I tried to get in touch when I came back. But like a lot of people at school, he'd left Wellington Point. No one knew where he lived, whether he'd gone interstate, whether he was still in Australia. So I don't know what happened to him, but I composed endless letters in my head."

His answer seemed to satisfy Merridy, who resumed her place. She poured milk into her tea and stirred. "Tell me, why does Ray call you Piers?"

He looked sharply at her. "You've been talking about me to Ray Grogan?"

She blushed.

His turn to come to the rescue. "Because Piers is my first name. But I never use it."

"Why not? It's a lovely name." So English – evoking buckets and spades and music-halls.

He breathed in. "It's the name I had when I lived here before."

CHAPTER NINE

ALEX HAD GROWN UP in Wellington Point until he was eleven. Sometimes he looked back, invariably without success, to his boyhood. He had pulped so many memories that whenever he tried to invoke his mother and father, a hopeless distortion overtook him. His parents sprang from their photographs on his bedroom wall, discoloured, in wool clothes saturated with a particular smell, and addressing each other in rotund voices by names that might have come from the movies that they saw at the Prince of Wales on their monthly excursions to Hobart. Marjorie. Basil. Piers.

It was not intentional, his name change. After the accident, he had gone to school in England but arriving at Sedbergh at the start of the Easter term, he was told by his housemaster: "You're not going to be called Piers, old chap. We've got four Pierses."

"My second name is Alexander."

"Alexander is toooo long."

So he became Alex. He even got used to it, wanting nothing more in a way than to live in the present tense. It was only when he came back to Wellington Point that he found himself having to explain to people that for reasons too silly to go into he was now actually Alex – in fact had been Alex longer than he had ever been Piers.

But he could not shake off that frowsy odour of old wool. He still caught a whiff of it when passing Agnes's charity shop. He did not know if the odour was soap or dead skin, or what it was, but whenever he smelled those "pre-loved" clothes he was jolted back to the sight of a wardrobe filled with his father's suits and, next to the bookie's tweeds from Bidencope's, his mother's cropped jackets and angora sheaths. Plus a blueberry Crimplene frock, bought in the Mather summer sale for the occasion of Prince Philip's visit to Hobart.

When, having been away more than a decade, Alex had returned to Tasmania, almost his first action after visiting the farm and observing its neglected state was to remove his parents' clothes from the house and drive the whole lot to Agnes.

Upon leaving her shop he had walked into a man getting out of a new Holden. He was a healthy-looking type, dressed in clerk-grey trousers and a plain white shirt with cufflinks.

"Piers Dove," cunning eyes evaluating him.

"Ray Grogan. I didn't recognise you . . . the moustache."

So they faced each other outside the Op-Shop.

"Fancy meeting you here, Piers," and patted the moustache that gave the impression of a bird hovering over his mouth.

"Living people often meet."

"What brings you back to Wellington Point?" and his green eyes looked searchingly at Alex.

"It's my home, Ray. I was born here," he said stiffly.

"Couldn't make it in the big smoke, eh?"

"Matter of fact, I'm about to go back there."

"How are you earning a crust these days?"

"I'm training to be a teacher."

"What, like Miss Pritchard? You know, that surprises me. You were so raw, Piers, I wouldn't have fed you to my chooks."

"How is Miss Pritchard by the way?"

"She carked it. But they're looking for a teacher. You should apply. You really should."

"Actually, Ray, I'm glad I bumped into you."

"What can I do for you, Piers?"

"I wanted to track down Cheele."

"Cheele? Who the heck's Cheele?" caressing his chin, in the guarded way that he used to do when Miss Pritchard asked him to spell out a word.

"You don't remember Cheele?"

But Ray had spotted something. "What happened to your hand, mate?"

Alex to his chagrin forgot Cheele and looked down at the black sock that he had taken off to bind his torn palm. "I was fixing a windmill," he muttered.

Ray contemplated the makeshift bandage. "Be careful of tetanus. It gives you lockjaw. You won't be able to speak. God, wouldn't that be great?" and the sun glinted gold on a cufflink.

Alex rubbed his hand.

But Ray was on a roll. "Talking of smoke, that place of yours ought to have a match put to it. That's what it wants. It puts me in mind of some of them people in Egypt."

"What, Moulting Lagoon Farm?"

"The house is back to buggery. Not worth a thing."

"You don't know that."

"Oh, yes, I do," and gave a husky chuckle. "I've been looking after it, mate."

"You? But Mr Tamlyn arranged the lease."

"One of my first jobs when I went to work for him was to take care of your place. And know what? I could hardly give it away with a tea bag."

So turning points come in plain clothes. The abysmal state of the crops and fences, the gates that wouldn't swing, the dilapidation of the house – all this, Alex understood, could be blamed on his schoolmate. Ray had had it in his power to walk around the property with the tenant and force him to put things to rights. Instead, he had done nothing with the asset but pocket his 10 per cent. One more thing for which he never would forgive Ray.

And having returned to Wellington Point steeled to get rid of the farm, Alex was all of a sudden determined to keep it.

"That's a pity because I was going to ask Mr Tamlyn to put it on the market."

"Is that so?" Ray leaned back against his car and folded his arms. "I suppose I could do a valuation. Mind you, nobody in their right mind would buy it except maybe a bloody Japanese – who are buying just about everything."

"You please yourself what you do, but if you ever come round there you won't walk away from the place."

"I said I could do a valuation."

"Save your precious time, Ray. I wouldn't wipe my arse with any valuation you did. Just ask Mr Tamlyn to send me back all the keys and papers to do with the lease. I've a damned good mind to give them to a lawyer."

"What? You're going to keep it now, are you?"

"Too right I am. And one more thing."

Ray waited.

"I'm not Piers any more. I'm Alex."

"Can you do that?" said Ray. "I suppose you can. Like a sex-change. But don't think giving a mongrel another name makes him less of a mongrel. You'll always be Piers to me. Always."

"Fuck you, Ray."

At this, Ray laughed. "Not while the dogs are still on the street."

"Hi, Ray."

"Hi, Agnes."

"I must say, it's grand to see Piers again," she smiled, locking up the shop and its new stock.

"I suppose."

They watched her cross the road to Talbot's.

Ray said almost wistfully: "I had a dig in that once," before his curiosity overcame his facetiousness.

But Alex was walking away.

He was passing the chemist's when he heard Ray call out in a different voice. "Hey, Piers? Why keep it?" And when Alex hesitated, he went on. "Hell, Piers . . . Alex . . . whoever you want to be. Why would anyone who's been lucky to get away from here look for a reason to come back? There's nothing to do in Wellington Point 'cept die."

Alex strode on. Into the view he had been about to renounce, and left Ray standing there, his arm frozen in a vague gesture at the bay.

Very possibly Ray was right. Unlike Swansea or Bicheno on the same coast, the town had not grown. Nothing commercial had made it sprawl larger than the backwater it was. Roads of red dirt leading to all sorts of futures, none of them enviable, and crawling with copperheads like Ray who took the colour of the country they lived in.

It had been down one of these roads that a 60-ton semi-articulated Scania log-truck came thundering as Alex's father, already going blind, and his wife beside him, nosed the family's Ford Zephyr out of their drive. Alex could never see a log-truck without imagining that moment: the dragonish smoke streaming from the two vertical exhausts, the air brakes screaming, the old-growth eucalypts tumbling.

The truck had killed his parents outright, picked them off clean like an artillery shell. In the crater that it had left behind, Alex had struggled ever since to find some battered meaning.

His parents had willed everything they owned to him. Instead of their possessions being dispersed, Alex inherited

78

their house, estate, belongings. Right down to a lifetime's subscription to *Bottleship* magazine.

All this he had abandoned until such a time as he felt equal to dealing with it. While in England, he had deliberately put any decision on hold. But by the time of his reappearance in Wellington Point on this hot, dry afternoon, he had made up his mind. He told Agnes that he planned to stay until the weekend, by which time he hoped to have washed his hands of the place.

"So you won't be coming back?" she said.

"No, Agnes. I don't think so."

That was before he bumped into Ray Grogan.

After the conversation outside the Op-Shop, to steady himself, Alex had taken one of his father's rods and driven in his hired car to the mouth of the Swan. The river broadened into an estuarial beach of white sand, dotted with tiny red crabs and patrolled over by pelicans. He walked along it, calculating. It was one thing to change his mind about selling Moulting Lagoon Farm, but what could he do with the property? His parents had lost enough money on the farm, and on a regular basis. Could he, with what little he had inherited, make it work?

Alex tried to bat away the thought. He put up the cane rod and caught a small bream with a prettyfish. He was eleven the last time he had stripped out a line or spent a quiet hour fishing. He could tell it was a bream by the black chevrons on the tail.

He buried the bream head down in the sand after gutting it. The fish flapped for a while on the beach amongst its guts, a headless, tailless, gutless creature trying to fly.

Am I being a pathetic bastard? he asked himself. He looked at the bream and then out across the bay, and there was not a nerve in his body that did not twitch like his line.

By the time he returned to his car an idea had formed. He knew what he was going to do.

Until this moment, Alex had assumed that he would continue to live and work in London. On coming down from Oxford with a degree in English he had enrolled at a teacher-training college in Putney. He lived in a rented one-bedroom flat on the sixth floor of a mansion block near Southfields Tube station, and had a girlfriend, Sarah, a teacher on the same course whom he described to his uncle-cum-guardian in Sedbergh as "good for me".

Even so, Moulting Lagoon Farm was always at the back of his mind a refuge; a place where he was in his heart while he was away. He might be living on the other side of the world, but on February nights in London, after two or three months of slanting grey rain, he recalled a jetty on the edge of some sea, and kept alive the notion that he would one day go back there for a visit or maybe longer; maybe even with Sarah.

Since his departure from Tasmania twelve years before, the house and paddocks had been let out to the neighbouring farmer. The call when it came was a letter from Mr Tamlyn, the managing agent, to say that Bill Molson had died and his estate had to sell up. As a result, the trustees wished to terminate the lease on Moulting Lagoon Farm.

The letter was a signal for Alex to face what he had left unresolved. But when he invited Sarah to accompany him to Tasmania, she declined: "I'd be getting in the way." Not until the night before he flew did she enquire with the seriousness of an oldest child what his plans were for the farm, and he went through the motions that he was returning to tidy up various odds and ends. But Sarah sensed the shape of his longing. She knew when he went out the door and stepped into the lift that he did not know what he was going to do.

A large part of her hoped that distance would lend clarity and he would arrive at a decision about their future as well. Nine days later he telephoned from Tasmania and said in a careful voice: "I have something to tell you." But rather than ask her to marry him he announced that he could not see a way of continuing their relationship unless she was prepared to abandon Southfields for the outermost margin of the earth.

"You? A farmer?" Sarah had shouted on the telephone. "I'll tell you one thing what you are. You're completely fucking nuts. All you've ever husbanded is a cold."

From Hobart, he had already called his uncle. "I'm going to do something quite mad."

"I'm so glad," said his uncle, "she sounds the right girl for you."

"No, no, I've decided to keep the farm."

At any rate, he had passed Merridy's peculiar test. She sat down and picked up her cup and looked at him over it.

"Well, whatever happened between you and Tildy, it no longer matters." On Thursday, out of the blue, Ray Grogan had invited Tildy to the Jazz Social at the Town Hall. "She asked me to pass on a message. She says her heart is spoken for."

It sounded like a phrase from one of Tildy's magazines. But what, Alex wanted to know, about Merridy's heart? "Tell me, why was Ray ringing you just now?"

"Oh, just being an idiot," and sat back.

"Did he hope you might change your mind?" Even at the last moment, with Tildy humming to her reflection: Your ship has come in, honey. Your. Ship. Has. Come. In.

"I don't know what Ray thought," Merridy said quickly.

Still, it nagged. "What made you crash his party – if you dislike him so?"

"I didn't crash. I was invited." Her eyes held his and a sly expression came into them. "And maybe I fancy him."

"Do you?"

"He has something."

"Do me a favour," Alex said. "Just explain to me for my peace of mind and my education, what was it between you and Ray? Everywhere I go in this town, I hear about you and that odious fucker."

"Oh, Alex. What is it with you people? He's not odious, he's footling."

"No, he's not footling, he's odious. He has one woman after another." And again saw Ray's face, in the moment when he squeezed Merridy's arm. His expression like that of a farmer in Cumbria who shot badgers in the stomach so that they crawled back to their sett and died there out of reach and without trace.

She tilted her head. Eyes glinting. Not knowing yet whether she found Alex attractive. But willing to concede that he was intelligent and generous and pleasant to look at, and dependable as the navigation-light beam that she saw from her bedroom, flashing on the tip of Schouten; and that something about him, while being tender beyond belief, was obviously strong enough to wrestle a steer to the ground, and even to punch it on the forehead if need be. And she could talk without strain to him.

"You really want me to tell you why women like Ray? Well, he's one of the few guys in this place who's on the make – and that's sexy. He's hustling, he's ambitious, he works hard, and that isn't very common here. He listens, which is always a bonus. And there's a bit of danger around him."

"Well, I'm sorry . . . I don't see it. I do not see it."

"Then can I ask you to keep this to yourself? I can't have Tildy knowing. At one time, yes, I did have a slight walking-out with Ray, but oh, my, how slight. Tildy wasn't in the picture and anyway she's my best friend. Well, it was appalling. You know what they're like, these men – the engineering faculty was full of them. They're so transparent, but you get used to them. I always knew that if I stopped dead and turned around and said: 'Take your trousers off, let's go to work,' they'd run a mile. Though Ray, I have to say, really got up my nose. I thought: OK, I'll do just that – and I did it. But what you probably don't know is what subsequently happened."

"No, that's not completely convincing."

"Oh, Alex!" shaking her head.

"What?"

She looked at him, then burst out laughing. He had never heard such a laugh. It reverberated through the whole building.

"I was on his bed down to my underpants and he ran away."

Ray would never forget the humiliation in his bedroom.

"I just want to have a cuddle," he told Merridy. "You could lie on top of me. It would be safe. I probably wouldn't even get an erection."

"But I want you to put your hand down my pants," she said hospitably.

Ray sat down heavily on his capacious bed and looked sideways at her. He had thought that he wanted her. But he was not feeling seductive.

He stared down between his legs with a ghostly expression. "I'm . . . not sure I can," he said brokenly.

83

She went on, musing: "Isn't it funny how we talk about vaginas as the sexual zone rather than the labia?"

It had never happened to him before. "I don't know why you dislike me. I just want to give you pleasure."

She sat in silent thought. "You know what would give me pleasure?"

"What?" His answer was edged with desperation.

"How long have we got?"

"As long as you want. All night – if you want." But his eye did not join in his smile. How fatally he had under-estimated Merridy. It would take more cannon-fire than he had bargained for to storm this citadel. A lot more.

"I remember you telling me that you liked to read poetry aloud."

"Yes," in a mossy whisper. And pawed his moustache with his fingers. He might have been checking to see if it was still there.

She sprang from the bed and opened the door and went into the main room. When she came back she was holding her coat. She patted its pockets. "Here we are," and produced a faded blue clothbound book that she handed to him.

He looked at the spine. "*A Book of Nonsense,* by Edward Lear," he mouthed. Already, he smelled the renewed stench of blazing pitch.

"Perhaps you could read to me?" she said.

It was not simply Ray's failure to perform that marked his rupture with Merridy. It was his inability to deal with what, remarkably for him, had not happened.

When, failing to hear from Ray-as-in-sunshine, Merridy paid a special visit to Tamlyn & Peppiatt two days later to assure him that he must not worry, it did not matter, he had addressed her in the tones of a stranger and refused to receive her comfort. His peremptoriness caused Merridy to question whether Ray had been attracted to her in the first place. It was a little blow to her pride and she went away feeling rather stupid, which was the cause of her preoccupied expression when a moment later she ran into Alex. She had got it wrong. She was arrogant. Why should Ray not fancy Tildy, who was, after all, easier and nicer? After that Merridy tried to be happy for her cousin – in fact, *was* happy for her. So that when Ray telephoned – just as she was washing her hands prior to leaving for the hotel – to apologise for behaving like a jerk, and to plead, even at this late hour, for Merridy to change her mind and come as his guest to the Jazz Social, she was grateful for the opportunity to turn him down flat.

Watched impassively by her father, whose bed she sat on to take the call, she informed Ray in an upbeat voice: "Nothing personal, no judgment intended, but it's been a really positive experience. It's taught me a lot to be at the end of a certain sort of behaviour, because it's made me realise it's not what I want right now."

The problem of Ray Grogan dispensed with, Merridy returned to her bedroom. She was late, she was late. That was all she could think as she slipped into her dress, called out goodbye to her parents and dashed from "Otranto", only to stop on the top of the steps – *Put this on and you'll see. You'll be a hit with it.*

Then, re-emerging a few moments later, she had run all the way along the main street to meet Alex Dove for dinner.

"I was also bored," she said, and straightened her back. She glanced around the restaurant at the paper napkins that earlier in the day she had folded into cones. "This isn't a place for anyone under fifty."

"It's not so bad," Alex said.

"I know what Dad would say if he could speak. He'd say it's a one-horse town where even the horse is on its last legs. Everyone's waiting around to die, and when they're not sitting in, waiting for death, or being poisoned by the water, they're waiting for you to fall flat on your face – and then they'll jump right on you. Mum's upset that she let herself be talked into bringing Dad here. She'd like to leave the island altogether. 'What has Tasmania produced except Errol Flynn and he got out as soon as he could,'" in Mrs Bowman's clipped voice.

Merridy's outburst took Alex by surprise. "Oh, come on. It's no different to anywhere else. It's all right once you get to know it."

"Tildy's been here two years. She says unless you have kids no one will talk to you. Then once you have kids, you're no longer part of the in-group. And if you stay on, then people who've left think you're a loser. She says there's no real jobs unless you want to work as a shop-girl in Talbot's or a waitress here." And sat back, breathing in quick breaths. She knew the details like an enemy.

"She says that?" All the same, Merridy's prejudices were ones that he himself had felt.

At Merton, Alex had come upon Henry James's description of Baltimore: "It affected me as a sort of perversely cheerful little city of the dead." There was a period after he reoccupied his childhood home when he looked at Wellington Point through adult eyes accustomed to the Oxford or London metropolis. And found it as depressing as a fairground. A town of flapping gums where no one escaped their neighbour's eye. "Don't do or say anything in this place if you don't want everyone else to know about it next morning," Harry Ford had warned Alex in his first week back, before adding: "Look close and you'll see this coast is full of quartzite. It's why the inhabitants are fractured and double-faced." In Wellington Point, any singularity or achievement – a little beauty or education – was regarded as an excess. In Talbot's, Alex overheard Joe Hollows, the boy who had been helping him fence a paddock, confide to the shop-girl: "He knows fuck all. What was he reading in so-called Oxford – litter-rat-ure? That's going to be all sorts of use down here." In that home of gossip, the Returned Servicemen's Club, local spite had it that Alex consorted with goats. Like any Pom left to himself. As any sensible person tended to leave Poms, which by dint of his parents and his slightly flattened accent Alex was regarded still.

"You can always leave," he told Merridy. He was not yet ready to admit that up until a few days ago he had been considering this option for himself. That when they met in the lane behind the school he was even then debating whether to go back to Southfields.

"Oh, I plan to. As soon as my father . . ." And stared at the backs of her hands that she was washing when Ray telephoned, flecked with the salve that she had rubbed on her father's lips. "He doesn't have long. He's left me an inheritance, not large, but enough to take me away from here." To create her tiny miracle, whatever that was.

"Where will you go?" conscious of a clatter of hooves in his heart.

"Back to Melbourne probably. My mother is pissed off with me for dropping out of uni."

"Do you want to go to Melbourne?"

"Not much. I'd prefer to go to Greece."

"Why Greece?"

"I don't know. I always wanted to go to Greece."

She wanted to find a partner. A Jumbly boy. She had not met anyone, there just had not been the click.

Most convent girls in their first year at uni went – as Tildy enviously had predicted – "besonkers". Engineering students were divided between "the Alfs" – the bogans who were rough as guts – and "the Ralphs", who attended lectures in ties and middle-class tweeds. For the second time in her life, Merridy recognised her power and it was heady. Plucky, slightly thin-skinned, but willing to take on anything, she had had two boyfriends at the same time: a raw and puppyish Ralph, whom she saw during the day, and a more experienced Alf, whom she tormented in the evenings. Unlike the majority of her contemporaries, she had not been to bed with her boyfriends. Part of her knew that they were "practice men". To sleep with either would risk raising the bar of complications and entail a commitment that Merridy was not prepared to make. She might have left Ulverstone and Randal Twelvetrees behind, but she could not forget her adolescent promise to herself. At twenty, she continued to feel her old antagonism to love; a suspicious fear of it that Ray Grogan had absolutely failed to lift, for all his persistence.

Alex Dove was another matter. So far their exchange had been tentative, but the young farmer had begun to spur in her emotions that Merridy suspected of being dangerously close to those she had guarded herself against.

At first, Alex had merely intrigued her. Then Ray told her about what had happened to Alex's parents. The effect was galvanic. She could not help but be attracted to a quality in him to which she responded in spite of herself; his candour and also his loss. She saw this vividly as the evening wore on: how his parents' death was a stone that dragged him down. It was an odd characteristic, unusually intense in both of them, that each would be drawn to a commensurate tragedy in the other.

Prominent in what was appealing about Alex was his instinct to blot out unpleasantness. He lived – it seemed to Merridy – with both feet planted in the present. He did not blame anything on his parents' death. He believed in putting the past behind him; in not looking back. She, on the other hand, only looked back. This was the difference between them. If there is an instinct to chain oneself to the past that leaves even the longest-serving convict howling for mercy, Merridy had it.

Towards the end of the meal a fantasy plucked at her. Somehow to whisk herself into Alex's slipstream and leave her history behind. She did not know what made life worth living, hadn't a clue, but Alex might.

She finished her meal before him. In the darkening room, she watched him chew his steak. "You're a slow eater."

"It's a family curse."

His father had chewed each mouthful sixty-four times, "like Mr Gladstone" – a habit that Alex could not shake. It had resulted in him having his plates endlessly taken away at school and university.

She said: "I still don't understand why you came back from London. I mean, don't you mind being so far away from everywhere? This is the end of the world."

He put down his knife and fork. "If you want to see the end of the world, go up Regent Street on a rainy Sunday afternoon."

"So where is the centre?"

"Wherever each one of us is." He raised his head. "Isn't it?"

"Is that what you believe?"

"Why not?"

"No, I mean, really believe." And suddenly her eyes were less playful than her mouth.

The question having appeared from nowhere hovered like a frightful moth between them.

Immediately, Alex was out of his depth. He had met Merridy two, three times. And yet he felt that somewhat more than the fate of the evening hung on his reply.

He pushed away his plate that had some meat still on it. "If you're talking about God, then no," he said quite fiercely. His heroes might have believed in God. Merridy's mother obviously did. But Alex could not lie, even if it meant losing her.

"I can see from a Darwinian point of view why the Church came into force," he went on, "because we need a body that is not the State to govern our morals. But all those wonderful con tricks about heaven and hell . . ."

Her eyes relaxed. "I think that's all a nonsense, too."

"You do?"

"Yes. I think we're just an accidental growth of moss that's appeared on a rock. To me, it's no coincidence that the vast majority of saints were created before the Middle Ages – when we can't check up on them."

"But you do believe in something?"

She considered his question. "The sea. I could believe in that."

"Any particular aspect of it?" He was smiling again. "It's quite a big place."

Another pause. "I believe that people who go away to sea always come back."

"That sounds poetic." For the first time, he could understand how she might irritate. "But what does it mean?"

"Does one's belief have to mean anything to anyone else? I suppose I have a residual superstition that when we

90

die, we don't die, we're still around somehow. But what about you? You haven't answered my question."

He picked at the candle wax. A piece fell away, the colour of dead flesh. Of something divine, perhaps. And though he did not have an answer, he was terrified to disappoint.

"I believe in bottles."

"You're an alcoholic?" she frowned.

"My father probably was," with humour. "No, not bottles with gin or wine in them. Not anything like that."

"What, then?"

"Ships."

"Ships?" She looked at him.

A chaffinch noise announced Debbie bringing the bill on a willow-pattern saucer. She started to clear the table when Alex reached across and seized all three satay sticks from Merridy's plate and slipped them without explanation into his jacket inside pocket.

The bill settled with a substantial tip, Alex was unwilling to tear himself away. He picked off a last piece of wax. The bottle was now bare of it and the candle shot up straight from the mouth. On the other side of the flame Merridy peered down into her cup.

"What are you looking at?"

She was insolently beautiful to him.

"Tea leaves. You can read the future." Another thing her father had taught her.

"What do they say?" leaning forward, immensely interested. But seeing only warm black wet flakes in the discoloured milk.

Her eyes fluttered towards him through the distorted air. "Not telling."

*

It was late when Alex walked her home. Past Sergeant Finter sitting in his Ford Falcon on the corner of Radley Street. The policeman looked at her and all but saluted. A woman to make you go crazy, his face said to Alex. Past the Town Hall. Barney Todman playing "Stranger on the Shore" and through tall windows a blur of faces nuzzling into necks and mascaraed eyes half-shut. Up Waterloo Street to Louisa Meredith House and the modest villa with its melon curtains closed and between the gap a bright light on.

He stood beneath the window, the light falling in a stripe across his nose. "Goodnight." Not daring to touch her for fear of bursting.

"Goodnight," said Merridy and for the first time trembled for him. For them both. "Love is a weakness. It peters out, it enfeebles, it has no mandate beyond the appeasement of lust; it is lent and snatched away." So did she remember the words of her mother, who lay on her bed behind the curtain, waiting.

But then her father's words returned:

> For day and night he was always there
> By the side of the Jumbly Girl so fair . . .

She looked with an intense expression at Alex's forehead where his hairline started. Quickly, she brushed his cheek with the back of her hand. "It's been fun, I must say."

"Will I see you again?" he said.

Merridy smiled at him. "What do you reckon? Small town."

The table radio was still on, playing Bach. Her father lay on his pneumatic bed, eyes closed and a muscle quivering under them. She switched off the motet and waited. When the head on the pillow failed to stir, she dimmed the light that her mother had kept on for the past four nights, ever since her evening with Ray Grogan.

In the Town Hall Barney Todman struck up a faster tune.

Merridy slipped into the room that she shared with her mother. She undressed and got into bed and stretched out, eyes on the ceiling, inhaling the music. The sound of the guitar escorted her back to a draughty barren hall of ugly red brick tacked onto the side of the Methodist church in Ulverstone, and the game that they played on Friday evenings, all the girls and boys; a sort of tribal mating ritual. The ripped copies of the *Advocate* strewn quite prettily about on the floor; the brass-rubbings pinned to the walls; and the surprisingly well-tuned piano on which Randal Twelvetrees, the repressed idiot who might have married her mother and into whose care Mrs Bowman out of some deformed sense of guilt now sought to deliver Merridy, played a jolly tune like "Coming Round the Mountain" that would stop abruptly in mid-note. She recalled the boys in an outer circle, each holding an *Advocate*, and the girls in an inner circle, skipping round in different directions, and – when the music stopped – the rush to grab hold of your partner and open up the newspaper and leap on it, standing very still, waiting for Randal to sweep back the gingerish hair from his eyes and shuffle over to turf off the last pair who had jumped on. She remembered with a cold shiver how he pressed his unblinking face against the bodies that in order to remain upright stood on tiptoe, inspecting for any stray foot that remained off the newspaper, or any part of a foot. The losing pair identified, the surviving couples each tore their newspaper in half and the music started up; and so on, down and down until there were just two couples left, circling each other around a shrinking island of shredded paper, an island no larger than a page, dancing closer and closer together until the piano fell silent. And she remembered what a strong connection you had with the other person if you happened to be one of these last two pairs, which repeatedly she was, so strong was her wish to escape the devouring ginger stare of Randal Twelvetrees. You were not a mob any longer, you were a couple. The girl perspiring under her little armpits and her nervous young breasts pushing against her partner's chest, and yet really enjoying it. The boy, too. It was superb. An ornate and deadly cocktail. "When it gets down to a tram-ticket, you're both of you dry-rooting," laughed Tildy. And then only one couple was left. And she remembered a boy with a massive erection who was too embarrassed to press himself up against her – and so he lost the game. Merridy had felt this thing and wondered what the hell had hit her, but it was nature sorting itself out. She had won him in a way and on those Friday evenings winning was everything. Afterwards, everyone walked home, although Merridy remembered one occasion when she had to plead with the boy to remain behind, until it was time for her mother to collect her, so that she would not be left alone with Randal. Sitting there in the hall beside the boy, not saying anything. Not doing anything either, beyond holding his hand while Randal cleared up bits of newspaper. There was a rural dorkiness about it all that she imagined when she thought of England, but also a thwarted passion.

Merridy remembered this, then looked across at her mother who lay awake, mouthing silent words at the ceiling and the beam that flashed from the lighthouse.

"I've found him."

Her mother's lips went on moving. Where had he got

to, her dearest boy, her firstborn? Was he in trouble? In pain? But he was strong. She wished that he could be here to protect her. Then stopped. "Who?"

"Who did you think?" sighed Merridy and threw back her head on the pillow. The surf boomed. Another spoke of light rotated on the ceiling, raking the night. "The bloody Dong?"

Walking back towards his ute, Alex resembled a bird at the top of its swoop, wings clipped to its side. Chesting the air like a bowsprit.

He drove home. North along the coast road and then down a small trunk road that led, five windy miles later, to his farm. Carrying in his head an image that he wanted never to fade. He hoarded up in his mind the smallest detail of their dinner. Her forthright way of speaking. Her sudden seriousness. Her mannish laugh that made him feel nothing so funny or delightful had ever happened to anyone. He had talked about his past in a way that he was not accustomed to talk with anyone, and said to her all the things that a young man might feel inspired to say who had lost his heart thoroughly. And yet when he pulled into the drive, he had, as inevitably he did on reaching this blind corner, a flashback of a white Ford Zephyr with his parents inside juddering forward.

Five drops of rain splashed onto the windscreen and then others. He shivered, struggling to invoke Merridy, and touched his cheek where she had brushed it with the back of her hand. But his younger self had ambushed him.

CHAPTER TEN

IT WAS FOUR YEARS before. He was twenty-three. He felt raw and nervous as he stood at the edge of the road where out of some superstition he had parked his hired car. Suddenly, he did not want to walk for half a mile up the worn-out drive of pale gravel that had lost its guts; past the windmill and the Oyster Bay pine, to find, as he knew he would, the house as he had left it; he did not want to squeak open the fly-screen into the kitchen; he did not want to stay.

So when he started up the drive, he was more resolved than ever to sell the place.

The house he climbed to was a low brick one with white-washed walls and a green corrugated-iron roof that sagged at the back. It was single storey and stood next to a farm-yard squared off by sheds and barns. On an unmowed lawn in front of it, obscuring the windows, was a large tree. The pine had grown enormous since his childhood, so that its lowermost branches reached out and all but brushed the roof.

He walked through the long grass to the base of the tree and stood before two slabs of Maria Island granite inscribed with the names and dates of his parents. He looked at the simple headstones and thought of his mother and father beneath, their bones blending with the roots.

Something was wrong with the iron windmill. The machinery creaked wildly and gouts of water streamed down from a pipe and into the yard. He delayed going into the house in order to fix the leak. For whatever reason, it was important that he stop the flow of water. But in trying to repair the windmill, he gashed his hand.

The blood oozed out of the cut. He washed his hand under the leaking pipe. Then took off his left boot and sock, and bound the sock around the wound.

He could anticipate Sarah's reaction.

The grassy air was scented with cow dung. He breathed it in and clenched his fingers to dull the throbbing. The water splashed from the pipe.

He leaned against the windmill and took a long look at his childhood home. The house had a flower bed around it overspilling with bottle-brushes and wild daisies. It lay in a hammock of barley fields and grazing paddocks that rose on either side to hills planted with black wattle and gums; and beyond, into Crown land of thicker bush and old-growth forest. Behind, paddocks sloped down to a windbreak of macrocarpa and through the trees a lagoon glittered. These were the smells and shapes to which he was first exposed. He knew their features better than his own.

He picked his way through the long grass, oppressed by the weight of memories. Their vividness had come to an end when he left Australia for England. Twelve years in that cold, foggy climate had blurred him. Everything that he had succeeded in keeping at bay behind a screen, as it were, of sycamore, beech and elm, threatened now to dart out into the open and overwhelm him.

His thoughts gallivanted off. He had the illusion that he could recall with extraordinary clarity almost every day of his childhood better than any day at boarding school or university. His memory struggled along a ditch. Was it here that he had sat with his father and watched the eels wriggling across the wet paddocks to the dam? He heard his father ruminating: "You know, no one has ever seen an eel mate." Or over there that the tiger-snake had wrapped itself about his father's leg and only uncoiled after being lured away with the glass of Beefeater that he happened to be holding? Afflicted with the memories, Alex trod across the lawn, ignoring the pain in his hand, ignoring the hives on his legs made by the grass, and opened the fly-screen to the kitchen and went in, to the damp and stringent odours of a house that had not been lived in since he was a boy.

He inhaled. Smells of dripping and Mortein insect spray. Another stink turned out to be a dead possum in the disused rainwater tank, heaving with a fleece of maggots.

Alex dug a hole in the flower bed and buried the rancid corpse with a rusted spade that he discovered in the shearing shed. Then he came back in and sat at the blackwood table and ate the sandwich that he had brought with him.

He looked around. Some things remained in the darkness beyond the lantern glow of memory. Though not the image of his parents playing Scrabble at this table. He heard their shouts as his father got up to refill his glass and upset the letters. His mother saying: "Piers, your legs are younger than mine. Run to my room and get the dictionary." She had been dead set against the idea of a dictionary on ideological grounds. But that was before her husband gave her one for their tenth wedding anniversary. From that moment on, she pored over her dictionary every night, ransacking it for obscure words. Especially words composed of two letters. She never knew what they meant, but was categorical that they did mean something. "Darling," she would say testily, "everyone knows that your luck is determined by the flow of qi" – although, when challenged, it usually transpired that she had confused the Chinese life force with the Egyptian spiritual self or a Vietnamese monetary unit.

Let to Bill Molson, who had lived the other side of Coombend and was interested only in grazing the land, the farmhouse did not show evidence of having been interfered with by any spiritual or human agency. Everything wore an aspect of distress and mismanagement.

There was a black telephone on the table. Alex finished eating his sandwich and picked it up. Dead. But sounds came back to him. The voices of the girls at the manual exchange. The party-line number: three short rings and one long. The occasions when he would listen carefully so as not to answer the neighbours' calls. He gently replaced the receiver.

Piles of mail lay where they had tumbled onto the kitchen floor. Alex started to open the envelopes, but his eyes only followed print that he did not take in. An appeal from Merton College for the renovation of the chapel. A brochure from a hotel in Cumbria addressed to his parents. A postcard from Sarah, sent ten days before he left London – *Hurry home, XXX S* – and bulletins from museums in Denmark and Germany that housed collections of ships in bottles. Plus forty-nine issues of *Bottleship* magazine that someone had stacked on the dresser.

This was the first hour. It caused a glugging in his heart to disentangle the kitchen from his rememberance of it. The sink against which he had groaned as a kid, a boy with the innocence rubbed off, hugging his elbows, watching the water running out clockwise – "In Cumbria," his father maintained, "it drains the other way." The windows that no one had cleaned since that horribly sad day. The Ruber calendar with Waterhouse's *Circe Individuosa* hanging behind the closed door, stuck fast in January 1972. His father liked to keep the grandfather clock half an hour forward, but his mother was the tardy one. She never flipped the page on the calendar until well into the following month. Another three weeks before she hurried into his bedroom on her way to the auction of fine furniture and linen in Campbell Town. "Your cricket whites are on the line, and, Piers, you can offer them breakfast if you like," while his father yelled from the kitchen, "Hista! Marjorie, hista! Unless we leave this *instant* we will miss the auction." About to close the door, his mother had darted back into the room and pulled open the curtains. "We should be back in time for tea," kissing him. "Good luck with the match. Who are you playing? Fingal? Bowl well." In her thick black hair a streak of white and on her breath the scent of something medicinal. Then, louder: "Coming." His last sight of her: from the back, the strong light splintering onto her peacock jacket before he retreated into sleep. The sleep in which he hoped to find the courage to tell Cheele how dreadfully sorry he was.

When he had opened all the mail, Alex stood up and went into the corridor that led to the two bedrooms and his father's workshop. His Blundstone boots were stiff, and the dry boards creaked like ice under his sockless foot. Alert, he avoided looking at the ratty frames of Huon pine that hung along both walls. He knew by heart their homespun wisdom. Occasionally in England, a sentence from within one of these frames had wormed its way into his head and stayed there. And he had gathered together homilies of his own that he might like to put behind glass.

No one reaches the end of their life and wishes they'd spent more time marking papers.

If you want to make the gods laugh, tell them your plans.

When you're skating on thin ice, you might as well dance.

Don't sleep with anyone who has bigger problems than you have.

Holding his breath, he creaked through the rooms. Saliva filled his mouth when he found his parents' clothes hanging in the oak wardrobe. His father's jacket and waistcoat fleece, his mother's blueberry frock. He pushed his face into the tweed suits and dresses, gulping in the odour of mothballs mingled with musty wool, and a shudder ran through him. "Oh, Dad, oh, Mum."

Alex unhooked the clothes from the rail and threw them onto the bed.

He fled into the living room and opened the curtains, sending up puffs of rodent-scented dust. The light slashed into strange, half-remembered furniture and paintings: a sewing machine, a watercolour of the River Tamar by Gladstone Eyre, a Lear lithograph of a cockatoo. Mice had eaten the arm of a red chair, revealing four springs.

He plumped up the cushions, shaking out the dead flies. He had inherited all this, down to the Brussels carpet, but he hardly knew anything about these objects. Except for those in the room at the end.

Alex turned the handle, pushed open the door. His heart pounding.

He stood on the threshold of what resembled an operating theatre. In the centre of the room was a worktop scattered with scalpels, tweezers, twist-drills, long scissors; all from the same surgical suppliers in Melbourne, all left where his father had put them down.

He rubbed his nose vigorously at the familiar smell of varnish and gave a slow look around. Sunlight winked through the window blind on shelves of gin bottles placed horizontally, of light bulbs and injection capsules. Each contained a miniature vessel under full sail.

Upright on the worktop, a bottle with a coin in its mouth.

At the sight of the coin, Alex started forward. His sudden movement disturbed a huntsman spider and a ghost in red braces who sat hunched over the bottle and stared intently at a match that burned at the bottom of it. On hearing Alex enter, the memory looked up and searched for him with fading eyesight: "You need to be original, you need to be different," in a voice curbed by exile. "Not like Johnny-round-the-corner."

*

It was to this room that Alex now made his way upon returning from his dinner with Merridy. His first act was to sit down at the worktop and retrieve the three satay sticks from his pocket. He reached over to the model of the ship that he had started to piece together and measured the sticks against the hull. Perfect.

Then, about to scrub off the legacy of the dried chicken, he noticed an orange trace on one of them. He pressed it to his lips.

And in the morning sketched a single enormous word on the green vane of the windmill. He read and reread the letters drying in the sun, then put the top back on the marker that he used for identifying sheep and climbed down the ladder.

When Alice came to clean on Monday, she found Alex trying on a new shirt that he had bought a year before and never worn.

"Anything the matter?" she asked, although she had heard some of it already from Debbie.

"No. Why?"

"You look like a washing machine set on spin."

CHAPTER ELEVEN

The WELLINGTON POINT READING GROUP met at the Bethel Teahouse on Tuesday last. The small audience was disappointing. However, the moment was rescued by a wonderful presentation by Mavis Pidd who in response to our suggestion that her talk be abandoned went on with enthusiasm to describe her vibrant and whimsical upbringing in Tomahawk.

Tildy stared across the counter of the cocktail bar and examined the face of her childhood friend with respectful astonishment. "Alex Dove took you to dinner? He's never taken anyone to dinner. You know what I reckon?"

"No."

"It was the lip gloss I lent you!"

"Very probably," laughed Merridy. Whatever had passed between her cousin and Alex, it relieved her to find that she was not upset.

"So. What did you make of him?"

Merridy picked up the brick and wiped the counter under it and put it down. "I liked him."

Tildy's eyes rattled in her head. "Oh, everybody likes Alex Dove. But Ray's right. Say what you want, he's still a Pom. And you know what they say about Poms. Where the heart should be there's a jellyfish."

"He was born in Australia, you goof," said Merridy. But she felt defenceless. Tildy was her employer's daughter. Not for the first time, Merridy resented the position this put her in. To be an object of Keith Framley's charity.

Tildy was not done. She rotated her glass. "Tell him about your brother, did you?"

Merridy frowned. "I did."

"You did?"

"Well, more or less."

"Oh, Merridy," she sighed. Then, matter-of-factly: "I don't think you'll ever get over it."

"Of course I will," flashed Merridy. "You can get over anything. You just have to put your mind to it."

Tildy was not ever going to be able to conceive of getting over Ray Grogan. Not in two hundred and ninety million years.

"Anyway, he'd understand," Merridy went on. Battling to keep the anguish from her voice. "After all, his parents . . . He got over that, didn't he?"

"I suppose so," said Tildy, and stood up. She was on her way to the Returned Servicemen's Club to meet Ray. "I suppose so," retrieving her handbag from the counter. "But you do like him?"

"Like, yes."

Impatient as she was to see Ray, Tildy paused. She had known her cousin long enough to be aware that Merridy's confidence was under siege. Something Tildy had not witnessed before.

"Would you *like* to be in love with him?" with exaggerated patience.

A dry silence. In which Tildy's father could be heard talking in the kitchen to Debbie.

". . . wind's started to blow again. Reckon if it'd stop, we'd fall over."

"We've had winter before we've even had it, Mr Framley . . ."

"Merridy?"

"Of course. Of course," in a whisper.

Tildy looked at the cousin she had danced with as a child and shook her head. "Oh, Merridy, you'd better start living. We're dead an awfully long time. You may not have liked Mr Twelvetrees, but sometimes he was right – 'Unknown makes unloved.'"

Her cousin's words ate into Merridy. She saw the regret in Tildy's eye and it moved her as umpteen young men's entreaties had not succeeded in doing. The following afternoon, she leaned against an ochre wall that suited her colour better than the dark jacket that Keith Framley obliged her to wear behind his bar, and stroked Alex's face again.

"Why do you touch me like that?" he wanted to know.

"Like what?"

He took her hand and showed her.

"It's a family thing. Don't all families do something? Yours must have had its idiosyncrasies. This is one of ours."

He moved forward at her inflection to read the intention in her mouth. Then they were kissing. He felt her breath inside him, warming and expanding, snapping the threads that bound him.

She pulled back. Fighting to catch her breath. And to keep above the surface. "Know what Ray Grogan says about you?"

"What?"

She struggled for distance, but something drew her to him once more. She touched his face with the tips of her fingers, the fair unprotected hairs at the borders of his temples. Like the hairs on a baby's legs.

"Go on," he said. "Tell me." Losing himself in her eyes.

She swallowed and tried to look mean. "He says you're the biggest spurt of piss ever let out of an English prick."

"He said that!"

"Also, you're so tight-arsed that if you rammed a bluegum up your bum it would come out wood chips," and her mouth, with the lipstick overrunning the lips, where she had kissed him, smiled as if he were something that she had in that instant decided to defend to the death.

In a sparsely decorated room less than a hundred yards away, Sister Surrage inspected a plate of melted ice cream. "How are we doing today, Mr Bowman? Not eating, I see." And clucked. "I suppose you know it's home-made?"

Propped up on blue cushions, Leonard Bowman had lost his appetite but not his taste for poetry. His gaze remained fixed to the wall of the bowls club opposite, and the couple kissing there. Unsuspecting on the other side of the wall, his wife scuttled forward two steps and released a black ball onto the grass under the critical eye of her plump partner.

"What's that you're saying?" Sister Surrage hovered with the tray.

He tried to speak, but the words were sewn to his tongue. A piece of doggerel memorised from the Talbot's *Newsletter,* and adapted.

Who do you see, sister, who do you see?
When you enter this room and stand looking at me:
Are you thinking: a crabby old man, not very wise
Uncertain of habit with faraway eyes
Who dribbles his food and makes no replies?
But inside this old carcass

A young man still dwells
And now and again his battered heart swells
I remember the joys, I remember the pain
And I'm loving and living life over again
So open your eyes, sister, open and see
Not a crabby old man, look closer – see me.

But all Sister Surrage heard was a low steady drone uttered through dry lips.

Moments later, the door handle turned and Merridy came into the room. "All right, nurse. I'll take over."

Once Sister Surrage had left, Merridy dragged over her Glory Box from the foot of the pneumatic bed and sat on it beside her father. She was conscious of the quickness of her breathing. She did not believe what her heart was telling her. The idea was absurd. It was only a kiss. And yet something remained, some strange tingling or taste, a presentiment even, that made her want to see Alex again already.

Another moment before it dawned.

She turned. "Dad, did you just see us?"

Seated in his wheelchair beside her, Mr Bowman had nothing to say. Even so, she heard his thoughts.

Good thing your mother's playing bowls! She wouldn't have understood what I witnessed. Once upon a time, perhaps. But I understand. It sweeps me back to my first sight of Leticia. On her way to a daffodil competition when this impatient young fellow overtakes her. Did I tell you ever about that afternoon? It was raining and we were both trying to get out of the wind. I noticed this girl in front of me, ducking her head and leaning forward at an angle as if she were running from a helicopter, and before I knew it I was tangled up in her legs. We fell head over heels, literally, but I was first on my feet. I pulled her up from the footpath and when I looked into those eyes I couldn't let go of her hand. Simple as that. I was heading out that afternoon to Burnie, but twenty minutes after meeting your mother I called up Mr Bathurst at the pulp mill to say I was crook and that night booked into a B & B – as it happened in the same part of town where she lived, though it took me a few days to track her down. Sometimes you have to act like that, straight away. If I had not cast caution to the wind, I might have missed out on a whole lot of heartbreak and bother, but I would not have had you. My own little miracle. That's what you are to me. You know that, don't you?

Some ice cream had dried on his jersey. Merridy licked the corner of her shirtsleeve and wiped it away. She switched on the table radio that she had bought him after his accident. The Tasmanian Symphony Orchestra playing Sibelius.

"It's all right, Dad. You can go to sleep. Unless you want to watch Mum losing at bowls."

Want your soon-to-be ex-wife's chattels or impedimenta moved to her mother's house? Or your grand piano? Contact THE LONG HAUL. No journey too far or too near. Phone: 62578583

Bang! A black shape tumbled from the gum tree in a blur and clatter of feathers. Bang! Another.

Alex was out with his father's shotgun, shooting crows before they picked out the eyes of the lambs. It gave him no pleasure to kill. Almost his first act on taking on the farm at Moulting Lagoon was to forbid the swan shooters from crossing his land. This had alienated an element in the community, foremost among them Ray Grogan, who had enjoyed unfettered access to the lagoon under Bill Molson's tenancy. Alex also banned 1080 poison, laid by other farmers to prevent marsupials from devouring the young plantations. This meant, though, that he had to cull. Unable to afford a wallaby-proof fence, he depended on his father's Purdey to protect his barley from anything that nibbled.

He left the dead crows for the devils. He picked up the plastic cartridge cases and put them in his pocket and walked home. At this hour, he usually made himself a sandwich, but he had no appetite.

Meanwhile, Alex's hunger for Merridy was a bread that he tore at. He had not expected love. For the first time, he began to find his isolated life depressing. The most trivial excuse took him back into town.

The following afternoon, he was at Nevin's garage filling the ute for the second time in two days, when he caught sight of Tildy's blonde head. She was squeezed into jeans and wore a man's white shirt with the gold cufflinks still in.

"Hi, Tildy," and nodded to her over the sack of Bismarck potatoes and jump-leads and rolls of wire. "How was the Jazz Social?"

"Wonderful," she breathed. She rested her arm on the side of his vehicle before deciding that it would dirty her elbow. "Just wonderful."

"I heard about you and Ray. That's great."

"Thank you," and stretched her arms. "It's the first time I've felt like this. It really is."

"Yes, I know."

She studied him. "OK, who is it?" cunningly.

"Merridy—" and stopped, embarrassed at having spoken – that it was so close to the surface.

Tildy fell silent at the mention of her cousin's name. She folded her arms and waited while Alex hooked the nozzle back on the pump. "Alex . . . a word in your shell-like," very seriously.

"What about?"

She rolled her eyes.

"C'mon. What is it?"

She exhaled. "Don't get involved," biting her lip.

"Who says I'm involved?"

"She's my oldest friend as well as my cousin. But it's not just her. It's the whole situation."

"What whole situation?" And tried to picture it from Tildy's angle. Merridy's father refusing to die; her mother a religious nutcase.

"Did she tell you about her brother?"

"She said that he disappeared."

"Explain what happened, did she?"

"No. Just that he disappeared."

"Well, I hate to say this, and of my own cousin too, but you've got to know something about Merridy." She whispered, as if to mock her own words: "The fact is, she's madder than a cut snake."

"Seems pretty normal to me," hunting around for the cap.

"Oh, she doesn't look mad, but she is. Don't believe me, have a word with Ray."

"Ray? Are you joking?"

CHAPTER TWELVE

KEITH FRAMLEY ALLOWED MERRIDY one afternoon off
a week. At 2.30 p.m. on Tuesday, Alex collected her from
the hotel.

It was a cutting cold day. Smells from a recent rain rose
from the paddocks and the sky was grey with flotillas of
thick cumulus. Early March and Wellington Point was still
exposed to sudden showers.

They talked pleasantly about not much at all on the
journey. But Alex felt nervous as he rounded Cerney Hill
and approached the last bend. It was raining again and he
wanted her to like what she was about to see. And Merridy,
sensing this, stared out through the windscreen with a
concentrated expression, her hands in their gloves of brown
wool laced in her lap.

The entrance to Alex's property was on a blind corner
concealed between two bluegums.

"I live by myself," he explained unnecessarily.

"Tildy said." But it was Ray who had told about the
Scania log-truck. In the Bethel Teahouse, he had described
for her the trailer stacked with gigantic eucalypts, careering
down this road as though the driver had but a moment to
live. She pictured the log-truck swiping the car that emerged
from between the trees, and scattering Alex's childhood
into fragments.

They jolted over the cattle-grid and up a long drive of
white gravel. She watched it dead-end into a tidy lawn in
the middle of which was a large and solitary pine. Like a

finger pointing upward in the Methodist Hall. Minister Twelvetrees's finger.

Alex parked beside a rotary clothes-line and they climbed out. It was raining heavily now.

She stood on the gravel, looked around, started to walk towards the house.

"No, this way," said Alex.

Ignoring the downpour, he insisted on first showing her the view. A veranda stretched around the back of the house, a deck of cedar planks which the sea salt had blackened. She stood beside him and cast her eyes out over Moulting Lagoon to Oyster Bay. It was, as Alex's father never tired of repeating, a top spot. But not on this day, perhaps.

Rain dripped from the gutters and leaves. A scratching and a whining sounded from inside. Alex opened a door and a young Border collie, jackdaw-coloured, bounded out.

"Hey, Flash!"

Merridy, who was unbuttoning her wet coat, sank to her haunches. "It's all right," shutting her eyes to the dog's tongue.

"I'm still training her."

In the tactile warmth of the kitchen, he twisted the stove on and offered her tea.

"It's Bushells." Not the Glen Valley that his mother insisted on.

"I'd love a cup," shaking the raindrops from her head and throwing off her coat. She wore a green jersey underneath with large yellow daisies knitted into it and the brown gloves that she would not take off.

He brought Merridy her tea, thinking of the tanned arm with the fair hairs.

"You heard about the prang?"

She nodded.

Silence. Just the rain.

"I was standing here," moving to the basin. "I'd just got out of bed and I saw a policeman outside and Miss Pritchard, our teacher. I thought: She's come with the cricket team and do we have enough bacon, and I went out in my pyjamas and I said: 'Hello,' and Miss Pritchard, white as a shirt, came towards me and lifted me up, and I said: 'My parents?'

"'Yes.'

"'Dead?'

"'Yes.'"

The accident had happened out of earshot after Alex had gone back to sleep. Composing an apology to Cheele.

"I must see them," he was moaning, and moaning.

The suddenly orphaned boy.

Merridy sipped her tea. Inside the kitchen, the grey light had solidified with the bacon fat from the stove. She was staring into herself and nodding. That expression again, at once absent and focused. He would have hated it if she had said anything.

"More?"

"I'm doing all right," and looked around. At the Welsh dresser painted green. The cherry pips in a saucer. The view through a rain-streaked window onto the solitary tree.

She moved and a yellow daisy rose. She had noticed the frames.

"My mother collected them," coming up behind.

"What are they?"

"Samplers. Young women made them on the voyage out as proof of a skill."

She stood before the first frame.

Alex went on: "To try and win themselves a husband, I suppose."

"Those were the days! But what kind of man would

fall for this one?" Merridy murmured the words, embroidered below deck in coloured wools: *"Emily Highmore, aged 13, December 4, 1840: Early will I seek thee/Now that my journey is just begun/My course but little trod/I'll stay before I further run/And give myself to God."*

Alex smiled. "Someone who's not going to see too much action outside a church?"

She passed to the next. *"Delay of repentance is a cheat upon ourselves."*

He said: "Mainly they sewed the alphabet. And numbers. My mother liked the ones with verses."

She put down her cup on a cabinet of white-bound *Encyclopaedia Britannica*s. Stitched in a frame above was the line: *Worked by Florrie Winch 1887: There is a mystery in every meeting, and that is God.*

"I like that," tapping the glass.

Excitement was in her now. The samplers drew her further into the leaden reaches of corridor, something in their faded colours arousing her to pause before each, read aloud, move on.

He who says all he knows does not know himself.

Beware the anger of the dove.

Remain a child so that your children will always love you.

At the bottom of the devil's bag, one always finds his bill.

When the moon is full she shines over all.

Beautiful are the heralds, crying, O traveller enter in.

Until she came to his bedroom.

She took in with a quiet glance the wide mahogany bed and the large wardrobe of dark oak with claws for feet.

"That's . . ." She had been about to say "a good piece of furniture", but it did not seem adequate.

"It's my mother's," Alex said. "She brought it with her on the ship from England. I don't know how old it is. She used to boast that it was older than Australia."

The wardrobe was the colour of a blackboard. One of the doors, she could not help noticing, was hinged back against the curtain, reflecting her and Alex, their two shapes.

She moved closer.

Some wind had filled her up and she skimmed over a surface where before she might have sunk. It was a novel sensation not to be repelling someone, a relief.

She closed the door, but it swung back on its hinge. She tested it again, with the same result.

"Doesn't it shut?"

"It was damaged in transit from England. They never got round to fixing it."

She pulled open the other door that was also pierced with a hollow heart and a cross above it, and heard her higher pitched voice: "No key?"

"My mother lost it." Or never had it.

Now both doors gaped. She stared inside at the divided interior: one side for hanging space, the other with five tray shelves.

This velvety darkness. It roused in Merridy a faint remembrance of something, right on the edge of memory. She searched her mind, but whatever it was stayed the other side.

She felt a tightening in her womb and at the same time a pleasant unravelling of herself, a clarity. "Do you want children?"

Merridy had never before said such a thing to a man and did not know how she had managed to utter it. But once the phrase was out of her mouth she followed it.

Beyond the curtain was the whirring of a windmill.

"I'd love children," she said. "Mobs of them." And poked in her head as if already she could hear them crying.

A little while later, she would carry away the soapy smell of his shirts; and the image of him in the tight white underpants, his cock straining.

Now, in the darkness of his folded clothes, she panicked. She wondered if anything she had could be important to Alex, anything at all about herself.

Sensing his gaze on her, she turned, hoping to catch him sneaking a look – at least to have that certainty – but his attention was trapped by the clawed legs of the wardrobe.

"What are they holding?" she wanted to know. "Is it a globe? Or just a ball?"

He might have been in their grip. "Do you always ask so many questions?"

"Don't ask, don't get," she replied in the words of her mother, who had herself mislaid the key to a number of things.

But his eyes daunted her. She looked back inside. Up a shelf. And saw something to make her raise her arms in a way that caught his breath.

"Hey, what have you got there?"

"Oh, those," of the bottles stacked on their sides. "They're my father's. Here, come and have a bopeep."

He piloted her to another room, at the end of the corridor. Opened the door.

"You made these?" staring at the shelves. Ship after ship. Each with its thorn-sized sails and cargo of dreams.

"My father taught me," Alex said, not yet adding that it was a way for him to preserve one of his few unfading impressions of a tall man with crinkled grey eyes who

Sunday mornings, early, would drive Alex to the canal in Lauderdale and launch his models in the company of enthusiasts; perhaps his only link, apart from a handful of isolated phrases and a distinct memory of the two of them both sitting under the stars on Barn Hill while his father, smelling richly of Balkan Sobranie, knocked his pipe against the ground and talked about white-throated swifts and eels and the uncommonly clear sky, damn well suited for an astronomer.

Less distinct was an excursion to New Norfolk when Alex was five or six, to visit the asylum where another fellow Cumbrian had been incarcerated. The composer John Woodcock Graves had written the words to the hunting song that Alex's father was always humming: "*Do you ken John Peel?*"

Otherwise, Basil Dove came to him second-hand through the memories of others, smoking a pipe as he swam in the river and holding a billycan filled with speckled trout. "Your father," Harry Ford said, "could catch fish in a bucket." It was not a memory you could argue with. Over the years Alex had constructed a less bucolic image of his parents. A middle-class English couple who sailed to Australia a decade after the war, married and settled in the outback, and when it ceased to suit them took their consolation in drink. Or so he understood from Harry, who fed him peppery morsels that added up to a depressing picture replicated all over Australia: exile, exacerbated by alcohol and a clinging to outdated habits. Like making ships in bottles. And thought of Harry, with his bomb-shaped head and a touch of malice about him, grinning at Alex over a large glass of South African port: "No shortage of empties!"

Across the room, something was stirring up in Merridy. She stared at a 1,000-watt light bulb that contained a minuscule ship.

Alex lifted the large glass bulb for her to see. "Five-masted clipper. Thirty sails in there. And you have to build them up one by one. I'm never doing that again. It's probably why my father went blind."

"How come it didn't explode?"

"Good luck," and smiled.

"Alex, tell me," impatient. "I know about light bulbs. It ought to have exploded."

He drew closer. "Right. You tap with a screwdriver on the contacts. There's a small sigh as the vacuum escapes," and imitated the sound. "Then you keep chipping till you get down to the filament. Once the filament is removed, you clean the rubbish out."

A vacuum was escaping in her, too. Solemnly, she said: "When I was the size of a deck-fitting, I once designed a boat."

There came back to her an afternoon in Wynyard less than a year after her brother's disappearance. She remembered burningly her mother's blank disinterest, her father's curiosity. "What's that, Merridy?"

"It's what the Jumblies went to sea in. Look, that's him steering."

Animated, her father set about making a model based on Merridy's design. It was a vision they shared. When he retired, he promised to build her a full-scale version. For years she had looked forward to it. His sea-going sieve.

It was not what Alex expected. He was braced for her laugh, not a fantastic floating colander. "This model, how big was it?"

"Oh, no bigger than that," and gestured at a bottle.

"I'd like to see."

"I lost it when my parents separated."

"That's a shame. What did you copy it from, a children's book?"

"It came out of my head. I don't know where it came from, I can't remember much about being six." But she had the original drawing in her Glory Box. A fuel-section measured to scale. The whole thing nearly sixty-five feet in diameter. And her brother at the wheel.

She elaborately averted her glance. "So this is where you work."

"I don't consider it as work," returning the light bulb to its shelf.

She listened to him, his face exposed and fragile in the smell of Super Glue and varnish, his voice the tinkle of something becalmed. Something in a bottle perhaps.

"Seems like work to me!"

He ran his finger over the surface of the table and inspected it. "I really should get Alice to clean this place." The words falling among the crumbs of wood and metal. He did not see that he required another sort of help. Or maybe he did, for his look would not retreat from the raft it had found.

"What's that for?" she asked, puzzled by the round smooth corner of an ice-cream stick pressed against his chin.

"This" – he brandished it like a crucifix – "I use for decks and for stuff that's out of sight, braces and bits and pieces that aren't going to take much weight."

There was the sound of his little stick on a bottle, the tap, tap, tap that she listened to, her heart catching the pulse on the vacant glass until the two sounds beat together.

"What about these?" Protruding out of the same jar she recognised one of the satay sticks that he had snatched so surprisingly from her plate. Still orange with Tildy's lip gloss.

"Satay sticks are good for masts."

It was only natural. People attracted to making boats

should be attracted to each other. An unfamiliar creature scampered up and down her ribcage.

On the scarred worktop a green ship lay on its side. She reached out and touched it.

"That's wet. Be careful!"

The sticky varnish was like sap from a black wattle on her wool fingertip, or honey.

Ever so respectful, he scooped the ship from the table and brought it to her.

"The *Otago*. A three-masted barque. Conrad's only command," noticing the fluff she had left on his ship.

"Conrad who?"

"Joseph Conrad. My father loved his novels. Conrad captained the *Otago* for a year and wrote a story about it. She was taken to Hobart and sold for scrap. Otago Bay – it's named after her." He tilted the ship. "See here? Over this side Captain Conrad was leaning when he saw a naked man looking up at him from the sea."

A picture of white legs and arms, desperate, floated into her mind. "Who was he?"

"He had killed a man and jumped overboard. Conrad hid him in his cabin. He risked his ship so that the murderer could swim to the China coast."

She sniffed her finger thoughtfully while Alex explained how he had crafted most of the hull out of Huon pine from the timber yard in Strahan. Two of her masts from Merridy's satay sticks and the main mast from kauri. And the deck out of ice-cream sticks that he had gathered from the bins behind the primary school.

"You saw me—" He started to speak, but she talked over him. She remembered.

"And what on earth are they?" rattling another glass jar.

"Kidney stones." His grandfather, a broom maker in

Sedbergh, had collected them, apparently. "They make good cannonballs."

Still the fusillade did not let up. She nodded at what he was cradling. "Where do you get your bottles?" She was thinking of her sieve. She had looked forward to it so idiotically.

"Your hotel, mainly."

"You go through the rubbish there as well?"

He blushed. "That's right."

"I've never seen you." She picked up the rum bottle that he had been tapping. Had she tossed it away herself, into a bin behind the hotel? Something grated and she peered inside. "What's that?"

"A penny." Alex's father had found it in a grave on the edge of his land. The blackened coin had belonged to a family of early settlers who had drowned in Moulting Lagoon, their boat overturning in a sudden gale. "It's old. You couldn't cash it in."

She rattled it. The coin had a face on it, but whether of a man or woman she could not make out. Her lips parted between curiosity to see the face and incredulity as to how it could have got there.

"Just how did you squeeze that in?"

"Ah, that *is* a secret." He spoke in such a serious way that she turned her head. And now she felt his eyes, how they stayed on her, and smiled confusedly.

"But Alex, I want to know. It couldn't possibly fit through this neck."

He stepped closer. Their arms brushing. "Take off your gloves, why don't you?" He wanted to stop her questions. To speak of things that had nothing to do with ships or bottles or coins that today would not pay for a telephone call.

She was staring into the rum bottle.

"Will you come to bed with me?" he said in a flat voice.

She could feel the bone in her denying smile. The horror of the black word forming in her throat. And looked for help at the grating penny.

"You never answered my question." She spoke at random, holding up the bottle and peering through the circular base at Alex. He was so unlike Ray. It was essential not to hurt him. "You *never* answer my questions."

"Which one?"

"Do you want children?" to her magnified brown palms. And thought again how uncanny it was that the uttering of her wish should have created it.

He nodded. Anything she wanted, he wanted too.

But she needed to be sure. "How many?"

"Oh, if they are like you, mobs of them." He took the bottle from her and laid it on the table.

She rubbed at her eye with the scratchy glove.

"Then you'll sleep with me?" His voice was flat, but his eyes shone. She could feel his fingers moving on her shoulders. And with no struggle at all her resolve fled out of her, a wave retreating from the ramparts of a child's sandcastle. She returned the pressure of his body.

Outside, what was going on was the chirring of the windmill.

She looked at him with the eyes of someone who was looking at all the children they would have. She peeled off her gloves and they went back along the corridor and into the bedroom.

Quickly, they undressed. At the touch of her warm skin he felt the blood startle in his hands and chest. His thought was not of the sea, but of the water that serpented along the dry furrow he had dug for his potatoes, the sun on its snake-dark back. It hurt.

She felt the tip of his cock on her chest and pressed herself against him.

In the darker room their bodies were the only light. She caught sight of her raised legs reflected in the patina of the ancient oak wardrobe, his back braced and then flowing into her into her. He could have been swimming for his life.

In shadow his face had grown thinner, his eyes rounder. Sound was the gasp as he replied to her with his whole body, the hiccup of flesh. Smell the varnish from his unfinished deck on her fingertips.

She pulled him to her breast so that he would not see her sadness. She felt no aversion to his neediness, no fear. Part of her had found a berth. Someone to share her obscure hurt. She looked over her arm that held him and envisaged in the colours that she could see through the crack in the curtain – a squalor of reds and blues in a grey sky – the children whom she would make happy with every scrap of love that had been denied her brother and, obviously, Alex.

"She'll be coming round the mountain," sang Mr Twelvetrees in the corner. "Singing Yi Yi Yippy Yippy Yi."

The dog sat under the bed, eating. Through the window, the sound of the windmill and the clack-clack-clack of the yellow-tailed black cockatoos pecking at damp pine cones.

Sometime later the face on the quilt took the shape of Alex.

"Hello," she smiled and sat up. She had been looking at something on the sheet.

With a finger he traced the scatter of moles on her shoulder as if he was connecting them.

She shivered happily. "Dad used to say that in another

life I must have been blasted by grapeshot through a sieve."

"What other life?"

Her silvery voice thinned out. "Don't you believe we were other things before?"

But he had been nailed in too straight; he had grown up in a period of thank-you letters and lace-up shoes and watches that you wound before you slept. At the bottom of his heart he had believed in his parents' love and, he supposed, their God. Until Miss Pritchard came into the kitchen and told him it was best that he stay up at the house, not leave, least not till the policeman returned.

He moved his head. "I don't know. I never really thought about it. Maybe I was something before." He looked down at the feet of his mother's wardrobe and it seemed to Alex that the talons were loosening their grip on whatever it was they had been clinging to.

He caressed her and she turned to him. In her need to be held, his to hold, to love.

They made love again and afterwards dozed. It was six thirty when he woke. Merridy no longer beside him.

His eyes darted around the room. She stood naked in the corner. Inspecting two frames on the wall – photographs of his parents.

Aware of his gaze, she said dutifully: "I can see a likeness. You take more after your mother."

Of greater interest was the hand-coloured lithograph of Baudin's cockatoo. Delicate, accurate, gleeful – it was Alex's favourite of their pictures.

"Edward Lear," she read. "Not the poet, surely?"

"He was a bird artist before he wrote limericks. He was eighteen when he painted that."

"I had no idea he painted birds! Australian birds!" and looked back at the soft undulating feathers, the unblinking eye. Another sign. A sermon could not have said more.

She returned to the bed and leaned over Alex, stroking his temple. "What can I tell you? Is there anything I can tell you?"

"No." Then: "Yes. I'd like to know how your brother died."

She gulped. Recovering herself, she rested her head on the dune of his chest and stared across it into the wardrobe.

"You don't have to tell me," he said.

"I know," and went on looking into the wardrobe.

CHAPTER THIRTEEN

FROM ACROSS THE ROOM she could see her mother at the basin, flannelling her brother's forehead. It was his seventh birthday. A Sunday morning at the family's shack near Wynyard on the north-west coast. The sun shining, the wattlebirds singing, the dry fresh scent of the eucalypts.

Nothing had happened, but she knew from a tenseness in her heart that something was about to happen.

"Mummy," he questioned the reflected face, "why is an island not a house?"

"I don't know, darling." Mrs Bowman squeezed out the flannel and rubbed it behind his ears.

In the mirror he caught sight of Merridy, stealing close to watch. With a quick flick of his wrist he dipped his fingers into the basin and splashed her.

"Hey!" closing her eyes and holding up her hands.

"Stop that this minute!" Mrs Bowman rammed a straw boater on his head and tried to fasten the strap under his chin, but gave up.

"Go and wait on the deck. Now, Merridy, your turn."

Her father had organised an outing to see the steam trains at Sheffield.

"We were in high spirits, my brother most of all. He had a new pair of Blundstones that he wanted to wear, a birthday present from Dad. Mum had given him a sailor's hat."

She could see her brother – out on the deck – toying with the strap and wiggling his toes to tell everyone how well his boots fitted.

"Mummy," she asked earnestly, "why is a house not an island?"

He leaned over the deck, staring at something.

"Oh, Merridy!" vigorously scrubbing her daughter's cheek.

What was he staring at?

At last, Merridy was all washed and dressed.

"Go and wait with your brother," and picked up the towel from the floor.

Merridy ran skipping out to join him. She loved her older brother. She looked up to his friends who came to the house, who sat in a row on the top step and flipped his Slinky towards her down the stairs. But not as much as she idolised him, sometimes to the point where she developed a stitch in her side. It did not matter that he believed in the silliest things. Things that existed, as she tried to explain to him, only in the imagination. Like the stalagmites they created out of wet sand that hardened into towers and battlements, where he patrolled with cobweb spear, a sentry visible only to his child's eye. Her brother was always sending his mind into places where she could not follow. At breakfast, when their father asked him: "Have you decided what you want to be, now you're seven?", he had answered with his most serious face that his life's ambition was to be a sailor in one of Edward Lear's drawings. He was a child enchanted by sandcastles and Jumblies.

But he was nowhere to be seen.

"As you yourself know," she said to Alex, "in life anything can happen, anything at all; you can be watching the person you love most in the world and you turn your head for the briefest moment and when you look back they are gone."

She shouted into the shack: "Mum, he's not here."

Mrs Bowman's first thought – he's run off. "Leonard, come quick."

Merridy's father, fiddling with a button on his shirt cuff, went down the steps three at a time. He called out into the bush.

Everyone stood still and listened. A wattlebird answered.

"We went looking through the bush, yelling for him."

The shack was on a sandstone bluff in lava-flow country. Potato fields interspersed with thick woods, along a cliff-face of rich volcanic soil that descended to a pebbled beach. The closest neighbours were a mile away, the closest town a twenty-minute drive in the family Holden. After searching for two hours, Merridy's father drove to Wynyard to get help. Soon a line of seventeen men and women – bushies, fallers, police constables, even some wives and children – fanned out from the deck and pushed their way knee-high through the potato crops and woods.

"We searched all that afternoon, and the next day. We were desperate. For three days, we searched. The only thing we found was his sailor's hat with the strap still loose on it that Mum had promised to mend."

At the sight of the straw hat Mrs Bowman burst into tears. She refused to eat or to sleep. She was aware that her son had not come back. Beyond that, her mind was a blank. She spoke of it as a "real shame" that he should have chosen to keep everyone waiting.

"It was weird at first, and then pretty scary. Everything, from what she was eating to the whole plot-line, was just gone. Daddy had to reiterate everything calmly, three to ten times – no exaggeration."

Eventually, she lost herself in household chores and made it clear that she anticipated her son's return at any moment. He would want his meal, a change of trousers.

"She cooked all his favourite dishes for him, put his best clothes out on his bed."

Then on the fourth day after her brother's disappearance, Merridy was trailing her father along the edge of a cliff about half a mile from the shack, when he halted, paralysed. His lips sucked tight. Like a man who had glugged down a bottle of gin in a minute and was trying to keep it in.

That summer it had rained heavily; the bush became a swamp of chocolate-coloured mud, ponds formed in the paddocks and along the cliff-tops holes appeared where tiger-snakes and devils had burrowed. One hole was bigger than the rest and suggested that an animal of some size had made its lair here. This was the hole before which her father stood.

"Daddy, is it him?" taking a step.

He whirled round. "No! Merridy, no!"

Too late. She had seen for herself the large round hole in the bank, as though something had shrugged its way into the earth – and, on the dead leaves to the side of it, her brother's Blundstone boot.

"Wait here."

Merridy watched him on all fours disappear into the burrow – if that is what it was. She pressed her brother's small boot to her face, recalling the way he had looked down at it, and prayed with every fibre in her body for his safe return. Presently her father reappeared. Shook his head.

She knew what she had to do. She had not kissed her brother goodbye. Thinking that he would always be there, wiggling his toes in his new boots. Or tearing, furious, after Merridy to retrieve a toy tractor that she had snatched. Or growing up to be a sailor in a drawing.

"Let me go," she said. She was small. She might be able to penetrate further.

She crept on, her father's black rubber torch between her teeth. The beam fell on dead leaves and violent green moss and the dartboards of torn cobwebs. Clay gave way to sand. Smells of fungus and mould to the damp marine scents of the sea. She lowered her head. The passage narrowed until she could crawl no further, ending in a wall of sand. The air was thicker, but when she stopped to catch her breath she could hear a tiny voice calling. It was barely audible and she did not know if it came from inside her head or where it came from. She removed the torch from her mouth and shouted his name. The two syllables rolled along the passage. She listened. Silence. Then a distant sound. The dull roar of the ocean sucking on its rocky teeth and sighing, and somewhere in the middle of this dull seductive roar a small voice persisting.

Merridy never forgot her mother's face when she received the news, the distorted look in her left eye. She seemed to stare at her husband through centuries-old glass.

For the next two days Mrs Bowman sat in a collapsible fisherman's chair and levelled her deranged gaze at the hole in the earth. The round dark entrance became the focal point of her worst fears, her wildest hopes. Her son had gone exploring. He only had to hear her anguished shouts and he would crawl back. It was simply a matter of hours before his sand-streaked face would emerge into the sunlight, and she kept a damp flannel at the ready. But as the hours piled up all sorts of extravagant theories stalked through her head. She feared that her son had been murdered or eaten. The detective from Wynyard had a brother in New Zealand where a feral pig – "as big as the trunk of your car" – attacked lambs and turkeys. Or else he had been plucked from the cliff-top by a bright blue Boss-Woss. Or a giant squid hunting for orange roughy. Or the monster marsupial *Wynyardia bassinia* whose fossil had been discovered in these selfsame cliffs by none other than Professor Theodore Flynn. More recently, the remains of a gigantic mollusc had washed ashore in Stanley, a cephalopod with eight arms each the length of the Bowmans' Holden and two tentacles forty feet long and covered with powerful suckers each larger than a man's palm. The scene tormented her. Her young son on the cliff-top in his golden morning. A kraken rising from the deep. Its dreadful arms encircling him. His unheard shrieks. The monster with its flailing prey sinking with a gargle beneath the waves, leaving behind a few bubbles.

An hour after the little boot was discovered, two policemen equipped with foot straps and waist harnesses, and holding spades and powerful torches, lowered themselves into the hole. A neighbour's Jack Russell was sent down, but picked up no scent. A thorough search revealed no lair of any animal, no trace of any boy; no clothes, no bones. When the search was called off, there was nothing of him to bring home or to bury, save for a straw hat and a scuffed right-footed Blundstone, size two. There was no body.

A month later, the entrance was blasted shut with dynamite and a stone left on the bank engraved with her brother's name.

Every unexplained death has its own peculiar horror. A reporter from the Burnie *Advocate* described the impact of the tragedy on the community: *The sight witnessed in Wynyard when the news became known was pathetic in the extreme. Strong men wept, hands trembled, lips quivered. Voices had an involuntary tremor in them and faces were filled with the deepest expressions of hopelessness.*

The *Advocate* editorialised that the young boy had been murdered and held out hope that the killer would soon be found: *Sooner or later the finger of Providence will point out him who has shed the blood of a fellow creature*. But in the absence of a suspect, or, of course, a body, the newspaper refrained from pointing its own finger.

Her father did all he could to protect Merridy from these speculations. He kept checking to see that she had something to do. She took to wearing her brother's clothes – his trousers and T-shirt that were too big for her – and to sleeping in his bed. His friends had been her friends. She feared that she would never see them again, because why would they come around with her big brother gone? As far as she was concerned, he had followed the noise of the sea, the sucking seductive roar. But his sudden absence degraded the whole of her life, an acid of loss inside her that she could not expel. When she realised that he might not be coming back, half of her was no more.

It was worse for Mrs Bowman.

Merridy was seven before her mother looked directly at her.

"You don't get over something like that," Merridy said. "The questions are always there. What happened to him? Who took him? A person, an animal? What did they do with him? Where are his bones? Or even – could he have survived? My mother still believes that he's alive somewhere."

"What do you think happened?" asked Alex.

Tears were running from her eyes. She had recoiled from thinking about her brother and had learned never to contrast her life then with her life as it was now; but in the recesses of the memories that she carried from childhood had grown a conviction. An idea gestating in a dark part of her that her brother would one day return, but it was not something she could actually say in words, only feel.

"My father told me the Jumblies had taken him. There

132

was no need to worry. He had gone with them on a great journey."

A fly buzzed into the room and flew out again.

"You haven't told me his name," Alex said.

She had not uttered it for many years. Out of a promise she had so far kept. She was full of ridiculous promises that she made to herself.

She hung her head, prepared, for Alex, to commit the sacrilege.

"Hector."

CHAPTER FOURTEEN

LOUISA MEREDITH NURSING HOME:
Invites community members on Thursday March 17th to
10.30 a.m. morning tea.
  Guest speaker: TBA. Topic: "Strokes".
  Phone 62578380 if transport is needed.
  Everyone welcome. So come along.

On a blustery day in the middle of March, Merridy took
Alex to "Otranto" and introduced him to her parents.

To conceal her nervousness, Merridy ran across the
room and hugged her mother from behind. Mrs Bowman,
in a yellow crocus knit, returned her daughter's greeting
with a metronomic pat on the arm while with her right
elbow she covered up a letter to her sister in Ulverstone.

In the large hesitant words that she forced herself to
write every week, she had revealed her concerns about
Merridy. "I won't deny it, Doss. I know that dread is a
sign of duty, but sometimes I fear that the crown of all
my ills is perched on her head." This was the paragraph
that her elbow hid.

"Mum, I want you to meet Alex, who I have told you
about," looking at him over the hand-knitted shoulder and
winking.

"Alex," repeated the sombre, lined face. The day
before she had sat on her reading glasses and today
peered out of a crushed frame. "I am grateful to you
for making Merridy happy at this time. Our family has

been spared its portion of happiness. I expect my daughter has said."

"She has, and I'm sorry."

She gave him a speculative look. "Are you a believer?"

"Mum!"

Alex glanced at Merridy. Her rueful expression.

"Do not ask, do not learn," Mrs Bowman reminded her.

"Well . . . in a manner of speaking. You could say, I suppose . . . that I believe in your daughter."

Mrs Bowman seemed to regroup, decided not to press further. The webbed feet tightened about her eyes as if her dryness was painful to her. She rolled her gaze down his right arm. If she was not likely to see him in the same pew at the Uniting Church, he might at least make a useful partner in the triples.

"I have been explaining you to Merridy's father," and nodded towards the window.

He sat slumped in a wheelchair in the alcove. His skin the shade of a peeled apple going brown, his neck swollen by steroids. He had the posture of someone in pain. A power cut the night before had caused the pneumatic headrest on his bed to snap down.

At Alex's greeting, he gave a slight, wincing nod, his eyes chained redly to the setting sun, where his sieve was – or his wife's God.

Mrs Bowman looked from Alex to Merridy as if she could see through the contours of the doom that awaited them: "I was sharing my opinion that Merridy should go back to university. She has talents that cannot be sharpened in Wellington Point. Nor, perhaps, in Tasmania."

"Not now, Mum."

"Well, that's what I was saying," and to herself: You're

going to be ruined like I was. You're going to go against your mother's wishes and be ruined.

Firmly locked at the end of her husband's pneumatic bed was the Huon pine steamer trunk that Mrs Bowman had prepared for Merridy in the hope of a devout future son-in-law – and that she took care to transport with her everywhere against such an eventuality.

The Glory Box was a Proudlock tradition. Into it every birthday, Mrs Bowman would pack an item to supplement Merridy's idiosyncratic dowry: scalloped cotton pillow-cases, lace tablecloths, bone-handled fish knives from Sheffield, a Bible and Prayer Book. Merridy called it her "Gory Box". On receipt of its key on her eighteenth birthday, she had added her own stuff. Tucked at the bottom in a plastic bag were her childhood drawing of a sea-going sieve, three scrapbooks, a photograph of her brother and a bright orange feather of a bird of paradise from Papua that had been one of Hector's cherished posses-sions. Plus a pornographic video that her partner from the dance class in Ulverstone had given her for safekeeping. She never wished to look at it and she never saw him again. But folded away in the linen sheets donated by her Aunt Doss, the presence of *Saucy Sally Sees it Through* took the edge off Merridy's embarrassment, and allowed her to smile in agreement whenever her mother started to voice plans for her.

Mrs Bowman had learned from her mistake in marrying Leonard. It was her unshakeable position that Merridy deserved a churchgoing mainlander with a salary, not a Pom farmer with the most peculiar hobby. Plus, worse – according to her enquiries – an agnostic.

"Of course, you can see that he's educated," Mrs Grogan

had remarked accusingly in the course of a conversation in the aisles of Talbot's. "Though goodness knows what he does all day in that house by himself. I mean, anyone can see he's no farmer. I won't even *begin* to tell you what Jack Fysshe says."

The bowls champion was searching for washing powder, but where the soaps used to be an unsmiling member of Albert Talbot's staff had stacked bread. "But getting back to what I was saying. I spoke to Ray and he doesn't once remember seeing him in church."

"No one will ever speak the truth about human nature," sighed Mrs Bowman.

"Ah, here we are!"

CHAPTER FIFTEEN

JUNIOR CRICKET TOURNAMENT
Saturday March 19th. Time: 9.30 a.m.
   Players should be able to bowl, bat and be able to score.
   Trophy donated by H. Ford.
   Dress: cricket attire. Ball and drinks provided.

On Saturday, Alex rode with Merridy over the farm.

It had rained in the night. Puddles everywhere. As if the sky had scraped itself on the ground and left rags of blue and white between the gums. Cattle eating stubble off the barley stood with fresh pats on their sides and mosquitoes bounced in the air.

Near the edge of the Crown forest on the top of Rossall Hill was a copse of four dark macrocarpa that in Alex's judgment boasted the finest view of his property. He dismounted and took Merridy's reins and tied them with his own to a branch.

He dragged over a large fallen bough and they sat on it while Flash rolled on her back between the grazing horses.

Merridy wrapped her arms about her knees and looked down over the clot of farm buildings to the sea. The landscape so different from Ulverstone and Zeehan. Her eyes had never seen anywhere more lovely. It was tremendous.

"See that thicket of gums?" Alex indicated with his riding crop. "A tiger was seen there."

Alex was six when Bill Molson encountered a young female thylacine, not more than ten yards from him.

"He heard a rustle, didn't think much of it, and then this creature emerged. He knew what it was because it had twelve stripes across its back. They stood gawping at each other, and after a few seconds the tiger turned and loped off, leaving only its scent behind."

It was a late February afternoon and Bill never forgot the sour smell: "He said it stank worse than his septic tank."

She peered into the eucalypts. "Do you believe it still exists?"

Alex picked up a pine needle. "It's like believing in anything you can't prove. It's like believing in ghosts. Or God."

"My father is convinced the tiger is extinct," and she imitated the voice that he had lost: "'The last thylacine died in Beaumaris zoo in 1936. Since then there has been no evidence whatsoever to indicate that the species has survived. No scat, no hair, no roadkill—'" And stopped. "I'm sorry. What a tactless thing to say."

"Oddly enough, my father *did* believe in the tiger." But then Basil Dove had believed in an awful lot of things.

CHAPTER SIXTEEN

BASIL DOVE WATCHED HIS olive trench coat – with a sausage roll in its pocket – jerk across the floor and out into the landing. A young cocker spaniel had come into his room in a northern hotel while he was packing. The dog belonged to a firm-bodied young woman in a thick red dress who was going downstairs to the bar. That was how he met his wife.

In Cumbria, his family owned a broom and brush factory. On the death of his father the running of the business was assumed by his eldest brother. Basil decided to emigrate. He was a passionate young man who could romanticise every situation and prosper with it. He had come of age in a rain-drenched valley in a period of blackouts, whale meat, egg powder and petrol coupons. After two years of National Service, he hankered for warmth, space and light.

He was making his way to Tilbury, to sail on the ten-pound scheme to Tasmania, when his coat with the crucial papers scurried from his room. The owner of the liver-and-white cocker was on her way home to Tewkesbury, where her parents dealt in antiques, after breaking off her engagement to an oboist in a Scottish radio orchestra. She was easy-going, but easily deceived and when she discovered that her affections were shared with at least two other female members of the orchestra she had become energetic and philosophical. At the hotel bar, she and Basil fell into conversation. They spoke frankly of their drooping circumstances. Marjorie wanted to make Basil laugh.

Bleakly convinced that she was, at twenty-two, washed up, she had on an impulse – and to the horror of her parents – accepted the oboist's offer of the puppy. She confessed to Basil that although she knew a certain amount about early English oak furniture and nineteenth-century paintings she had never before looked after a dog. Basil fed him the rest of his sausage roll, asked his name, and when informed that he did not have one, and was only three months old, suggested Tethera, in Cumbrian dialect the word for three, and advised her to have his tail docked. "He'll wag it like that and scratch it and then he'll go through brambles and the callus will fall off and he'll be permanently flapping blood, and the sore will never heal." He pointed down with the stem of his pipe: "The skin there is like the skin on your shins," and hoisted his gaze up her leg. "It's that thin."

Marjorie stared wide-eyed. She was persuaded.

Basil had a sympathetic laugh and a fondness for board games. They played Scrabble into the night. Marjorie won.

In the morning they exchanged addresses.

"But why Tasmania?"

He said: "I hear it's a place where you can go away and bury yourself."

Marjorie laughed.

Ten weeks later a letter arrived from Hobart with details of Basil's journey on the *Strathaird* to Aden, Ceylon and Fremantle and then on a Port Line apple boat to Tasmania. He had been one of seventeen passengers on a ship taking out Leyland buses and Morris Oxfords – "There was a great palaver because the leather seats went mouldy in the hold" – and returning to England with fruit. He was full of the sight of a queue of trucks stretching from the wharf into Davey Street, all piled high with apples and pears. He had taken lodgings in Battery Point to plot his next move.

Over the months ahead, Basil's family in Cumbria learned of his intentions to become a fruit-farmer, a boat-builder, a cattle-breeder. He might even open a bookshop or a coffee house where customers could play Scrabble all day. Or a museum devoted to ships in bottles.

"That's Basil," said his older brother. "Full of brisk, emphatic plans that never materialise."

Only in his plans for Marjorie Fulmar did Basil succeed in realising his wishes. For eight months, the pair wrote weekly letters to one another, until one night the telephone rang in a cluttered hall outside Tewkesbury. A long-distance call from Hobart. By the time Marjorie put down the receiver she was engaged.

"What about Tethera?" her mother asked.

"I'm not leaving him behind. Tethera introduced us."

Fourteen months after their first meeting, Basil Dove waved to his fiancée from the wharf in front of the Henry Jones jam factory. Then Tethera shot down the gangplank and all hell broke loose.

"I see you didn't take my advice," Basil said, returning the cocker to Marjorie, after seeing the long, frantically wagging tail. That was before a terse official whisked the dog away. Another three months before they were able to collect Tethera from the kennels in Quarantine Bay. By then they were Mr and Mrs Dove.

They had married in St David's, and after spending their wedding night at Hadley's Hotel drove out to the east coast. Basil still had no house. He had dithered since his arrival, enthusiastically inspecting properties and then rejecting them. In the end, he had needed Marjorie's approval before he committed himself, as well as the small amount of capital that she brought with her.

Within a month, they had completed the purchase on Moulting Lagoon Farm. He set about building a barn and bought his wife a docile piebald to ride along the beach, and for himself decked out a room where he could indulge in the passion that he had had since boyhood for crafting ships to fit into glass bottles.

The couple envisaged a quality of life that had been denied them in a country ground down by six years of war and years of rationing.

"But they didn't transplant well," Alex said. "My mother never worked – she haunted antique shops. Nor was my father cut-out to be a horny-handed son of toil. Fitting little bits of cedar into bottles was his pastime, that and reading. They soon realised farming wasn't for them and yet they didn't want to return to England. Instead of trying to address the problem they just floated along. Then my father started to go blind."

Basil's last years were dispiriting. His romanticism of himself was quite vast, but fragile at the same time. A self-appointed remittance man, he had deliberately washed up in a place where there was nobody who understood him or how he spoke, save for an ex-journalist in the nearby town. So when his grey eyes that once had seen for ever started to fail him, he took refuge in gin – which he drank with a token dash of tonic – and in his ships. In the bottle, as Harry Ford put it to Alex on more than one occasion, as well as a lot of other things. "Best present your father ever gave you – to die young. Or have I told you that?"

"Several times."

Ten days after the log-truck barrelled into their car, Alex's parents were buried in the lawn beneath the Oyster Bay pine. There was no one to tend the farm. Several months later, the chief stock inspector came on a police launch from Hobart to inspect for disease and parasites. The old white-footed piebald was still in the triangular paddock next to the house, its ribs like the contours of a shipwreck, but pleased to see people; as were the cats. The chickens had been eaten and four cows in Rough Run were so wild they had to be shot. Alex learned these details only on his return.

Alex would have needed to live in Wellington Point a year to soak up the goodwill that his new circumstances created, but within a fortnight his godmother, a midwife who had met his father aboard the *Strathaird*, scooped him off to Sydney. Stranded on the mainland, he spent two terms at a school in Vaucluse. At the start of the following Easter term, his uncle in the north of England paid for Alex to attend a similar establishment in Sedbergh famed for its austerity – "You'll like the motto," he joked. "*Hardness is the nurse of men.*"

He arrived in Sedbergh at night, dressed in his father's National Service trench coat, leather buttons done up against the cold. Only next morning did he see that he had come to a place surrounded by high fells. Where the stone walls ended, grass paths led up to long open ridges from where Alex looked down on a landscape a little like Tasmania: mountainous, close-knit and monarchist, with some farmers still travelling about in horse and cart.

At the time of his arrival, these hills belonged to West Riding, a district of Yorkshire. By the end of the year, to the tremendous indignation of his uncle, they were claimed for the new county of Cumbria. It gave Alex a strange but definite relief to move among a rural population that was itself having to forge an unfamiliar identity and adjust to shifted boundaries.

The school was less austere than its motto suggested. It encouraged pupils to get out and engage with their surroundings. On Sundays after chapel, Alex could take a sandwich lunch and, as long as he did not use a wheeled vehicle, he might go anywhere he liked. Over the next four years, he climbed Winder many times and walked the banks of the Lune, and ran ten-mile cross-country runs. His abiding memory was the smell of sheep shit and the sound of curlews in spring, a sonorous bubbling absolutely lovely cry that echoed all round the fells. He never forgot, either, the friendliness of the people. Caught out in a downpour on Firbank Fell, he was ushered into a low-ceilinged house by a farmer who, noting his drenched blue jersey, introduced Alex to his family as "one of them scholar lads" and a month later invited him to his daughter's wedding. But although outwardly very friendly, Cumbrians shared with Tasmanians a resistance to outsiders. They might welcome him into their homes and dry his clothes before a peat fire, but no matter how passionately he immersed himself in their landscape, no matter how often he bathed the perspiration from his face in the Rawthey or hunted for fossils and dippers and otter trails, to the locals he would always be an off-comer. Someone from off.

Off began fifteen miles from Sedbergh. Tasmania was very off. One or two of the masters had the habit of confusing it with Tanzania.

In Hart House, a forbidding grey stone building on the south side of the cricket pitch, Alex caught his first English flu – deeper, darker and wetter than anything he could remember. On the windowsill in his dormitory, the thermometer recorded minus twenty-one.

It was at Sedbergh, too, that Alex discovered the authors whom he would study again and more at university: Henry James, Joseph Conrad, Samuel Johnson. But he was not convinced of a deeper purpose other than to study and to smile and – after a rain-soaked afternoon on the rugger pitch – to strip off his mud-caked shorts and brown shirt. His time at the school served to intensify a sense he already had of running about a playing field that was parallel to the rest of the world. He might wave at others, and they might see him, but he was never able to reach out and tackle them – however far he stretched, whatever name he was called. This sense, almost of weightlessness, could not wholly be put down to the sudden loss of his parents or to the fact that he arrived at Sedbergh a term late and took longer than others in his year to adapt to the school's idiosyncratic rituals and language; or even to the arbitrary shedding of his first name at the request of a jocular house-master. It had to do as well with where he was from.

An Australian educated in England, Alex found himself trapped between suppressing emotion and trumpeting it. Prone to fits of impatience, he rarely cried when he hurt himself. He held his breath until he fainted rather than kick out or lose physical control. In scrums and skirmishes, other boys left him alone. Wary of a swallowed-up pain that seemed at odds with the soft-spoken orphan from Down Under.

He went up to Oxford on a scholarship endowed for Tasmanian students. At Merton, when not working hard, he clowned and had girlfriends and gambled and got drunk. But he could never find an intimate circle, the one, two or three friends with whom he might be himself. Somehow it eluded him.

On coming down from Oxford, he was offered an apprenticeship in the broom factory by his uncle. Alex declined. Perhaps hoping to master his reticence, he trained to be a teacher, and was halfway through his course when he abandoned it. He was then twenty-three.

Those he left behind in England were not persuaded that Alex's temperament was suited to live alone behind a stock-fence. The view prevailed that he would soon be back, once he had sorted out certain things. "He's gone to Australia really to learn about England," was how one

Merton friend explained his behaviour to Sarah (who wrote Alex an irritated postcard, wondering what to do with his stuff. *Keep it,* he wrote back. *Maybe send me my trench coat*). On others, it had never dawned that Alex could be Australian: "He's living *there*? In Van Diemen's Land? Isn't that where people were packed off who'd done something awful?" But 14,000 miles away, pride and enjoyment in his farm took Alex unawares. In a way that he had not anticipated, it exhilarated him to watch his animals grow fat and healthy above the barley, the blood on the frost at lambing time, and to lay a fresh drive of white gravel that emphasised anyone walking up it.

Even so, his passage into countryman had not been smooth. Unmonitored by Ray Grogan, his tenant Bill Molson had raped the land, flogged it to death. Nor had he made any effort to maintain the buildings. The property was so lamentably run down that a farmer up the road, Jack Fysshe, warned Alex that only a mad rabbit would take it on. "Don't do it, mate, it's not worth the candle," Fysshe said, bumping into Alex outside Talbot's. "But I'm there if you need me. And if you do decide to do it, I had a thing going with your dad. We used to rent a combine harvester together, three of us." The third was Tom Pidd, who farmed towards Bicheno. "Really, we liked your dad. A useless farmer, but a nice man. If you want my advice, sell your farm – if you can get any money for it – and go back to Putney, England. But if I can be of any help, ring and I'll be there."

Alex was slightly surprised when, back a month, none of these neighbours had appeared to help him. They just had not turned up.

During his first days home, as he began to think of it, farming was as baffling to him as the pink and green lists at Sedbergh. Twelve years since he had last ridden a tractor or a horse. After five weeks, he decided to call on Fysshe.

The farmer was hardly more encouraging than before. "Now you're back – I couldn't say this when Bill was alive – well, the fact of the matter is he wasn't fair to the land, he took the top right off it. I used to look at your farm and think: When I buy it – which I'm inevitably going to have to do – I shall make an offer for nothing, considering the fortune I'll have to spend on fertiliser."

Eventually, after two or three years, the two of them worked out an arrangement to share a semi-trailer for ewes, but Alex would never scold Jack Fysshe for his generosity.

On Fysshe's advice, Alex spread a load of phosphates on the paddocks and hired a young man out of school to help him repair the fences. On the fifth day, Joe Hollows failed to show up.

"Par for the course," said Fysshe. "Workmen are hard to keep round here."

His own ineffectualness brought Alex closer to his parents. He understood how local traders could have fleeced them with such depressing regularity and cheerfulness. The severest case was a builder he contracted to repair the shearing shed, who ordered an excessive quantity of sandstone, only to abscond with half of it to build himself a house in Marion Bay.

And Alex made plenty of mistakes of his own.

He first thought to plant flax for tanning, but it did not take. Nor did the cash crops that he sowed the following year. A storm blew the oats down. Rust got into the spring barley and the seeds failed to germinate. Misled by climate conditions that were warmer here than in the Central Highlands, he had sowed too late. So in his second year home he started running cattle and sheep.

Alex bought Corriedale and Poleworth as his father had

– another mistake, since they were not ideal for wool. Two years on, he was in the process of changing the flock, using merinos from the stud in Triabunna.

Thirty paddocks stretched away down the hill. "I move a mob every two days to a different paddock. That way the grass grows back quickly."

"How many sheep do you have?" asked Merridy.

"Three thousand all up. Plus thirty cows and a bull." The herd of Aberdeen Angus was self-replacing, and caused him the least headache. He sold the calves straight off the cow, keeping five. If there were one or two dry cows, he sold those. He was shortly to get rid of the bull after three years – "Otherwise he'll be going over his daughters."

The ride had loosened Merridy's hair. She unpinned it, threw back her head. "Are you a good farmer?" with the tortoiseshell comb in her mouth. She had met few farmers.

Alex laughed. "Good? No. Tell the truth, I was thinking of chucking it in."

"You mustn't do that," she said involuntarily.

"I don't know, Merridy. Farming's hard. It takes everything out of you."

"Everything? Surely not."

"Well, maybe more than I'm prepared to give. It's a lot of uneducated people, mainly families, trying to live off the land. It's not treated as a business, but it is. And I'm not a businessman. I depend on the goodwill of the bank to survive – utterly."

"I don't care. You can't sell this," nodding at the view.

He was surprised at her vehemence, and pleased. "Perhaps I won't have to," and tossed away the pine needle with which he had dug clean his fingernails. "It could be I've just hit my straps." Three days after he first encountered Merridy, Alex had secured a contract to sell barley to Cascades brewery. "As of next year, I might even stand to break even."

149

She pretended to finish mending her hair, but she was admiring his competence. She had guessed that he was hard-working, and that he was strong because he was running this farm all by himself. What she had not appreciated was that he was dying to stay alive. He had no help, and yet help was what he needed.

Alex whistled to Flash, and they rode to where he had knocked down the scrub and burned it; where he had banked and drained the marsh; and where in rough winds the south end still overflowed with salt water.

The hills west of the marsh ran up to Masterman's Tier and paddocks of rich volcanic soil; beyond was all sags and tussocks where the sheep hid themselves. In four years, he had taught himself to be a tolerable counter. When his rams went missing he took a bottle of cold tea and stalked through the kangaroo grass that grew thick as the hair on Flash's back, and down through gullies of red ochre which the Oyster Bay tribe had patted into their faces and hair.

Love made him expansive and articulate. They cantered to the summit of Treasure Hill where in the 1920s a travelling cattle-buyer was discovered dead beside the track. Alex did not know the whole story, but the man was reputed to have been carrying a satchel of gold. To Rough Run, where his first summer back Alex bumped into a seal in the ripened corn. "At full moon, the old fur seals come over from the Isle des Foques to die." He described for her a still winter evening, a grizzled leopard seal and its bellow on being disturbed. And on to Barn Hill, where his father had put up a Cumbrian bank-barn. "He was walking here one clear day, nothing in the sky, when he heard a terrific wind and was struck on the elbow by a hard black object. I've still got the meteorite." Alex paused to unwind a strand of wool caught on a wire. "Lucky it didn't take his arm off."

It was past noon when they galloped back to the homestead. In the field above the house a sheep licked at the umbilical cord of a lamb as it nuzzled to suck its mother's engorged teats.

Merridy swivelled in her stock saddle. "Lambs in March?"

"You can have lambs throughout the year – as long as there's a bit of green feed for the ewes."

Alex watched her fascination rather than the drama enacted on the grass. For him, the lamb's birth was not convincing any more than his parents' car accident had been. But Merridy convinced. As if she had fallen to earth and caused a gale and burned the grass all around.

"Let's have some tucker."

They ate in the kitchen, sandwiches that he had prepared with leftover chicken from his dinner the night before. Half an hour later, he shut the fly-screen behind them, and after checking his dog – gulping at a bone beneath the table – resumed the tour.

The land absorbed Alex's energies, but had he the money he planned to renovate the farm buildings. Beyond a sagging fence stood the convict-built shearers' quarters, put up in the 1870s by an old lag called Fazerlacky who had exchanged his wife for a pair of boots. The shingles on the roof were kept in by wooden staples. Several were adrift and the sky, glimpsed in blue splinters, reminded Alex of yet another thing he had to fix. "The shearers have been complaining that the possums piss in their faces."

To the rear of the building lay the shearing shed. Shears in leather cases and an old turkey-stone, originally the property, it was said, of Wellington Point Sam who could drink a bottle of beer standing on his head and who never sharpened his shears in the open air in case the wind scraped the edge off them.

The lime had drained from the bricks, giving to the exterior a dejected look, but inside it smelled of sweat and dung and wool from the June shearing.

He guided her between stalls carved from thin beams of Oyster Bay pine – and back out again into the open, where meanwhile a warm wind had blown up, a northerly that bowed the macrocarpa on Rossall Hill and skittered through the farmyard. It was answered by the shriek of agonised machinery.

She said, to help: "That sounds crook."

What grated and gnashed was the green-painted windmill.

"It's been crook since I can remember."

According to the angle of the wind, the blades worked intermittently – as now – blurring the field behind into a circle of widening ripples.

He followed her gaze. Propped up against the windmill, a ramshackle ladder led to a narrow viewing platform protected on three sides by a rail, and on the fourth by two strands of wire.

"You can see Oyster Bay from up there," he said.

"Can I look?"

"Here. Let me go first." He took hold of the rungs and the ladder all but toppled from the sky.

Alex's voice climbed ahead of him, explaining the windmill's provenance. His father had bought it on the recommendation of an Anglo-Argentine whom he had met in Hobart, and had it shipped from an *estancia* in Entre Ríos. Two rungs below, Merridy did not catch every word but she gathered that Alex had haggled with its innards since he was a boy.

She hauled herself after him onto the platform and he lifted up a wire for her to crawl under.

The platform had the narrow shape of a ship's bridge and was large enough, just, for the two of them to stand side by side. The motion of the wind made it vibrate. She licked from her mouth a strand of dark hair, and held on to the rail.

Then as abruptly as it had blown up the wind dropped. The blades creaked to a halt and shuddered and with one last grumble fell silent.

She turned her head. Wanting a sudden look at him. Over his shoulder through watery eyes she made out a bright smudge. On the vane in an orange marker, her name.

"Alex. What's that doing there?"

"I wrote it," he said, bashful.

"What does it mean?"

He took her hand. She saw that his nails were clean. "I love you."

She withdrew her hand. "Please don't say that."

"Why, have too many men said it to you?"

She looked down. The platform had shrunk to the size of a newspaper.

"Have you said it?" he wanted to know.

"Yes. I have."

"Lots of times?"

"No. Not very often."

"Last time was when?"

"When I was five."

She twisted away before he could see the consternation on her face. Leaning against the rail, she breathed in. The air smelled as if cleaned in rainwater. It had the stillness of something that had cried itself out.

"I'm sorry."

"It's all right." Then: "It's not you who should be sorry. It has nothing to do with you." Whatever it was.

Subdued, Alex followed her gaze to the scrub that led in one direction to low hills of wattle where Tethera had bitten a snake and been bitten and died, and in the other to shimmery fields over the top of which Oyster Bay unravelled in a turquoise thread.

"Ten miles to civilisation," he murmured.

It was so quiet they could hear a pigeon drooling. Far away, the drilling of a speedboat grated on the sea.

"What?" she was laughing again. "Wellington Point?"

"No, the Hazards," rallying.

"I was going to say. You can't even drink the water."

At her laugh, the prospect of early autumn tinged the distant mountains with a pink glowing promise. "You asked why I stayed," he said. "I'll show you."

They walked along the lagoon towards the beach.

On a slope overlooking the shore was a fenced-off area containing four gravestones with the grass growing over them. He waited for Merridy to read the inscriptions. The names of the family of settlers who had drowned in 1843.

"What happened?"

"They were a couple with two children. They'd been at sea eight months. This was the very last leg. The father took off his shirt to sunbathe when a wind came up and blew it into the lagoon. He dived in to retrieve it and got into difficulties and began to sink. His son stood up to jump in, but the convicts held him back – they thought they'd be charged with his murder. He was watching his father die when the wind capsized the boat. His mother and brother are also buried here, so I presume they saw it all, too. The father's body was never found."

Alex pointed. "My father was tidying up the graves one day when the penny surfaced."

Merridy wanted to linger. She had questions to ask. But Alex was anxious to press on. He grabbed her hand and led the way to a low scalp of lichen-covered rock where, he said, he escaped to sit in the numb days following his parents' car crash, watching the waves in their steady regiments charge in, wanting to be older.

She tensed herself to sit, but he took her arm and guided her away through the emerald boobyalla until they came to a dune weed-choked with startling red flowers.

"There," he said.

They stood on the sand.

The earlier wind had chased a pack of clouds to the horizon so that there appeared no distinction between sky and water.

"What?" he asked.

"I was listening to the sea," and rubbed her sandy heel against his leg.

> *I am tired of living singly*
> *On this coast so wild and shingly.*

He stared back out at the bay. "Almost every day I see something, a cloud, a tree, a bird – and say to myself: Four years ago I wouldn't have looked at that. And I can't help thinking what a chump I was. I was so concerned, I'd forgotten how to look at land or sky or sea. When at last I did open my eyes that was a real moment. I'd just caught a bream, over there" – and waved in the direction of the river mouth – "but instead of the fish I saw hills and space and weather, and it made me want to look at it for a long time."

Alex wondered if he might regret the remark, or if she

had ever met a more tedious man, but she touched his face.

He held her hand. "See, you're doing it again."

"Electricity," she explained.

"Electricity?"

Her father had taught her to touch everything with the back of her hand. "Otherwise," and flattened her palm on his wrist, "the hand contracts around the shock." She gripped tight. "And never lets go."

She led him by the hand and they lay down in a clearing in the marram grass. The sun blazed in the absence of wind. She stretched out in the sunlight and felt no shame or shadow as he dusted the sand from her arms and her knees. The two boys she had kissed at uni had touched her with greedy hands and no tenderness. They did not tickle her spine like Alex or stare into her eye as though they wanted to rake the bottom of it, or promise an answer to the dark questions that she would like put to them.

What she felt for the others with whom she had tried to envisage a future had leeched away until all she remembered was something synthetic and mildewed. Her feelings for Alex sprang from her intestines.

The sand squeaked beneath them. The colours poured from him into the sky, the waves hissed out and somewhere in the parrot-feathered dusk a black swan honked its way across the water.

When Alex got to his feet the sun was setting.

In silence they picked their way back to the house. They were halfway across the lawn when she heard the scrape of claws on wire.

"Can you drive me back? My parents will be worrying."

CHAPTER SEVENTEEN

HER FATHER DIED ON Sunday. Merridy sat beside his wheel-chair in the alcove, waiting for the next breath. He seemed to come up a long way to search for it. But there was nothing there. His mouth lay open on yellow teeth, his eyes in frozen gaze at the window, as if one of the bulldozers he had made for his son had wound down.

The funeral service was at the Uniting Church. A handful of mourners filled three pews, including a latecomer who was whispered to have been Albert Talbot. Keith Framley, dressed in a suit too tight for him, read the eulogy in which he opined that "death is a turning off of the electric light before dawn", and afterwards there was a wake at the bowls club where Debbie handed out lukewarm sausage rolls and hamburgers that tasted of roo.

TWILIGHT BOWLS – It's already started. Wednesday for 5.00 p.m. and only $3.00 to enter. So come along and have some fun.

Not for another four days did Merridy visit Moulting Lagoon, driving from Wellington Point with her mother in Leonard's 1968 green Peugeot. Mrs Bowman, not trusting their mission to her headstrong daughter, was adamant that she come too. She waited in the car, sitting upright and stiff in the passenger seat and glaring at the tree on the lawn, while Merridy sought out Alex.

Merridy spotted him up a ladder against the shearers' quarters, hammering nails into the shingles. The clouds had speckled over and a pair of wedge-tailed eagles scoured the poppies in a paddock behind.

"Merridy!" He took hold of his pliers and hammer and clambered down the ladder two rungs at a time and ran to her.

But her eye would not fit into his. Tomorrow, her mother was taking Merridy to Ulverstone to visit her aunt.

He looked over her shoulder at the gaunt face peering at them from the parked car, the lank grey hair. "You're back when?"

"In a fortnight."

"That's a very long time."

"No, Alex. To pack up. I'm going back to uni." Obedience to Mrs Bowman's wishes had given her an air of unreality. "I've come to say goodbye."

Numbly, he absorbed the news. "Oh no, that's a disappointment."

"Isn't that the way it is? You meet. You say goodbye. I was always going back to Melbourne. You knew that."

With an injured laugh, he quoted Robert Louis Stevenson. "*I think of Melbourne and I vomit.*"

"Well, it's what my mother wants," said her mouth in the same dutiful voice. "We've put the unit on the market."

He inspected his pliers, opening and closing them. It ought not to have surprised him. She had never concealed her intention to go back to university eventually. She had only stayed on to look after her father, and now she was free. "Isn't there anything that would keep you?"

"Like what?"

He told her. He put his question to her and she felt the pins and needles returning to her heart.

She did not answer. Looked away. A branch dipped on the Oyster Bay pine, releasing a fat black bird.

From the car, a bark: "Merridy!"

She made a strange sound. He thought she was laughing, but stepping closer he saw the tears streaming.

She smiled through them. That enigmatic face. She said with all the conviction that she could muster: "No, Alex. I'm not good for you."

"Rubbish, Merridy, of course you are."

But the promise she had made to herself, it did not permit her to believe in what he offered. She went on in a beseeching voice: "What do you want? I bet it includes a quiet life."

"I suppose so, yes." He was an implicit disciple of the seasons. The security of crops grown and harvested. He would like something durable.

"Then you shouldn't be with me." And remembered Randal Twelvetrees: "You're like your mother. You shouldn't be with anyone – you'll only destroy them."

Or maybe children would stabilise her.

"*Merridy!*"

"Listen, I have to go."

"But I love you," his heart aching for her. He put everything else out of his mind. Her mother calling in a reproachful voice from the car. His leaking roof, his cattle and sheep, his barley and clover, his bottled ships. All his care on the young woman who stood before him and wiped her cheek.

"How can I?" she said, miserable. "I'm not in love with you."

"It'll come, you know, it'll come."

She thought that he was trying to boost her up. She thought that she could easily extract herself as she had done in the past. She did not know what she thought.

"Are you serious, Alex?"

"Yes. I am deadly, deadly serious."

She looked at him and saw the faces of all the men she had repudiated.

Meanwhile, the face that leaned from the car window had never been more contorted. "Merridy! Are. You. Coming?"

His expression sabotaged her. She felt the gummy tentacles of his need. And hers.

"Let me think about it. I'll tell you when I get back."

FOR SALE: 1 pre-loved hospital bed and wheelchair. Enquiries to Sister Surrage at Louisa Meredith.

In her father's cocktail bar that night Tildy could not control her excitement. Someone had seen Ray Grogan in Sargison's jeweller's in Hobart. Buying a ring.

"Is that good news, then?" asked Merridy. Her final evening behind this counter.

"Just so long as it's for me!" and splashed herself another incautious measure of Captain Morgan.

"Silly," putting on a smile. "Who else could it be for?"

"Oh, Merridy, will you be my bridesmaid? I've never told you this, but I know how much I owe you."

"If you didn't ask, I'd never speak to you again."

Tildy drew out a compact from her handbag. Her large eyes looked larger still as – mouth open – she applied her mascara. "By the way, how did Alex take the news?"

On the other side of the counter, Merridy checked the level of the upturned rum bottle.

Tildy glanced up. "Well? You did tell him you're leaving, didn't you? How did he take it?"

Merridy gave a crimped smile. "He asked me to marry him."

"No!" Tildy snapped the compact shut, tucked it back in her bag and brought her stool forward. "Tell me, tell me, tell me. Of course, you've said yes."

"Oh, I don't know." She had never thought she would marry. Even if that was in her mind, she had not thought it through.

"But you like him, you said."

"Like, yes. But I'm not in love with him. You mustn't think that," and put the bottle into the bin. Anyway, twenty was too young.

"It will come, you know, it will come."

"Funny, that's what Alex said," quite pensive.

"Then maybe he listened to me. It's what I told him. It's what I keep telling Ray," and leaned over the counter. "Hey, are you sure that bottle was empty?"

LADIES BIBLE STUDY. If you would like to know about Christianity and/or have fellowship with other ladies then you are invited to the Bethel Teahouse, Monday 6 p.m. Supper (finger food only). New members welcome.

It was strange. Mrs Bowman had had a premonition that Alex was about to propose.

In Ulverstone, she had called on the minister at her old church in Hortle Place, the one to whose son she had been engaged when she met Leonard, and asked him about the advisability of her daughter marrying this Alex Dove boy. Minister Twelvetrees was a wise old man with a long narrow face so worn by the sins it had heard that he had come to resemble a tawny frogmouth. His son Randal had settled down eventually with a girl from Albany and they lived in the bush, more or less content. He studied the photograph that Mrs Bowman showed him, a formal portrait of Alex in Oxford after taking his degree, and replied in a voice that sounded as if it had just sipped communion wine, rich and sweet: "If Mr Dove holds out one hand, you should hold out two."

Merridy was grim-faced for much of the fortnight in Ulverstone. She had felt like a sorcerer's apprentice, handing over to her mother the only photograph that she possessed of Alex. She repeated: "Everyone in Wellington Point speaks well of him, except Ray Grogan, and that's a commendation in itself, God knows."

"Mind your tongue, girl." Mrs Bowman gave a little sniff. "*Woe unto thee when all men shall speak well of thee.*"

In Ulverstone, they stayed with Mrs Bowman's younger sister. Doss had been stricken by polio when an epidemic swept through the state. After she became crippled, having been beautiful, her husband decided to disappear. She lived in a crescent lined with pear trees in what had once been a brothel, subsequently bought by a Mayor of Ulverstone. The house had black-stained wooden banisters; dark varnished doors that caught the dull overhead light – beamed through glass bowls from the 1950s; worn green carpets that reminded Merridy of the Louisa Meredith Nursing Home; and peeling grey wallpaper. It was cold at night. Unable to sleep, she combed her mother's Bible for ammunition. The small print revived her father's grumble: "You can find proof of anything you like in that book. You can prove that Edward Lear wrote *Hamlet*."

One morning beside her breakfast plate, Mrs Bowman discovered a card with handwriting on it.

"What is this, Merridy?"

"Just read, Mum."

She put on her warped glasses. "*Cast thy cares upon Him for He careth for thee.*"

"Letty, will you have some of this?" interrupted her sister. Her false teeth shining like the two rows of encyclopaedias in her hall. She had bought them in an extravagant fit after her husband left her and was still paying for them.

"Now, Doss, you know I never eat cream."

Her sister skimmed a wink across the table to Merridy: "*Whatsoever is set before thee, eat, asking no questions, for conscience sake.*"

WELLINGTON POINT RSL & EX-SERVICEMEN'S CLUB
Former intelligence officer (MI5 et alia) reveals "A Life of Intrigue".
In the Clubrooms on Friday 25th beginning at 7.30 p.m. Members are urged to attend.
Ask the friendly staff about becoming a member. Tom Pidd (Hon. Sec.).

The fortnight stretched away like fourteen years. Alex waxed the sand-scratched floors of the corridor and kitchen; he finished painting details on the deck and hull of his latest model boat, and to the side of the bridge glued a white life-ring, the size of a Polo mint, with the ship's name, *Otago;* and chores had accumulated in the garden. On the morning that Merridy was due back from Ulverstone, he cleaned out the lime-tinted gunge of a wasps' nest caught in the water tank after February's heavy rain. A few wasps buzzed at the moist green overlap, spiralling on angry wings towards the mouth – which he had blocked off. Clots of soggy drones circulated the surface when he stirred. He netted them out and sprayed with mosquito repellent the pipe that he had taped up, and after a day the mass of them did not return, save for one straggler.

All the time, the thought of Merridy shifted like a heat-wave in distorting currents.

He was looking forward to her return so much that he did not hear the car. That evening, a tap on the window as he sat in his workroom. Preoccupied with the ship that he had launched into its rum bottle.

In the kitchen, he turned on the stove.

She did not take off her coat. "What have you been doing?"

"I was working on the *Otago*, mostly."

"Did you finish it?"

He fetched the bottle and laid it on the dresser. Ever prone to expecting the worst, he did not look at her but gabbled.

"This part of the hull is made from the original ship, a piece of timber offcut, would you believe it, from a sawhorse that was still there."

She looked into the glass, a quiet, steady gaze. On deck, a cat sat on the penny and her kittens all in a circle.

"If you want, I could tell you more about ships, as I did the other day . . ." But he was as nervous as she.

"I dare say we'll have time."

"You mean . . ." and his eyes brimmed over with pleasure above a six-inch grin.

There was only one condition. Before giving her consent, Mrs Bowman insisted on viewing the house.

MENOPAUSE INFORMATION SESSIONS. You are not alone. The Pit Stop tent will be erected outside the nursing home between Monday and Friday next week. If you are interested, please drop by to browse or contact Cheryl Surrage on 62578380.

Merridy's mother arrived at Moulting Lagoon Farm dressed in a blouse of hailstone black muslin that had the mysterious effect of making her look a good deal younger than her years. She had come on her own and walked alertly through the rooms, taking everything in. If she had been a man, thought Alex, she would have been a cavalry officer, straight-backed, with a mouth like a tight strap keeping her chin in place. But something in her relaxed to observe the God-fearing gene advertised in the frames along the corridor. Her hostile religious spirit placated by the sight of the samplers, she continued into the living room where Alex had set out tea.

He produced his parents' best china, but Mrs Bowman was not to be bowled over by Spode.

"Mr Dove, I won't beat around the bush. My daughter ought to be at university."

"I quite agree."

"You do not know her yet as I know her, but I am concerned how she will behave if her mind is not occupied."

"Maybe she could do a correspondence course? But do you mind if we get the farm up and running before that? I give you my commitment that then she can not only explore, but achieve."

His promise appeared to mollify Mrs Bowman. She drank her tea and the talk was of her plans, after the marriage ceremony and the sale of "Otranto", to return to Ulverstone where she planned to take up again with her sister.

The single other reference to Merridy was made as she was leaving. Her hand polished the air – she might have been cleaning a candlestick in church.

"My daughter is slovenly, Mr Dove."

"I think she's extremely beautiful."

She gave him a Pentecostal glance. "It's frightening what we think is beautiful."

He opened the door of the Peugeot and she gathered up her black skirt and settled in.

She sat there, gripping the wheel.

"I would be grateful if you could make arrangements to collect Merridy's Glory Box. Naturally, I will meet the costs of the wedding. And, Mr Dove –?" reaching for the door handle. "You should know that her father has left her a small legacy."

In the aisles of Talbot's and at the counters and tables of the Bethel Teahouse they acclaimed the engagement as one of the excitements of the autumn. Agnes wrote a commemorative poem for Talbot's *Newsletter* and the vicar in Swansea was in regular communication with Minister Twelvetrees over arrangements for the wedding service.

They married in the third week of May in the red-roofed Uniting Church at the bottom of Radley Street where, not so long before, a small gathering of nurses and patients had buried her father. Minister Twelvetrees officiated and Mrs Bowman's sister came down from Ulverstone. Alex turned to see Merridy on Keith Framley's arm, and was conscious of everyone craning their necks to catch his own expression: Agnes, Jack Fysshe, Tom Pidd, Abbygail, Dr Musgrove, Sergeant Finter, Sister Surrage, Mrs Grogan, Debbie, Tildy.

The rain stayed away, as did Ray-as-in-sunshine Grogan.

Alex had not wanted to invite him. Merridy was relieved, but it worried her that Ray had still not proposed to her cousin, a prevarication that was the source of comment in the RSL and of a degree of panic in Tildy herself. Invited to be Merridy's bridesmaid, she had caught the bouquet – "as if she was fielding at gully," remarked Sergeant Finter afterwards at the reception in the Freycinet Court Hotel.

It was dark when Alex drove Merridy home. He had to swerve twice to avoid dead animals. Sitting beside him, his wife of three hours looked into the passing trees and remarked that her mother had found it indecent the amount of roadkill that she had had to put up with in Wellington Point. Alex smiled. In his opinion, so much roadkill was proof of a nature in rude health.

Not even at the reception had Mrs Bowman let up, tackling Merridy as she helped to carry the wedding gifts into the back of the ute. "Are you really not going back to uni? How are you going to keep your head alive?"

"I. Will. Manage. Mum."

"Well, I'm going to give you as a wedding present *Engineering World*. Because your father would really want you to finish your degree. This is my way of saying: Please keep using your brain."

At the bottom of the drive Merridy reached over and switched off the headlights. The better to look at the night sky with its gunpowder of stars. At a slow walking pace, the ute crunched up the white gravel that seemed to glow as the vehicle approached the house.

That night the couple made a pact that they would keep for the next sixteen years. The idea was Merridy's. She kept looking at the door ajar on the wardrobe, blackboard-coloured on which to chalk the sum of her wishes. Some memory was hiding there. Like a face she knew but had forgotten from where.

She leaped out of bed and stood before the wardrobe. "We must never shut this door," in her most serious voice. "Ever." She could make out the reflection of her hand, pointing.

"I'm not certain that you *can* shut it."

"Well, from now on we always keep it open."

"Regardless of the consequences?" amused by her earnestness. It reminded him, with some reason, of a parlour game.

"Regardless of the consequences."

Again they made love. Afterwards, she brushed his face with the palm of her hand.

"You're so precious to me," he said huskily.

His heart was so open, his longing so unsettling to her, that she had to close her eyes.

He held her palm against his face. "What do you want to know? Ask me anything."

"Anything?" It would come, hadn't he promised? It would come.

He was stroking the back of her hand. "In the whole wide world and I'll tell you," he said.

She opened her eyes. "How did you get that penny into the bottle?"

"No," and tried to twist away, but she pinned him down.

"You promised!" straddling him.

He studied her face for a long second. "You'll never tell?"

"On my brother's name."

"I'll have to whisper it."

She raised the hair from her ear and lay forward on top of him, her cheek against his face. "Alex, I'm listening," into the pillow.

His fingers running up and down her naked spine –
"Oh, yes," she wriggled – Alex breathed into her ear the
secret that his father had taught him.

She said nothing.

"Merridy?"

Asleep. With the most tender expression.

PART II

Moulting Lagoon Farm,
1988–2004

CHAPTER ONE

REFURBISHMENT SALE. 5 piece older-style lounge suite $80. Brussels carpet $20. Westinghouse stove and Robin Hood canopy $30. Good condition. Contact: Merridy Dove, PO Box 311.

For a great many months there was nothing wrong with their marriage.

If she thought of herself on occasions like Alex's penny, squeezed by a force beyond her comprehension into an impossibly tight and airless space, Merridy felt safe. She perceived in Alex the outline of an anchor. He had taken away her fear, and though what she felt for him was not love necessarily but comfort, she had trusted him when he had assured her that love – and with it passion – would come.

In the meantime, she threw her energies into renovating the house.

Four years since Alex reoccupied Moulting Lagoon Farm and he had done nothing in the way of decorating. The rooms cried out for her care. The house was cold, even in summer. There were no mirrors and frequently no electric light because of power cuts. In the bad light, it had become natural for Alex to ignore the ramshackle state of things.

First, Merridy unpacked her Gory Box – or most of it. Then two cardboard boxes containing her father's cook books and engineering manuals, plus his first editions of

Edward Lear, Lewis Carroll, Charles Kingsley. All these she stacked in the spare bedroom.

Next, she sorted out their wedding presents, and with Alex's help distributed them through the house. She spread Tildy's possum rug before the log fire and moved the Lear cockatoo into the living room, hanging it over the fireplace. She bought new mirrors and Electricare plug-in radiators. She removed her father-in-law's bottles from the sock trays in the wardrobe and rearranged them on shelves in Alex's workshop. By tactful degrees, she tidied up his bachelor's detritus.

"Guess how many cherry pips I threw away today."

"I can't. Ten?"

"Two hundred and forty-seven."

"You counted?"

"It's a habit."

"But your mother warned me how untidy you were."

"My mother specialises in warnings."

"She called you *slovenly*."

"Only around her."

Merridy had the corridor and bedrooms repainted in bright yellows and reds. She stencilled luminous stars on the ceiling of the spare room – for which she ordered a new bed from Hobart – and above the bookshelves that had doubled as his father's drinks cabinet replaced Alex's print of Merton College gardens with her pencil drawing, at the age of six, of a sixty-four-foot steel sieve, for which Alex made the frame.

She installed her father's radio in the kitchen that she refurbished from top to bottom, and set about as one of her goals to learn to cook. In particular, she taught herself how to make pastas that her father might have appreciated. She looked with suspicion at the "Easy Asian" and "Fabulous French" recipes in the *Women's Weekly* that

Tildy lent her, and which called for Oxo cubes. Disregarding Alex's indifference to food, she devoted herself to creating the ultimate red sauce, using fresh tomatoes from her garden that she boiled and peeled.

In the garden, too, she stamped her mark. She did not like to think of other hands putting in the seeds and bulbs; she ripped out the wild daisies from the flower bed around the house and planted stylidium and native correa to attract the birds, and deep red peonies that she bought from a nursery near Hobart. As a last touch, she positioned two she-oaks in terracotta pots beside the kitchen entrance.

So in fits and starts did Merridy create an environment – the first that she had known since childhood – where children and friends would be made welcome.

Tildy came often. The cousins spoke regularly on the telephone in the days and weeks after Ray at last, at last proposed. Ray did not visit. Alex never said anything, either to Merridy or Tildy, about how Ray had damagingly neglected the farm, but he kept it in his mind.

In the same way, Merridy never admitted to Alex about the times when she surprised herself thinking about the real-estate agent.

On the first occasion, she was washing her hair in rainwater when there was a power cut. She lit a candle and was shocked to see in the new bathroom mirror just how long her hair had grown. She was trying to cut it herself when the lights flashed on again and she looked down and noticed her hairy legs. It was Ray's moustache that she saw as she shaved them.

And once as she stood planting seeds outside the living-room window in the pearl of winter, the pine trembling, she found herself playing Ray's game and imagining how he might describe Moulting Lagoon Farm in the wholly improbable event of the property coming onto his books.

The quiet private location. The classic, balconied home with leadlight windows that could be mistaken for a gamekeeper's cottage in the English countryside. The exceptional views of the sea.

A most welcoming entrance foyer leads to rooms of generous proportions with the character of yesteryear. The master bedroom has high raked ceilings with exposed beams and powder room off. Within easy access, and ideal for the growing family, are two further bedrooms, one at present in use as a workshop . . .

CHAPTER TWO

THE MORE TO LEARN the valley, she walked for an hour, sometimes two, each day, or rode on the pony that Alex had given her. Clutching a discarded hickory rake-shaft for her stick, and with Flash at her side, she strolled out in the early morning or evening, with the breeze at its lowest. She took her bearings from the windmill. Whenever she was down on the beach she could see its blurring blades above the boobyalla line. The green vane that had her name on it.

Merridy spent the best part of a fortnight exploring the property. She sat on Alex's orange, lichen-covered rock and picked the marram grass seeds from her feet, picturing her husband at the age of eleven. She revisited the graveyard on the edge of Moulting Lagoon where Alex's father had found the coin. And several times returned to the copse where Basil Dove's neighbour had encountered the thylacine. The only fragrance she detected was euculyptus.

She discovered the trembling jetty from which Basil Dove had liked to swim. On the far side of the stream an eddy of air on an otherwise calm day caused a splash. She thought it might be a platypus in the reeds, but it furred the surface, then crossed the water and ruffled the grass on the near bank, coiling it with the force of a small cyclone. Or a spirit passing, she could not help wondering, as she watched the grass twisting up the bank, outside a disused shed and into the field. The grass greener than a mallard's breast and on the hill an ochre shiver of grain.

On her way back to the house, a black horse running wild in a field of yellow grass reminded her of how it was possible to feel.

Away from people, she let her hair grow below her shoulders. She took to wearing the same jumpers and trousers. So relieved to be out of her mother's oppressive clutches, leave aside Keith Framley's uniform, that she stopped seeing herself – to a point where she almost forgot that she was female. It was enough to focus her attention on Alex and her project of turning a dilapidated Federation post office into a late twentieth-century home. A home fit for a young farmer and his family.

When it was breezy, the sounds of the animals reached her in the house. They carried through the fresh-painted rooms with tremendous clarity, like the sounds of something lost. She heard the bellows of the herd, the lowings of the new bull and the clicking of horns. She had never lived close to animals. It took her a while to get used to them.

Three months into her marriage a black swan pecked at Merridy's hand, breaking the skin. She was feeding it corn on the edge of Moulting Lagoon and the swan arched its neck and struck, removing the hard yellow grain pinched from one of Alex's cobs, and leaving a bruise on her palm the size and shape of a postage stamp, a purple one from somewhere foreign.

A month later, she ran into the kitchen with a shower of white excrement on her hair and clothes. A wedge-tailed eagle had shat on her. She had disturbed it in the field below the sheep-race and the droppings on her shirt put Merridy in mind of the bottle in the restaurant where Alex had courted her. She stripped off and threw her shirt in the wash, but the stain did not come out and no amount of soap could remove it. Still, she refused to see it as a sign. Until the day when a cheerful plumber came from Swansea to fix a mixer tap that persisted in clogging with silt.

He was under the sink so long that she asked if he knew a good solution to remove eagle shit from clothes.

"I leave that to me wife, love. She's got a remedy for every stain – and with the kids there's a lot."

Packing his tools back into a bag, he remarked on the tidiness in the kitchen. "Obviously, you don't have kids."

She coughed. The salt air often woke her with a dry throat. "No. I've only been married for four months."

"Wife got up the stick right away. Maybe before!" He closed his bag and looked at her. "Or don't you want children? Some don't."

Merridy was affected by the question. She saw by his expression that he felt sympathy for her, and yet she did not – until that moment – feel sorry for herself. His words upset her and soon afterwards she came off the pill and took notice of her cycles.

Her mother never visited. Mrs Bowman's sense of release following her husband's death did not survive the winter. She used her daughter's marriage as a staircase into a long cathedral of depression. She wrote on the first Sunday of the month, a single-sided letter containing meagre news and the hope that Merridy was enjoying *Engineering World*. On reflection, it had been a mistake to live with her sister; she was looking for a house to rent in Devonport; she had found one. And a PS in which she asked to be remembered to Mrs Grogan and sometimes to Alex. Nothing about grandchildren.

*

179

In a moment of happy tension she called him Piers.

They sat on the back deck facing the sea, between them a bottle of Coombend Riesling, empty. An autumn evening in April. They had been married almost a year.

He reached for her hand. "Is that what you'd like to call him?"

"Why not?"

"What about Hector?"

He felt the involuntary tug of her arm.

"What if he's a girl?" she said, and left her hand where it was.

He contemplated the Hazards. South, towards Maria Island and the Antarctic, the dragon-coloured sea went from green to scuffled blue. "Piera sounds nice. Piera Dove."

He was teasing, of course. Or was he? She squeezed his hand, but was intertwined, she felt, with a riddle. Not that she minded, or doubted that he was her answer. "Piers Dove. Piera Dove." She said it lightly. Remembering a book of her father's, of pale Italian frescoes. "I'll settle for either."

He opened her fingers, stared at the mark, like a stigma on her palm. "Does that hurt still?"

"It doesn't hurt at all."

There was a flat croak. They watched the birds passing

overhead, their eyes hooked to the rim. They looked as if they had been burned into the sky with a hot blade.

So the sun fell in the menacing pink of Tildy's eyeshadow and the lighthouse glowed earlier and earlier from the tip of Schouten and autumn became winter.

LIONS CLUB OF WELLINGTON POINT have horse manure for sale by the trailer load. For orders and enquiries: phone J. Fysshe 63245668.

Then there were mornings when the wind blew even the clouds away and the sky had the translucence of a membrane. From the kitchen, it stretched so thin that a tap of her hand could break it and the oceans it kept back would tumble her in angry torrents. On these days, walking the nine-mile beach with Flash, she felt that the whole sea was chasing her, flaring with a cold anger to protect its secrets.

Not that she denied herself the vivid pleasure of picking up whatever the sea had dropped. Jellyfish in the shape of Tildy's bras. Mutton-bird feathers pressed into the sand. Necklaces of kelp attached to a single stone that it thrilled her to hurl back at the waves.

In Agnes's Op-Shop, she bought a book on seashells and looked up those that she had collected. They might have been characters from her father's unpublished stories: hairy arks, southern gapers, shining wentletraps, flaming dog cockles, exotic boring venerids. There were also mud-oyster shells from an Aboriginal midden, with round holes punctured into them by borer parasites through which she surveyed the horizon. Reciting to herself preposterously: *He went to sea in a sieve.*

The prettiest oyster shells she brought home to her

bedroom and laid out on a blue cloth on her Gory Box. She blocked her ears to the sound of the waves, like pebbles in a drum reminding her: There is no God there is no God there is no God.

DEEP-SEA DIVER GIVES LESSONS. *Contact: J. S. Phone 62578583.*

She was often alone. Once the kitchen-fitters and decorators had departed, fewer visitors came to the house. Despite her radio, she began to feel out of the eye of the town. It was not an uncomfortable feeling, not to begin with.

When the hay was on, Alex was up at six. Through the bedroom wall, she heard him in the kitchen eating his unvarying breakfast. Three pieces of toast: one Vegemite, one butter, one marmalade. Then the careful closing of the fly-screen and kitchen door and after a few minutes the noise of a machine starting up. She lay in bed, savouring the image of her husband cutting and binding the hay and leaving stooks in the paddocks in the shape of the hourglass with which her grandmother in Ulverstone used to time her husband's eggs. When Alex was cutting hay, it was full on from November to January.

In the early morning, the sun pressed on the southward-facing slopes of Barn Hill. She liked to watch it from the bed, flattening the paddocks and gullies into a long spreading curve. The kangaroo grass that grew in thick clumps along the summit was yellower than custard. Her eyes hunted for the man who had left his shape in the sheets. Who would return for dinner at noon and sometimes not until sunset.

Because, as she quite soon learned to appreciate, Alex was

forever occupied. Judging fairs. Buying and selling cattle. Planting and harvesting crops. In January, he dipped the sheep. In February, he drenched for flukey. In March, he sowed for barley. In the first week of April, he prepared his heifers for the autumn calf sale at Pawrenna, to which he brought along Merridy. In May, he sprayed for grubs. She could understand why he declined repeated invitations to become a councillor or a firey or go on a whale-stranding course. He had no time. There was only himself on the farm, and now Merridy – who took it upon herself to look after the horses, cleaning the tackle and boots. And though she suspected that the land had not yet worked itself into her husband's bones, she knew that the management of it consumed him as exhaustively as it consumed every farmer on this coast. He was part of a network of landowners all with the same agent, an unprepossessing fellow with a toupee and false teeth who drove around to see each of his clients every three weeks on what Jack Fysshe drily referred to as the Suicide Run: to stop any of them committing suicide after one of their number a few years back threw himself down a well.

RAY GROGAN is proud to announce the opening of his new office at 7 Waterloo St. "I am always in need of rental properties for short and long lets. I have a long and proven history of providing landlords with good reliable tenants."

What was left poking through the froth once her memory simmered away the first months at Moulting Lagoon Farm was less the deepening dread that she would never conceive, nor the moments when she thought with a pang of Melbourne and her university contemporaries, but the evenings, early on, when they made love on the living-room floor.

183

Alex lay underneath her, his sandy head on the thick possum rug. He had never seen the colour of firelight on a woman's cheeks. He could not keep it from his smile. How she edified the place.

"What did you do today?" He loved to hear everything. Down to the most basic detail. He welcomed the upset that she brought to his routine. The sight of her tights on the clothes-line. Her finger stirring a red sauce; her inevitable frown when she licked it. Plus, in the days when she was renovating the house, the never-ending trail of plumbers and carpenters who had traipsed through the rooms under her direction, even if Alex took great care to conceal his anxiety when their bills arrived. He drew the money out of his fast-shrinking savings, refusing to let Merridy touch her father's inheritance. It was an article of faith with him. Anyway, the farm remained on track to make a profit. They were in love. It would turn out fine.

"Let's see," rising and falling above him, "I made bread. I finished painting the laundry room. I spoke to Alice about getting some bleach. Oh yes, and started *The Shadow Line . . .*"

She edited out the two letters that she had written to friends in Melbourne, urging them to come and stay (they never did). Or the wistful feeling that she experienced whenever she looked into Alex's study, or opened *Engineering World*, or read one of Alex's books.

In the hard bright sun of those first months the possum rug stood out. She remembered his tongue on her eyelids, between her legs, and was almost persuaded. Love was not sober nor static. It was the supreme example of tenderness in motion. And Alex had taught her.

"You've taken a prune and made it a plum." So she told him.

She kept busy. Thinking of the interaction of their bodies.

Thinking of their child. She saw, they saw, a baby plucking daisies off her jersey and staring up at a terracotta ceiling spangled with yellowy green stars that twinkled in the darkness. The Christmas trees they would decorate with cut-outs of shiny paper. The toys they would wrap – water pistols, little red Wellington boots, black felt Tasmanian devils from a shop in Bicheno.

"We are going to have a baby."

Tildy's jaw dropped.

"No, no, I don't mean I'm pregnant. Just that I've gone off the pill."

But it did not come. It was so simple: they could make love, but no child.

Unlike Tildy who now had Zac.

"You will be a godmother, won't you?" looking up from her hospital pillows, barely ten minutes after his birth.

"I'd be hurt if you hadn't asked."

"Here. Hold him, why don't you?"

CHAPTER THREE

ONE MORNING, MERRIDY JOINED her husband at his dawn breakfast.

"You're up early," cheerfully.

"Alex," clearing her throat. She tightened the cord of her dressing gown and sat down. "I'm going to Launceston for a test."

"A Test? Are England playing?"

"To see if there's something wrong, silly. Dr Musgrove has arranged it."

Alex looked hurt. He was a fierce dog where the body was concerned and certainly not going to submit himself to inspections.

"Well?" he asked ten days later.

She held up the letter from the clinic in Canning Street. "They say nothing's the matter. Not so far as they can tell."

He looked away. "So maybe there isn't." And came and wrapped his arms around her waist, as if she was a mast that he would never let go. "We'll just have to go on rooting like rabbits."

Winter came and Alex exchanged his T-shirt for a dark brown jersey and the trench coat that Sarah had sent back.

He had not thought much about Sarah until in his second year of marriage a letter arrived to say that she was coming out to Australia with a group of teachers, and any chance of their seeing each other? Her schedule was tight. She doubted whether she could make it to Tasmania. Perhaps Alex could hop up to Sydney?

"What, like a kangaroo?" said Merridy, feeling a prickle of jealousy. "Has she looked at the map?"

"She was always hopeless about directions," Alex said.

When he telephoned the number that Sarah had given, she had already left for Australia. They never did meet up.

Meanwhile, there was dribbly-eye in the roos. In June, barely a day went by when he did not press his gun to his shoulder and shoot a wallaby or rabbit. Over on Barn Hill, their neighbour's sheep got into a paddock and spread lice into Alex's flock. He decided to dip the lot, not that it made any difference. All his fleeces had a bit of discoloration that year. Wool prices were the lowest he could remember. He had shorn the ewes in May before lambing, but the market had fallen further by October, when he sheared the wethers. "We need another Cold War, that's what we need," grumbled the classer from Kempton, rubbing a fleece between two blunt oily fingers. The Cold War had been good for wool, the Korean War better still. Peace was an effing disaster.

Once again, children from the local school gathered in the shed to watch. They loved to be there on shearing day – "Getting in the way," grizzled Pat, a stout Aboriginal woman from Flinders, who was very patronising to Merridy, who quite liked her.

The children stood gaping at all the noise and activity: Pat and two other shearers stooped over the sheep; the morose classer feeling the fleeces for strength and texture, eyeing the wool for colour; the wool-roller sorting out the fribs and skin pieces to one side, and the stained wool that he threw into a bin.

"It's all done by feel and eyesight," Alex explained, leading them over to the shearers. He was quite sweet on Pat.

Merridy cooked a big mutton roast for the shed-hands. She would look at them, who had never had to cook in their lives, and see the possum shit in their eyes.

The hurry of the shearers, their pace and physicality – Pat could sweep a sheep from the pen with one arm and on a good day shear 130 fleeces – never failed to impress Merridy, but nothing impressed her more than Alex's natural ability to send children into excitement. In Wellington Point, all round town, there were kids who would walk up to him and say: "Good day, Mr Dove," after spending a morning or afternoon at Moulting Lagoon Farm.

Not only the farm excited the children's curiosity. Once, coming into the shed with a tray of lemonade, Merridy overheard Alex in conversation with two boys and a lanky girl who watched transfixed as he held down a shorn lamb for the taller of the boys to daub with an orange D.

"Oh, Mr Dove, what muscles!" the girl joked admiringly.

"Why don't you have children?" piped up the boy with the marker, and Merridy recognised Rob, who had stood in the Bethel Teahouse.

"Oh, I don't know, I'm doing my best."

"What does doing your best mean?" pressed the girl. "You're obviously not doing it right."

Alex looked up and caught Merridy's eye. "Hi, love," blushing, and released the lamb, which dashed its head against the central pine beam and then shot off, slipping and scratching along the wooden grating. "Here, let me take that."

Wool prices were so low that year that Alex toyed with the idea of going organic and then rejected it. He would persevere. At the end of October, Cascade brewery renewed the contract for his barley.

*

WELLINGTON POINT MODEL YACHT CLUB.
All those who are interested in forming and joining are
invited to attend the inaugural meeting to establish Where
and When. 4.30 Tuesday 15th. Greer Street jetty.

Like Mrs Bowman, Ray never came to visit. But Tildy did.
Bringing Zac and magazines with recipes.

"I must say, you've done a great job, Merridy," tracing
a finger over the new ceramic cooktop. "A great job. But
don't you find it dull up here?"

"Not enough moments," borrowing Alex's words. She
bent over the pram. "How's his sleep going?"

"I only have to turn over and he wakes." Tildy scanned
the novel that Merridy had left open on the dresser. "But
who do you speak to? Apart from Alex."

"Oh, the sea, the animals." They had a cat now and
some ducks. "Does he need another blanket?"

"No, he's mad for the one you gave him. In fact, Ray's
got a mind to cut it in half in case he loses it." The book
reminded Tildy. "You know, I went to bed with him."

"Who?" stroking Zac's mottled arm.

"Your husband, sweetie. Who do you think?"

"Oh, Tildy."

"There's me shooting my big mouth off," sighed Tildy,
and wondered if she had been on the brink of uttering
something profound.

But Merridy was amused. "You forget. You already
told me."

"Do you – still?"

"What?" looking up.

Tildy's hair was no longer blonde, after she met a man
in flippers who remarked of her dye that the anti-foul he
painted on his boat contained less poison. And she was

pregnant again. So fat that her arms came out at right angles.

"Like rabbits, you said."

"Oh, yes. Absolutely."

"He wasn't a rabbit before," and Tildy cackled before falling contemplative. "You must have made him one."

Merridy turned back to Zac. Who had the preoccupied smile of a baby filling its nappy.

"I think a new Huggie's in order."

Tildy looked at her cousin without rancour. To think that Merridy anticipated Zac's needs before she did. "There should be one under his pillow."

"Zac just needs a little fuss," said Merridy, changing him.

Tildy sighed. "You're a much finer mother than I am. You connect better. He's just like his father."

Merridy felt her face turning hot. She was tugged away from the pram, like any dog from a smell. "And you, Tildy. What about Ray?"

The Grogans had married two months after them. Tildy had worn black boots under her dress with four-inch heels. "I could only find them high enough in black." The Doves had given as their wedding present a pewter tray.

"Is he what you wanted?" persisted Merridy.

"Oh, and more." Tildy's eyes fell again on the book. "Hey, that reminds me. I need your help. What should I read? I was thinking of joining Agnes's reading group."

"I'll ask Alex."

"Would you? I want to branch out."

"We'll make a list. It'll be fun." It was what they did most evenings, read. They had built up a small library.

Tildy folded her arms. "I must say, I really would go mad up here on my own. But, of course, the way you two carry on you'll soon have family responsibilities."

"I know, I know," and smoothed her stomach. She was not going to tell Tildy, but she would have her baby before long. She had missed her period and already she imagined the shape and growth in her uncorrected body.

She did not tell anyone, not even Alex. She bought a test at the chemist's. It was negative. A week later she bought another test. In the slow days ahead she haunted the bathroom, her excitement intensifying. Her periods were usually very regular. Even so, she was conscious that she lacked Tildy's wholesome peaceful expression.

Draggedy draggedy. Day after dragging day. Like her mother's first steps across the room after her stroke.

One Tuesday, Alex came home late from Launceston to find her standing on the counter, scrubbing the top shelves of the dresser.

"What are you doing, love?"

"Alice never gets up here."

Then the frosty morning, a fortnight after Tildy's visit, when she detected the spotting. Next day her period started. Not a child after all, but a phantom. And felt her womb heavier than ever, a black, empty, bottle-shaped presence inside her.

The next meeting of the poetry group will be on Wednesday August 9th at 2.30 p.m. at Agnes Lettsom's house. The subject is: "Sea" – a word to conjure with!

The end of another August and the boobyalla were covered with little yellow caterpillars of blossom. She collected pine needles to put on the path and lay down the silverweed and old copies of the *Mercury* as mulch, and kept the mulch away from her fruit trees so as not to rot them. She wrapped her apple trees against codlin moth. She sprinkled blood and bone around the roses. She started a herb garden down near the beach – pepperberries, lemon verbena, chives – where she also planted tomatoes, strawberries and rhubarb. Her fingers gloved in dirt, she kneeled on the earth and pressed each seed into the ground. And once or twice lifted her eyes to catch a blue-tongue lizard with a taste for strawberries watching her.

She looked for pleasure in predictability. The daisies – purple and white – that opened during the day and snapped shut in late afternoon. The spinach flopping in large green spades. Her flowers that grew around the house in the colours, it suddenly struck her, of Alex's samplers: in reds, blues and yellows.

Merridy was happiest, though, in the garden that she had created behind the dunes. Nipping the flower stalks in the rhubarb, she thought of the child that they would have. She pictured a boy somewhat like Alex and looked forward to the day when she would be leading him by the hand to inspect her herbs and vegetables. "Your great-grandmother, who was a bit of a battleaxe, used to say to me: 'God gives a herb for every ill.' This is hoarhound for coughs. That's comfrey for bones and bruises. Over there that's broccoli, the everlasting vegetable. High on the list for needing lots of poo." So would she converse with him, and not only about plants. "That's a huntsman spider. They get active before the rain. Take your attention off them and they go away. But they're harmless, unlike a red-back. See under that pot? Never put your fingers in anywhere you can't see." She smiled to contemplate anyone she had known at uni overhearing these private conversations. They would conclude that country life had turned Merridy Bowman Dove quite potty.

And in the evening after they had eaten, she gave herself to Alex in firelight.

"Oh, and I polished your boots," she reminded him one memorable night, opening his hand and pressing his palm against her stomach. Not because he needed to know, or cared even; but it was part of the fabric that wove them. A reason to listen to his plans for the next day.

"That's good," Alex said, looking up at her, serious all of a sudden. "Since I have to go to Hobart."

Her immediate thought – the windmill was playing up again. The complexity of the female body was as mysterious as the guts of Alex's windmill, and as liable to go wrong at any time. His journey, she imagined, was to fetch a spare part. "Can't East Coast Freight deliver?"

"I'm going to take a test."

She stared at him, the meaning of his words reaching her. And was impelled to bend down and squeeze his face so tight that he cried out.

He had made an appointment at the Royal Hobart, combining it with a visit to his bank manager, who for some time had been requesting a meeting, and also to J. R. Stephenson in Campbell Street to buy a new water pump and spear pipe. Plus a feed of oysters for Merridy: "I know – it's insane that you can't get oysters in Oyster Bay."

On his return, Alex laughed at how easy the procedure had been. The soft-lit room, the pile of magazines, the glass jar – and the shutter that opened in the wall and the anonymous white gloves that took away the jar. In a fortnight or so Dr Macbeth would send the results.

And when the envelope came. "Same as yours." A five-inch grin. "Sperm count normal. Motility, too. No reason at all."

"What's motility?"

"I think it's how zippy they are."

Next morning, he was up early for the store-sheep auction at Quoiba. On waking, she rolled over onto his cold side of the bed and hankered for the rocking applause of the springs. It was an enormous relief. To think they might leave it to nature, to the forces that regulated the lambs and the black swans and the wedge-tailed eagles and tiger-snakes. And also not a relief.

CHAPTER FOUR

WELLINGTON POINT PRIMARY SCHOOL is now taking enrolments for children who will be 4 years old on January 1. Enrolment packs are available from the school office.

Two years on and the itinerant workers he employed to shear his sheep had grown balder. The cars roared by with boats on trailers, the names on the sterns sillier and sillier. And still nothing for them to christen Piers or Piera.

The simplest act for some had become very complex. Merridy tried not to indicate to Alex that she was at the most fertile part of the month because she did not want to appear utilitarian, but she found herself seducing him mid-cycle. She shied from looking at his temple, and took her tongue to where she would not have to see his face.

Wild flames they were her lips and hands, but her heart was dark to him. It hovered and seemed not to land. Very occasionally Alex stared down at her neck and the chevron of black hair – and mourned that she did not return his love. Instead, it was her brother's disappearance that ran through her veins like a thick red sauce, and everything always, in the end, came back to it. On these occasions, he was crushed by the idea when he wrapped her in his arms that he was holding nothing more than the locked Glory Box of someone who inwardly fell away to the core of the earth.

Most of the time, though, he believed that they were

destined to be together. They transformed loss into trust, disbelief into gratitude. They loved one another.

CHILD CARE CENTRE. Advanced photographer will be taking family portraits at Centre on Friday evening for just $10!

Christmas approached. They attended the Cranbrook Fair, a sunny day in a bowl of hills. She watched Alex and Flash in the sheepdog trials and afterwards paid two dollars for a long-bearded man on a turquoise hot rod to give a ride to her godson. "That's from Santa," she told Zac. Afterwards, she bought the boy an Abel Tasman pancake from the side of a van. And bumping into the Welsh sisters, in a tent selling lemon marmalade, accepted their invitation to a girls' night out.

In her garden, cultivating life in terracotta pots, she brushed the back of her hands against the fine hairs of the growing leaves. When a little frog hopped out from underneath a saucer, she helped it off its back. One afternoon, a lamb in the field behind the windmill was stung by a tiger-snake and died within minutes. She watched the snake trickle off through the grass with the gleam of hot tar. Between the bite and the bleat, she thought, I take my pulse, and felt again the heavy vacancy inside her.

Next time she saw a baby copperhead undulating across the drive she took a stone and crashed it down. The snake writhed up bleeding, half its body pinned useless to the gravel in a silvery-red smear. She walked back to the house in erratic steps. Hostile and frightened and also jubilant.

*

FOR SALE: Toyota diesel 1984. 8 months rego. Cheap reliable car. Lots of history, very clean. Red. $800 Phone: 63456776.

Then there were little things she looked forward to. The long afternoons gazing out to sea. Listening to the radio in the kitchen. The ritual of reading the *Mercury*, especially the crime column and its list of thefts that told her that something was happening in the world. ("Oh, Alex," she would say, her voice rising to a tremolo, "just look at this. Someone's stolen a wheelbarrow in Orford!" He would always chuckle.) The dinner with Rhiannon and Myfanwy, at which Rhiannon served mussels. ("Everything's so phallic," Myfanwy said, squeezing a shell. "It's important to eat girlie food, too.")

There were other dinners, too. With their neighbours, the Macdonalds, from Queensland, who had bought Bill Molson's property and kept a motorboat in Coles Bay on which, twice a year, the two families sped over to Schouten to picnic on a sheltered beach of smooth pebbles. With a pale, shy potter and his wife who lived across the river in Swanwick. With the rather trying Harry Ford, the friend of Alex's parents, in his bungalow opposite the school. Every so often, Keith Framley treated her and Alex to a large dinner at the RSL. Sometimes Tildy joined them – always when Ray could not.

How it evolved, neither party examined too closely, but it became an unspoken agreement whereby it never entered Tildy's mind to invite the Doves to a meal that might involve Ray; nor did Merridy ever ask Ray to Moulting Lagoon Farm. She sometimes caught sight of him over the grey heads, like blown dandelions, on ANZAC day; or pushing a pram into the golf club; or in line at the chicken counter in Talbot's. But they never spoke. They nodded hello, but they did not speak.

This did not stop Merridy from looking, though. Ray's office was opposite Talbot's and she would guiltily catch herself gazing after him if ever he came into the street, and know that she was lingering too long and try to convince herself that it was an accident. As the years went by he filled out, but even his little paunch suited him. The appeal of a big-boned man.

Once – to her considerable shame – Alex caught her standing red-faced outside the store. Her eyes on a figure down by the jetty who winched a new-looking boat onto a trailer. She had thought that Alex was putting the groceries away in the ute round the back, but he was watching her watching Ray.

"Ray-spotting again?"

She turned round horrified, but he was smiling. He winked at her. "Can't keep your eye off him, can you?"

An uncertain look crept into his face when Alex registered her dismay. It perplexed him. He knew that it was innocent.

Ray accelerated up the ramp as they loaded the last of the shopping bags. Alex braced himself, but the real-estate agent was in no mood to stop. Alex's first impression was of a gold chain around a thick tanned neck. That was before he saw Ray's face. He had a black eye and a cut under his jaw criss-crossed with stitches.

"Did you see that?" after Ray sped off.

"I did."

"I'm surprised someone hasn't clubbed him to death before now."

No one was able to tell Alex who had done it.

Ray Grogan apart, Merridy's life at this period of her marriage was more social than later it became, and certainly more social than she had been accustomed to in Ulverstone or Melbourne. There was an element in town that would never accept her as a resident but part of the geriatric flash-tide who came to Wellington Point, took advantage of the facilities and left; but there was another group, much smaller, who invited her to things: to raise funds for the day care or to meet over a capuccino at the Bethel.

Her ability to get around improved enormously after Alex bought her a second-hand Toyota — until then she had had to rely on his ute. For a time, she helped out Agnes twice a week at the Op-Shop, even if she said no to joining her reading group. She assisted in the Summer Flow Show and in Meals on Wheels when Abbygail fell ill. And though neither she nor Alex went regularly to church, they did religiously attend the ANZAC service at the Uniting Church and afterwards stood on the footpath outside Talbot's to watch the procession of old men in ribboned medals shuffling past like a squad of prisoners.

So the days levelled out. Summer yellowed into autumn and the noise of the wind through the tree on the lawn kept her awake. Sleepless, she conceived further plans for the house, for the garden, for her potager by the sea.

CHAPTER FIVE

RAY GROGAN is proud to announce that he is expanding his services from sales, rentals and property management to professional loans. "Let me help you become a stakeholder in your community!"

One Monday morning a truck arrived from Wellington Point and unloaded oyster shells onto the drive. Merridy had taken the idea from Mrs Macdonald. The shells were soon crunched into fragments, several barrows of which Merridy scattered on the graves of Alex's parents under the Oyster Bay pine, where children played on them, trampling the brittle surface in delighted whoops.

And still the only children to chase each other through the bright painted corridors were the ones who came to visit. The junior class from the primary school – she had let the teacher know that pupils would always be welcome to ride the ponies. The two small Macdonald boys, Don and Mike. And Tildy's children, of course.

"What do ducks eat?" said Zac, the elder, who had been discovered by Tildy at the age of eighteen months with a large spider sticking out of his mouth. The only effect of swallowing the huntsman, so far as Tildy could tell, had been to make Zac fart. Dr Musgrove had said: "Better not make a habit of it."

"Grass, water-beetles," Merridy suggested, although really she had no idea. She was Zac's godmother, but she could never look at his mouth without seeing hairy legs protruding. "Ask Alex, why don't you?"

Alex had an affinity with Zac. He would take the boy on his tractor or into the shearing shed. Zac's greatest pleasure was to race through the stalls, and then stand and shriek at his gargoyle's reflection in the central pillar, a thick beam of Oyster Bay pine that the backs of wriggling sheep had oiled to a dark shine. Leaving Tildy a few moments' peace to push her pram on the lawn.

Once upon hearing Zac's hysterical shrieks, Tildy told her with the tactlessness of an adoring mother: "When something's really bad, you hear silence."

"You're so lucky, Tildy. They're beautiful."

Her tone made Tildy look up sharply. "Well, the more time you spend with them, the more time you want to spend with them. You just want to gobble them up."

"Like peanuts!"

"Exactly!"

Inside the pram the new baby gurgled, woken by her brother's screams. Tildy poked a hand under the hood and adjusted something. "Though where this one's button chin comes from, I don't know." This one was called Montana. She continued to make her noise, like a sleepwalker on the verge of speaking, and then stopped. "It's only in the last two days she's begun sucking her thumb. It's as if she's discovered God."

On another visit, Tildy noticed the sagging fence and said: "Oh, I forgot. Ray told me to tell you that one of his farmers has thirty rolls of chicken wire he doesn't need."

"Alex will be thrilled." Or, would he? She no longer knew with Alex, she had stopped trying to gauge his thoughts from his expression. It pained her to notice how the two of them had settled into a kind of acceptance over the past months. Their words careful and deflective.

Kind without being intimate. In the unchanged air of their marriage.

"Then I'll let Ray know, shall I?"

"That would be kind." Merridy looked at her cousin. "How is Ray?"

His photograph appeared every week in the *Mercury's* property supplement. A beaming mouth and, below it, his telephone number and the words: *Phone now to be spoiled.* He had bought out Tamlyn & Peppiatt the year before and operated under his own name. He specialised in loans over $150,000, under the questionable motto: *Ray's solutions. Why not settle for more?*

"Oh, you know Ray. Busy as a bee. He's even thinking of standing for the council," but Merridy saw in Tildy the beginning of a disenchantment.

"Come on. What's the matter?" They had trusted each other when they lived in Ulverstone. She was able to tell Tildy not to be such a slut, and Tildy could tick her off for acting like a cock-teasing Vestal Virgin.

Tildy had never spoken ill of Ray, had always been protective of him. But once she started, the floodgates opened. She seemed to relish recounting the worst of their marriage. He was always on his boat when she needed him – "He says he bought it to escape the children's screams, for God's sake. And what am I supposed to do?" When he did come home, he was demanding and took her for granted. "Sometimes I have the feeling he'd like me to peel his grapes for him – and if I don't, he'll trade me in for a spanking new condo."

"Oh, he wouldn't do that," Merridy said. "Not Ray."

"Don't be so sure. He just might. When he's in one of his moods." As he seemed to be in right now.

"What kind of mood?"

"It's like he's had a quarrel with himself and neither

side has spoken for a while. He's only truly happy when he's out in the middle of the bay with a rod in his hand."

"It will sort itself out."

"Hah!" said Tildy bitterly. "And Alex?" she added in her new stirred-up mood. It had not escaped her notice. Something unhatched in Merridy's eyes.

"He's good," said Merridy. She took off her wide-brimmed floppy sun hat and wiped her forehead. And looked down into the pram. "Hey, is there a fragrance?"

Zac rubbed his red eyes. "She's done a poo."

"It's all right, I'll go," said Merridy, relieved to have an excuse. She put her sun hat back on and went to fetch a Huggie from the supply that she kept handy in the spare bedroom. At the back of the nappy cupboard was a basket of toys and puzzles from the Op-Shop and a second-hand travel cot in case anyone stayed over. Tildy often dropped her kids off to play. Merridy dug out a Huggie and a Winnie-the-Pooh as an afterthought, and came back outside.

Tildy was content to watch Merridy change Montana's nappy. "Spoon it in one end, mop it up the other. Zac was two before he laid his first firm turds. Weren't you, darling?"

Then Zac came up and grabbed the bear and started pinching his sister's leg.

"If you don't stop doing that," said Tildy seriously, "I'm going to kill you. Slowly. No one will know it's me."

He pinched again.

"Stop it, Zac, you're just tired."

"I'm not tired," he shouted, pressing his knuckles to his tired eyes. Looking in that moment like his father, save that he did not have a moustache or a bangle around his wrist, for by now it was an open secret, how Ray flashed with a new item of gold jewellery every time he sold a sizeable property.

"Well, I am," snapped Tildy. She minded that Zac would not let her hug him. That he answered back. That he used sleep as a weapon in the jealous battle which he raged against his sister. And explained through clenched jaws: "If Ray gets up to give him milk, he won't drink it. So I get up three times every night to give him milk. I've never been so knackered, Merridy. Frankly, it's a stake through the foot." Staring into the pram where the one with Merridy's nappy on had resumed her screaming. "Two stakes, in point of fact."

And suddenly Tildy felt all elephantine and red-faced from the sun, her naturally auburn hair too much in a mess to be tamed by her chemist's comb. "I'm not a stressed person, I don't easily wobble, you know that. But I'll tell you this, Merridy Dove – and it's something you'll discover soon enough – children are crap."

"You don't mean that," Merridy said.

"The crappiest version of yourself. The self you thought you'd left behind but keep on meeting." Tildy stopped herself. "You know, I'd never go on like this with anyone else who didn't have kids. But you're different. You're the only person with no children I could bore like this."

"Oh, I don't mind." And she really didn't. She took an interest in children because she still did expect that she was going to have them. She could afford to be generous with her ear.

In her motherly way, Merridy went to fetch some warm milk for Montana.

"It's her birthday soon, isn't it?" coming back.

"That's right. The twenty-third."

"I'll get her something from Pumpkin Patch."

"You can't keep away from that shop!"

Merridy loved the store in Hobart with its simple

fresh colours. She was always buying Tildy's children new outfits. She said: "It even has a maternity section now."

"Nothing I could squeeze into. I always get so huge."

Moments later there was a sudden quiet, as if a mosquito was feeding.

Tildy broke it. "You know Rose-Maree's pregnant?"

And Merridy felt her smile droop. Slacker than the fence and the brim of her shapeless sun hat. "But I thought she never wanted children."

"I don't think she felt comfortable talking to you about it. Oh, God, sorry," noticing Merridy's face. "What an insensitive cow I am."

A girl who worked sometimes at the Op-Shop had told Merridy a few months back of her two abortions. At the time, Merridy did not judge her. Now she found herself hating her. It was one reason why she stopped working for Agnes. She began to nurse a resentment against Indians and Chinese, all those who seemed to multiply like rabbits or took it for granted.

She hated, as well, others' discomfort over her affliction.

"What, you don't have children – oh, I'm sorry," and the person would get embarrassed and she would have to counsel them, as if she were missing an arm or a leg.

"I'm not childless," she taught herself to say. "I'm child-free."

But six months on she passed Rose-Maree's pram unattended outside Talbot's and had the strongest urge to snatch the baby.

*

This freedom was infrequently discussed with Alex. Maybe it was his English blood to overlook what had not happened. At any rate, he seemed to take it much less to heart than she did. He treated her concerns in the manner of his sheepdog, as things to be herded and corralled. While Merridy fretted, Alex buried himself deeper into his patch of east coast soil, his hopes hinged on rain and an upturn in the wool price. Somehow they never got round to talking about adoption.

But Tildy talked. It irritated Alex, who once glumly observed, "Why does she have to keep two mouths open all the time?"

Now that she had started to discuss Ray, Tildy seemed unable to stop. Each visit or telephone call updated Merridy on Ray's latest mood, their last fight.

"What is it about us that we want nothing so much as to be married, then, no sooner is the ring on our finger than it pops out through our nose? We've been fucked over, Merridy. I never yelled before I had kids. Now listen to me. I've become a screamer." And lifted her head in the direction of the Oyster Bay pine where, in the elliptical shade beneath, two shapes stamped with glee on the oyster shells.

"Zac! Montana!" she brayed. "Here, *now*!"

The children slouched across the lawn towards them. Yes, Montana was her daughter, but sometimes Tildy felt no greater attachment to the girl than if she spouted through a blowhole. As for Zac, he could ignite in her an anger such as she had never imagined a human being capable of. "Ray says it's like having a couple of blue-fin permanently on the line. Right until the last day of your life. If you ask me, they're more aggressive than tuna. They're like tumours. Or mutating viruses," and watched Zac, all thread and chicken bone, try to push the crushed oyster shells down Montana's knickers. But the virus, plainly, was catching. With a fondling look: "He only does that to girls he likes."

In the next breath, Tildy was fierce in wanting Merridy to be a mother. Then she forgot about how her children diminished her, eager for the day when Merridy likewise would be clutched at by a monster with four outstretched arms and two yelling faces tarred with Vegemite. Or six arms and three faces, since, lo and behold, Tildy was pregnant again.

"Why don't you get more tests? What's the problem, Merridy? Why are you so passive? You were never passive before."

"Tildy, we're trying," in a thick voice.

"Well, you'd better go about it in a different way. You could have IVF. I've read about this forty-four-year-old woman in Perth—"

"Listen, this is what we've been dealt. I have a marriage in which I'm happy; you have two lovely children."

"You're not unhappy, then?"

"I'm not unhappy, no, I can honestly say that."

"So it's worked out?"

"Yes," she laughed sadly. "It has worked out."

But for Tildy, who conceived so easily, it was not understandable. "You could always do it on your own, you know. You don't need a man."

"You speak as though it is Alex's fault. It's neither of our faults."

"That is the biggest lorry-load of horse manure I ever heard, girl. You could spread it on your veggie garden for a year."

"Oh, Tildy," and wondered if in fact she did not prefer her cousin in the days when she was single.

*

207

Merridy knew that she had not covered all the ground. There were better doctors out there, someone who could tell her what to do, what was wrong. We are in the hinterland here, she thought, with not exactly the latest technology, assigned to a form of ignorance.

She booked another test, in Sydney this time, where Alex, through a medical friend of his godmother, now retired to the Blue Mountains, arranged for Merridy to meet a foetal–maternal specialist in King's Cross. But neither could the doctors on the mainland find anything untoward. Two laparoscopies had revealed her tubes all in place, no past infection, no scarring.

"Sometimes there is no explanation," relaying to Alex what the specialist had said. And yet it upset her to think that there was no obvious physiological reason. A certain sperm and egg had got together and biology had declared this combination was not to be. What did that say for the relationship? Perhaps it was nature's way of saying: Not a good pairing. Perhaps as she had recently read somewhere, their DNA was too alike.

"The doctor did suggest IVF," she said carefully.

Alex gave a groan.

She looked sharply up. "Why not, you do it for cows?"

"You're not a cow."

But the initials had been planted.

In the days ahead, Merridy found out all that she could about IVF. Through Dr Musgrove, she made an appointment with the director of the unit at the Royal Hobart and took Alex to meet him and they both underwent tests. The only sticking point was the fee. She would have to pay, but some of the cost could be reclaimed on Medicare.

Alex asked for a fortnight's grace to raise the amount. She felt guilty. "Listen, Alex, maybe we can't afford it."

"Don't worry. I can take it out of the farm account."

"There is my father's legacy."

"Absolutely not."

It was another three weeks before he was able to send off the cheque. Within a few days she began her injections. They were self-administered – two in the morning, one at night, and no alcohol, coffee or tea. It all seemed to need precise timing, and Alex had to swallow vitamin pills.

A month later they drove down to St John's in Cascade Road for the egg collection. The anaesthetist led Merridy into the operating theatre. She lay back in the stirrup chair in the most humiliating position she could remember and had her eggs removed – which was excruciatingly painful. As the needle passed through the vaginal walls and into the ovaries, Alex was despatched to provide sperm. Less of a novelty this time. A nurse supplied him with a paper bag and a plastic jar with a label on it that had his wife's name and date of birth. She asked Alex to check to see if the details were correct and showed him where the staff toilet was. He thought, looking around: How am I going to do this? But there were magazines jammed in with the cleaning fluids underneath the sink. Ten minutes later, he popped the sample into the paper bag and wandered along the corridor until he found the nurse.

The pain from the needle was forgotten next morning when the embryologist telephoned to say that of the fifteen eggs collected eight had fertilised. He kept in touch over the next three days, ringing morning and night until the afternoon of the embryo transfer. Alex was allowed with her into the operating theatre. The embryologist brought in a dish containing two embryos and projected them onto a screen. At the sight of the cells splitting and dividing, Merridy looked at Alex and looked away. Then the embryos were put in a large test tube and given to the doctor who injected them into the wall of her womb.

"Take it easy for the next few days," the doctor said afterwards.

"Is that it?" asked Alex.

"Pretty much, that's it. We'll know within a fortnight."

Another two weeks. More injections. Suppositories. Blood-thinners twice a day and a powerful intramuscular in the evening. Another drive to Hobart. Another blood test. And two mornings later, Alex feeding the dog when he heard Merridy dragging her bare feet into the kitchen. Her hands fretted at the table and her eyes had begun to swell.

"I've started my period."

Alex crushed her, sobbing and drivelling, to his chest. "Oh, my darling."

So they tried again. Alex scraped the money together and off they went to Hobart.

Afterwards, she would liken the experience to a roller coaster that she had been on with her father and brother when the Royal Show came to Launceston. She could not get off.

The same result.

"It doesn't matter," through her phlegm and tears, "I never was much good with children. I don't think I ever understood them. Not really." Maybe it was another thing that was not meant to be resolved.

"We'll try again. Of course, we'll try again. You'll think differently in a month."

But after the third occasion Alex could see that she was distressed and something in her eye incinerated. When the nurse telephoned to confirm, very gently, what they already knew – "Sorry, you haven't been lucky this time. It's a negative result" – Merridy could not face going through it all a fourth time. It was too disappointing. They stopped.

CHAPTER SIX

THE MANIFESTATION OF THEIR barrenness dawned more slowly on Alex. It had taken until now for him to understand how deep ran his desire to put something into the future. Imperceptibly but steadily, the thought had developed that he could replace his parents with a son or a daughter. Now, as his father would have put it, he looked forward to neither chick nor child.

Once he had absorbed it, the prospect of not having children attacked him at unexpected moments with the violence of a kidney blow.

He tried to keep it from her, but she noticed. How he hummed to himself as though nothing was amiss. How he walked fast past the spare bedroom. He was a long corridor of doors shut and locked.

And while he bowed to her moods and was tolerant and protective towards her, she was irked by his refusal to communicate. The deeper he burrowed into himself, the more snappish she became.

"Wouldn't you prefer someone else?" she said in one sour moment in the wake of a trivial argument.

"Absolutely not," he spluttered.

"I warned you I wouldn't make you happy."

"But you do!" exasperated.

"You could go off. I'd understand. You must feel free."

"What are you talking about, Merridy?"

"You wanted a child. Lots of children. Mobs of them, as I remember."

"Only because you did."

But she noticed that he had not touched his ships for months.

Instead, it was she who went off.

One cloudless Thursday morning, while Alex was repairing a fence at the bottom of Barn Hill, she slipped out of the house wearing a yellow oilskin, walking down the drive, not once looking back until she reached the bus shelter in Wellington Point.

On the bus to Hobart she listened to a garrulous blonde talk of her bad experience with a guru, a French-Peruvian who called himself Pachamama.

"I met him at a night-class in Battery Point. He'd read a few New Age books and saw this as a way of seducing women, so he started a class in which he told us: 'Your first choice is yourself.' Certain women need to hear that. It gives them permission to be totally selfish. Me, I'm no exception. That's why he was so attractive. 'You should only do things you really want to do. In your heart.' But it's just a bunch of shit. Like his claim he could get it up four times a night. He dressed all in white because white was more – spiritually speaking – enlightening, and never wore sunglasses so that people could always see into the window of his soul. And white tennis shorts, winter through summer. I used to see him sunning his gut – ill-fitting dentures and long greasy hair in a tail. Immigration wouldn't let him in because he's such an old goat. If you bump into him and he asks to live with you, don't. He's only after a permanent visa."

The girl was an ex-hippy from Byron Bay with dead eyes and scars on her wrists.

Merridy had not told Alex, but she had gone to Hobart for a last meeting with a last consultant. In the private

213

clinic in West Hobart, the doctor went straight to the point: "I don't think it's going to work other than by sheer accident. Look, there's not a thing wrong with either of you, but many people have come here and said: 'You're the last port of call; we have a completely clean bill of health, what can we do?' and I say what I'm going to say to you: 'Nothing. It's in God's hands. It's in the lap of the gods.'"

It was a very rum fate being in the lap of the gods. But later that morning, Merridy walked through St David's Park to Salamanca Place. And found herself hunting for a ponytail dressed in white.

The brilliant day drew her down to the sea. She thought: I'll find somewhere to sit for an hour to watch the bay and then I shall buy myself a dress and go home.

The water rocking against the wharves infected her. She picked her way along the dockside, taking in the fishing trawlers and yachts, until she stood outside a chandler's shop. Through the window, a boyish-looking man looked up, and she thought for a fleeting second that it was Alex as she had first seen him, coming out of the school yard with his plastic bag of ice-cream sticks, and her heart began to drum and she felt a surge of anxiety and excitement.

She walked in. Smell of pitch and glints of brass and in a back yard a boat being built.

He was locking up. He had his back to her and was sorting through keys.

"Hi," in her emancipating laugh.

"Good day. How are you doing? How can I be of service?"

"I'm thinking of the sea."

"The sea? What is it exactly you're looking for?"

"I don't know. I was just drawn to the sea."

He looked around, a stranger in a chandler's shop, smiling. "Let's see what we can see."

The young man was due to go out on a trial run, testing an outboard. "I'll show you how it works."

She remembered stepping into the sleek black-hulled boat, putting on the life jacket that he held up, the splutter and take of the engine.

He steered the boat into the Derwent and out of the mouth of the river and into Storm Bay. It had become a blazing hot day. They were halfway to Bruny when he cut the engine. A swell came up and she did not feel terribly good. She stood to take off her life jacket and then her oilskin.

"Are you sure you're all right?"

"Nothing a swim won't cure."

Stripped to her bra and underpants, she went overboard and swam around the boat as he watched. For the first time in her married life she was away from something, anything, that she recognised as her world. She was out in someone else's world.

He helped her back in and the swell toppled them against one another.

She remembered the beat of her pulse and the sweat that oiled his hair and a sense she had that he may have been here before.

They undressed, she in a daze. He had a mole on his foreskin and a small hairless oasis on his scalp. To which she pressed her cheek as he rammed into her.

Afterwards, she said: "We will never see each other again, will we?"

When she came home she found a letter for her tucked under the bottle with the *Otago* in it. In Alex's educated, neat, upright hand. *Without you I am so unhappy, I am.* It was the first letter that he had written to Merridy and she had wondered if he had forgotten how to write, his words saved for sheep and cattle and creatures.

RAY'S SOLUTIONS. *Why not settle for more? Phone now to be spoiled. Everything I touch turns to SOLD.*

They settled back. Each day another drop of wet sand accumulating beneath her cupped hands into a rising tower from which she gazed out with tightening desperation.

Marriage had been a false passport to tranquillity. She was quite miserable. As was Alex. Neither of them had ever believed that they would find a companion in the storm; when they did find each other, they supposed that a child would be a way out of it, and into a region refreshed by what they had suffered. Instead, it was her father's books that seemed so childish, the little group of six or seven verses which aroused her. In this way, she punished herself.

Silence invaded the house. She was the rustle of the paper, looking for crimes. A tightrope-walker in Zeehan had missed the net. An article on Southend Pier, the longest in the world, reprinted from an English newspaper: *The hunger for piers is strictly nostalgic.* An advertisement that featured a bland-looking man in a suit, staring out: "*Is your memory a sieve?*"

She did her best to forget about the chandler and their moment of frenzy on the bottom of his fast black boat.

While on its shelf on the kitchen dresser, the *Otago* sailed on. A consoling empty bottle with its ship and its obsolete coin. Through the curved glass of which she saw a murderer swimming in the sea look up at her.

Meanwhile, Alex was out on the farm somewhere. That

was his achievement. He was off on his own; unwinding strands of wool from the fence, left there by rubbed necks; or painting slats of red cedar with Madison oil, or at a clearance sale, bargain-hunting for old farm machinery. Or counting sheep in Cumbrian: yan tan tethera methera funf aerter slaerter lowra dowra dick yandick tandick . . .

Like this, he subdued himself further into his land. He had his fields to sow that made it easier to accept his uselessness. He had his barley and his herd of cows. The grazing grass that brushed his legs into hives. The green-painted windmill that had taken on the shape of a mystery whose meaning stayed withheld. But now and again in the shape of a lost animal he caught a glimpse of the mob of children that he had not had, and it slayed him.

About Merridy, he felt a spent resignation. Where had she gone, the forthright girl? He thought of Samuel Johnson on marriage, meaningless to him until now: "The dislike hourly increased by causes too slender for complaint and too numerous for removal." Small acts of will kept him on her side and his love alive. But they were in a new stretch of life and the stubble began to show in their relationship. Their eyes tangled and looked away. Their lips rusted together. Before, they had conversations; now they had arguments. "Dumb stuff, as it usually is," she confided to Tildy. Some comment made the wrong way that boiled up. Some cold exchange, its words worn so thin with repetition as to be transparent.

"Don't put that there," she fluctuated, angry, concerned: under it all, bored. Her husband was a good man. She knew well enough his gentle innocence, but his vision was unpolluted by their sterility; what it was doing to her. She felt her boredom dragging at the corner of her mouth. At the sight of an unwashed plate, she wanted to scream.

Alex, for his part, responded by not touching her, perhaps

because he had touched her too much; he scratched his nose and looked at the saucepan heating their minestrone and moved his mug of tea off the neat, clean tablecloth and onto the bare blackwood. And thought of the letters that he kept receiving from the ANZ in Hobart, to advise him that interest rates had risen to 18 per cent, 19 per cent, 20 per cent . . .

Now at night beneath the quilt their bodies lay apart. To Merridy, the hand and mouth that had touched her with such intimacy were nothing but a hard limb and an empty hole smelling of what she had fed him. She piled all her blame on the wardrobe that had filled her with a desire she had never sought and could not satisfy. She had sensations of vertigo, when she wanted nothing so much as to curl up inside and seal the door. But there was also a vital part of her that wanted to remain faithful to the promise which she and Alex had made on their wedding night.

In the meantime, the future lay open and darker than the inside of any Jacobean wardrobe. A future to which neither held the key.

CHAPTER SEVEN

TALBOT'S STORE will be closed on Christmas and Boxing Day. The owner and staff wish all our customers a safe and happy Christmas and New Year. And remember – give the Emergency Services Workers a Christmas present. "Go easy on the Grog" and "Take care with Fires". Cheers everybody. A.T.

The talk that summer was of the drought. It was a time of red poppies and grasshoppers that hiccuped through the barley stalks. In the blaze of sun and salt, conversations flapped and fell, and lips became drier for the heat or worry. A mile up the road a sixteen-year-old girl had twins eight weeks prematurely in a shack that no one had known was there. That summer, it was so hot that it seemed to Merridy everyone was giving birth. Save for the Welsh sisters, who announced what many in the community had all along suspected: they were not sisters.

On an oyster shell in the shade of the pine, the cat paralysed a dragon lizard. Merridy found the lizard going black. She held the shrivelled creature by the tail and was looking around for a place to put it when a hoot sounded from the bottom of the drive and the next moment Tildy's white Honda sped into view.

Merridy had been married six years on the morning in late December when Tildy appeared with Zac, Montana and Savannah for the Doves to babysit during the New Year long weekend. At the very last moment a grateful client of Ray's had presented him with a three-night package at the Freycinet Lodge in Coles Bay. Tildy was looking forward to her first weekend alone with her husband since Zac's birth. All she had to do was find a babysitter.

In the early days, when she assumed that it would happen, Merridy had felt kindly to others and did not mind if Tildy took advantage. Now she experienced a flicker of resentment before agreeing to give up her New Year to childmind her godson and his two sisters.

"We've never had all three to stay at once."

"It's the same as looking after one. And they do adore you."

Merridy came out from the shade of the tree as Zac and Montana spilled from the car and ran to torment the horses. She helped Tildy, who held a sleeping Savannah, to carry the bags into the house.

In the kitchen, it was a lot cooler. Merridy had made little iced muffins, laid out on the table on a plastic sheet, and prepared a jug of lemonade. "You've chosen the hottest day of the year," pouring out five plastic cups. "Any plans?"

"I can't speak for Ray, but I don't intend to leave our room. We're going to go at it," Tildy promised, "like you and Alex. At least, I presume you still . . ." And scrutinised her friend.

"Hey, look at my tail," laughed Merridy, and turned. As much to conceal her face.

Meanwhile, Tildy had spied a wickedness taking place through the window. "Zac!" putting down her cup. "Don't DO that to Montana!" And streaked from the kitchen.

Moments later, she shepherded her children in. Montana wore a top that Merridy had bought her from

Pumpkin Patch, now stained brown with banana. She was sobbing: "He said he was going to kill my belly button."

"Zac, wish Merridy a Happy New Year."

"Happy New Year," said Zac sepulchrally.

"Now, I want you all to behave with Merridy," Tildy said, plonking Savannah on the table beside three baskets stuffed with clothes and squidgy toys. "I want no repeat of Christmas."

"Why, what happened at Christmas?"

Tildy rolled her eyeballs. "I decided this year we wouldn't go to church, I'd take them to Louisa Meredith House." Succumbing in a foolish moment to a charitable instinct, Tildy had introduced her children into the nursing home, Zac encased in a scarlet Spider-Man outfit with prominent pectorals, Montana in a fluffy bear suit and Savannah dressed as a fairy. But instead of cheering up the inmates, her son and daughters proceeded to terrorise them. They had punched the emergency button in Doris Prosser's bathroom, switched off the live carol service from King's College, Cambridge, that had mesmerised Sadie Wentworth into a contented rhapsody, and stolen Mr Carr's burgundy fez. No one had seen the hat since.

Tildy inspected the baskets with unseeing eyes. "I reckon you have everything you need. Seeyah all Monday."

Over that weekend, Merridy reached a deeper understanding of why people who had children so often looked distraught; much the same as people desperate to have them.

Barely had Tildy's car disappeared from the drive than Zac vomited. The vomit splashed up from the kitchen floor and a speck of it landed in her mouth.

Montana's nose meanwhile was stubbornly charred with dried snot, infecting Alex with a touch of gastro and a streaming cold that he would not shake off until March.

As for Savannah, she had to be restrained from rushing up to her siblings and plucking at handfuls of hair and then sinking her teeth into their backsides.

"They get on very well," Tildy had said. "They're inseparable, in fact. It's me they have the problem with. Zac *still* won't let me hug him."

Away from their mother, the children did not get on. At lunch Zac pulled away Montana's cup of lemonade. She reacted by tipping it over his head.

"All girls are princesses," Merridy reminded Zac, towelling his carrot-coloured hair. "Boys have to understand that."

"She's not a princess," glowered Zac. "She's a big, fat, hairy triceratops, and I'm going to kill her belly button," and lunging from Merridy's grasp, he slapped Montana on the stomach, hard, with the bread knife.

"Please be nicer to your sister," Merridy implored. The most hopeful words in the English language.

As Montana howled, Zac began tugging at Merridy, speaking with sudden seriousness in a grown-up voice. "Merridy, I think Savannah has a pooey bum."

Savannah had not stopped smelling since her mother deposited her on the kitchen table. But Tildy in her haste to join Ray at Freycinet Lodge had forgotten to leave nappies. By four in the afternoon, Merridy discovered that she had run out of her reserve supply, and so, to distract the children with an expedition, she loaded them into her car, a challenge in itself, and drove to Talbot's where Rose-Maree reacted with a look of feral curiosity to be asked about nappies.

"Row four – where cereals used to be."

Talbot's had sold out of Huggies for girls. The boy's Huggies that Merridy bought would keep slipping down over the weekend.

Merridy had left the three children sitting peacefully in the car, but two of them had managed to undo their seat belts. She found Montana at the wheel and Zac with a gleeful expression switching on and off the head-lights and the windscreen wipers going full tilt. With a terrific struggle, she strapped both children back in their seats.

For the rest of the weekend, she supervised the children in the garden, trying to encourage them to paint and fielding questions.

"What's this?" asked Zac.

"A dragon lizard."

"It's not moving."

"No," she agreed. "Bring it over to paint, if you like."

"No thanks," said Zac, who looked as if he might prefer to eat it. He tossed the shrivelled thing behind one of the gravestones. "What about that?"

She gazed at the thin stalk in the earth. "A geranium," she said. And to herself: Still hanging on. Foolishly.

"Looks dead," exultant.

And at breakfast, squinting at the contents of the glass dish: "What's that?"

"Lemon marmalade. Here, have some."

"It's got weeds in it. I don't like weeds."

And at lunch: "I don't like sea-horse tails."

"That's pasta."

"No, it's not. It's sea-horse tails."

"What would you prefer?"

"I'd like Coco Pops."

"But you had them for breakfast."

"No, I didn't."

She glared back at him. Shocked at the distance between this face and the face that she had stroked moments after his birth in the Royal Hobart. You uttered bird-like squawks and when I smelled your breath it was as if it had come up through a dank rock. You opened an eye and it was by far the most ancient thing I'd ever seen. You . . .

But Zac did not appreciate being looked at. It was then that he landed his punch. She was removing his plate when he asked: "Where are your children?"

"I don't have any."

"Why not?"

"Because I don't want them." And sensing herself ill-equipped to be in the presence of a child to whom she had not spoken the truth, she stood up and carried her godson's plate to the sink. But when she turned around Zac's mouth hung open and the hairy legs of his words flailed out of it.

"Does Alex have one?"

"No, he has . . . he has . . ." But what did he have, her husband? Zac's question made her frightened. She had a powerful image of Alex going off with someone as she had gone off with the chandler. She saw her fate with absolute clarity of vision, as described with such relish each week in Tildy's magazines. He would trade her in for a younger model and she would join the great confederacy of unused women.

Her eye stabilised on the Welsh dresser. "He has his ships."

But Zac, staring down into his mug of rainwater, had spotted something floating.

"What's that?" for the first time wanting to know.

She took the mug from him. "A wasp, it looks like."

"I don't like wasps." He pushed back his hair and she caught sight of an ugly scab.

In a new voice full of concern she asked: "Zac, how did you get that?"

At night, she calmed them with stories. She did her best to interest Zac in Edward Lear, but he was not having it. Tildy had packed his favourite book. He wanted to be read that.

"Where did your mother find this?"

"The Op-Shop." Like many of Tildy's things.

"Then before I begin, I'm going to ask again. How did you get that scratch?"

"Mummy bit me," looking uncomfortable.

"What do you mean, she bit you?"

"She did. She bit me."

"I don't believe you, Zac."

"It's true," Tildy confirmed later with not a smidgen of shame. "His ear was next to my face. I was so annoyed, I bit it."

Her sleeve was being tugged at. "Get on."

He was asleep before she reached the end. She looked at the smile on the pillow and saw that he did not have his father's mouth but Tildy's and was glad. She read on anyway, reluctant to leave a story unfinished. Even one so derivative.

"*The rider of an old horse who had galloped through the darkness slowed to a canter and then to a trot and reined in above the bay. The man looked down and took brief note of the unusual colours, then spurred his horse and rode off across the sea.*"

On New Year's Eve, Merridy was woken by Zac screaming. The boy stared at her through a veil of sleep and horror and threw an arm across his eyes, moaning. She coaxed him back to sleep in the bed that she had bought in the first months of her marriage, a different child in mind, and thought of Ray and Tildy, in all probability making their fourth baby, and for the first time admitted to herself: Who in their right mind would want *this*? What if it's better the way it is?

Soon it was safe to close the door. On couches in the living room, Tildy's two younger children snored through blocked noses. She opened the window and breathed in. The clear air affronted by the smell of Savannah's nappy.

She crawled back to bed and hugged her husband. The children would be leaving the next day.

"What's wrong?" he sniffled, half-succumbed to Savannah's cold.

"It's all right."

"What's all right?"

"We have each other."

But if she thought it was over, it was not. At breakfast, Tildy telephoned to say that Ray had developed kidney stones. "We have to take him to Hobart. Isn't it typical? They say this is something that comes the moment you start to relax." The ambulance was on its way. He would have to be operated on immediately.

Tildy went on: "Listen, I've used up all my red chips with Ray's mother. The truth is, Merridy, no one will take my children. Could you look after them? Please? It'll only be for a few days. And they do adore you."

CHAPTER EIGHT

WELLINGTON POINT SUMMER FLOWER SHOW:
Vegetable and fruit: onions over 8oz – H. Ford.
Flower arranging (themed arrangement) – Garden of Eden.
Joint First: Rose-Maree Kemp, Merridy Dove.

Thereafter, the subject of their childlessness was added to the list of no-go areas that included Ray Grogan, Merridy's university course, the Doves' car crash, Alex's penny and Hector's disappearance. Something that they did not mention. Like a couple who years before had come to an agreement never to talk about it.

When exactly nine months later, Tildy gave birth to Cherokee, Alex and Merridy consoled themselves in the same unspoken way: They could not afford a child, it would wreck the shape of their lives, it was not meant to be.

Nonetheless, they had had a tough trot, and it might have continued. Alex had his land, and this gave him satisfaction. But what about her? The solidity he found in his farmwork was denied Merridy. It was not enough to redecorate the house, or replant the garden, or potter around in the dunes, or seek the ultimate in red pasta sauces, or once a year cook big mutton roasts for the shearers, or make the daily journey into Wellington Point to collect the *Mercury* and milk, plus a blueberry muffin over which to read the crime column.

But what to do? Her abbreviated time at uni was a broken arrowhead inside her and more excruciating than any kidney stone. She had cancelled her subscription to *Engineering World*, but if ever she glanced at the spines in the spare room – the two shelves of textbooks and, above them, the single row of children's books – a complicated regret assailed her. She felt her father's disappointment that she had not achieved her tiny miracle. Worse, she had not given herself the chance to know even what she would have been good at. And yet too late to go back to college. Besides, to leave Alex on his own was out of the question. So she tried to entertain visions of herself driving the elderly at the wheel of the community bus. As a firey. Or a volunteer for the ambulance service. Or reading stories to children at the day care. But none of these options excited her.

She had become conscious, too, of another no-go area. They were running out of money.

It remained a source of pride with Alex that he had not merely broken even during the first years of their marriage but had steered the farm into modest profit. Then, he could still afford a cleaner once a week: Alice, who brought her blonde, curly-headed daughter to play on the lawn while she ironed his shirts and trousers, or dusted his bottle collection. In the expectation of continued profits, Alex had supported Merridy in her makeover of the house. He had footed the bills for three rounds of IVF treatment and bought her a car and paid her a monthly allowance. But he concealed from his wife that money had since become an issue.

Like other farmers Alex lived on an overdraft, but interest rates had risen so steeply that he was overstretched. He had looked into harvesting different crops – poppies, walnuts, wine, peas – but it would almost certainly take several years before he generated the sort of turnover to satisfy his bank. Meanwhile, income came in twice a year, barley at a different time from cattle and wool sales. And it was not enough.

While Alex had made his share of mistakes, there was no avoiding some costs. He had had to raise the dam by a metre after a bad drought in which the barley failed to come up. A pivot irrigator set him back the equivalent of a year's income. And when his father's ancient tractor expired halfway up Barn Hill, he had little option but to replace it with a John Deere, bought second-hand off Jack Fysshe. That tractor was nearing the end of its life, as often on a block in Nevin's garage as in the paddocks. He could not see any way to affording a new one.

Little by little, Alex had gnawed away at the investments left him by his parents until less than $7,000 remained. A further fall in the price of wool or a hefty garage bill could wipe him out. On top of it all, his bank was making persistent demands that he find ways to reduce his overdraft.

TALBOT'S STORE. Applications are invited for a temporary holiday worker. Some experience in the service industry desirable.

One Thursday towards the end of January, Alice failed to turn up.

"That's unlike her," Merridy said at lunch, and kept turning her eyes to the window.

Until Alex looked from his plate. "I've let her go."

Merridy failed to understand. "Go where?"

In a flat voice, he explained. His father's folks had paid

for his education. Now Uncle Matt was dead in Sedbergh, and there was no one in the family whom he could draw on for a loan. "We don't have a brass razoo and the ANZ is saying: 'We own 67 per cent of your farm and we are thinking of making this asset of ours a little bit liquid.'"

"What about Ray? Doesn't he specialise in loans?"

No sooner had she blurted the words than she was chiding herself. Alex would never seek a solution with Ray Grogan, who according to Tildy had made a complete recovery and roared across the bay at the helm of an even faster boat.

In the evening, Merridy came to where Alex sat in the living room.

She reached for his hand. "How's that sunspot?" turning it over and inspecting the back of it. "You should let Dr Musgrove take a look." Then: "Listen, Alex, I've been thinking. Maybe I can kick in."

"You?" moving his stare from the fire. He needed spectacles now, and orange flames licked his lens where she expected to meet his eye. "How?"

She had her father's inheritance, she reminded him. "Take it."

"I can't, Merridy," in a dismal voice.

"Oh, don't be so proud, Alex. I want to help."

"How much is it?"

She told him. And glimpsed behind the reflected firelight the painful modesty of the sum.

"No, Merridy. That's for you. I'll have a word with my agent. He's lent money to Jack before. I'm certain he'll let me borrow off him."

Nonetheless, from this moment she cast about for a way to support her husband.

*

Alice had been a tolerable cleaner, but her broom rarely troubled anything suspended on a wall. A week after Alex dispensed with Alice's services, Merridy was dusting the mantelpiece in the living room when she observed a cobweb trailing from Lear's cockatoo. The discovery motivated her to take a damp cloth and sponge down each and every picture in the house.

So she washed the samplers in the corridor, the Ackermann of Merton College gardens, the foxed print of Sedbergh chapel, until she progressed to her own pencil drawing in the spare bedroom. She wiped the glass frame – and for the first time in many years found herself rereading her childish handwriting.

Plans of a sieve, series 6. General arrangement. Dimensions: 64ft 3 inches diameter; depth 7ft 6 inches; draft: 6ft.

She was tidying the angle of the frame when the urge overwhelmed her to leave the room, get out of the house.

Merridy walked down to Moulting Lagoon. It was seven weeks after her encounter with the chandler and nothing had happened. Her period had come three weeks later, since when she had tucked him away.

Where the lagoon fed into the river was a picnic spot with a wooden hut and the old jetty from which Alex's father had dived and fished. The lagoon was a part of his property, a part of his life, that Alex was not remotely interested in, and so Merridy had made it hers. She had taken to going there more and more.

Put put put. She was sitting at the end of the jetty when coming up the river was a speedboat with a buoyant-looking face at the wheel. She thought for a heart-stopping moment: What am I going to do?

But it was not the chandler.

She watched the boat approach. There was something odd about the man who threw out the line. He was dressed in a black rubber suit, so he must have been skin-diving.

He stepped onto the deck of yellowed planks, each board scratched and bouncing underfoot, and tied the rope with a dripping hand. Under his wetsuit, it was impossible to gauge how old he was.

Out in the river, something large came to the surface and slurped. For a second, he forgot all about Merridy. "Oh look, oh look," to himself, "a Fizzgiggious Fish."

". . . *who always walked about upon Stilts because he had no legs.*"

The man turned, surprised, and the smile on his face broadened. "Hey!"

He sat down heavily beside her. He had an accent like Alex's, only more pronounced. A Pom for sure.

"I've always liked the look of this place. Yours, I suppose?"

"My husband's."

"Do you know what, if it were mine, I would do here?" kicking out his rubber legs and contemplating the slightly hairy toes that protruded.

"What would you do?" She was perfectly open, utterly unprepared.

"To my eye, I think it's crying out for oysters."

"I'm just brewing a cup of tea. Would you like one? I've only one cup."

"Don't you worry, madam. I'll take it out of the kettle!"

"Don't be silly."

She lifted the kettle off the Primus stove and poured. They settled down, sipping from the same cup, passing it back and forth.

"What makes you say oysters?" she said.

"Well, it's sheltered, the right size. You've got the ocean and the river. Best of all, it's undisturbed. I've been past here many a time and I've never seen anyone near here."

"Why is your boat called the *Lobster*? Do you fish for them?"

"I used to, in another life, but it keeps me in mind of a French poet, mad as a hatter, who used to walk a lobster on a lead up the Champs-Elysées. Someone asked him what the fuck . . . and he said: 'It doesn't bark and it knows the secrets of the sea.' Rather charming. But what you need right here in this ideal spit is to farm oysters."

"What would one have to do to make an oyster?"

"Not much. A female oyster spawns forty million eggs. The sea does the rest. You need a vessel, low flung, something you can stick things on. As for the tackle, I've got a mucker who's getting out of scallops in Triabunna and would sell his stuff. I was with him two days ago and he said to me: 'How in God's name can I get rid of all this?' He's moving into mussels and throwing out ropes, floats, scallop lanterns, everything you need. I'll ring him tonight, if you like. It's not going to be expensive, and I could collect it in my van and drop it off next time I'm passing."

She looked at him long and hard. This man who had come up out of the sea with a solution. Because in the last seven weeks she had nursed the bubbling hope that an unknown person might have given her a last chance. But it had not happened.

"You could have had his boat, too," he said, handing her back her cup, "except that someone smashed into it. The thing is, you should get it properly made. Design it yourself and it's all yours."

She flew back to the house on eagle's wings. It was so obvious, what he suggested. She had been staring at it ever since her second visit to the farm when she climbed the ladder to the windmill. The view down to Oyster Bay was something that she never tired of, whatever its moods or hers. Why should it *not* contain her future?

That evening Alex came home from drenching the sheep and saw her face. "What?"

"I've decided what to do with Dad's inheritance."

He implored her: "Please don't say you're going to open a B & B?"

She worried that the man in the boat would forget, but a fortnight later there it all was, in a heap inside the shed. Together with a note in a waterproof folded envelope: "Dear Madam, wishing you all the luck in the world. If you would be kind enough to send a cheque to this man . . ." Signed: "Joseph Silkleigh."

She sent off the cheque to Triabunna. She would love to have been able to say thank you. But she never saw Mr Silkleigh again, this strange-looking, slightly scholarly *deus ex aqua* who had seeded in her an idea.

CHAPTER NINE

SHE SPENT A DAY at an oyster farm outside St Helen's, led around by a skinny, introverted man with thinning white hair that the wind blew about, and a patch over his right eye. He had skewered his eyeball when clearing boobyalla on a block near Wellington Point. Les Gatenby knew right enough where she lived. He had started his farm twenty years ago and was happy to lend Merridy all his papers and books – most of which originated in British Columbia, where they had been harvesting Pacific oysters since before the Second World War.

Over the following months, Merridy read everything that she could about oysters. In a way that she never managed to feel when researching into IVF, she had the impression of picking up the degree she had left off. Not since her first term at uni had she experienced such a longing to study, such an elating sense of purpose.

Her confidence returned. Once it grew warm, she moved into Alex's old workshop. He had transferred his office to the post room, a brick building behind the shearing shed. Years had passed since he had occasion to hide himself away among his father's ship collection.

She tidied away the tools onto the shelves, next to the bottles. She took down her father's engineering manuals and spread them on the worktable. And over the following days designed an aluminium catamaran: ten metres long with a big, broad beam and pointed bow, a crane to hold the lanterns, a cabin to keep out the weather, and gutters to make it easier for her to clean the deck.

The naval architect in Launceston to whom she showed her plans was approving. "This one will take on anything."

"That's the idea."

For economy, he would shave out the gutters and cabin. Otherwise, he kept faithfully to her drawings. A month later, his design was ready.

Spending half of her father's inheritance, Merridy commissioned a boat yard in Launceston to build the boat; not Hobart, which was identified in her mind with her last despairing fling.

She named her the *Zemmery Fidd*.

"Where the Oblong Oysters grow," she explained to Alex.

The boat was the main expense. Thanks to Mr Silkleigh she already had tackle. Next to sort out was the lease. The Department of Sea and Fisheries was encouraging. For $2,500 a year, she bought a thirty-year lease from the Crown.

If Alex had misgivings, he suppressed them. It was obvious that his wife's mind was set. Long ago, he had given a promise to her mother. And it took the edge off his worries to support her in a venture about which she felt more and more involved. Merridy's oyster farm would be, as she put it to Tildy, her baby.

The *Zemmery Fidd* was already being built in a ship-yard on the Tamar when she arranged the construction of a new shed on the banks of Moulting Lagoon. She looked at seeding her own oysters, but Gatenby warned: "You'll need alarms and water controls and temperature gauges – plus you'll have to work seven days a week." Seedlings were dirt cheap anyway. For an investment of $2,000 she bought 8,000 dozen, two months old, from Shellfish Culture in Bicheno, and spent a weekend rolling them in plastic mesh. Then stapled the ends and floated them temporarily from the jetty in scallop lanterns.

The lanterns were partitioned, with individual trays at different levels, and compactable. They reminded Merridy of her brother's Slinky.

One noon, hauling them up, she heard a shout. "That's a sheila doing that!" Men from the power company, down having their lunch. She waved back, chuffed. Oysters was a blokey industry, like salmon. Not too many sheilas doing handlings.

Everything on the river was done by hand, the labour back-breaking. Initially, she wore baggy men's clothes, but in her second season Merridy found a New Zealand firm to make her a pair of bright green overalls. "I want to feel flattered."

Not that tighter overalls made her feel especially feminine. She felt dirty and ugly and different. And in a way she was different. She changed physically. Around her chest and shoulders she grew bulkier from lifting the ten-kilo lanterns. She found it hard to squeeze into her old clothes.

Regulations forbade Merridy to work on her own, so she employed an assistant, Jason, an absent-minded bass guitarist from Cranbrook who accompanied her on the *Zemmery Fidd*.

The oysters required handling every couple of months. She and Jason hoisted them from the river and sieved them and progressively stored the seedlings in larger meshes until they were ready for the sea. Then they were packed back into the lanterns and loaded onto the boat and relocated to Oyster Bay, where they put on a spurt of growth. At thirty months her first oysters were ready to sell.

Sometimes she imagined Mr Silkleigh coming back up the creek. Merridy would like to have told him about where his suggestion had led. To have shared just a fraction of her exasperation. But he never did reappear. Nor was there anyone she could hire as a consultant – save for Les Gatenby, and he very soon became her competitor. She had to learn by herself.

To begin with, she felt that she was holding the whole project together with nothing stronger than wire. The shed had no electric power. Her first job every morning was to light a fire.

She had no idea how to tie knots. The octopuses were adept at unpicking her ropes, until she met a cray-fisherman in Coles Bay who taught her a slip knot that he called a Grinner. "Just tie this one on everything."

She could not tell the wind direction; it might be blowing on her face and she would not know whether it was a south-easterly or northerly, or what it was.

She knew nothing about tides. That before a sudden change of weather the tide sometimes failed to go out; and sometimes it went out and did not come back in for a couple of days.

"And I never ever seem to have enough gear," she complained to Alex. It was not simply that if she left anything out, a float or a rope, thieves would take it. The oysters grew so fast that she found herself lacking the equipment to put them back in the water.

A lot of the equipment she made herself. She cut out the mesh and folded it into baskets. She unearthed a sewing machine that had belonged to Alex's mother and stitched up the ends of sacks. Life on the jetty improved in the second year when she bought a small generator from the Macdonalds.

There was a dirt track to the shed, but only people who had lost their way ever travelled down it. Because of its location, no one liked to come in to Oblong Oysters. If the outboard engines packed up, she piled them into the flat tray of her Toyota and drove to Gravelly Beach Marine on the Tamar.

Then there were the storms that blasted through and tore up her lines, plunging the lanterns to the bottom. The banks in Hobart and Launceston that told her to go away – "because we don't have any data on your industry". The daunting paperwork that she was required to submit to the Department of Sea and Fisheries.

"Don't you love these abbreviations, especially if you don't read the first paragraph and go skimming. What do you think a tassqap is?"

Alex could not recall it from the Scrabble dictionary. "A native sea slug?"

"A Tasmanian Shellfish Quality Assurance Programme."

Like this, it was nearly two years after Merridy registered her business before she made her first sale. To a wholesaler in Victoria chosen with a pin from an old Melbourne telephone directory.

"No worries, send me two hundred dozen."

Merridy was so particular that it took her all day to pack eight bags. Soon she would be able to pack two hundred dozen oysters in an hour. Not that Anton seemed overly impressed by the stuff she was sending.

They had done business for five months when he telephoned to cancel an order: "We've had to throw out your last shipment."

"Why?"

"It smelled."

"What of?"

"I don't know, a customer didn't like the smell."

"What does that mean?"

"It means we're not paying for it," with an offsider's laugh.

"But, Anton, I've got the POD with your signature. Why wait two weeks to tell me?"

"Sorry, Mrs Dove. If you don't like what I'm saying, feel free to go elsewhere."

"Well, I *don't* like it."

One thousand one hundred dollars down the drain. Another six weeks before she found a new wholesaler, this time through Les Gatenby.

That throughout this period Merridy kept her head above water was chiefly thanks to Alex, who knew about the pitfalls of trespassing into new and unknown territory when you are fired up with passion but have zero expertise. With her husband's support, the goad of her father's memory and the painstaking stewardship of her inheritance, Merridy built up the oyster farm. Until four years after the launch of the *Zemmery Fidd*, Alex discovered a curly-headed young woman in the kitchen ironing his shirts.

He continued down the corridor to his old workroom.

Merridy sat on a swivel chair behind a large new desk, writing. Pinned to a corkboard was a mud-map showing the distribution of her lanterns. Otherwise, the same view through the window onto the edge of the lawn and the Oyster Bay pine. The same fleet of ships on the shelves. And her Gory Box in the corner.

He coughed. "Isn't that Alice's daughter?"

"It is." She signed her name and handed the rectangular piece of paper to Alex.

"What's this?"

"Just read."

He dug his spectacles out of his shirt pocket and put them on. A cheque. Enormous. Made out to P. A. Dove.

"What's this for?"

"A tractor."

*

Merridy suspended her oysters in the sea for their last six months. In the centre of the bay, she laid out seven long lines, made from 600 metres of polypropylene rope. At a man's depth below the surface, she tied the scallop lanterns full of oysters. She floated them with the oysters evenly spaced apart. She had inherited her meticulousness from her father, her stubbornness from her mother.

She had chosen Pacific over natives because of the latter's higher mortality rate. The hole through which she repeatedly had scanned the southern horizon for a fugitive pea-green sail was bored, she learned, by a ferocious little parasite that attached itself to the top of the native shell and killed it, exactly as it had killed off the flat native oysters of England. Pacifics were not susceptible to so many predators. Only if they touched the bottom of the bay.

"If they get to touch bottom, then the whole world comes. It's like a biology lesson," she explained to Alex.

Not just octopus and stingrays and dough-boy scallops galore, but skates and sea urchins and – worst of all – starfish. From now on, scarcely a summer went by without her grizzling to Alex about the starfish. They were like flies, vomiting stomach juices onto the young oyster and breaking down the shell so that the starfish could suck it up.

Protective of her oysters, she regarded Moulting Lagoon

as their natural home, but during her fifth season a natural disaster startled Merridy into a realisation that she could not have been more mistaken: the lagoon was holding them back.

A bad rain in the middle of January wiped out 95 per cent of her seedlings. The river grew too hot. Not only that: the rain flooded the river with fresh water and this streamed into Moulting Lagoon. The oysters took a little sip to check if the salt water had returned, and when they discovered that it had not, closed up. Ten days on, and still only fresh water in the lagoon.

Alex could not have been more relieved, but for Merridy the rain that raised the level of his dam and replenished the aquifer beneath Dolphin Sands spelled catastrophe.

In normal conditions, the fresh water sat on top and the seawater ran in underneath. Even during a storm, the salt water would sneak in. This time, no such luck. The lagoon was not emptying. Metres of rain kept coming down, kept flowing from the mountains into the river. More water coming down the mountains than upriver, and no wind to stir it. And the oysters could not wait any longer, they had to feed. But hunger was not their sole concern.

"They think the end of the world's come. They think this is their last chance to reproduce."

Panicked, the oysters opened their shells and drank and tried to spawn. But to drink hot, fresh water was not a good combo.

Exhausted by their premature spawning, the oysters succumbed to bacteria in the hot water. They died at the speed of the bush fire that in the same year raced through Friendly Beaches. Merridy's losses were huge.

She despaired about what to do with the surviving seedlings, only ten weeks old. As a last resort, she telephoned Jason, and they loaded the *Zemmery Fidd*. Merridy had little reason for optimism. She had taken it as Gospel that the species was not evolved enough to survive on pure salt water. That the Pacific oyster did not exist which grew all its life in the ocean. More or less everyone in the industry shared Gatenby's belief: "If you're stupid enough to grow your seedlings in the sea, they'll die in a day." As she dropped the seedlings overboard, she had the notion that she was burying them.

But out in Oyster Bay a miracle happened.

It gave her more intense pleasure even than to buy Alex a tractor. Fifteen months after the flood that all but destroyed her harvest, Merridy brought home a bucket containing two dozen live oysters. The first that she had cultivated from seed in Oyster Bay.

"I guess you could say they're really pretty-looking," passing one to Alex. "A lot more water flow. Not with mud and silt settling on them. I'm getting into feeling glad it happened."

And watching her husband inspect the craggy, purple-white oyster that she had grown in the sea she was overcome by the certainty of her affection for him. They had come out of their tangle and the road stretched ahead; it was not the road they had started on, but she could see where it led and the knowledge no longer made her despondent.

Merridy's decision to relocate her lanterns in the bay did more than safeguard the oyster farm: it guaranteed a demand for her produce that was unstoppable. Sure, the rough water rumbled the topmost trays. The oysters in those trays were smaller as a result, their shells more friable.

She passed anxious days worrying in case the trade rejected them. On the contrary. The splitters in Melbourne found that they could shuck twice as many of Merridy's thinner-shelled oysters. Around Christmas time, it was her sea-grown oysters that the restaurateurs in St Kilda savoured above their Tasmanian river cousins. Their salty ocean taste and sharpness of flavour and distinct colouring. Most important of all, the customers clamoured for Oblong Oysters – although this would take a while for Merridy to discover.

Dmitri, her new wholesaler in Melbourne, was a Greek of few words, and these reluctantly spoken during their fortnightly telephone conversations. Les Gatenby had recommended him as "a real straight-shooter". They had yet to meet, but Dmitri had made a verbal agreement to take a pallet of 600 dozen a week.

On Monday afternoons, Merridy watched the shipment leave her shed in the East Coast Freight van – always with a tinge of sadness at the sight of the door rolling down on the pallet. The oysters were now out of her care, and she pictured their onward journey with the involved concern of any guardian. Van to Hobart. Into a container. Trucked to Devonport. Across on the *Spirit* and landing at 11.00 a.m. Wednesday in Melbourne fish market where Dmitri's splitters waited.

She had no idea if her competitors bothered much about what happened to their produce once it left their sheds, but Merridy cared. Dmitri's lack of feedback maddened her. "You're a customer, Dmitri, but you're not the final customer. What did you think of that shipment? Was it the right size? What are customers saying?"

"Beautiful oysters – and send me some more next week. Oh, and I like the hessian packaging."

"That's as far as he goes," she raged to Alex. "When I

send him crackerjack oysters and he goes, 'Yeah, they're all right, can you send me two extra pallets?' – that's when I know they're fantastic."

One night – he must have been drinking – Dmitri telephoned, and this time verged on the loquacious. He talked about his health and daughter, and towards the end of his call invited Merridy to Melbourne to discuss a business proposition.

"I don't have time to go to Melbourne, Dmitri. Let's talk about it now."

This was not Dmitri's method. Always in their telephone conversations thereafter he was sure to raise the subject of a meeting – "One to one, no lawyers, just you-me."

His persistence began to irritate. One evening, she declared: "I will never come back to Melbourne – not until you tell me what your customers think of my oysters."

Silence. Then in his grave surly voice: "You ask what the customers say? They say your oysters are so good, you get a stiff neck when you eat them!"

At some point she would have to yield to Dmitri's pleas and fly to Melbourne. For the moment, though, she was happy with their arrangement. Dmitri's guarantee to buy a pallet and a half every week ensured that money flowed in on a regular basis, easing the pressure on Alex. But money was the least of Merridy's pleasures. Every time she emptied out a lantern filled with her Pacific oysters, she felt like a pioneer in the early days of a new industry; and there was the pride she took in her boat.

Because the *Zemmery Fidd* had such a wide beam, she was safe in most weathers. This meant that Merridy was called out to help vessels in distress if the police launch in Bicheno could not reach them in time, or if the sea was too rough for the 18-foot coastguard boat in Swansea.

When a high-speed rubber dinghy, on a joyride in Coles Bay, tipped off six people – and there were a few broken bones besides – Sergeant Finter had no sympathy. He chewed out the survivors: "You'd have drowned if it hadn't been for Mrs Dove."

FREYCINET COURT HOTEL. Talbot's Newsletter would like to extend a warm welcome to Murray Went, the new proprietor. Two licensed bars and restaurant. Open for bookings. "We look forward to seeing you."

That same summer they lost Flash. The restorative air had given the creature a new lease of life. The lifespan of a Border collie was generally no more than twelve years. Smelly, blind, lame, Flash was almost seventeen when Alex pressed the cold barrel of his Purdey to her trusting neck.

He and Merridy were left desolate. For six weeks, Alex could not bring himself even to begin looking for a replacement. But the farm needed a working dog and he used the occasion of Merridy's birthday to give her a puppy that was part collie, part golden retriever. Rusty had a pedigree from Europe on both sides, said the woman at the Kennel Club – who added what an ass Jennifer was to have left a champion bitch on heat playing behind the clubhouse with Sally's retriever. She pointed out Rusty's extraordinary feet, built to run on sand, and remarked how sensible of Alex to choose this combination of breeds. "I have known this mixture before and they give endless pleasure to children."

She did not have children, but at thirty-six Merridy had never felt so clear-headed, so precise in her thoughts and movements. Whereas before she had melted from life, now

246

she strode towards it. She was confident that her stripe of grief had been removed. Perhaps removed messily as a gland is removed. But removed.

Until one mild early morning when she was steering the *Zemmery Fidd* across the bay, the same uneventful and endless stretch of sea that her marriage had become, the realisation came to her that she was uncomplicatedly content. After so many years of fretfulness and frustration, her anxieties seemed resolved into the sea. At last, it suited her to be on this rim of the world. She no longer scanned the horizon for a phantom sail. She looked down into the sea. At her achievement. There might not be a God, but there was the sound of the waves, now hushed, now loud, galloping on through the day and night forever.

PART III

Oyster Bay, 12–16
December 2004

CHAPTER ONE

OBSERVATIONS FROM THE FRONT LINE. We have noticed with alarm the growing pilfering by young boys of goods in shops. Maybe names should be named. The editor will give thought to this matter. A.T.

No one forecast the storm. Not on Merridy's radio nor in the *Mercury*. It came out of a day so calm and bright and blue that Ray Grogan had locked his office three hours early to go fishing.

It was such a rare afternoon that as soon as Albert Talbot observed Ray's trailer approaching the ramp, he did what he had not done in a long while. He put down his binoculars, abandoned his customary position at the top-storey porthole and shuffled down the back staircase to watch at close quarters. Ray's gleaming craft was the envy of Talbot's proprietor and put the former coast-watcher in mind of the American patrol-boat that had dropped him ashore in New Britain. Even though it was his basic rule that any time you went down to the coast you struck trouble, there was also a tricky matter that he needed to broach with Ray, about his son Zac. Hired by Talbot's for the holiday season, Merridy's fourteen-year-old godson had been caught in the act of removing a wad of notes from the till.

In the event, Albert did not manage to speak to Ray, but he inched his way along the jetty in time to overhear the following conversation.

Ray stood, hands on the hips of his shorts, beside a

white van, waiting for a man in a wetsuit to haul his speedboat out of the water.

"You all done for the day?" Ray called impatiently.

"That's right," said the diver, who had an oxygen cylinder strung from his shoulder and goggles pushed up over his head.

"A bit early in the season to be packing up, isn't it?" and screwed up his eyes to read the make of the boat.

"Well, don't take the blindest piece of notice of me, but there's a gale up ahead, and one you won't want to mess with, you mark my words."

But Ray was more interested in the man's boat. "What is she, actually?"

"A Cobalt runabout with a 260-horsepower Volvo inboard engine. Sometimes known as a Bow Rider because you can sit in front. Really, she's a lake boat, although I do find she's terrific for reefs."

"But there are no reefs around here," objected Ray.

The man stared at him with a strange frankness and replied in a tone of sacramental gravity: "There are reefs, old soul, everywhere."

Ray looked up from the boat to the side of the van. *THE LONG HAUL*. The words reminded him of his marriage. "Where are you from?" puzzled, and tugged at the gold chain around his neck. "You're clearly not from here or you'd still be out there."

The man waved a yellow snorkel at Ray's trailer. "Trust me, you should be keeping yours out, not putting her in."

"Never! You blow-ins don't know your arses from your elbows. If ever there was a perfect afternoon to go and drown a few worms this is it."

"Then all I'm going to say to you, old soul, is slacken your guy ropes."

When Grogan's boat *Follow Me* smashed into the jetty

less than two hours later, everyone except Albert was taken by surprise. The old man watched the gusts of wind needling his window, packed with sea-spray and sand to obliterate his view, and mumbled to himself: "I wonder who that clever dick was? How did he know what no one else knew?"

The storm thundered in like a log-truck. It hit the beach late afternoon, the cold wind moaning as it passed through the telegraph wires, clattering off a loose sheet of tin from the shearing shed and popping out the wooden stays.

Its vindictiveness alarmed Merridy. The lagoon had thrown back a clear, pale sky when the van collected the oysters at five. She had left Jason to lock up and driven home to take a shower and afterwards sit in the kitchen, as she liked to do, reading the *Mercury*. She had changed into the soft green jersey that she had bought years before at a trekking shop in Hobart, though it felt small on her, and a pair of new trainers; her long, fine face lined against the no longer transparent afternoon light.

A breeze blew up from the beach, slamming the door, but she was accustomed to strong winds in December. She hardly noticed it filling out Alex's shirts and trousers into bloated equivalents of himself that tossed and twisted against the greying clouds. Nor the new puppy that shivered in its basket.

She turned the pages. The Pope was dying – this time there really was no way back, the doctors were saying; the Navy had intercepted near Broome a second vessel filled with boat people, all claiming to be Afghans; a report on Tasmania's increasing appeal for Japanese property speculators; and a photograph of a two-masted ship under full sail.

Something blundered against the fly-screen. She knew

what it would be. Bogan moths with red eyes that liked the rain and banged against the windows and stuck to her when she tried to bat them away. Nor did she bother to look up when another door slammed. A good old southerly buster, that was all.

Soon the Crime Stoppers column absorbed her attention.

Sometime on Saturday, Elle Macpherson underwear was stolen from a garden in Lindisfarne. Her mind tiptoed after the thief to a house in North Hobart, snatching a neckwarmer, ski goggles and a centenary medal. And was emerging from a shed in Moonah tugging a Victa lawn-mower when she heard a tremendous clatter.

This time Merridy reacted. She raced outside and saw that the rotary clothes-line was down, the tug of the wind so strong that Alex's airborne trousers and shirts had uprooted the Hills Hoist's concrete base. Her trainers crunched across the gravel to where her husband's clothes lay in the grass. She gathered them up and was running back to the house, arms full and her mouth stuffed with pegs, when she glanced out over the deck. Strung along the south horizon a noose of cloud was drawing in. She looked at Schouten for a telltale flash, but there was none. Only the long low cloud advancing.

Still the wind pounded up the slope to a jingling of tin. It moved at great velocity, filled with grit and dust, quar-relling with all that it touched, frittering her flower beds and unclenching the green fists of the pine tree.

Only when she stepped back inside did Merridy hear the telephone ringing above the gale.

"Mrs Dove?" came the urgent voice. "Pete Finter here."

Groggy from a bout of flu, Alex had not wanted to leave his bed, but the day was so exceptionally mild and sparkling

254

– glisky, they would have called it in Cumbria, one of those bright borrowed days of early autumn – that he had taken advantage of the rain which had fallen in the night to plough a field on the east edge of Moulting Lagoon. For most of the afternoon he had sat warmly wrapped in the cabin of his tractor. The earth felt both squashy and hard, as if cardboard boxes were laid out underneath it and the land was a temporary thing.

Not until he stopped the tractor to swallow down a Paracetamol with a cup of Thermos tea did Alex appreciate how humid it had grown suddenly. How thick and hazy.

Wick wick wick. A large flock of swifts passed fast over-head. He could hear the wings and the clack clack of their beaks as they fed on a hatch of insects. He was too congested to dwell on the reason for their appearance. He sipped his over-stewed tea, watching them rake the sky against a lens-shaped cloud. Then he screwed the top back on his flask and returned to ploughing the field.

Protected by the pine break, Alex did not feel the force of the wind until he drove his tractor onto the road an hour later. But it was not the wind that made him slam on the brakes.

Less than fifty yards away, right on the edge of David Macdonald's property, a ghost shambled between the gums.

Alex stared into the bush. Heart chugging at the bright white figure that he saw there. The puzzle was the colour. Bill Molson confided to Alex's father that he had seen a blue child hasten along the marshes where the black swans laid their eggs. Possibly he had. Not Alex, though some-times he looked out for it on those evenings when he walked home beside the lagoon.

He slipped the tractor into neutral and applied the hand-brake, mesmerised by the pristine colour. Even as he stepped down, he recalled a matron at his house in Sedbergh who had believed in the Radiant Boy, a luminous apparition that made its appearance with dire results. Now Alex found himself speculating, with all the rational instincts of a forty-three-year-old farmer educated at Oxford, whether the ghost might be one of the family of settlers who had drowned.

A pine cone dropped at his feet. Over the fence, the spirit moved behind a thick trunk of macrocarpa, and Alex saw it for what it was: a Friesian cow with a vertical white mark on its coat that it was easy to mistake for a human being.

He kicked the cone into the bush and climbed back onto his tractor and drove on. But the mark on the cow went with him; it remained silhouetted in his head like the flash when a strong light goes out, and it was still there when he turned into his drive.

Alex watched the house come nearer through the tractor's windscreen. A grey cloud wrapping the ripple-iron roof. The fallen clothes-line. And through the window, Merridy, in oilskins, speaking in heated tones to someone, her hands winnowing the air as always when excited.

In the comfort of his cabin, he considered: What would he tell her, that he had been startled out of his skin by one of their neighbours' cows?

He parked the tractor next to the ute and walked towards the kitchen door, head down, hands pinching the bottom of his Driza-Bone pocket and pushing his smile against the gritty wind. The force of it bent back the pine on the lawn and clacked the blades of the windmill into words that belted out across the distance between Alex and the light in the kitchen, and chided him for his credulity.

Through the window Merridy caught sight of Alex struggling up the drive. The pressure of battling against the gale gave him the exaggerated totter of a crippled person.

"Listen, there's Alex. Let me work on him," and slammed down the receiver. She ran across the kitchen and flung open the door.

He raised his head. "You'll never guess—"

Her pressing voice competed with the windmill. "Alex, there's been an accident."

A ship was going down between the Hen and Chicks. The Marine Police in Hobart had picked up the call. They were requesting local volunteers to get into the water without delay. All the professional rescuers were indisposed.

"Finter's asked if we'd take the *Zemmery Fidd*."

"Where's the police launch?" Alex asked.

"In Hobart for repairs."

"And the Devil cat?"

"Answering another distress call."

"What about Trevor?" Trevor was the fisherman in Coles Bay who had taught Merridy her knot and owned a cray-boat.

"On holiday."

"And David?"

"I just rang him. He's sold his boat." She was unhooking Alex's oilskins from the back door.

"You think we can? What if it's too large a sea?"

"I'm prepared to have a go – if you'll come. How are you feeling?"

"Fine," he said. "Fine."

"Here. I'll go and shut Rusty away. He'll be a wreck with this wind."

Squeezed into his oilskins, Alex followed Merridy outside to the ute. The weather that morning had been unnaturally still and warm when he left the house, the bay the smooth opaque green of a perfume bottle. Now he felt the angry smack of the wind. A sheep rolled over in the next paddock and a kookaburra that had nested in the Oyster

Bay pine flew off in a twisted parasol of black and grey feathers.

He climbed in beside Merridy and turned the ignition. He was driving off when he heard a resounding crack.

In the rear-view mirror, the lawn capered and twisted. Then burst apart in a dark clot of roots and earth. The tree had toppled over.

Alex drove fast along the edge of Moulting Lagoon towards the jetty, gravel pinging against the windscreen. The storm was ripening. He had never known such a wind.

"What kind of ship?"

"A brigantine, could it be?"

"A brigantine? In Oyster Bay?"

"She's a replica. It's all over the *Mercury*. She's sailing around the island."

Bored by the idea of yet another project to do with the island's bicentenary, she had glanced at the article only out of respect for her husband and the anachronistic image of a ship that might have sailed straight out of one of his bottles. The *Buffalo* had arrived from Sydney the previous day in George Town, and was modelled on the brigantine that had landed two hundred years ago at the mouth of the Tamar, carrying the first European settlers. *Hoods at sea* ran the headline of the article, which she had not bothered to finish but reminded herself to show to Alex.

He skidded to a halt at the entrance to the oyster shed while Merridy leaped out, unlocked the gate, raced ahead.

In less than five minutes, Alex was reversing the *Zemmery Fidd*, with Merridy on board, down the bank. He aimed the stern at the lagoon and steered the ute, its wheels churning the seaweed and mud, until the aluminium hull clanked loose of its pivot and slid into the choppy water.

Merridy started the engines and nodded at Alex. By the time he had parked the ute at the top of the bank, the *Zemmery Fidd* was rocking at the jetty.

He jumped onto the deck, untied the rope. "OK."

Merridy opened the throttle and the force of the engines threw him against the crane. He held on as the boat sped into the river.

Soon they were out of the river. The *Zemmery Fidd* slammed over the bar-way and twisted into the breakers, the spray falling in heavy sheets.

Merridy punched out towards the tip of Freycinet, keeping close to the shore. The sky had darkened further. The clouds overhead a mass of shadows, now dense, now thinning, and tortured into antedeluvian shapes: hippogriffs, bulls, unicorns.

She yelled: "See anything?"

One arm hugging the crane, Alex looked out. The sea roughened and agitated. The bay rutted with deep waves. The waves not advancing in orderly lines, but frenzied like wild cattle. In the fading light, they came on at a gallop, horns down and backs tossing, sweeping water up the beach in a vivid white foam.

She called to him again. The sea had matted his thinning hair so that the skull shone through. "Well?"

He shook his head. As far as the eye could see waves kicked and reared, churning the horizon.

The boat thumped into a trough, lashing salt water into Alex's face. He ascended higher up the crane. At the crest of the next rise, he picked out Maria Island, the Isle des Foques. Then, to the right of Schouten, before a wave hid it, a tangle of white and black.

259

"Over there," he bellowed in the direction of the rigging. But the wind grabbed his words. "Merridy, over there."

It took the *Zemmery Fidd* twenty minutes more to reach the *Buffalo*. The brigantine was heeled in to land and lying on her side, the sea breaking over her in all directions.

A yellow shape rolled up and down the quarterdeck. Alex saw with a sick heart that it was a body.

The wind blasted fiercer. He felt his shirt heavy and wet under his oilskin and a cold razor of air slashing his face and hard bullets of rain. The waves frothed and seethed as though flames were burning under them, and the wind swooped the sea up into the sky.

"Look, Alex!" Merridy was pointing.

A dark blue figure clung to the flapping ratlines halfway up the mizzen mast.

Alex shouted.

No response.

Above the stampede, the sky had turned the colour of black lava.

He waved a hand, shouted again. His hoarse throat aching from his flu.

A head turned. A hand detached itself from the mast. And this time waved back.

CHAPTER TWO

IT WAS, EVERYONE AGREED — although they were quite surprised, too – an amazing physical achievement. Nobody but a halfwit would have got out of that boat.

Even as Merridy brought the *Zemmery Fidd* alongside, the *Buffalo* began to tilt. The mast that a moment before had pointed up at the sky now stretched at the angle of the horizon, in the direction of Moulting Lagoon Farm. The waves rose in a boiling fountain, snatching and whipping at the man who held on, one leg crossed over the other, one arm over the other, in the stoical attitude, Alex could not help thinking, of a grub clinging under the seed head of a stalk of barley.

"Jump in!" he yelled. "Jump in!" the words funnelling off.

Less than twenty yards away, the mizzen mast juddered. It sank further, towards the grasping sea. Quite soon, it would be pointing down.

A wave licked up and there was a splash.

Already, Alex was stripping off his life jacket, his oilskins. He tugged his shirt over his head and belted his life jacket back on and leaped overboard.

The cold kicked the air out of him. He went up to take a huge breath and was slapped by a wave, inhaling it. He desperately tried to climb to the top of the water, dimly aware at the back of his mind that this was how people drowned, and broke the surface coughing.

Vast waves crashed into the existing swell and lifted him away from the *Zemmery Fidd*, towards the sinking ship.

Ten yards away an arm rose out of the sea. He flopped in its direction.

"You all right?" through his throatful of water, approaching from behind. He knew that a drowning person had nothing to fear. They pushed you down to get themselves up. But the man appeared unconscious. Alex front-crawled towards him and reached an arm under his shoulder. When he lifted the head to clear the airway vomit spewed from the mouth. He started towing the man back, one knee up in case he had to thrust him away. At every second ready for him to revive and thrash around and drag Alex under in his panic.

Alex had indeed nearly drowned, bringing in the man. He was sixteen minutes in the sea with him, before he got him onto the *Zemmery Fidd*, Alex shoving, Merridy tugging, having tied herself to the crane. At last the man rolled under the rail, into the boat.

He was so relieved to let go that Alex was caught unprepared for the wave that knocked him back. The sea filled his mouth and he started to sink. He could make out Merridy's distorted face above him, oscillating, coming and going in particles. He reached up his arm, but already he was subsiding. His fingers were grabbed just as he felt himself disconnecting.

When Alex hung his hands on the rail, he went to jelly, but with a wave helping, he held onto Merridy's wrist and hauled himself as close as possible to the stern.

Merridy pulled Alex into the boat, settling him between the engines, and returned to the body. She had laid him out on the bottom of the *Zemmery Fidd*. She knelt down, a knee on either side, water swilling everywhere, and pressed her head to the cold blue lips and inserted a few puffs of air.

"Is he alive?" between breaths. Feeling the heat of the engines on his skin.

The sea banged into the side, lurching Alex onto her.

She pushed herself up, wiping her mouth. "Have a look while I grab the wheel."

CHAPTER THREE

IN ALEX'S CHILDHOOD, SOUTH-EASTERLIES had cast ashore a giant squid, a sunfish and on one occasion the stringy orange remains of what might have been a coelacanth. But nothing was stranger than the young man whom the Doves rescued from the bay that evening and brought back to the farm. As Merridy later explained to Sergeant Finter: "It would've been madness to try for Wellington Point, the sea running as it was."

They laid him on the bed beneath the stars that she had stencilled all those years before. Small drops of perspiration sprang from his forehead and down his neck, and the breath bubbled awkward under his tongue.

Merridy was put in mind of a horse's nose, tender and pale.

"Where do you think he's from?" unfastening the brass buttons on his jacket of heavy serge. His numbed arms and legs belonged not to any port he might have sailed from, but to some region of his own.

"Could he be a stowaway?" Alex wondered aloud. "One of those Afghans?"

Whoever he was, he looked pretty odd in his uniform, a striped sailor's top under the jacket and navy-blue trousers cut in the style of another century.

But he did not strike Merridy as Afghan. His darkness came off with a flannel, revealing a white man in his late teens. Average height. Short spiky hair dyed blond, and on his left ear a gold earring that made her think of Ray.

Alex looked at his watch. Eleven p.m. They had been away four hours. "I'd better telephone Finter."

"Yes, he ought to be told," squeezing out the flannel into a bowl of hot water.

Merridy had twice radioed Sergeant Finter from the *Zemmery Fidd*. The storm causing so much interference on the VHF that she understood nothing the policeman had said.

At the door, Alex hesitated. "Could we have done more?"

She gave him a brave smile. Remembering his expression as he sank beneath the surface. How she reached down with her whole body to catch his upraised hand. Something told her that if she failed to catch it Alex might not reappear. "No."

Alex left the room and she continued mopping the face. Eyes tight shut and streaks of tar on the scratched cheeks.

His lips opened, sucking in another laboured breath.

With great care, she rubbed at the corner of his mouth where the sand had compacted. His teeth were slanted outwards and chipped, the colour of dirty crabshell, and there was an ugly bump on his forehead.

Another breath. The way he gasped for air, he might have been crawling out from the *Buffalo*'s dark hold.

When she had finished washing his face, she raised him by the shoulders and removed the sailor's top from his limp arms, revealing the surprise of a purple T-shirt printed with a skull and a cigarette dangling from its mouth. She slipped the shirt over his head and shook off his soaked trousers.

His legs. They could have been the flanks of a horse.

And felt the weight of something.

Still he lay there, eyes closed, as Merridy drew it out of his pocket.

A silver rigging knife, well-oiled and sharp. She tested

her thumb on it and winced. Then closed the 4-inch steel switchblade and carefully put it on the bedside table.

She covered him with a duvet and went to fetch some disinfectant to dab on that forehead.

The storm blew itself out in the early hours. Rain replaced the wind and then the rain stopped and there was a damp silence. Outside, the windmill stood motionless. The only sound to penetrate the curtain the nervous cough of a foal.

It was still dark when Alex got up.

Merridy smelled his metallic breath before he kissed her cheek, but did not open her eyes. She heard him let Rusty out of the living room. Their footsteps – the scrabbling of a pent-up, excitable animal and her husband's more measured tread – passed along the corridor to the kitchen.

He took down the torch from the Welsh dresser and pushed open the fly-screen and went out. Around the house, pandemonium, as if an angry Zac had thrown a tantrum on the landscape – loose sheets of tin, tree limbs everywhere and dotted here and there in the darkness the white blur of a dead sheep. The most dramatic casualty was the Oyster Bay pine. Its topmost branches had crashed onto the drive a few yards short of the living room. Flashing his torch up and down, Alex saw his parents' gravestones lopsided.

He whistled Rusty away from the exposed earth. Then crossed the lawn and walked through the farm buildings, making an inventory of the damage.

Inside the house, the silence unnerved Merridy. She lay awake, worn out but unable to sleep. Moments later, she heard a throat being cleared and quickly pulled on her clothes and stepped barefoot along the corridor.

The young man sat up as she entered. He glanced over

the room, the ceiling. Rubbing his head and turning it in her direction.

She switched on the light.

His mouth hung open, red and vulnerable like a child's shoe. The face of someone who might have become a man too soon. And Merridy half-expected a neigh or a bawl.

"You're awake," looking into his eyes. But there was no bottom to them.

He peered back. With his spiky hair and unseeing eyes, he seemed like something hallucinated.

Then she understood. "Can't you see?"

"My specs," he mumbled. The accent Australian. "I lost them."

She went and fetched Alex's spare glasses.

"Here," she said. "Will these do?" They did. They fitted. They seemed to be made for him.

Glasses on, his eyes prised into her. The sabre of a smile guarding his thin, hesitant face. His eyes particularly white under her husband's lenses.

"Hello," she smiled. "I'm Merridy," and held out a hand. "Merridy Dove."

A long arm rose from the bed. Shaking hands, she could have been gripping a tiller. Then all at once he released his hold and leaned forward, fingers touching her face. Ripped by the splintery wheel or mast, their tips had the feeling of shells.

She heard her young girl's giggle. "No," she hooted, closing her eyes. As if a young boy was splashing water at her.

The kitchen door slammed.

"Alex . . ." fluting. "Could you put on the kettle?" And to him, her hand hiding her flushed throat: "Would you like some tea?"

"I . . . I don't recall."

267

"Then I would."

At the sound of footsteps coming down the corridor he snatched back his hand and his eyes moved to the door where Alex stood.

With Alex, his mouth was adrift; he had abandoned the certainties of speech.

"What do they call you, mate?" Alex asked, dragging up a chair and sitting down.

Without Merridy in the room, the young man looked worried, alert.

"Kish," he whispered.

When Rusty tried to lick him, he shied back.

"Come on, he's not going to eat you," Alex said gently. "Hey, Rusty, get out."

And when the dog had left: "Where were you heading, Kish?" It was strange to see someone wearing his glasses.

"Hobart Town." Rolling out his gaze from under the overhanging brows and scanning the ceiling for a path out.

Alex gave a surprised snort. "Oh, come on," he said. "Hobart."

"We were told Hobart Town. That's what the captain said."

Alex thought: The bump on his head has caused these convolutions and made him lose his place.

"How long have you been at sea?" he asked.

"We left Port Jackson . . ."

"Port Jackson? Oh, Sydney."

". . . on November the sixteenth, eighteen hundred and four."

Alex looked at him kindly. "It's OK, Kish, you're on dry land now. You can relax."

They were still at it when Merridy came back with the tea.

She poured for him and Alex resumed. "Where were you heading?"

"China. I don't know."

"You mean like those escaped convicts from Sarah Island?" said Alex cleverly.

"Or maybe it was Chile," said Kish.

This game he was playing, it had begun to annoy Alex. The young fellow behaving as though he might have been blown forever by icy gales in a purgatory of white ridges and penguin crap. His fate to go round and round the pole.

Nonetheless, whoever had instructed him had done their work. The boy had learned his lines so well, they might have become ingrown.

Alex tried to catch him out, but Kish had an answer to everything. Where he did not reply, he deflected Alex's questions with a sawing laugh.

"Speak Dutch, do you?" Alex joked, playing his game.

Kish looked at him over his mug of tea, not speaking. His eyes unreadable. His silence tightening its hold.

Still congested by his flu and now by lack of sleep, Alex leaned forward, trying to anchor and clarify his thoughts.

Was this man having him on? Or did he seriously believe that he was a sailor from the year 1804? If he did, then he was lost in a region where no one could reach him, and certainly no one in Wellington Point. They needed to get him to a doctor.

If Kish was a ghost, his currency was worthless. Worth nothing to anyone. Like an old penny found in a grave. And Alex thought of the cow in the wood and Kish drooling in the pine needles; superfluous and dribbling.

No, he was simple, that's what he was. A simpleton.

One of those street kids they took aboard ships to teach teamwork.

But Merridy did not think so. To her, Kish was a lost soul. She wanted to lead him off into a quiet corner and read his face.

"I think he needs to sleep, Alex."

Her husband took another look at the young man he had saved. He stood up. "I spoke to Finter again. He's been in touch with the coastguard. It looks like three of the eleven crew are missing."

The sun had climbed over the Hazards by the time Alex stepped onto Dolphin Sands. He looked towards Maria Island. The sky red as a devil's ear. But no sign of the *Buffalo*. The only vestige of the night before, the iodine seaweed smell and the havoc on the shoreline.

Down on the severely eroded beach, the dunes had the shapes of cliffs. Scattered all along the sand like small alligators were the blue legs of starfish, ripped from their bodies by the battering surf. And grey sea slugs – dead men's dicks, as Pam the shearer called them. And the most shiny, perfect shells: yellow, with scribbly-gum motifs, some with the red suckers of the whelk protruding, still alive.

Alex followed two gulls. They picked their way through the seaweed, too bloated to fly until Rusty chased them. Clots of kelp lay drying in rubbery brown wigs or floated in submerged rafts close to shore. At the far end of the beach where it met the Swan River stood a solitary figure by a white van. Someone down early, no doubt to see what they could muster.

He discovered the bodies rolling in a gentle surf. Two young men, both dressed in the same naval uniforms as Kish, and the corpse of an older man, togged up in yellow wet-weather gear and heavy sea-boots with electrical tape on the tops.

Already the sun had reddened the faces, and large flies rose and fell from their lips and eyes.

The tide was coming in, so Alex, with great difficulty, propped them upright, over his shoulder, and one by one carried the bodies to the ute where he covered them with a blue tarp against the flies. He scanned the water for a further hour. The calm procession of waves for some reason reviving a fragment of a poem that his father had liked.

Between the sob and clubbing of gunfire
Someone, it seems, has time for this,
To pluck them from the shallows and bury them in
  burrows
And tread the sand upon their nakedness . . .

At 7 a.m. Alex drove back to the house. He left the engine running and Rusty panting on the front seat while he went inside to telephone Sergeant Finter.

The *Mercury* was open on the table and the aroma of bacon filled the kitchen. Merridy had prepared a cooked breakfast on the stove. She must have returned to bed.

He was devouring with his fingers a second warm strap of bacon when Finter answered.

"Pete, it's Alex. I have three bodies in the back of my ute."

The policeman was the only copper on this stretch of coast. He had been up all night and his reaction was not what Alex expected. "Hey, you should have left them where you found them and let us deal with that."

"Then you should have warned me about the effing gale," with a streak of irritation. "Anyway, I'd have needed sandbags."

"Fuck you, mate, nobody told me either."

"That storm, Pete, had the ingredients of a hurricane."

"Well, what I'm being told is that it was too compact and fast-moving for anyone to have predicted." Then, calming down: "Listen, Alex, thanks for finding those bodies. I'll let Emergency Services know."

"What about the boy? He needs to see a doctor."

"Can't you bring him in as well?"

"He's the one who shouldn't be moved. Not till someone's seen him."

"Leave him, he'll be right. I'll speak to Dr Musgrove. In the meantime, get those bodies over here."

Alex waited in case Finter had anything further to say, but he did not.

"How are you doing, Pete?" he asked.

Finter's laugh rattled with exhaustion. "It's a fuck-up, Alex. And if it isn't, I reckon I'll keep my eye on it till you get here."

Half an hour later, Alex drove into Wellington Point. He found the policeman's car outside the hotel, parked behind the community ambulance. He drew up alongside and climbed out and rapped on the window.

Sergeant Finter sat slumped behind the wheel. His head at an angle on his large chest. His badged blue shirt covered with sand.

"Hey, Alex," blinking, and shook his head. "Boy, I needed that."

From far away up the street, faces pressed against Talbot's ground-floor window watched Alex and Finter unload the bodies into the hotel.

They carried the dead men across the lobby to the kitchen, their passage over the carpet leaving a widening trail of seawater. They were bringing in the third and heaviest body when a total stranger ran into Alex.

272

"Hi, Murray," panted Finter. "Hey, have you met Alex Dove?"

"Hi," nodded Alex.

But Murray, a burly man with darting eyes, was in no mood for introductions. "Could you fetch a towel?" he snapped at Debbie who appeared in the lobby at that moment. Then padded after Alex into the kitchen, blenching when he saw the two bodies stretched out on the tiled floor.

"Murray's the new owner," explained Finter, unshouldering the dead man. "He's from near Canberra."

"Congratulations," said Alex.

Tildy's father had died three months previously, since when Ray Grogan had been advertising for a buyer.

In a drained tone, Murray asked Finter: "How long might you want to keep them here?"

"Hard to tell. The captain's got to identify them. Then you've got the coroner, and maybe a pathologist."

"It's not ideal for business, you know."

"No, probably it isn't," agreed Finter.

"How many survived?" asked Alex after Murray had gone to mop up the carpet.

"Seven altogether. With the boy you rescued, eight. They were eleven in total, with these three." Finter studied the bloated, sunburned faces. "Poor bastards. They'd have been better off playing cricket, not going to sea in a fucking brig."

Alex looked down. The skin was starting to peel from a pair of puffed-up lips. "Why did you want them in here?"

"I didn't. Nor did Murray. But Dr Musgrove does. It's the only place with an industrial fridge. The coroner's van isn't due for another few hours and Musgrove's worried about the heat."

"What, you're going to put them in with the wallaby and ice cream?"

Finter laughed. "Who's going to notice? Have you eaten here ever? Anyway, it's up to Musgrove to decide where they go."

"And the survivors?"

"In bed. Where I'd swap this badge to be."

Finter had lodged the captain in a suite in the courtyard; the six remaining crew, who were suffering from hypothermia, in the Louisa Meredith, which was now full. He hunted around for a dishcloth. "Lucky it didn't happen at Easter or I'd be having to unlock the cells," trying to be humorous.

"Have you spoken to the captain?"

"Not yet," wiping the sand from his sleeves. "I was down on Cowrie Beach when he landed in the rowboat. But I need his statement. Ah, that may even be him," at the sound of synthetic birdsong.

Alex followed him into the lobby where Murray was wringing out a towel into a washing-up bowl. "Mind if I listen in?"

Finter stopped. "I don't think so, Alex."

"Come on, Pete."

Finter looked at him and he was no longer a policeman but a boy who used to bowl Alex seamers in the nets behind the school.

"I'd like to hear what happened," Alex persisted.

"That's not the point." Then: "Hell, what am I saying – after what you did last night . . . Actually, I'd be glad of someone with a little nous myself, to help me work out what the fuck happened," and opened the door into the restaurant, setting off a trill of chaffinches. "Jesus fucking Christ, how I abominate that noise."

At a table in the corner, Debbie flustered over the captain, trying to interest him in tea and scones.

274

He had removed his frock coat and sat tightly wrapped in one of the hotel's green blankets, his body shaking like a rope ladder down which feet continued to trample. His expression shambolic and frayed.

"Thanks," he muttered to Debbie. His mind still at the helm of the *Buffalo*.

"You'll be relieved to know we have another survivor."

At the sound of Sergeant Finter's abrasive voice, he jerked his head. A light flickered in the dazed brown eyes. "Oh, yes?" and looked at Alex as though he might be the one.

"This is Alex Dove. He and his wife rescued one of your crew last night. At considerable risk to themselves."

At Finter's urging, Alex described the young man in his spare bedroom.

"That'll be Kish," and nodded to himself. "So he's alive," subsiding ever so slightly into his blanket. He looked like the leftovers of someone.

"Kish?" said the policeman. "How do you spell it?"

"Oh, that's not his real name," the captain said dully. "It's the name he was given. I don't know what his real name is."

In childish capital letters Sergeant Finter wrote KISH. "Like that?" showing the captain. And the troubled look on the policeman's face brought back a memory of Finter in class, sitting at a desk in front, labouring to spell the name of a medieval English king.

"I suppose so."

"I have to be accurate."

"It was a name that was invented," the captain said, moodily. "If you want to know his real name, ask Mrs Wellard."

"Mrs Wellard?"

"She's the one in charge."

"Wellard." Sergeant Finter slowly wrote out the name and looked at it. "Like it sounds?"

"Fucked if I remember," and screwed up his eyes.

The policeman selected a scone and popped it whole into his mouth. "Why don't I take your statement now?" sitting down. "Debbie, if you would – two more cups."

Debbie looked at Alex and left. Already in the street, through the window that she had obscured, small clumps of dog-walkers discussed the drama of the night and every now and then peered out to sea or pointed.

Alex brought his chair closer.

He pieced together the story from the *Mercury* and from Kish and from the captain's statement.

The three dead men were part of a sixteen-week course run by the Bilgola Mission in Sydney for disadvantaged kids. "A shipload of crims," in Finter's estimation. "People not right in the head who didn't know a boat from a banjo. Frankly, it's a sodding marvel any one of them survived."

The idea was to generate self-esteem and responsibility by sending the boys away for a period of outdoor activity. Some rock-climbed, others chose white-water rafting. This year, seven had seized the chance of joining the *Buffalo* on her circumnavigation of Tasmania. The captain had given Mrs Wellard every confidence that he could handle these "hoodlums", mainly from suburban areas around Sydney who were having trouble at home or with the law. He had led similar excursions in the Caribbean with black kids and Cubans. On such trips, generally speaking, everything went well. There was nowhere to escape to; they had to learn to work together, and while it could take several days to understand that they had to rely on each other, the outcome was nearly always positive.

Because the *Buffalo*'s expedition formed part of Tasmania's bicentenary celebrations, the captain made it his project to be as authentic as possible. He had borrowed the idea from the museum at Port Arthur. His crew were to live on board ship as if the previous two centuries had not been. "It was a lark. To get them interested." He provided each boy with a fresh identity and a biography from the convict era. He had dressed them in authentic uniforms from the period. And had issued his crew, as part of their first-day equipment, with a marine rigger's knife – "so if they fell overboard and got tangled up in ropes, they could cut themselves free. 'Just don't use it on each other,' I urged them."

Sailing down from Sydney, he taught them how to tie knots and splice and to shake out the reefs; to learn the difference between a dolphin-striker, a fore topgallant studding-sail and a spanker-peak halyard; and to calculate their position by the stars, even though he had on board a Global Positioning System.

"Otherwise, I was just there to point and shout and scream. You wait a couple of days to see who's agile and put them on the wheel. The difficult ones peel potatoes."

"What about Kish?" Alex interrupted. "What did he do?"

On the subject of Kish's duties, the captain was evasive. "He joined us late."

"Why?"

"That you'll have to ask Mrs Wellard. But he didn't have time to settle in."

"Who was Kish?" Alex suddenly wanted to know.

"What?"

"Who was Kish in your game?"

"Alex, I do think this can wait," Sergeant Finter said. More pressing for him to know were details of the shipwreck, what had happened.

Required to relive the events of the past twelve hours, the captain shrank deeper into his green blanket. In a squashed tone he explained how he had sheltered from the south-easterly on the northern side of Maria Island. Then a change in the wind forced him to look for another anchorage. His crew being inexperienced sailors, he had not dared to send them closer on beam than 90 degrees.

"The storm front hit us at 6 p.m.," and recalled the noise, the big sea breathing, the wind shrieking through the rigging. The wind had come in so hard and sudden that the dragging anchor snapped its fluke. "I just didn't want a knock-down. I ordered the others below, all except Reg—"

"Reg?" cut in Finter. He did not need help in spelling that.

"The skipper's mate. I needed him to secure the boom while I kept at the wheel. I was steering through the breakers with water coming up over the bow at me. The wind was meeting the current and it all went to lumping up the waves."

In a small voice, he described how his mate was swept from the mast, onto the deck.

"Reg was crawling along topside when he hit the jackstay. It ran like a dog on a wire and it snarled his legs as a breaking crest hit the boat and he went out straight over the top of the boom, a perfect dive . . ."

The captain managed to bring the ship around, but as he moved to grab hold of Reg, who had plummeted to the deck, the *Buffalo* dropped into a trough and in the next moment struck the unmarked rock. "That rock – it wasn't on the charts, you know."

After an interval, Finter asked: "Do you suppose you could have done anything differently?"

The captain fixed his eyes on the glass bowl of strawberry

jam. He wished he had cut away the mast when the *Buffalo* first struck, but the axe was in the hold. Otherwise, no, nothing could have been done. The waves were washing fore and aft the deck. It was as much as grown persons could do to hold on. As for Reg: "I did reach him and keep him on board." But his mate had perished in his arms while the ship broke up about them.

"Why didn't you get the kids to shore at the first signs of the storm?"

"If I could have, I would have," shaking his head. He had been twenty-nine years at sea. He had never experienced such a gale. Nor seen a vessel and people in a more dangerous position.

"And they've been in dangerous positions," noted the policeman.

With the captain's assistance, Finter wrote down the names of the six other survivors. He would take their statements later. "And I'd better speak to this woman at the Bilgola Mission. Mrs . . ." flicking back several pages in his notebook.

"Wellard," said the captain.

There was one further duty to perform. Before leaving the hotel, Alex accompanied the captain and Sergeant Finter into the kitchen to identify the drowned men. The two bodies in their nineteenth-century sailor's breeches looked sad and wet on the floor.

Dead seamen, gone in search of the same landfall . . .

"That's him. That's Reg Hull," the captain said, his features buckling at the sight of his mate propped up against the fridge.

They all stared at the face. The lids had started to swell up and close over bulging bloodshot eyes. Finter said to Alex in a contemplative way: "Know who he reminds me of? Cheele. Remember Cheele?"

"Yes," a little surprised to hear the name.

A yard away, a hand trembled out from under the captain's blanket and touched the sunburned, flyblown forehead. "I held him for ten minutes after he was dead. He'd got more brains than you can imagine."

CHAPTER FOUR

No sooner had she cooked Alex's breakfast than Merridy felt exhausted and went back to bed. On waking several hours later, she telephoned her assistant and left a message on his machine. "Could you grade those lanterns? Oh, and Jayce – I won't be coming out."

It was now after ten. Along the corridor, Kish had lapsed back into sleep, sprawled across the bed, snoring. She watched him breathing. From far away she felt something running towards her, and shivered.

She picked out some of Alex's clothes from the wardrobe and laid them on the chair by Kish's bed, and after a while fitted on her gloves and went into the garden to begin the task of clearing the debris.

When he opened his eyes the first thing he saw were the lemony stars on the ceiling. He put on the spectacles that he had left folded on the bedside table and then the white shirt and the pair of green moleskins, and opened the door into the corridor. He peered into the kitchen. A pan with a cold egg on the stove. Newspaper on the table. He looked at the advertisement on the front page and turned a few pages and closed the newspaper. He opened the fridge and looked inside and sniffed and shut it and went over to the sink. He poured himself a mug of water and drank it and then walked back down the corridor into the living room and sat in a chair with his feet stretched out on the dog-basket. The sun shining onto the cockatoo. He stared at himself in the glass.

An hour later, she came upon him in the kitchen. He stood at the Welsh dresser with his back to her. Alex's shirt stretched across his body.

She waited. Then: "How's your head?"

He said nothing. Touching with awe something high up.

Merridy took off her gloves. "I made some bacon and eggs. I can heat them up."

He remained on tiptoe. "What's this?" and held up the shiny black rock.

"A meteorite. Alex's father found it." And Alex's voice came to her: "One of twenty-four million a day that enters the atmosphere."

He replaced it on the shelf. "Alex – he's your husband?"

"Yes."

Still the corner of the dresser attracted his attention. "And that?"

He squinted into the bottle, at the hull of cracked green paint.

"She's called the *Otago*. My husband made her."

"Where is your husband?"

"He went into town."

But it was the ship that interested him. He took off Alex's glasses, wiped them on his shirt and put them back on again. Polishing the lens had not unclouded his eye.

He placed the bottle on the table and gazed into it. He folded his arms and leaned forward and sat there, gazing.

"Insane," he said approvingly.

She skirted past him and heated the pan and served him his plate.

He picked up two straps of bacon, swallowed them.

"You must be hungry," she said.

"I could eat this all in one gobble."

She watched his mouth open and close. "I'm afraid some of your crew – they weren't so lucky," she said after a while.

"You think I'm lucky?" hurling her an abusive look, but it was a pebble that fell short.

"You could have drowned," she pointed out.

"Yes," and laughed.

She tried another tack. "What about your parents?"

"What about them?"

"Don't you want to telephone them? Tell them you're safe."

"No," he said, chewing. "Not especially."

"Do you have brothers, sisters?"

Again, that sawing laugh. "Not that I know of."

He made her feel that her questions were indecent. As if she had asked a man to show her pictures of his mother naked.

Her tiredness dragged at her all of a sudden. "It's all right, Kish. Don't if you don't want," and opened the door to the corridor.

"Hey, Mrs Dove," slyly.

"What?"

"I like your sneakers."

She looked down. She had bought them in Hobart for her forthcoming trip to Melbourne. "Thank you."

Alex arrived home just before noon. He parked the ute the other side of the fallen pine and climbed over the tree and went inside. Merridy was loading the drier with Kish's sodden clothes.

"Where is he?" Alex asked, anxious.

283

"I sent him down to the beach. What are we going to do with him? I don't want him here."

He followed her into the kitchen and watched her squeeze out a dishcloth.

"It's all right. Finter's coming with Dr Musgrove to see him."

"When?" Angry as the cloth that attacked the dresser and tabletop and dabbed at the dried bacon fat. Anywhere he might have touched.

"I don't know. This afternoon."

"It doesn't take all day to drive out here, Alex."

"Love, they've got seven others to attend to." But her anger surprised him.

Late in the afternoon Kish returned to the house, bringing from the beach a twisted piece of tidewood. He went to his room and stretched out on the bed. He flicked open his knife and started to whittle the wood and only gave any sign of life when Merridy knocked on his door to tell him that the doctor was here to see him.

Sergeant Finter waited with Alex and Merridy in the living room while Dr Musgrove examined Kish.

"Where will he go?" Merridy wanted to know.

"A woman's coming from the Bilgola Mission," Finter said vaguely. "She'll be here Friday." He was a little over-whelmed. Nothing like this had ever happened in Wellington Point. Nothing remotely like it.

"Not till Friday?"

Alex said: "I'm sure he can stay here. If push comes to shove."

But Finter had registered Merridy's face. "No, no. He'll need to be in touch with his probation officer."

"Where is his probation officer?"

"In Hobart – for a check-up."

"Is he seriously injured?"

"I haven't a clue, but it does mean there's no one to look after Kish."

"Shouldn't he be with his mates?" Merridy said.

"The problem is," said Finter thickly, "the hotel's full."

"Full?" Alex did not believe it.

"I had to reserve rooms for the coroner and his clerk. Plus the dive squad." Four divers were driving up to survey and assess the wreck, whether it was a hazard to navigation.

"Surely, they can squeeze in one more person," said Merridy.

"The press have taken every other bed. I should have moved sooner." Finter thought. "Maybe I could try the Malvern."

"Please do," said Merridy, and pointed to the telephone.

Finter dialled the Malvern, but the bed & breakfast, too, had stopped taking bookings. The owner suggested Tasman Cottages. No vacancies there, either.

"He might have to go in the cells after all," Finter said. Wanly, he explained to Merridy: "I was joking to Alex a little while back that if it was Easter I'd have to open up the cells."

Merridy nodded.

At last, a room was found at the Oyster Bay guest house in Swansea. But it would not be free until the morning.

So did Merridy accept the inevitable. "I suppose we *could* look after him for another night."

A knock, and now Dr Musgrove entered. Slightly concerned about the bump on Kish's forehead – it would need watching. Otherwise, his patient seemed as well as could be expected under the circumstances.

Confused by lack of sleep, Sergeant Finter flipped open his notebook. "My turn."

Kish remained seated at the kitchen table after the visitors had left. He got out his knife and flipped it open and started assaulting the stump of driftwood.

Merridy leaned, arms crossed, against the dresser while Alex explained: "A room has been reserved for you from tomorrow in Swansea."

Kish did not look up, but twisted his head as if reacting to some buzzing or twittering that only he could hear.

"Swansea's just across the bay," Alex said.

Kish scraped a sliver onto the floor. Sullenly, he said: "I'd rather stay here." Which surprised them. "Maybe I could sweep up some leaves."

"Leaves?" said Merridy.

"Why not?" asked Alex.

"You heard what Sergeant Finter said. It's not suitable—"

Kish stabbed his knife into the table.

"Hey, don't do that!" Merridy leaped forward. She seized the knife and snapped shut the blade. "I'm taking this away," and marched out of the kitchen, down the corridor, not knowing where she was going, where to hide the weapon.

Kish looked at her when she came back in, but said nothing. Rusty's head on his lap and his index finger caressing the length of her puppy's muzzle, from the nose to between the eyes, back and forth.

She cupped her hand and swept the shavings into it and dropped them in the bin under the sink. It was clear to her: Kish's good points had died in him some while ago.

"Here, Rusty."

At dinner, he ate with his mouth open. She wanted to smack him. It was a face that was made to look the other way, not like Alex's. The violence of her reaction, what she felt, shocked her. She did not like the way that Rusty had attached himself to Kish.

"What do you think he did?" she asked Alex later in bed.

"No idea. It's like adoption, the same procedure. They don't let you know the sin any more than they tell you the father or mother." And she wondered how he knew.

"That knife will have something to do with it," she said. "I bet you it does."

"He's only had it since he joined the ship," Alex pointed out.

"I wonder if he's quite right in the head?" remembering the way he had batted away something invisible. A gesture – thinking of her mother – that was the prerogative of the insane.

Alex swallowed two Nurofen and switched off his bedside light. "He's probably no different to any of these kids from halfway houses. He goes into pubs and has fights and works things out, and one time he gets caught." He did not tell her about the captain's uncomfortable reaction. Nor about his conversation with Finter as he saw the policeman to his car.

Finter had said: "You'll keep your eye on him, Alex? Strictly speaking, he shouldn't be staying here 'without supervision'. Those were the words. But everything's gone to buggery."

"Then find somewhere else for him to go."

"At any rate, the probation officer has promised to come out to see Kish once the hospital release him, which should be any minute."

"Did you find out what he'd done to be on that boat?"

"He doesn't have a record, if that's what Merridy's doing her melon about."

"Why was he late joining the *Buffalo*?"

"I don't know that, Alex," rubbing his eyes. "He didn't tell me. Nor did I get anything out of the Wellard woman. That was the excuse – that they wanted to help him – but I don't know what went on and I don't want to know either. Right now, I just want to catch a few zeds."

That night Merridy lay awake. She felt a heightened alertness since Kish's arrival. He was hard to understand, but he seemed to express something that she could not articulate. Sitting next to him at dinner, she had felt out of breath.

Beside her, also awake, his thoughts inflamed by the Nurofen, Alex indulged himself. The idea was ridiculous, but supposing just for a moment that this man – this Kish – was who he said he was . . . what could Alex tell him that had been learned by men and women over the last two hundred years?

In the room across the corridor, a light was still on. Kish had taken off his borrowed shirt and lay on the bed. He was looking at Merridy's drawing of a sieve and remembering something.

Alex rose later than normal. He ate his three pieces of toast and went outside to start sawing up the tree that blocked the drive. A moment later, he was back.

"Chainsaw's out of fuel, I'll have to go to Swansea hardware," collecting the keys to the ute. "Is he up?"

"No."

"Darling . . ."

She saw his concern and was touched. "I'll be fine. And Alex – I don't see why he can't stay on here. He's spent two nights already. It's only till Friday."

He tossed the keys in the air and caught them. "I'll tell Finter, then."

She watched his ute disappear behind the tree and was wondering what to do about Kish when the telephone rang. Jason, speaking from the boathouse. He had got her message and had graded the oysters. He had also been down on the beach, collecting the remains of oyster trays that the wild weather had broken apart. But he was calling for another reason. A mate had been in touch who worked for Les Gatenby. "He says they've started spawning."

"When?"

"Last week."

Merridy swore. "That's early." She had been hoping that St Helen's would not spawn at least for another fortnight, until after her trip to Melbourne. But if the water temperature and conditions were right anything was possible.

"Do you want a holiday?" without thinking. It would be two or three months at least before her oysters were back in condition and she could resume selling them to Dmitri. It was a phenomenon that she had mentioned before to Alex: "Once St Helen's goes, it's a rule of thumb that within ten days the jellyfish start turning up in Oyster Bay – and bang, we're gone."

Jason laughed. "Since you ask, I wouldn't mind going up to Flinders." And she remembered a girl at the Taste of Tasmania, a singer in a band from Lady Barron. His utter excitement.

"OK. Take the next fortnight off. You'll love Flinders."

"I didn't know you'd been."

"On my honeymoon, Jayce."

Preoccupied, she returned to her bedroom, where she found Kish.

"Get back from there!"

He stepped away from the wardrobe, Alex's shirt undone on him and pleated from being too big. His eyes alarmed at the fury in her voice.

He touched his earring. "I . . . I was looking for a shower," without conviction.

"Down there," sounding just like her mother.

But instead of reacting to her imperious voice, he walked over to the wardrobe and looked inside.

"Hey, what's wrong with the door?"

"It's always been like that."

She would have told her husband anything, had he asked. Even about the chandler. But he never asked.

"You should get it fixed," Kish said, and poked his fingers through the hollow heart, the cross.

It was uncanny. Dressed in Alex's glasses and clothes, he gave her the distinct impression that he was Alex, only younger. She was looking back through her husband's eyes to a parallel time where what was dead lived.

"Maybe I could fix it."

"Out!"

Still, he lingered. His gaze locked on the wardrobe at which he stared long and hard. Until some inkling of obedience led him in the direction of her pointing hand and into the corridor.

She left the door to her study ajar so that she could monitor him taking his shower. Any other day, she might have driven to the oyster shed. But she was not prepared to leave Kish alone in the house. Friday stretched too far away.

It therefore dumbfounded her to see the transformation

in the young man who emerged from the spare bathroom. His shirt buttoned and his blond hair brushed back. Lean and narrow-shouldered – with his chipped teeth concealed behind tight-drawn lips – he had the look and smell of a clean, oiled knife.

"Wait here," she relented, and went into her bedroom. She retrieved it from its hiding place and returned to where she had left him standing beside her desk, and gave it back to him.

He opened and closed the blade. He believed in his knife quite fiercely, she could tell. It was his crucifix.

Satisfied, he slipped it into his hip pocket.

She followed him down the corridor to the kitchen.

Restless, he opened the fridge and took out a carton of milk and sniffed it. He put it back and rummaged some more.

"What are these?"

"Oysters." Then: "I grow them."

He looked interested. "You grow scallops too?"

"No."

"Oh," disappointed. He picked one up and studied it. "Get pearls from these?"

"Unfortunately not. Different oyster and warmer water. These are for eating." She shut the fridge door. "Have you eaten them ever?"

"Course I have."

He took out his knife and started to open the one in his hand and all but ripped his thumb.

She showed him how. "Stab it vertically at the end, then work the blade back under the muscle."

He studied the watery grey flesh streaked with black.

"Try it," she urged.

He looked reluctant.

"Go on."

With great caution, he raised it to his lips.

Then spat into the sink.

"Your first one?" amused.

"Course not. But the other was nicer."

"Oh, you won't get nicer than these." Her eyes sparkled. "Our oysters are so good, you get a stiff neck when you eat them."

"Is that all, Mrs Dove?" he said. "Then I'd be pretty right as an oyster farmer. I'd be like walking around with a horn all the time."

She ignored the look that had come into his face, but he was not to be put off. "Aren't oysters supposed to be good for you or something?"

"They have amino acids that you won't find in other foods," in a neutral voice.

For something to do, she opened the cupboard and took out the bread-maker. But even as she prepared ingredients, Merridy was conscious of the watchful eyes behind her husband's spectacles.

Presently, a regular rasping sound made her turn. Kish sat facing her. He was honing his stump of wood and had made a point of creating out of the shavings a neat pile on the table.

"What are you making?"

He twisted his head, and once again Merridy had the idea that he was responding to a noise audible only to him.

"What are you making?" she repeated.

"Nothing," he said, and investigated the thin scrap of driftwood that he had pared down to an entrail.

There was something unplumbable about this young man. At the same time she recognised in his face some sign unknown to Alex, belonging to a sect of which only they were initiates, and it did not make her comfortable. She stepped closer. "Show me."

He held up the fragile length of sassafras for her to see, and snapped it.

Minutes later, Rusty burst into the kitchen, followed by Alex, who scattered onto the table the *Mercury* and a bundle of post. And a black bin liner stuffed with something.

He pushed it towards Kish.

Kish glared over his cup at the bag, suspicious.

"Clothes for you." And to Merridy: "I bumped into Agnes."

Kish showed no desire to inspect this donation from the Op-Shop.

Alex turned to him. "It's probably just as well you're up here. You can't budge in town for journalists and photographers." And when Kish did not say anything: "I spoke to Sergeant Finter. He's put in a request to the Bilgola Mission that you stay here till Mrs Wellard comes on Friday. If we don't hear back by this afternoon, we'll assume it's OK."

Merridy smiled; it seemed the best thing to do. "That's settled then." She held up the pot. "I've just made a brew. Want some?"

"Give me half a cup," Alex said.

"If you don't draw it a bit more, it'll be like possum piss," Kish scowled, and went on stroking Rusty whose head had popped up from under the table.

"Sleep well?" Alex asked benevolently.

"I suppose."

"How are you feeling?"

"All right."

"Want to make yourself useful?"

"How?"

"Come and help me cut up that tree."

"No," Kish said, and picked up a magazine that he had noticed in among the bundle.

"What, it's only leaves you sweep?"

Kish opened the magazine.

Alex exchanged glances with his wife. He accepted the cup from her. "I'll be on the lawn. Come on, Rusty."

Outside, the jaded growl of Alex's chainsaw.

Merridy unfolded the *Mercury*. The front page devoted to the disaster at sea.

Sitting opposite, Kish flicked through the pages of *Bottleship*, the magazine of the European Association of Ships in Bottles.

Why Alex had not cancelled the subscription, Merridy could not fathom. He never looked at it. The only journal he liked to read was the *Wilderness*.

Kish pushed back the magazine as though it might be one of her mother's Methodist tracts.

"Mrs Dove?"

"Yes?"

"Come on, the truth. How do you get it in there?"

"What?" She tore herself from the photographs of the *Buffalo* floating raft-like beneath the water.

"That coin," and swivelled back in his chair, pointing his knife at the bottle on the dresser.

So that was it.

"Oh, that. You'll have to ask Alex."

He observed her with his hard, white inscrutable eyes. "It's against the natural law of things."

"You'll find a lot of things are like that. Especially in Tasmania." As Harry Ford once told her: "We're too far out of reach here to be touched by any God or man-made laws, or even scientific ones." She said to Kish: "In Tasmania, everyone is left to be as idiotic as they please."

"But you know, don't you?"

"I might."

"Then tell me."

"No."

"Why not?"

"Because I promised," she flared.

"Is that all?"

She studied him over the top of the *Mercury*. "First," she said, "you tell me what you did to be on this boat."

He met her stare. "And then you'll tell me?"

"No."

Merridy had the distinct idea that Alex had once explained it to her. Too many years had gone by for her to confess that she had forgotten.

Behind their lenses, Kish's eyes had a tarnished, brash look, and there were dark specks under them like burned spots on a pan. He reminded her of someone, but no longer Alex.

"I could tell you and you'd go white sitting there. You don't want to know, Mrs Dove."

But she did. "What did you do, Kish?"

He gave her an aggressive single-fingered salute and stood.

"Catch yez later," and slammed the door.

Shaken, Merridy flicked through the *Mercury*. "*Is your memory a sieve?*" The same bland-looking man in a suit stared out, his black-and-white features unchanged over almost two decades. Next to the advertisement, a study on earthquakes. Men's greatest fear was to be thrown up in the air, women's to be gobbled up by the earth. And all of a sudden a bank of sandy soil stretched out on her inner eye, covered in roots and dried-out leaves, and a hole smelling of must, darker than any wardrobe.

She stood unsteadily and poured herself a glass of water. Again, she was conscious of the silent windmill. It was the constant wind that made her feel silly. You never realised how much it irritated till it stopped. But the noise of the chainsaw had ceased as well. The only sound, the grind and groan of the bread-maker.

On the lawn she saw him talking to Alex.

Her husband had put down the chainsaw and removed his earplugs. He gestured at the fallen pine, the thick trunk that he was cutting into neat slices. Behind them, Rusty had found an interesting smell in the foliage.

Kish sank on his haunches and tentatively reached out a hand to touch the single eyeball of exposed wood. Alex squatted next to him, explaining something, and Kish listened, running his hand up and down over the white surface. He appeared to make a request.

Alex nodded and started up the chainsaw.

"What were you two talking about?" she asked him later.

Alex told her. "There was a lovely, rare treecreeper caught in the branches. I couldn't resist showing it to him. Know what he said? 'That may make your life, Mr Dove, but what I like is a police siren.' Then in the next breath he was asking questions about the tree – why it was called an Oyster Bay pine, whether it grows in groves."

"And does it?" She was so accustomed to the lone pine that she had never bothered to ask.

"Well, you don't often see one independent like this, or so bushy. Normally, they grow up in preference to branching out."

She pondered this. "You cut him a piece, I saw."

"He asked for something to hew." Then, with a boyish conspiratorial smile: "I have an idea that he wants to make a ship."

After dinner, Alex took down the dusty rum bottle covered with dried wasp wings and spiders' droppings that once had contained his horizon.

Childlike, all aggression fled, Kish sat rapt by the fire in the living room as Alex explained how he had crafted the *Otago*. And Merridy, reading the novel that she had put down weeks before, overheard them. Her husband remembering his passion; the young man bombarding him with questions.

"All sailing ships go out of the bottle. See? This is sailing in."

"Why is it sailing in?"

In case Merridy had refused him. But had he ever told her? He looked over at his wife. "Just to be different," he said fondly.

"Did you design it?"

"It was built from a half-mould, so no original plans. I had to draw them and blow them up and cut them to shape."

"What do you make the sails from?"

"Cotton japara, stiffened with water."

"What tools do you use?"

"This pair of tweezers is all I need. You touch them to the neck of the bottle to stop your hand shaking, then put in the sail."

"What's the sea made of?"

"My father used putty. I prefer children's blue plasticine."

"And the deck?"

"Ice-cream sticks. Just like the bowsprit."

"You're kidding!"

"I'm not. Am I, love?"

"No, he isn't," said Merridy from her chair across the room. Years ago she had had the same conversation, asked the same question.

"Ice-cream sticks," repeated Kish, and brought his face closer. "Jeez, man."

And the pleasure in his eyes transported Alex back further than a drizzly day in a playground to a period before he met Merridy. It's absurd, he thought. A man spends his first forty years trying to escape childhood; his next forty, trying to retrieve it. We grow up, only to want to become children.

"What about the coin, Mr Dove?" The intensity of Kish's question made Merridy look up.

Alex put down the bottle. "That's just something my father found. So much rubbish we use as model builders. You need to be original, you need to be different. Not like Johnny-round-the-corner."

That night she lay curled on her side, legs tucked under, asleep, when she became aware of a pressure on her heel. Alex had it in his palm. In his touch she felt the heat of his desire. He followed the line of her leg up, tracking her, almost like a doctor, following the lineaments, making sure everything was there. When she stirred, he moved his hand to her knee, squeezing it, and there was a safety in that and in the weight of his arm on the outside of her thigh. He rested his chin on her hip and then moved up and pressed her shoulder in the same way, emphasising it. He might have been looking for all the ways to fit himself around her, to find her contours. He cupped her ear and held her forehead with his other palm as if to silence the silence. Barely moving, they slipped together under water. Not wishing to make any sound that Kish would hear. Only when needing to taste his breath she turned and rose above him, thighs, breasts, hair, and caused him at last to shudder, hurting – as though a heel pressed into his heart. While she could have been straddling some bowsprit that he had made for her, rising and falling through the phosphorescent waves. Until she floated.

In the morning, Alex had to leave early to meet his agent in Launceston.

"I ought to ring Finter," he said. "I don't know why the probation officer hasn't been in touch."

"Go. I'll be fine."

"You've got his number. Maybe you could call him?"

"Alex. I'll be fine."

She found Kish lying, legs crossed, on his bed, whittling his piece of pine. He wore a blue-and-white striped shirt from the Op-Shop, an oversized grey cable-knit jersey and a pair of faded brown corduroys the colour of dried figs. Merridy caught the frowsy aroma of dead skin and old wool and too much soap. She had preferred it when he smelled of the sea.

In a voice that she tried to keep vague, she asked: "Why is it called an Oyster Bay pine?"

He laughed. "You don't know?"

She blushed to be caught out. She would know if she had grown up on this coast and not in Ulverstone. He was always catching her out. "Of course, I do."

He went on honing.

"Are you making a ship?" It had upset her when Kish

snapped his piece of driftwood. The audacity of his look had made her shudder. She said: "Haven't you had enough of ships?"

He ignored her needling tone. "You have to wait for the wood to tell you what to do with it. That's what Mr Dove says. I'm waiting for it to tell me."

"Well, until it does," she said tartly, "maybe you'd like to help out on a real boat."

A day cooped up in the house and she fretted to be back on the *Zemmery Fidd*.

It was Alex's idea for Kish to join her. Before her husband set off for Launceston she had shared with him her concerns for the fate of her oysters. "I ought to check the lanterns. The storm might have damaged them. But who can I get to help?"

"Why, what's happened to Jason?"

"I've just given him a fortnight off. I can't ring and say I didn't mean it. Anyway, he's gone to Flinders with a girl he's crazy about."

"Take Kish, why not?"

The idea had not crossed her mind. "Kish? Would that be allowed?"

"I don't see anyone rushing to stop you. Until that probation officer turns up, I reckon we can do what we like."

"But won't Kish be terrified?"

"He can always say no. And what else is he going to do until Friday? You could try asking him to repair the Hill's Hoist. But I tell you, he's not going to help me take out that tree unless I'm standing right behind him with a chainsaw in his back."

Against Merridy's every expectation Kish accepted her

offer. "OK, Mrs Dove, if you want a hand, I'll give you a hand," and folded away his knife.

Once inside the shed, she fitted him with the orange life jacket that normally Alex wore. For someone who had all but drowned in the bay two days earlier, Kish showed remarkably little apprehension about returning to sea.

"We'll take these lanterns," she pointed. "I'll start the crane, you loop them onto the hook and I'll raise them onto the deck."

The scallop lanterns were stacked adjacent to a large metal perforated tube, through which Kish poked a finger. "What's this for?"

"Do you really want to know?" He was always poking fingers.

"I asked, didn't I?"

The answer shamed her. "That's the rotary grader. It knocks their shells about and stresses them. They think: 'Oh, God, I'm dying, I need to sort myself out.' It makes them concentrate on the inside."

Kish ran his hand over the perforations. He had revealed the same interest in Alex's bottles.

She added: "We call it the wheel of fortune, because it's fortuitous if they survive."

If Merridy feared that her talk would bore him, she was mistaken: his curiosity had only sharpened.

She undid the stitching and plucked an oyster from the lantern. Very well, if he wanted a lesson . . . She indicated the ridges on the shell. "Oysters get handled about ten times in their lives. That's ten shocks. Each touching leaves a stress mark like a tree."

"Why would you want to shock an oyster?"

"Shock is good for them. Gets them working, stops them

301

being lazy, wakes them up. Otherwise, they just grow their shells to be beautiful, but their insides go yukky."

"What does yukky look like?"

"Not much, thin and grey. Here, let me show you."

She opened a couple of oysters until she found one with the telltale watery flesh. She handed it to him. "This one's lazy, needs a bit of a shock."

Kish lifted up the oyster until it was level with his spectacles. "Boo!" he yelled. Then ate it.

Soon the *Zemmery Fidd* was banging out towards the mouth of the Swan. Kish sat in the stern, between the two engines, and looked with a baleful expression at the white breakers curling along the far side of the sandbar.

He nodded at the engines and muttered something.

"What?" Tense, she leaned towards him.

"That's a lot of grunt."

"Seen a Suzuki Ingus on the road?" she shouted. "One of them is one of those."

The boat slammed over the sandbar and twisted into the breakers. Then they were through.

Beyond, the sea stretched calm and windless and it was impossible to conceive that this tranquil plain was where the *Buffalo* had splintered apart. Maria Island sat like a hat on the horizon and a sulphur-crested cockatoo flapped alone through the warm blue sky.

Kish lapsed into silence.

"Better than lying on your back," she shouted, and opened the throttle.

She steered west, parallel with Dolphin Sands towards Wellington Point. The water so clear that she could gaze all the way down to the sandy bed. Ahead, she kept her eye out for the orange buoys that supported her lines.

But something was wrong with the sea.

"Hey!" Kish tapped her shoulder. He had sprung to his feet. An expression of wonder in his face.

She looked around. And suddenly there was no end to the whiteness in which they floated.

Kish leaped forward and gripped the bow-rail, leaning over. "It's like something's burning underwater," excited.

Merridy cut the engine and stared into the white cloud that was the colour and consistency of moonlit fog. Mirages enveloped her. Sea-green faces and sky-blue hands. She tried to pull her eyes away, but an inexpressible longing tugged at her. A vertigo that made her want to jump into the water and dive down, down into the centre of this awful whiteness. Then it dawned. "The oysters are spawning."

"It's like snot," Kish had decided.

In a distant voice, she heard herself say: "It's no different to when coral releases its seeds, or a squid lets go its ink. The same deal. Except white."

Still, it bewildered him. "What is it, actually?"

"Eggs mainly, plus some gonad."

"Gonad?"

"Sperm."

The word carved a raw gap in the air. She burbled on to plug it. "Like everything else, they're born to spawn. Their whole life, they're looking to cast their germ-cells into the water. There may be more living creatures in that cloud than there are human beings on the face of the earth."

Kish peered into the white water and his eyes struggled to penetrate the cloud that could contain so much life. The cocky leer had vanished from his expression. He had a child's thoughtful clear face. A child who listens to everything, sees everything.

"How long do they spawn for?" in a fascinated tone.

"What we're seeing will only last an hour. After this

303

they'll be unsellable for three months. They go without telling you. Don't even leave a note on the fridge."

What Merridy knew of the phenomenon she had learned from Les Gatenby, who had witnessed it once in the shallows off Bruny. But she had never seen it for herself until now. Perhaps the storm was responsible.

She was content to let the boat drift. The only sound the gentle slop against the hull. Even so, she flinched from the whiteness. The sea that was blinding her.

Kish remained at the bow-rail, looking over the side of the boat, his back to her so that she was unable to make out his expression. Every now and then he expelled a moan, like a child calling out to itself in its sleep. She pretended not to notice, but she could not help what she felt: a strange and intensely painful sensation, not to be compared with anything she had experienced. His stance so like her brother when he looked over the deck that it produced the illusion of Kish being the same person. It seemed to her, at that moment, as if Hector had not died and was standing in front of her, staring over the edge.

"Can you eat them?" he asked.

She retrieved the answer from somewhere. "The French like them, apparently, but no one in Australia will touch them."

He came back and joined her behind the windscreen. "And those eggs" – he might have been waving at all the men, women, children who ever lived – "what happens to them now?"

Hastily, she started the engine. "Let me tell you something interesting about oysters," clinging to the lesson that she had resolved to give him. She knew it by heart.

"In the normal course of events, the egg will spend the next few days trying to get it together with a sperm.

Once fertilised, it's called an eye larva. It has one eye and a foot and wanders around for up to three weeks until with its little eye it sees something that it can settle on, like a rock. Then this foot attaches itself to the rock and puts a secretion around the side of it like Super Glue, and for ever after it is attached to that rock. The foot and eye disappear and it changes completely from a free-floating creature to a fixed, sedentary critter. It changes anatomy end to end."

Kish was still listening. As if he had never wanted to know anything so much.

"They trick them in the hatchery," she went on. "They put down ground scallop shell, and the eye larva settles on an individual microscopic piece thinking it's settled on a rock. But out here the process is interrupted. Something stops the larva, so it doesn't get to settling. I don't know what happens. A combination of the wind and grazing. Like everything else in the sea, something's eating something. And in Oyster Bay something's eating an awful lot of larvae – probably zoo plankton that floats on the surface and scoffs them down at a fantastic rate."

She wondered if she had lost him, but he was still there. "Hanging onto your every word," as Tildy used to say of Randal Twelvetrees.

"Something else I'll tell you about oysters. They change sex."

"No!"

"It's true. When I buy them as two-millimetre seedlings they're fifty-fifty male and female. But after eighteen months, there are twenty-three females to each male. The males have converted straight across to female."

"You mean, like Sydney boys at Mardi Gras?"

Merridy burst out laughing. "If you like."

She returned her gaze to the sea, but the cloud had dissolved and the water was almost clear again.

Over to starboard on the western side of the oyster lease Kish had spotted something. "Hey, Mrs Dove, what are those people doing?"

"People?" What was he on about?

Kish flattened his hand against the sun. "Over there – those heads."

Her initial thought: It's a flock of gannets sitting around. Only as the *Zemmery Fidd* motored close did she realise the extent of the carnage. So taken up by the white sea and her lesson to Kish that she had failed to notice the mess of orange floats bunched together on the perimeter line.

"They're not heads," slowly. Rather, evidence that her oyster farm was not unscathed after all. "Stand here, Kish. When I hold up my hand, put this into neutral."

Kish took her place behind the wheel. She picked up a grappling hook and moved to the bow-rail.

Far below, a hideous tangle of rope, buoy and lantern.

It would take a day or two fully to understand what had happened. The storm that had sunk the *Buffalo* had ripped one of Merridy's polypropylene lines from its anchor and swung it south to north, enmeshing all its lanterns around the neighbouring six lines. They criss-crossed in every direction, the web of an aquatic spider.

Merridy hooked what resembled a coffin suspended below the surface and winched it up, the lantern suddenly shrinking as it emerged from the sea.

She made a rapid calculation. "We've got three thousand dozen oysters down there."

"What do you want to do?"

"We'll have to load the lanterns into the boat and transfer them to another line and put them straight back down."

"How long will that take?"

"Three or four full days – of good weather, too."

"Then we'd better not hang around, Mrs Dove. I leave tomorrow, remember?"

They worked until sunset. Tucked behind the windscreen on a plastic-covered clipboard was the mud-map, marking one hundred and thirty-three lanterns on the line. They picked up the easiest, until what they were doing made sense.

Each time she saw a lantern she raised her hand.

"Now reverse. Enough! Got him." And with the grappling hook scooped the line expertly from the water, hitching it over the Kabuki roller.

In this way, they raised and relocated thirty lanterns. They paused once, to refuel from the emergency tank on board.

It was shortly after six o'clock when Merridy cupped a hand into the sea and splashed the sweat from her face. "OK, Kish, let's call it a day."

She replaced the mud-map behind the windscreen and steered the *Zemmery Fidd* towards the river mouth. A hundred lanterns still to untangle. And tomorrow Kish was leaving.

In bed that night, Alex said to her: "Have you noticed a change in him?"

"Not really." Why she did not tell the truth, it was difficult to say.

"You know his course is supposed to last another three months?"

"How does that concern us?"

"I don't think he wants to go back."

She sat bolt upright. "He must. We're not probation officers!"

"He could help finish sorting out your lines. And I could use him on the farm. Anyway, it's not up to us."

Separated from them by the corridor of samplers, Kish lay on his bed with an illustrated book of verse. He had discovered it on the top shelf. He flicked through the pages, looking at the drawings, and when he came to the end he turned out the light and stared at the luminous stars on the ceiling.

CHAPTER FIVE

LATE ON FRIDAY AFTERNOON, a raspberry Hyundai with an Avis sticker on the windscreen advanced hesitantly up the drive and parked at the second attempt. A slender woman with a dumpy face climbed out. She stood and moved her eyes over the ruined lawn, the fallen tree and the figure of Kish on the edge of the grass, spading earth around the base of a clothes-line.

Kish had spent all day with Merridy on the *Zemmery Fidd*. They had been back at the house less than an hour. Before he left Moulting Lagoon Farm for good, he had promised her that he would mend the Hill's Hoist.

Mrs Wellard had flown down from Sydney. In fact, she had been on holiday in Cairns when she heard the news of the shipwreck. She was accompanied by the probation officer who had been on board. He had survived with nothing more serious than a bruised ankle.

Through the kitchen window, Merridy saw them ordering Kish to get ready.

While Kish went to his bedroom, Merridy brought the visitors tea in the living room. The door into the corridor was open and she overheard the man speak in a rough whisper. He was talking about Kish.

"Didn't I warn you? Sheepish as a first-timer."

"I didn't notice."

"I did. I tell you, Mrs Wellard, he's cunning, he's innocent, he's scum. The judge was wrong."

"We don't know if it was him or someone else. Maybe it was the one who drowned?"

"Believe you me, he sent in the razor gangs, cut, cut, cut, no apprentices – though I have to say he did like the sheilas. In Sydney, he was shoving everything."

"Shoving? Say that again, Ricky. I don't recognise the term."

"Local dialect, Mrs Wellard, that's what it is. A wonder he didn't wear his pecker out."

"What do you want me to do, ask him if he screws around? I'm not going to do that, it's a leading question—"

"I hope you don't mind Bushells," Merridy broke in cheerily, nudging open the door with the tray.

She had left the window open; the collar blew up around the man's neck.

"Nothing wrong with Bushells," he said, watching her put the tray down. "Nothing at all."

She pulled Rusty's basket away from the sofa and went to close the window latch. "I'm sorry if it's stuffy. We tend to use this room only in winter. In summer, we keep the dog in here."

The woman sat back as Merridy poured the tea. "A dreadful tragedy," she kept saying. She had plucked at the phrase so often over the past four days that her words sounded loose and twangy. She was called Annette. Her breasts had nudged together like croquet balls under her green wool trouser suit. In Sydney, they had warned that Tasmania would be cold. "But he's as well as could be hoped. Didn't you think so, Ricky?"

"Oh, he seemed fine."

Gangell was the probation officer's name. He was unpleasant and young and had a lean face that emphasised his brown eyes and sharp nose. He looked like a possum.

"We've been expecting you for the last two days, Mr Gangell," Merridy rebuked him.

He shifted uncomfortably, stretching out a leg. "Yes, well, there have been some crossed wires."

It fell to Mrs Wellard to explain. "You see, we were given to understand that a colleague from Child Welfare would be standing in for Ricky."

"I don't know what the trouble was," Merridy said. "I rather think he was waiting for you to contact him. Or maybe it was us. But, yes, it's all been rather chaotic. As you may imagine."

"I hope this hasn't put you out," said Mrs Wellard, "having Kish staying."

"Oh, no. Not at all."

"I was in Hobart for tests," Gangell piped up moodily.

"Nothing serious, I hope."

"Not so far. Not so far."

"How long have you been a probation officer, Mr Gangell?" Merridy asked politely. As anxious to put off the subject of Kish.

"Five years." Before that he had trained as a psychiatric nurse at a remand centre in Brisbane. Screening inmates for suicide risk.

"That must have been hard."

Gangell's palpable relief to be alive made him talkative. "We assessed them, but they got wise to telling us what we wanted to know. 'Oh, I'm cruising, seven out of ten.' Then they killed themselves." Three men had done so, apparently, who had spoken their last words to Gangell. He evinced a horror of being summoned to a coroner's court. "I'd book a ticket to Norway!" In Gangell's hardened opinion the men had been on speed. "Even in the straits they'd find drugs to be on."

"Straits?" said Merridy, and wondered what on earth people in Gangell's charge might be doing in Bass Strait.

"Straitjacket," Gangell explained, accepting a biscuit.

He sat back and bit into it, looking above the fireplace at the Lear lithograph. "Is it me or is something wrong with that parrot?"

"I think it's you, Ricky," said Mrs Wellard quickly.

She put down her cup. She could not stop thinking of the dreadful tragedy. "So awful about those boys . . ." Her bony hands were agitated and her face was the colour of bread mix. Unlike Gangell, she was eager to convey to Merridy just how much the young men had looked forward to their expedition on the *Buffalo*.

"They were terribly excited about the characters they were going to be. You should have seen them rehearsing!"

"It's Reg I feel sorry for," said Gangell. "He used to give me a turn at the wheel. 'Come on, Ricky, why don't you have a go?' He was anxious for everyone to be a part of it. 'Hey, boy, want to take this? Come on, lend a hand here.' If a slack-arse, he'd kick his arse. And there were some slack-arses."

"Really?" said Merridy.

"Oh, yeah. Redfern Aborigines. Rich kids from Bilgola. Some quite savage – knifings and car thefts, all that hoonery." And chewed his biscuit.

"And Kish," Mrs Wellard said at last, picking puppy hair off her green wool knee. "How have you found Kish, Mrs Dove?"

"He was strange to begin with, but he's become friendlier."

"He does find it hard, sometimes, to mix."

"I don't know, he seems to like it here, on the farm."

"Oh, one can never be sure what they like," Gangell said with a grimace. In stretching out his leg he had hit his bad ankle against the dog-basket.

"My husband tells me that Kish is not his real name."

Gangell flashed a significant look at Mrs Wellard. "It's a policy we have."

"I gather he was late in joining the boat."

"That is the case, yes," nodded Gangell, attacking a second biscuit.

"Is it too much to ask what he's done?" This short-sighted knifer.

Gangell looked for a fleeting moment as though nothing would give him greater pleasure than to be able to divulge this to Merridy, but before he could speak Mrs Wellard intervened. A professional tone had returned to her voice. "You will, I am sure, appreciate that we are not at liberty to say."

"Oh," said Merridy, and found herself gazing at the cockatoo. "Then I suppose you're here to take him back?"

Mrs Wellard rocked forward. Her long arms crossed like mallets against her chest. "We are right now in the process of sorting things out. If I may be absolutely truthful with you, Mrs Dove, the whole thing has been rather diffi-cult. You see, the *Buffalo* wasn't expected home for another three months. Most of our regular staff are on leave and it's taking time to organise. None of us could have foreseen such a dreadful . . ."

All at once the painted bird was ruffling its feathers. Merridy turned and looked at Mrs Wellard. "You mean, it might be more convenient if he stayed here?"

On the sofa the thin woman with the fat face blathered on. "That wouldn't be legal. There'd be a lot of admin-istration. You see, when he's not at the Mission he ought to be under supervision."

"*Would* it help if Kish stayed here?"

Mrs Wellard looked at Gangell. "Funnily enough, we were talking about that, weren't we, Ricky?"

"It would not be regular," shaking his head. "For one

thing, Mrs Dove, you're not a qualified handler, and Kish, as I ought to make clear, is someone who very much needs careful handling. Anyway, I doubt if he'd want to—"

"Ask him," Merridy interrupted reasonably. "We don't mind looking after him – that is, until you are ready to take him back."

"But what if that's not for several weeks . . . ?" fussed Mrs Wellard.

"I've discussed it with my husband. If Kish does any work for us we'd pay him a wage."

For the first time since Mrs Wellard had sat down a modicum of cheerfulness animated her rotund features.

"What do you think, Ricky? Of course, we would have to get clearance."

Gangell looked at the possum rug and frowned. "I don't know, Annette. This lad, he's not like the rest of them. If I were here to keep tabs on things, it would be different."

"Ricky is taking a sabbatical," Mrs Wellard quickly explained. Which for some reason annoyed Merridy.

"A *sabbatical*?" she said.

"It's actually really rather interesting. I'm going to do a course in biodynamics." And that annoyed her even more. All at once she saw him for what he was. Lackadaisical. There for the trip. Issuing institutionalised warnings to the effect that Kish would never be any better than he was, a savage little bastard.

"Ricky kindly agreed to look after the boys for the first fortnight, until they got their sea legs, so to speak."

Merridy was no longer interested in Gangell or his bio-dynamics. "If Kish likes it here, why not give him a chance?"

But did he like it?

"Why not, Ricky?" Mrs Wellard echoed. Pleading, almost. "If we get clearance, why not?" And Merridy could see her thinking: If it was a libertine house full of fourteen-year-olds . . . But a nice, childless couple on a farm!

Besides, they wanted to be rid of him, that was obvious. One less statistic.

"Because, in my opinion," Gangell said gruffly, "he needs supervision."

"You could always delay your sabbatical," Merridy suggested brightly.

"Mind you, if he did stay here," said Gangell, beginning, at last, to see certain advantages, "it couldn't be for any longer than the duration of the course."

"I understand," Merridy said. She stood up. "But please, before we go any further, shouldn't we ask Kish?"

She found him, glasses off, lying on his bed. He was wearing his purple T-shirt with its gruesome insignia, and had folded his uniform that Merridy had washed, hung on the line and ironed, into the bin liner. On the floor at the foot of the bed in two neat piles were Alex's clothes that he had borrowed, plus Alex's spectacles on top; and the clothes that Agnes had donated. He was shed of all his possessions save those that he had worn in the sea.

Merridy led him into the living room. She realised that she had no idea what his answer would be.

Mrs Wellard had adopted a formal attitude before the fireplace. "Mrs Dove has kindly invited you to remain at Moulting Lagoon Farm for the moment. Subject to what you would say if this could be arranged."

Kish stood with his mouth open. Uneasy, he turned to Merridy. "You mean you don't want me to go?"

"If you'd like to stay, you may stay – for a little while. You'll have to go eventually, obviously."

"It's only for the time being," Gangell said. "An interim period."

"Sure," he said slowly. "I'll stay."

"Well, that's settled then," said Merridy.

Two hours later Mrs Wellard telephoned from Wellington Point. She had spoken to her superiors. Provided that a probation officer could be in touch once a week, there was no objection to Kish remaining at Moulting Lagoon Farm until 23 March, the date on which the *Buffalo* had been due to drop anchor in Sydney.

PART IV

Moulting Lagoon Farm, 17–20 December 2004

CHAPTER ONE

UNITING CHURCH, WELLINGTON POINT.
Memorial Service next Sunday at 10.00 a.m. All visitors
welcome. Captain Vamplugh and his crew again extend
their appreciation for the lovely knitted items they have
received. With your generous donations of goods and
money we raised $940.45. We also have 100 Wellington
Point tea-towels for sale with pictures of the village drawn
by Myfanwy Davies. Any profits go towards the Bilgola
City Mission. Phone to place your order: Rev. Chris Mantle
63526836.

Sister Surrage kept telling him: "You're lucky to be alive."
He nodded. He could not forget the force of the waves that
had dashed his speedboat against one of the pylons of the
jetty, or the fury of the wind that tumbled her up the concrete
ramp, to burst apart the hull against Mr Talbot's garage –
at which point he had jumped unceremoniously out and
run, stumbled and collapsed. All the same, his concussion
was not so severe that he could ignore the unprecedented
publicity that the storm had attracted in its wake. Despite
the constraint of his bandages, he was eager to tap into it.

From his bed in the Louisa Meredith Nursing Home,
Ray Grogan, who was now on the council, sent instruc-
tions to Tildy to open up the school kitchen and for the
playing field to be made available to all camper vans. So
many of these vehicles had converged on the promontory
that the kids had nicknamed the area behind their playground
Winnebago City.

Wellington Point, meanwhile, blinked in the glare of an attention that old-timers could not recall since an aeroplane decapitated two locals in the 1930s. Day-trippers came from Hobart and Launceston. Bushies who never much liked to travel beyond sight of their shacks came from Royal George and Green Ponds and Llandaff, and combed the shore to see if they could spot a few deck boards, as often as not mistaking a fragment of Ray's speedboat for a piece of the *Buffalo*. Eventually, a recovery barge anchored off Schouten and hauled away the wreck.

There were those who pretended to dislike the publicity, but no longer Murray Went, who was forced to bus in extra staff from Swansea after promoting Debbie to manageress; nor anyone else in the hospitality business, for whom the sinking of the *Buffalo* was a bonanza. It was a novel sight for Alex to read the "No vacancy" signs outside the bed & breakfasts, and quite a few houses as well. As for the people thronging the street, Alex had never known such an invasion. The hotel's restaurant and its two bars overspilled with reporters and photographers who had flown in from the mainland and even from abroad, a television crew from the BBC competing with one from Southern Cross to interview eyewitnesses and survivors. Agnes had filled a bin liner of clothes for each and every one of these – whom Merridy could not help remarking that Kish showed no inclination to seek out – so that the captain and his crew resembled members of a visiting cricket team as they sat in the hotel restaurant, dressed in baggy, white, moth-eaten jerseys, some of them from a batch donated by Harry Ford, and struggled to find different answers to the same questions posed over and over again.

In this avid atmosphere, it was inevitable that stories began to circulate of Alex's heroism.

Late one morning, he came up from Moulting Lagoon to find a journalist tapping on the living-room window. The man – mid-forties, brown shoes, pot belly – had paid Rose-Maree the equivalent of a week's salary to drive him out to the farm. She sat in her car, radio blaring, engrossed in *Who Weekly* and a feature about actresses with moles.

"Can I help?"

"Alex Dove?" jerking round. He had a beard and was bald.

"No," said Alex.

"Where could I find Mr Dove?"

"Who are you?"

"Oh, friend of a friend." His brown shoes stepped across the herbaceous border that Merridy had created, squashing a red peony and a white trigger-plant. "Marty Ponting. The *Advocate*." And held out a hand.

"He's out at sea, he won't be back till late."

"I see," and inspected a spiral-bound pad with panicked ferocity. "Actually, it was Mr Cash I wanted to speak to." He frowned at what he had written. "Or Cosh, could it be?"

"They're in the same boat."

Mr Ponting looked at Alex. "Who are you?"

"A friend of Mrs Dove," said Alex for some reason.

"Could you ask either of them to ring this number?" and with his still-unshaken hand opened a wallet that bulged with receipts.

Alex suspected Harry of priming this Ponting. The ex-Fleet Streeter could never forget the heavenly days of his journalistic calling that ill-health had cut short. Alex remembered that Harry, fond as he no doubt was of his mother and father, had orchestrated the newspaper coverage following their death. The morals of an alley cat.

He watched the beard duck back into Rose-Maree's car. Then went inside before she looked up. He ripped up Marty Ponting's card and put the pieces in the compost bin.

CHAPTER TWO

THREE DAYS ON AND the journalists had begun to seep away, leaving their smears behind. And still the Oyster Bay pine disfigured the lawn.

A pile of roots extended over the crater, tangled with stones and clay and Aboriginal shells. The roots had forced things down over the years. Alex picked out animal bones, farm equipment and an old whaling blubber-cutter that had lost its handle. He dreaded to investigate the dark hollow beneath his parents' tombstones. He would attend to their graves once he had dealt with the tree.

Already, he had chainsawed the topmost branches that obstructed the drive; the rest of the trunk balanced in an amputated column on its crushed foliage, a huge evergreen umbrella blown inside out.

Even so, Alex felt a curious reluctance to dispose of the pine on his own. The tree could wait; there were fences to right and roofs to mend and sheep and cattle to find. The thought of Kish out in the bay with Merridy intensified the young man's absence.

Not until Sunday morning late did Merridy and Kish untangle the last lantern. On Monday, it became Alex's turn to claim him.

In the hour before dawn, as he drove his tractor across the darkened fields, Alex startled a bloated devil gorging on a dead cow on the other side of a fallen fence. He discovered the putrefying corpse a yard or two inside the adjacent

Crown forest where the animal had blundered in the storm, its hide tined by fangs of barbed wire and a sheet of rusted tin embedded in its neck. He repaired the fence and afterwards dug a trench. Playing with the notion and then dismissing it that this was the very cow he had mistaken for a ghost. He levered the remains into the trench and covered it over with bark and leaves.

The crude burial reminded him of the task that he had postponed, for which he would be glad of Kish's assistance.

Down the corridor he heard a mannish laugh. As he had not heard it in years. He refilled Rusty's bowl with water and sat at the table and finished a piece of cold toast that he had left uneaten, and picking at the marmalade label waited for her to come into the kitchen.

He stood up and kissed her.

"What's that smell?" she said gaily.

He told her about the cow in the wood and the devil that had emerged from its backside, teeth clamped around an intestine.

"Let me wash your clothes," and started to unbutton his shirt.

But he held her hand.

"What's wrong?" noticing his face.

"You're wearing mascara."

"I saw myself in the glass, I look so old."

But the lilt in her voice did not sound right. Her face above her green jersey over-bright and the make-up drawing attention.

"Aren't you going to your shed?" he asked. She was usually out of the house by now, dressed in her work clothes. There were nets and baskets to stitch with baling twine, mud-maps to fill in, outboards to mend. In spawning time, she often told him, you needed to get everything ready for the next run.

"I have to ring Panasonic."

"What the hell for?" releasing her.

She looked at him, surprised at his tone. "I lost a blade."

"What blade?" asked Alex. Her face seemed slimmer under her make-up.

"For the bread-maker. Second time, too! I'm going to have Panasonic send two this time. Oh, and Alex, I almost forgot – the new cleaner's coming today." Alice's daughter having moved with her partner to Longford. "She should have been here at eight."

Alex heard Kish knocking around somewhere in the house and went to talk to him.

By the time he came back in, Merridy had moved to the sink. Both hands held onto his plate that she had dried.

"What's up with Kish?" Alex wanted to know.

"Why? Where is he, anyway?"

"He refuses to leave his room, but right now I could do with his help."

"Just go and tell him you need him," carefully stacking the plate.

"It's that lump of wood I gave him. He can't keep his hands off it."

"A bit obsessive, isn't he?"

The sound of a vehicle brought Alex to the window. "Your cleaner's here."

CHAPTER THREE

HER NAME WAS MADASUN, a Catholic from Devonport. She had advertised in Talbot's *Newsletter*.

She parked at an angle on the far side of the tree and tripped from her car, spilling keys onto the gravel. Her round face obscured by frizzy auburn ringlets that she brushed from wide trusting eyes. She had only recently moved to Wellington Point and had overshot the entrance to the house, ending up 30 kilometres away in Bicheno. She was dressed in blue dungarees and had a large watch on her wrist.

"I was listening about the Pope, poor man."

Merridy showed her where the cleaning things were, and around the house, and introduced her to the figure who stepped into the corridor.

"This is Kish."

"That's a nice name," not put off by the skull on his T-shirt. "Unusual."

"I'll be in here if you want me," said Merridy, and opened the last door.

Barely twenty minutes had passed when the vacuum cleaner was switched off to be replaced by the sound of Madasun's resonant voice. She was conversing with Kish in his bedroom and what they were saying, on that cool, overcast day, reached Merridy in Alex's old workshop. It was clear that Madasun was not going to be efficient in the tradition of Alice or her daughter.

"Where were you heading?"

"Hobart Town."

"No, really?"

"I was, too."

"What were you going to do in Hobart?"

"I dunno, spear a whale or two."

"I thought they'd banned whaling. You're not Japanese, are you?"

He laughed.

"I bet you're a Virgo. I always get on with Virgos."

"Who are they?"

"Oh, come on. When were you born?"

He gave a date.

The girl giggled. He was funny, Kish. "I don't think even whales live that long. I'm serious, when were you born? What month?"

He told her again.

"Then that would make you, let's see . . . a Pisces."

Suddenly, he did not want to play her game. He mumbled something.

"Look, if you'd rather not tell, that's OK," she said concerned. "It's not important."

But there was something, clearly, he did want to reveal. He spoke in a halting voice. Too low for Merridy to hear.

"That sounds like head lice," said Madasun. "Maybe you should go to the chemist's."

But it was of a different category, evidently, from nits.

"I know what you mean," Madasun sighed. "I feel like that sometimes. Utterly lost. And with a fiancé, too."

So far as Merridy was able to gather, her fiancé was a fireplace installer from Beaconsfield who had a child by a previous partner. Her parents disapproved, but probably they would marry in October. If not, she had other plans. She would like to write science fiction. She would like to study Aboriginal art. She would like to travel.

Until Merridy got up from her desk.

"Maybe you'd like to get the cobwebs out from behind the fridge," interrupting.

Madasun jumped up from the end of the bed, impervious. "Oh, Mrs Dove, gosh, I was so enjoying listening to Kish that I forgot myself."

Kish lay across the unmade bed. He watched Madasun unplug the vacuum cleaner. Then he folded his knife, picked up his piece of wood and left the room.

Merridy called after him: "Kish, where are you going?"

Over his shoulder: "To help Mr Dove."

Merridy returned to her desk and flung herself into the mundane tasks that she had put off for the spawning season. After ordering the blades for the bread-maker, she compiled a list:
   – sort out cleaning schedules
   – sign and date harvests
   – order seedlings
By ten o'clock, she had drawn a fresh mud-map, marking the new positions of the lanterns, and composed letters to the Department of Primary Industries and to Dmitri, apologising for having to postpone her visit to Melbourne. To leave the farm right now was impossible. *I am still dealing with fallout from the storm,* she wrote. *Perhaps I could come next week?*

But it was sand to halt the tide.

In Sydney, he was shoving everything. A wonder he didn't wear his pecker out.

The room she sat in was at the end of the house and the window at an angle to the lawn so that she could only see a tantalising portion of the grass. On another day she might have been too preoccupied to look out. But this morning her eyes kept straying. She watched the lawn as dutifully and carefully as Tildy used to watch Zac. The fallen tree with its massive claw of roots and stones and soil.

Did he notice her figure, her eyes? Some men did and the idea of it made them stupid.

A figure approached the tree. Kish! But it was her husband. He stood talking to someone out of sight.

She watched the familiar face that time had nicked and hollowed. He bore the scars of two carcinoma operations, on his right cheek and right hand where he faced the sun when driving the ute. And all at once had no control over her emotions. Dark thoughts flapped around her.

She forced her eyes to the tree. The simplicity of the fall was dreadful, the massive finger aimed at the sky in the angle of a benediction now pointed, stunted and accusing, at her.

Alex said something and came on towards the house. She heard the fly-screen open and close. The sound of the cistern flushing. Her hands tightened into fists. In that instant she hated him that he could still pull a chain, still shut the fly-screen. He was like the air which she had expelled. And she hated herself even more – for this sudden and unexpected ill-will, this deadness towards her loving, decent husband.

She picked up her pen again. Appalled and shaken that she could be capable of feeling like this. She took a fresh sheet of paper and started writing. *Dear Mum . . .* Drawing in the whole assembly of her mother's church to her sense of shame and guilt. *It has been months since I last wrote*. And rummaged further into herself as if she was the wardrobe in their bedroom, to throw her sinful feelings out and leave only what was pure. But her pen did not know how to go on. What could she tell her mother? She looked outside to find the words – and found Kish.

"*A young man washed up on the beach the other day,*" she murmured aloud. "*En route to harpoon a whale in Hobart Town. I've hexed him with my lantern and he has sky-blue limbs, a shiny silver knife and a ring in his ear, his ear. I surprise myself in the uncomfortable position of wanting to sleep with this man, to taste the sea in his mouth. Do you see my quandary? Please advise, your otherwise faithful daughter, Merridy.*"

Her gaze did not move from the enigmatic figure who had appeared from behind the fallen tree. In Alex's jeans and denim hat. He was playing with Rusty.

"Know what you are, Merridy Dove?" she said. "You are a silly, silly cow." But still her eyes fumbled after him.

Partially concealed by foliage, Kish snapped off a branch and threw it across the lawn. Then as Rusty ran to fetch he leaned back against a bough and took something from his hip pocket.

She rolled her chair forward. What was he carving? Whenever she woke, she could hear him through the bedroom wall, working on it. But if she asked what he was making, he told her it was a secret. She had little doubt that it had – obviously – to do with ships. Something about the *Otago* obsessed him. Once, on her way to collect firewood, she had startled him poking his rigger's knife into the bottle, but the blade was too wide. He had leaped back, as when she had found him by the wardrobe.

This time she smiled. "Still trying to get that penny out?"

"Hey, Kish!" It was Alex, reeling him in again. Carrying across the lawn not the chainsaw, but two spades. "Come over here."

They walked to the base of the tree and the pine's roots obscured them.

She looked down and wrote quickly: *It is very sad about the Pope. It doesn't look as though he will survive much longer. I realise he has been a constant all my life.*

After a while her serenity returned.

"Mrs Dove?"

Madasun, knocking on the door. Her three hours up.

Merridy scraped together forty-five dollars from her purse.

"We need some bleach," said Madasun. "If you like, I can get it."

"No, I'll get it."

She had decided to tell Madasun not to come again. But what came out was: "Same time next week?"

After the grateful girl had flustered her relief, Merridy returned to the letter that she was halfway through writing to her mother. *Alex is still counting the damage from the storm. He lost eleven sheep and the roof of the shearers' quarters. I wonder if the winds reached you in Devonport . . .*

By noon Merridy had covered six sides. She folded them into an envelope and went into the kitchen. Kish must have finished whatever he was doing with Alex because his silver knife lay on the Welsh dresser. Engraved into its handle, a name – Marlow – that she had not noticed before. Of the manufacturer, perhaps. Once again she tested its blade. This knife to cut ropes that threatened to entangle him, or her.

"Hey! That's mine."

She had not seen him come in.

He snatched it back. Settled his buttocks in a chair.

"Hungry?" she asked.

"I suppose."

He put his legs up on the table and she felt like a woman in a Western when she snapped at him to get them off.

"I thought of making some pasta," she said.

He yawned.

"Does that mean you don't like pasta?"

"No."

"What do you eat in Sydney?"

"I dunno, meat."

She filled a pot with water and put it on the stove. "Weren't you going to saw up the tree?" staring out of the window. That stagey tree she had never liked for its insistence upon itself. She had supposed that getting rid of it was the priority. So she understood.

"Maybe this afternoon."

"What were you doing just now?"

"Righting some stones."

"Oh," before realising that he meant the granite gravestones.

"Didn't Mr Dove tell you? They were popping out of the ground."

"I know. I could see them from here." She turned back into the room. "Something to drink?"

"I wouldn't say no to some moo-juice."

She opened the fridge and poured him a glass of milk, which he drank down in one gulp.

Her breasts filled out her jersey.

"Hey, don't," he said, over the top of his glass.

"Don't what?"

"Look at me like that."

She took his glass from him, colouring.

Tak, tak, tak. From over by the sink she watched him persecute the wood with his gleaming blade, and compressed her lips. She had worked hard with Kish in the bay, lifting and dropping oysters and altogether too busy for

332

conversation. But after the quiet communion at sea, he had reverted to his former prickliness. All his childish seriousness transferred to Alex.

"What's that you're making? Is it a ship for Alex?" Who had never, she realised, taught her how to put a ship in a bottle. Not even tried to.

He rolled it over in his hand. It could have been a naked man swimming. Or drowning. "It still hasn't told me."

"Then it had better get a move on or there'll be nothing left."

Tak, tak, tak.

"You know, Kish," carefully. "It's not good to tell stories."

"I don't," he frowned.

"I overheard what you said to Madasun. That stuff about you being a long-lost sailor, well, it's not really very funny."

"I wasn't trying to be funny, Mrs Dove." He was giving her a hard time, that was all.

"She's an impressionable girl, Madasun. She might believe you."

"So?"

"It's just that . . . Look, Alex and I, we want to help."

He said nothing. He had pulled into himself.

"How old are you, Kish?"

"Nineteen. How old are you?"

"Thirty-six," she shot back.

"How long have you been married, Mrs Dove?"

She looked at her fingers. There was ink on them. "Almost seventeen years."

"Why don't you have children?"

That fucking question. Again. Always. She hunted around for some soap and picked it up, but it had stuck to the dish.

"Didn't want them." Her answer so harsh that he turned his head.

He studied her face, whiter than the soap dish. "You'd like a child, wouldn't you?"

The energy had retreated from her shoulders and legs into her face. Her eyes shone like a sick person's. She picked up a shaving that he had missed. "What I would like," she said from within her invisible hole, "is for you to throw away your mess into that bin."

At the sound of her distress, he laughed. His sawing laugh that kept away questions.

"Want to know what this is?" He held up his stick of wood, the colour of a dirty collar. "It's a key."

"A key to what?"

"Your wardrobe, I reckon."

On the stove the water bubbled away.

Holding onto the table. "It doesn't need a key."

She'd wanted to wait for Alex but her wish to shut Kish up was stronger. In silence, she prepared his lunch and served it to him.

Two mouthfuls into the meal, Kish poked his fork at something on his plate. "What's this?"

"Anchovies." As her father had taught her.

"I don't think I want antchervees."

"But you've got them, haven't you?"

In which position Alex interrupted them.

"Ah, Kish. Do you have a second?"

"I suppose."

"It's that bloody windmill," to Merridy.

"I thought you'd fixed it."

"Yeah, but it's gone again. I reckon it hasn't worked for days. The storm must have buggered it."

"I've made some seafood pasta." This being Alex's favourite.

"It can keep, love, can't it?"

Merridy looked hard at the bowl. "I suppose."

She waited for him to leave the room. His unshaven chin, his reek of dead cow.

Guided by the snorts of thirsty cattle, their heads scraping empty tin and feed on their damp noses, Alex had only now discovered that the windmill was not pumping water to the troughs.

He hoped that the fault lay with the spear beneath; with Kish's help he pulled up the black plastic tube and staring down saw a little rear-mirror of light and his face taut and stubbly.

It puzzled Alex. "Plenty of water there."

"Can I look?"

Kish kneeled, screwing up his face like a photographer at his reflection. Then he twisted round and nodded at the windmill. "Bet you London to a brick the problem's up there."

"It's always caused grief," Alex acknowledged. Most probably, the storm had been the final straw, the wind pumping the machinery into a frenzy so that a vital part had snapped inside the maze of rods and pistons. This time, Alex was determined to get the thing properly repaired.

As he struggled to his feet, he noticed Kish's eyes still on the ladder. "Want a look?"

They climbed to the viewing platform.

Kish took off the denim sun hat that Alex had lent him and raked a hand through his spiky hair, then put it back on, and shook his head. "Good view, Mr Dove."

The grey sky had gone and the sun was out. From far below, Rusty whined up at them.

"Hi, Rusty!"

His back to the rail, Kish turned and looked the other way.

"Hey, what's that?"

Before Alex could stop him, he bent forward and ran his fingers over the faded orange letters that the wind and salt had all but burned off.

It was hard to believe that this was the same angry and confused young man whose lunch he had interrupted. Unlike Merridy, Alex had not warmed to the arrogance contained in the skull shirt, but as he watched him puzzle out her name that had bled into the rust he was glad that he had insisted on Kish staying.

"Been on a farm before?"

"I have been on one, I think," straightening up. His eyes did not budge from the vane. "But I can't say it was anywhere like this."

Alex checked his watch. Now that he had made his decision, he was impatient to press on, find the right person to fix the windmill. And there was still the pine to clear from the lawn. But he had forgotten how pleasant it was to have company.

He looked at Kish. "Ever sat on a horse?"

For the rest of that afternoon, as he had with Merridy half a lifetime before, Alex rode Kish over the farm.

"Just hang on, he's a tame boy."

Alex led the way, opening and closing gates.

The far side of Barn Hill, a piece of wood came away in his hand. He reined in. Legs the larger for a pair of his own trousers kicked Merridy's horse until it came up beside him.

"Look," showing Kish the decayed fence post. "Mayfly caddis."

Splashing across the rivulet where his father liked to swim, they saw a cormorant take a trout on the wing. Kish watched the bird flash through the air and the wriggling silver fish.

"That's a beaut," a sly respect in his eye. The sun glinted on the lens of the borrowed glasses and on his smooth cheeks. One week on and still no beard.

"Better than a police siren?" asked Alex.

"I reckon."

And Alex, on the horse beside him, felt a shot of paternal pride at how this confused Sydney boy responded to his land, his animals. He indulged in the extravagant idea that he had plucked from the sea a child he had never had. He had stuck a life jacket on him and now he had put him on horseback. And he admitted to himself how much he would have liked as a parent to teach Kish a whole lot more.

Three months, though, would be ample. Because what would Kish turn into if he stayed? He would pick walnuts, work for Nevin at the garage, peddle porn DVDs. Or worse. Look at Zac, loved to death and caught stealing from Talbot's. Or so the rumour had it at the RSL. No, three months would be ample, and sucked on his blade of grass at the prospect.

Over by Moulting Lagoon, Kish watched Alex and Rusty move the herd between paddocks. The cows bellowed, stretching black necks, and swayed reluctantly through the gate.

Alex could hear Kish talking to his horse as he closed the gate. He swung back into his saddle.

"Let's go before it breezes up again."

*

High up in the clear sky, a flock of tiny birds dipped steeply up and down like a shoal of fish in the air. Alex scratched between his horse's ears and the animal quietened into a lope.

"They're fast," Kish remarked, staring at the birds.

"You'd be fast, too, if you flew a hundred miles an hour."

They rode on at walking pace. The birds' twittering audible above the squeak of leather.

"What are they, actually?" Kish leaned forward in the stock saddle; the jolting had sifted away any last trace of discontent.

"Magic birds. White-throated needletail swifts. They fly everywhere, except the ice cap. And you know the most amazing thing about them? They sleep in the air, they feed in the air – even mate in the air."

"No way!" said Kish.

"It's true. They spend their nights up there on the wing. And only come to earth to perch or nest."

"Where do they nest?"

"Treetops in north Asia. They find a hollow and go down deep into it, or cling to vertical, rough bark. But it has to be vertical."

"What, you mean they don't land on the ground?" in a marvelling tone that reminded Alex of his own reaction as a boy on first hearing this fact.

"Their legs are so tiny, they couldn't stand up. They wouldn't be able to fly off. You could say being on the ground doesn't suit them."

Once again it struck Alex that he had no one to talk to; on his own for most of the time, he lacked opportunities to share his thoughts, his enthusiasms. He had Merridy, but Merridy was not always enough. Especially after she discovered oysters. Not for the first time, it made Alex think that he needed another person about the place.

"What I love about those swifts is that we know so little about them," he said. "There's a lot of people hell-bent on taking the mystery out of life. Bit of a shame, really."

On hearing this, Kish seemed to fall into deep contemplation. He did not speak again for the rest of the ride home.

Growing restless after the two men trotted off, Merridy put on her Driza-Bone and went outside. She had no destination in mind, but once on the lawn she walked across it until she stood before the graves of Alex's parents. The stones upright again, the neat earth patted around and sprinkled with the oyster-shell fragments that always reminded her of chicken claws. Her shoes crunched on the mended soil before the names. Basil. Marjorie.

And without warning thought of Hector.

It was not, in fact, the inscriptions that brought her brother clattering up from under the seashells and pine needles and small woody cones, but the touch of grey feathers.

Merridy hauled herself onto the fallen tree that she had never bothered to climb when it was aimed at the sky, and was rubbing her fingers over the abbreviated trunk, exploring the scarred wood from which Alex had sawed Kish's fragment – when she looked down.

Hemmed in beneath a mattress of browning twigs, the mangled body of a kookaburra.

She had not brooded on her brother since her marriage, nor discussed him with anyone, not even Tildy. Instead, she had created a space where he could not enter. But the longer she had refused to think about him, the more insistent – in a cavity of her mind – the memory of him became. It seemed to Merridy, leaning down to discover the snarl of feathers and crushed bones, that Hector was still there, trapped in the amber. Trapped like this sheltering bird.

So she walked back to the house, as isolated in her thoughts as the two men riding towards her. More isolated even than in the painful months and years when she nursed the infantile idea that her brother might return a stranger from another place and time, but would she recognise him?

Twenty minutes later, she discovered Kish sitting in her chair in the kitchen. He was bent over a white cereal bowl and stabbed at something in it with the tip of his knife.

"I thought I heard the phone. Where's Alex?"

"In his office."

"Enjoy the ride?"

"It was good. Real good."

She looked over his shoulder. A few seconds passed before she absorbed the latest object of his persecution.

"What are you doing, Kish?"

"You don't understand how small we are, Mrs Dove. We want to walk big. Be important. Someone dying, people have this idea it affects the whole world. And yet we're not so much as the smallest scraping off this piece of sand. We're so small, God doesn't even know we're here."

"Don't be silly."

"He doesn't."

"I don't know what He knows and I don't suppose you do either."

"What do you reckon God looks like, Mrs Dove?"

"How would I know? I don't think like that any more."

"You're not listening to me," he said to Merridy who

340

thought that she was. "What do you think He looks like?"

"That's not the point," irritated. "Why? Do you have any good ideas?"

Kish stood up and walked over to the Welsh dresser and took down the *Otago* from the shelf. He held up the ship as though it were a telescope and investigated her through it.

"I'd say He could look like anything. He could look like the face on this coin."

"You don't mean that."

He put down the bottle on the table and stared at the coin. He stared at it and he thought about it. "I do."

"Tea?"

"You know, I'm sick of tea, Mrs Dove." He turned to her. "Ever heard of Rudolf Steiner?"

"No," surprised by this turn in the conversation.

"He must be close to whoever made us. He discovered that when you bury a cow horn with cow manure at a certain time, the manure is fifty times more powerful. It's the same with iron. Gearboxes made for Ford cars in 1977 last for ever. Those made in 1978 go to pieces."

"Honestly, Kish! Where did you hear this?"

"Gangell told me."

She remembered the probation officer with the gammy leg and the face of a possum, how she had disliked him.

At that moment the door opened and Alex strode in, smiling broadly. "It's all on," he said, addressing Kish as much as her. "I've spoken to my agent and he's put me in touch with this bloke in Woolnorth."

She was lost. She had no idea what her husband was talking about. "What bloke?"

He took a bucket from under the sink and filled it with water. "The windmill expert. I caught him in the nick of

341

time. He's about to go to Alice Springs for three months, but he can look at it tomorrow. Only snag is, he refuses to leave Woolnorth. I'll have to take it to him."

"What, dismantle the whole thing? Isn't that excessive?"

"That's what he says. Hey, Kish, fancy a trip to the north-west?"

"You want to do this now?" she said.

"Come on, love, you should see the state of the animals. What choice do we have? Kish and I can drive it up tomorrow."

"But is that allowed – I mean, for Kish to leave here?"

He turned off the tap. "I don't see why not. Not if I'm there to look after him. It's no different to you having him out on the *Zemmery Fidd*. And we'll be back for dinner."

CHAPTER FOUR

IT TOOK UNTIL NINE the next morning to unbolt and collapse the windmill.

With a sense of relief for which she chided herself, Merridy watched Alex and Kish load it onto the ute and leave. "It's not a bad thing that you're going," when Alex asked if she would look after Rusty. There was tack to clean, her trip to organise. "I can spend the rest of the day preparing for Melbourne."

For Dmitri had now insisted on a date. "We want to do promotion. Send photographs, anything you've got to make you look good."

They had been gone four hours when the woman telephoned.

"Mrs Dove?" That mainland voice.

"Mrs Wellard."

"I've rung about Kish. How is he?"

"Kish is fine." Although he had seemed awfully glad to be getting out of the house.

"I spoke to Sean."

"Sean?"

"From Child Welfare."

"Oh, Sean." On Sunday afternoon, Sergeant Finter had arrived with a man who stayed for coffee and had a word with Kish and left.

"He sees no reason why the arrangement can't continue. If you're happy, that is."

"Oh, we're happy," said Merridy.

"Could I speak to Kish?"

"I'm afraid not." Licking her lip. "He's away with my husband."

A pause. "I see. He'll be back when?"

"I'm expecting them for dinner."

"Then I'll ring tonight."

Merridy put down the receiver and returned to the stove.

The onions were almost caramelised. She smashed some garlic under the flat of a knife and chopped it up and added a pinch of coarse salt and a tin of Italian tomatoes. She pureed the tomatoes and the onions with the potato masher so that Kish would not be able to see them. She was making the kind of sauce she used to make for Tildy's children. Simple, with no evidence of onions. She was an expert in hiding onions.

CHAPTER FIVE

Kish spoke hardly at all on the journey to Woolnorth, content to stare out the window. The further north they travelled, the more extreme the impact of the previous week's storm on the landscape. The trees on the east coast were hardened to strong winds from the south-east, had grown to face them. But north beyond Longford, the vegetation faced in the opposite direction, towards Bass Strait. Unaccustomed to fast-bowling gales from the south, the gums and wattles had been spun out of the ground like cricket stumps.

They stopped in Stanley and ate fish and chips on a triangle of grass surrounded by seagulls. Kish soon finished his meal. He watched Alex chewing.

At last, he spoke. "Harry says you can get wonderful pork pies in the north, just like he ate in his youth in England."

"When did you talk to Harry?"

"He came up yesterday to see you."

"Where was I?"

Kish shrugged. "He says Tasmania is a place where you can get things that have vanished from England."

"You shouldn't listen to Harry. What did he want?"

"He didn't say."

Trailed by seagulls, Alex took his paper plate and dropped it into the bin with the remains of the battered trevalla. Across the road, a she-oak had collapsed onto a house.

Alex looked at his watch. "I said we'd be there by two."

The windmill expert lived near Cape Grim, a small cove of black sand. Below, a treacherous sea receded from the cliff in white rags.

"Does it ever get calm?" Alex asked the man, who was called Scantlebury.

"Oh, flat as."

Mr Scantlebury had a well-trimmed beard and a serious face protected by rimless glasses, and was employed at the wind farm. He was in his workshop when they arrived, a converted hangar next to a whitewashed stone cottage. He walked out to the ute and lifted the tarp and nodded.

"Probably the bearings." He was familiar with the model. He had serviced an identical machine in Gladstone. "The bearings go and no one does anything with them."

Only one thing about Alex's windmill puzzled him.

"You live by a highway or something?"

"No, why?"

He reached out a leathery hand and shifted the vane to reveal the bright, fresh orange letters.

"Reckon someone's been hooning around with a spray can."

It was almost four o'clock when Alex called from Smithton.

He was in a buoyant mood. Mr Scantlebury had inspected the windmill and was confident that he could repair it; furthermore, was prepared to work late to do so. But it would not be ready to collect until the following morning. Rather than waste a journey, Alex planned to stay overnight with Kish in the north. "We should be back by lunch."

"Where will you sleep?"

"Scantlebury's recommending a B & B in Alexandria."

He had not sounded so happy in months.

346

"So you'll be back by lunch," she said slowly.

"What are you doing?"

"I was making you dinner."

"Then we'll have it tomorrow. We can eat it tomorrow, can't we, love?"

"Oh, I should think so," without force.

"Did you finish all you had to do?"

"Yes, I got everything sorted."

But she felt dowdy. She took the sauce off the stove and the cake out of the oven – it looked cooked through – and went into her bedroom. Nauseated suddenly by the kitchen smells on her clothes, she stripped. *Anything you've got to make you look good.*

As Merridy had not done since a teenager, she found herself appealing to her reflection in the bathroom mirror. She combed back her hair, squirted some three-year-old scent beneath her jaw-line, polished her nails and put on a bit of make-up. Then rolled on a pair of new stockings and unhooked from the wardrobe the cornflower dress that she had picked out in the Myer winter sale for her trip to Melbourne. And as the clock chimed four on the radio shut Rusty in the living room and climbed into her car to drive to Wellington Point.

She was strapping herself in when she heard the telephone ring in the kitchen. She was on the verge of taking off her seat belt when it crossed her mind that the caller would be Mrs Wellard. So she drove away.

RECENT TRAGIC EVENTS
From Sgt Pete Finter: "The recent tragic events in Oyster Bay have highlighted the necessity of having a suitable

*local rescue boat in our area, as in Swansea. It's fright-
ening to think that without Alex and Merridy Dove there
would have been another death. Merridy's handling of
the <u>Zemmery Fidd</u> (which the young lady designed with
her very own hand) was an amazing feat of seawom-
anship. No less exceptional was Alex Dove's dramatic
rescue of a drowning Sydneysider. I know that the whole
community takes pride in this brave act. Well done, both
of you!"*

In Talbot's, Merridy took a *Newsletter* from the stand
next to the till, and then a *Mercury*. On the front page,
the same bland-looking man stared out at her with the
same unwavering expression: "*Is your memory a sieve?*"
Next to him, the photograph of a five-metre boat un-
covered in Marion Bay.

*Watch out for ghost ships! The wild weather and giant
swell which battered Tasmania's coast earlier in the week
have already bared the wreck of this long rowing boat in
Marion Bay. Anyone who sees a wreck should get in touch
with the Parks and Wildlife Service.*

Merridy folded the newspaper into her trolley – and
turned to Rose-Maree. "Where do I find bleach?"

"Sorry?"

"Bleach, Rose-Maree. Where is the bleach?"

"Oh, it's you, Mrs Dove," said Rose-Maree, thawing.
"You look amazing." She pointed out the aisle.

And, searching for bleach, bumped into Tildy.

For a fraction of a second, they failed to recognise each
other.

"Merridy!" laughed the oversized figure in a grey coat.
The freckles were hard dots in her cheeks and around the
thick neck was twisted an orange scarf.

"Tildy!"

"How are you? You look well."

"And you."

"Off somewhere special?"

"Oh, no, not really."

"I like the dress!" rubbing her fingers over the lapel. Her hand was puffy and her face had a peaky look. "Why don't I ever see you?"

"I know, it's ridiculous."

"My God, how long has it been?"

"Your father's funeral, was it?"

Tildy touched Merridy's arm. "But that's three months ago! I reckon we saw each other more when you were in Melbourne."

"There's a lot to catch up on," agreed Merridy and felt a warmth returning. There was so much, suddenly, that she did want to say. "How are the kids?"

"How long have you got?" Tildy groaned.

Now it was her hand on Tildy's arm. "Hey, what are you doing now?"

"You mean right this moment? I've got an X-ray at five, but after that—"

"An X-ray? Is something wrong?"

"No, no. It's the Breast Bus." Ever since Tuesday, a converted coach offering free scans had been parked outside the Louisa Meredith Home. "Ray thought I should go – seeing it doesn't cost a cent. Plus it gets me out of the house."

"Then let's meet afterwards."

"Where would you like? I'd ask you home, except Ray's got Albert Talbot coming round for a chat that's apparently so bloody important we've all had to skedaddle. The girls are having a sleepover. I'll be free as soon as I've dropped them off."

"What about the hotel?"

Tildy hesitated, as Merridy remembered once hesitating. "I suppose we could."

"Say six o'clock?"

Merridy had parked outside Talbot's. She looked across the street, but no one moved in Ray Grogan's office. With an hour to kill, she put her shopping in the trunk and walked towards the Bethel Teahouse. She longed for a strong coffee.

It was that time of afternoon when the wind had paused and the bay was a plate of blue. Out beyond the jetty a gannet mortared the water for black-backed salmon.

But the tearoom was locked.

Disappointed, Merridy peered through a Gothic window at the sombre interior and recalled the afternoon when she had pressed her face to this very pane probably, and searching inside for her mother spotted Alex.

She did not want to think of her mother, but now that she was reminded she was comforted by the maternal presence. Whatever her warm feelings towards Wellington Point, Merridy had never forgotten her mother's opinion of country people. "There's a jealous streak running through this town, Merridy. There are plenty here who hate success. The slightest cut and they're in there – feeding. Mrs Grogan will tell you no different." (This after Mrs Bowman overheard Rose-Maree caution a woman in Talbot's: "You don't want to have coffee in that place, you might get contaminated.") And now the Bethel Teahouse had chairs stacked high on the tables and a black-and-yellow board outside.

A premonition of this same sign planted outside Oblong Oysters hastened Merridy across the road. She walked up the hill, away from the tearoom. If she could not have a coffee, she would spend the next hour exploring her town.

It was not so often that Merridy found reason to stray from the waterfront. Her traditional goat path was the main street. On this still afternoon, striking out up Malvern Road, it struck her forcibly the degree to which Wellington Point had altered.

Early on in their courtship, Alex had walked her around, sketching in the history of the settlement. As if repeating fragments told him by his father.

"That" – the golf course – "is where Captain Greer cut down the trees that reminded him of his dead soldiers at Waterloo."

"No, that's where Tildy lost her virginity."

"What, to a golfer?"

"If you must know – Pete Finter."

"Swansea," pointing seven miles across the bay.

"That's where Ray Grogan really would like to live."

His hand cut the air, encompassing the horizon. "Over there, Maria Island . . . The Hazards . . . Oyster Bay."

"Which those who have never been there bravely liken to the Bay of Naples!"

"Ssshhh."

So had she surrendered herself to his silence. She had been on death-watch ever since driving her father and mother down from Zeehan, and had failed to take in her surroundings. But then she stood beside Alex and made an effort to look at the view through his eyes – and saw that it was indeed spectacularly lovely.

In the intervening years, the weatherboard houses had transformed themselves into spic, modern brick homes: "Wivenhoe" and "Cherwell", and "Bliss House" and "Gay Bowers", with gleaming 4x4s behind their security gates. Some of their owners were unknown to Merridy as were the owners of two or three small businesses that had mushroomed on the fringe of town, employing handfuls of people, filling the school, electing Ray to the council. In the first years of her marriage she had known by name nearly everyone in the community. This afternoon almost the only name that she recognised was the one proliferating on the wasp-striped boards visible up and down the street.

She walked on fast and turned into Worcester Crescent, but neither here could she escape the signs. Wherever she looked the same name rose to challenge her.

Ray Grogan. Why not settle for more? Everything I touch turns to SOLD.

On the dot of six Merridy stepped into the old cocktail bar. She frowned at the room. Seen from the entrance, the place was a chaos of fume and noise. There was a large television screen bracketed to a wall. There was the bray of relaxed males and women squealing, with low lights to bathe the faces. She imagined everyone's breath a different colour, the spewing tangle.

Merridy ordered a tomato juice from a woman with lavender-tinted hair whom she recognised but could not place. Behind the bar, where in her first week working for Tildy's father Merridy had had to pin a postcard of Mount Vesuvius, was a photograph of a log-truck, captioned: *Doze a Greenie*. But it pleased her to see the convict brick on the counter. Still filled with matches.

She paid for her tomato juice and made her way to an empty table under the television.

In the artificial light, a stud on a dog's collar winked. Largely unnoticed on screen, the Pope got on with dying. A spectre in a wheelchair appeared at the Vatican balcony.

The twin of a Francis Bacon portrait, a poster of which she had had Blu-Tacked to her wall at uni.

"The world is standing by," a commentator gravely intoned.

"No, we are not, pisspot," snarled a tall, emaciated figure in an old cricket jersey – the only other person watching. And to his dog: "We're not standing by anyone, are we, Paddy?"

He caught Merridy looking at the animal.

"Hi, Harry."

"Do I know you?" in an English accent. He stared at her uncertain. Long years had pushed back his eyes. In the pulsing light they were the colour of the oysters that she once grew in the river. "Ah, Mrs Dove, if I'm not mistaken?" and abruptly grinned.

"That's right. How are you?"

"My days are numbered. I saw my specialist in Hobart," and caught his breath. "It's likely to be soon – and sudden."

"I'm sorry to hear that." Harry Ford had come to Wellington Point in 1957 to die, but . . .

He nodded at the screen. "Pope and I, we're in the same boat," and scowled out of his lined, grey cheeks. "But answer me this, Mrs Dove, if he's going to Heaven, why are they weeping?"

"For themselves, I imagine."

"Hypocrites!" he rasped. "Hypocrites!" and held the dog lead tighter. "And Alex? How's that fine husband of yours?"

"He's good," she said, withdrawing. She had never enjoyed moments spent alone with Harry.

But he was not letting go. "I heard . . . I heard that you have a lodger." And his breathlessness reminded her of the chandler in Hobart and a rocking boat.

"That's right. His name is Kish."

He leaned over her. His teeth were slimy and the pupils in his eyes were black. "You do know that's not his name."

"I do."

"As hot a yo-yo as the world produces. So I'm told. As hot as a pistol."

"Is that right, Harry?" angrily smoothing her dress. And remembered Alex: "If a martian landed on Dolphin Sands, Harry would do his best to interview it for the *Daily Express*."

"And you, my dear, how do you find Mr Kish?"

"He's been a great help to me on my boat."

"So I understand. So I understand." At his feet, eyes bulging at the tightened lead, the dog alone watched the pontiff dying. "But take care. My grandmother used to say: 'Save a thief from the gallows and he will cut your throat.'"

"I don't think Sergeant Finter would have allowed him to stay at Moulting Lagoon Farm if he was worried."

"My dear girl, Pete Finter never solved a crime in his life. You might tell Alex—" But the effort of speaking was too much and his face collapsed in a coughing fit.

"Are you all right, Harry?" Overcoming her distaste, she stood to clap between his shoulder-blades.

But he waved her away. He covered his mouth, and jerking his dog after him beat a retreat through the drinkers in the direction of a door with the outline of a beaming man in a top hat with a cane.

Merridy was left looking at the crowd that seemed to expand even as it swallowed up Harry; at the row of men and women at the bar who sat or stood over their stubbies, talking. She recognised barely any of them: the vet, a tapering man with a wife who tore off bottle caps with her teeth; and the lugubrious, bearded face of Sammy the Serb who was said to eat roadkill – Alex had once discovered him plucking a crow. These were all that she knew.

"The insurance salesman came out in me. I rang the Kempton pub and asked: 'Who in Kempton is having a baby?'"

"Harry says the coppers sat on it and the driver kept mum. They're doing sixteen hours a day, those drivers."

"One of the great pontiffs in Vatican history."

"She's so fat now, you could slap her in the dough to make gorilla biscuits."

Merridy stood and listened. She could not quite believe it. This room where she had worked all those years ago, and which she remembered as habitually deserted, was now a thriving bar where the whole of Wellington Point seemed to have convened. Paying no attention to a dying Pope.

Merridy caught the sweet, thick smell of a home-grown joint – not unpleasant – and coughed.

She sat down again. Tildy was late. She sipped the tomato juice and watched out for her cousin. But her image of Tildy was impaired by the suspicious, monitoring faces that stared back at her. Until she was no longer looking for the woman whom she had bumped into earlier in Talbot's, the one with pendulous breasts and chicken's feet scratching at her eyes, but a girl with varnished cedar curls and a Cupid's bow mouth who leans over a garden gate in west Ulverstone and holds out a brown paper bag.

"Hey, want one?"

The bag, Merridy cannot help noticing, is spotted with wet purple bruises. She walks up and reaches in her hand and casts about for a cherry that will not stain her gingham dress.

"Going to the dance tonight?" says the mouth made for love.

"That's right."

"There you are!"

She was waved out of her thoughts by Tildy. Her puffy hand above the sea of drinkers' heads. Her wool scarf like a shred of orange peel.

"Hi."

"Sorry I'm late."

Thirty-six again, she watched her cousin push her large body through the throng. A face on which the eyes of men no longer clung.

Once upon a time Tildy's father had owned this place, but that counted for nothing now.

Merridy heard a voice say: "You won't hear the telephone ring in that!"

"I couldn't see you," Tildy apologised, bursting free. She put two glasses full of something down on the table. "That'll give a spurt to our juices."

She subsided onto the stool and clinked glasses. "To us."

Merridy reached out, happy to see her again. She did not normally drink alcohol. But she had finished her tomato juice and the hot, smoky room made her thirsty.

"To us," and swallowed. "Mmm. What is it?"

"What you used to serve me. Rum and tonic. Oh, I've wiped myself a couple of times on that, I can tell you – between Captain Morgan's and Bacardi. I don't do it any more. Not since I've been off the slops. But tonight I will make an exception." Tildy crossed two thick legs beneath the India cotton dress. And looked directly at Merridy. "Well?"

"How was the Breast Bus?"

"There's nothing to tell," shrugged Tildy and clutched at her bosoms which moments before a disaffected

Canadian nurse had rested on cold glass plates. "She was so bored she might have been arranging fruit. They're bloody freezing still."

"Lump free?"

"Think so – you ought to nip in. Anyway, I have plenty of other things to worry about. Plenty." Tildy poked around in her handbag. "Thank God, you can still smoke in here."

She put a scuffed paperback onto the table and then a packet of cigarettes.

"I didn't know you smoked," Merridy said.

Tildy shrugged. "I just lied on the mammogram questionnaire. Why, do you want one?"

"No."

Tildy tapped one out for herself and went on ferreting in her bag. "At school, I have to stand out in the yard," in a voice distorted by the cigarette between her lips. "But not for much longer."

"What, are you giving that up?"

"Certain aspects of my daily intake are no longer satisfied by catering. I want to do something for myself."

"Like what?"

Very seriously, Tildy said: "You're not to laugh, but I am toying with the idea of going into politics."

"Politics," Merridy repeated, wondering if she had misheard.

"Now don't you sound like that, Merridy Bowman Dove. You are looking at the person who organised our entry for last year's Tidy Town competition. In which, may I remind you, Wellington Point came proximay something or other." She leaned forward. "I'm going to put my name down for the council election in April. Listen, it makes sense. I know everyone. I've fed them all. They can vote for me. At the very least, I'd make a better politician than Ray."

It all seemed odd to Merridy. "Tell me, how's Zac?" falling back on a more reliable subject. In the past, when the two cousins had had nothing to say to each other, they would talk about Tildy's children.

Tildy winced. "Later." But unable to restrain herself, she plucked the unlit cigarette from her mouth. "It was his birthday on Tuesday. Guess how old he is? How old do you think Zac is?"

"He must be—"

"Fifteen!"

"Fifteen . . . And Montana?" Merridy said quickly, to tide her over the fact that she had forgotten Zac's birthday.

"Just started grade eight."

"Alex loves Montana."

"Everyone loves Montana," with that blend of pride and resentment which mothers reserve for daughters who seem to enjoy greater luck with the opposite sex than they can remember having had themselves. "Shit, I was in such a hurry to leave the house I left my lighter behind. I'll get a match."

While she waited for Tildy, Merridy rotated the paperback so she could read the title. *The Shadow Line,* with mild surprise. The girl she knew from Ulverstone was not merely politically illiterate but voraciously unread. Interested only in magazines like *New Idea.* Who whenever she saw someone reading a book felt impelled to distract them.

"I started it on the Breast Bus," Tildy explained, resettling herself. "I remember Alex discussing it." It had stayed with her, his expression as he talked about the book. His concentration fastened on the mystery in his hand that Tildy could not hope to match by undressing. But the passion with which he spoke had made her want to glimpse it for herself, even if it had taken her all this time.

"What do you think of it?" Merridy asked.

"There's a bit of packing. But all writers use packing. Have to make up the numbers. But you just skip and keep on going," and drew on her cigarette.

"I'd no idea you liked Conrad." And yet Merridy had known that there were seams in her.

"Sweetie, you'd know a heap more about me if you bothered to ask. It's all I do now, read." She looked for somewhere to put the dead match before squeezing it under the wrap of her cigarette packet. "Reading gives you four eyes."

"When did this happen?"

"It might have happened a darn sight earlier if you and Alex had got your fingers out. Remember I was thinking of joining Agnes's reading group?"

Now Merridy did. "That's right. And we were going to write you a list. Oh, Tildy, I'm sorry."

"You never gave me a solitary title, either of you," Tildy scolded. "So in the end I was left to make the discovery for myself." She took in a long draught and blew out the smoke through her nostrils, smiling. "I'll tell you and you won't believe it. That New Year when you looked after the children?"

"When you and Ray went to Coles Bay?"

"That's right, for our fuckathon," and her eyes sparkled at the irony. "Well, Ray drank too much and afterwards fell asleep on top of me. Next morning he went out to fish. I was so bored and upset. That's when I found this paperback under the bed. *A Fringe of Leaves*. Well, I didn't have a clue what it was, it could have been a gardening book, but I read the first page, for something to do, I suppose, and flicked through the pages to see if they were the same colour. Anyway, when Ray came back with his flat-head and his kisses I was still reading. At last, I had an idea of what so excited you and Alex. Merridy, I never understood before. It was more exciting than anything Ray could offer. It meant that I had something to occupy myself when he woke up next morning with kidney stones, and we had to rush to Hobart in the ambulance." She coughed. "Smoking, it's worse than snakebite," and took a sip to quell her throat. "Actually, over the years I've meant to ask you for books to borrow."

"Why didn't you?"

"I thought you'd laugh at me. But it's one of the reasons I haven't been out and about so much." She put down her glass and cast her eyes around. "In fact, this is the first time I've been in here since Dad died."

"I don't think I've been here since my wedding reception."

"It's where Ray always comes," Tildy said.

"How is Ray?" Still trying to accommodate the novelty of Tildy the Reader. "I heard he was in the Louisa Meredith."

"Only with a minor concussion. I suppose you know what my fat-head of a husband did? Smashed his *Follow* bloody *Me* all over the boat ramp. Mark you, he learned this morning he'll get 120 per cent of the cost of the frigging thing from the insurance. And did you hear? He'd been bloody *warned* not to go out that afternoon and he told this very kind English gentleman to go and pee all over himself. The pity of it is that he didn't get drowned himself . . ."

"Oh, Tildy, you can't mean that."

"Yes, I do." The weight of her body made the stool squeak.

"I see his name everywhere. *The David Boon of real estate*."

Tildy nodded. "Listen to him and he's single-handedly responsible for the property boom!"

From the street came the sound of a car horn and the scream of brakes.

"Bloody bogans," someone muttered.

A girl giggled, the enthusiastic giggle of the marijuana smoker.

Tildy cradled her glass with both hands and grew thoughtful. "I meant to say this before. You were right about Ray."

"What makes you say that?" doing her best to remember whatever it was she might have said.

"The way he carries on. He's changed, Merridy," and bit her lip. "Or maybe he is what he always was and only you had the smarts to see it."

"Maybe he's under pressure at work?"

Tildy sipped at her rum. "Only pressure I'm aware of is from other women's cleavages."

"Oh, no."

"Oh, yes," and made a motion with her glass. "Only yesterday I'm having my hair coloured and he comes in and starts carrying on with the hairdresser, who used to work in his office. So there he is, talking to his buxom, hard-headed friend, not knowing it's me sitting across the room with Glad wrap about my head. He's probably been shagging her on the floor of the Bethel or wherever he's meant to be selling."

"Tildy, you don't have proof."

"Don't think she's the only one." Tildy blew out smoke. Cooling the hot dish of her anger. And all at once looked oppressed. "I think one of his tarts has had a baby," in a small voice.

"Good grief!"

"Not anyone we know." Her pink tongue licked an upper lip. "A Japanese girl he met last year," and she gave a mirth-less smile. "At a real-estate convention in Melbourne, for pity's sake."

Tildy had received a letter from this woman asking her

to release Ray from his marital vows so that they might live together – "'I love him so much, blah, blah, so if you care for him in the slightest, blah, blah, you'll let him be with me, blah, blah, blah'" – and enclosing a photograph of a baby girl looking vaguely like Ray, except with oriental eyes and straight black hair.

"Ray denies it's his, of course. But I don't believe him. Frankly, I've reached a point where I don't care one way or the other. I tell you, when I looked at the photo of that baby I felt the battery acid run through my love channels and I knew that our relationship was busted forever. But Zac's taken it none too well. He heard us rowing about it and found me all in a heap. I honestly believe that's what made him behave as he did. You heard about Zac, I suppose?"

Merridy nodded. Everyone had heard about her godson. Caught with his fingers in the Talbot's till. "Zac's five-finger discount," Agnes was calling it.

"It was dreadful." Tildy looked around. Then, recognising someone, leaned close. "It wasn't much money, but Ray was furious . . ." Her voice trailed off. Her Cupid's bow snapped. "Mr Talbot's coming around tonight to discuss it. That's why Ray wanted the whole family out of the house. Montana, Savannah, Cherokee, me. All except Zac."

Merridy put an arm around her shoulder. "Oh, Tildy," as two women passed.

"Hi," one of them called out to Tildy.

"Hi," rubbing her nose.

"Who are *they*?" asked Merridy after they had gone by.

"Search me," Tildy said, pulling herself together. "Oh Christ, don't look now. There's Harry Ford."

"I know. I've been talking to him already."

"How is he?"

"Dying, he says."

"He's always dying. He's been given extreme unction so many times the priest in Campbell Town now sends a bill."

It revived Tildy, to laugh at her own joke. She found a tissue in her bag and blew her nose.

"He reminds me a lot of someone," Merridy mused. "But I can't think who."

"Mr Twelvetrees, could it be?"

"Tildy, that's exactly who!"

"Remember his face, how he used to stare?"

"'Miss Framley, I think that's your foot on the floor.'"

"That's him! That's him!"

"'Please remove yourself, Miss Framley. Meanwhile, will all other couples tear their newspapers in half.'"

"Just want to get by you, mate." A man lurched past. She was pushed against Tildy. They were joined again at the shoulder and for a second there was a unity of lines in their faces and conflicting thoughts, and they were friends again. Her hand touched Tildy's skin. They were reconnected.

"She'll be coming round the mountain when she comes," Tildy sang, her face lapped by the television light.

They were both laughing now; rubbing the tears that rolled down their cheeks and causing Harry's dog to bark. They laughed so much, thinking of the Friday dances. Girls again.

"And you were always the one left standing," said Tildy. "You were so attractive. You still are, of course. Everyone wanted you, Master Twelvetrees most of all."

"They did not."

But Tildy was right. Randal Twelvetrees had believed that the two of them were destined. Had got it into his head that her mother's rejection of him years before was God's way of preparing him for his inevitable union with Merridy. There was suddenly projected onto her memory

363

the day that the Minister's son had taken Merridy to a church near Penguin to make a brass rubbing. She saw him kneeling on the floor and the peculiar movement of his Adam's apple as he brushed the lock of red hair from his eyes and declared himself. "You think there isn't a pattern, Merridy. You think we're just a blank sheet to be drawn on. But there *is* a pattern. You only have to rub on it like this. And then it takes shape, what was there all along. Our whole life. Stretching before our eyes. Just waiting to be rubbed over with a piece of black crayon."

"Listen," Tildy said, "I'm getting us another drink. I want to hear your news."

Tildy came back with fresh glasses. She leaned an elbow on the table; she could have been leaning on a garden gate, contemplating cherries. And lifted an eyebrow.

"So tell me, Merridy. About yourself."

They sat awkward, at an angle to each other.

"I don't know there's much to tell," stalling.

"Everyone's talking. That boy you rescued. I hear Alex was so brave."

"He was. He was incredible." And fidgeting on the stool described for her cousin the night at sea; how Alex threw himself into the waves, and how Kish almost dragged him under as they swam back to the *Zemmery Fidd*.

"They're not talking only about Alex's bravery." Tildy picked her words with care.

"How do you mean?"

Across the table, two eyes shone. "Talk is that you and the boy, you're actually quite close."

"Me and Kish?" She felt the dried tears on her cheek.

"There's me shooting my big mouth off."

The hubbub had receded and the faces of the drinkers

bathed in television light and smoke, and the denim-covered legs.

"What are they saying?"

So Tildy repeated what she had heard, about their sordid trampolinings and how Merridy was so sweet on Kish that she hung a white shirt out when it was safe to visit, a purple T-shirt when not.

"But that's absurd," Merridy said, and reached for her glass.

"Oh, I've crossed too many dry creek beds to worry about Wellington Point gossip." Again, an eyebrow raised itself. "Even so, something's wrong, Merridy. I know it is."

"No, it isn't." She finished her drink.

Tildy stood up.

"Hey, where are you off to?" said Merridy.

"I'm getting us another."

"I'm going."

"Stay where you are," Tildy commanded.

"I've had enough," but Merridy sat down.

Tildy went away and presently came back.

Merridy watched her put down two more glasses on the table.

Tildy touched her arm. "Come on, sweetie. Share." This time the cigarette she offered was hand-rolled.

Merridy shook her head. "I don't smoke."

"You don't drink, and you're drinking. C'mon, it'll relax you. Ray used to grow it himself until he became a councillor."

Dully, Merridy accepted the joint. Inhaled.

She looked up at her cousin. Tildy had seen her childhood; to everyone else, even Alex, she covered it up. Miserable, she pushed the words out with the thick, sweet smoke: "I don't know. He reminds me of . . ."

"Of who?" Taking her hand away.

"No, it's stupid. I know it is."

Everyone at that bar, which had shrunk with the crowd of people and the enormous screen and the dimness of the lighting, everyone began to fade.

"Not him?" And Tildy saw that she had hit the mark. "That's crazy, Merridy. Hector is dead," very sharply.

"I know," flinching at the name.

"Well, then." Almost angry now.

"But what if . . . what if he didn't die?"

"Well, he'd be almost forty for a start."

"What if—"

"Oh, tommyrot. He died. I don't know how he died, but he died. Full stop," and sat there in glowing annoyance.

Merridy sucked on the cigarette. She was not strong enough for these memories. "He's dead, of course. It's just that when I'm with Kish . . . this sounds idiotic, but . . ."

"But what?"

"I feel, I don't know . . ." She could not stop them. Tears coloured with mascara and rouge. Tears that followed lines which had not been there when they were young. "I feel like I did when Hector was alive."

"That's a very, very long time ago," Tildy said in a voice that had never sounded so grown-up. And raised her glass.

Merridy was matching Tildy sip for sip. Swallowing more than rum. She was swallowing her fear, her pride, her guilt.

"My turn," said Tildy in a jollier voice and took the joint from her.

Merridy borrowed Tildy's tissue and dabbed at her cheeks. "Have you ever wanted anyone – apart from Ray?"

"Oh, Merridy, aren't you getting any?"

"It's not that," in what had become a trembling whisper. "I know that look, and it's not what you're thinking."

366

Over Tildy's shoulder she could see Harry eyeing them. "Don't you know . . ." but the shame was welling, to suppose that Kish might be any resolution to her hidden anguish.

"Of course I know," Tildy sighed. "But that's in the past now, darling." And tapped the grotty paperback. "This gives me everything I need. Well, almost."

Merridy slumped back. "I don't know why I'm talking about this. It never leads to a good place. Let's forget it."

But Tildy was on a jag. "For God's sake, when *are* we going to talk about it? You know one thing reading has taught me? It's that you may as well talk about it because it's *there*. Everyone has felt dreadful for you over the years, but at a certain point your refusal to talk about Hector has turned to poison. To be honest, until you talk about him no one will ever know you – and can you tell me what is so great about not being known? I bet you don't talk about it with Alex. In fact, I bet you chose Alex because you knew you wouldn't have to talk about it with him." She took a final puff and stubbed it out and picked up her empty glass. "Another?"

At last, Merridy pulled herself to her feet. "I really must go."

"Well, go then."

"You're not staying, are you?"

"I don't know, I might. Just for a little. Like I said, it's been ages. Anyway, Ray's probably not finished his oh-so-important business with Mr Talbot," with an embittered laugh.

"Then I'll say goodbye." She moved unsteadily to kiss Tildy's cheek, but their heads bumped and they were kissing on the lips.

Tildy clung to her. "It was lovely to see you, Merridy. You're still my best friend."

Merridy left her there.

It was dark outside. A harvest moon was slung between the Norfolk pines. The white chips of the whittled clouds that the south-easterly gathered across it provoked a dread in her.

Merridy walked on legs that felt drugged. Gulping the air, she stumbled towards her car when she saw a dog in the middle of the road, hunched over something. And observing the dog, a tall figure silhouetted against the moon.

The English voice spoke half to itself. "Pretends he's deaf when he's eating roadkill. He is deaf anyway, but he's even more deaf then."

"Goodnight, Harry."

"Goodnight, Mrs Dove. Don't forget – my affectionate regards to Alex."

CHAPTER SIX

ALEX WAS SURPRISED THAT there were no other cars at the Alexandria Beach Retreat. All was explained. The guests had fled the convict-built cottages because of the stinking whale.

The owner, a small and talkative nurse from Burnley, had lived twenty-five years on this spit. She was relieved to greet two clients who did not appear to mind the stench.

"I live on a farm," Alex said.

"It got so bad I had to spray the room every half-hour. You had to cover your face. You can still smell it faintly," and sniffed. "There." She stepped back from the reception desk and pointed through French windows to where the adult sperm whale had rolled onto the shore, yards from her hotel. "That whiteness on the rocks was made by the oil. See the sea eagles?" Two grey smudges on the pines at the end of the beach. "I think that's some of the intestines over there. Yes. Bits of intestine are sitting over there."

Cormorants wandered along the sand with pieces of blubber in their beaks.

"It was fifty foot long when Parks and Wildlife did their post-mortem. They think it was the storm that made him lose his way, poor thing."

"Is there a toilet?" asked Kish, face taut.

"Over there." And to Alex: "I'll just get the keys."

She went into another small room. Kish headed straight for the lavatory while Alex looked at the newspaper that she had been reading.

A black-and-white photograph on the front page caught his attention.

He was still arched over the *Advocate* when the woman came back.

"I'm putting you both in the deluxe cottage. It has a spa-bath. I assume you don't mind sharing with your son."

Alex looked up. The colour had drained from his face. "I'm sorry. We are going to have to leave at once. I really am sorry, but this is an emergency. Could I use your phone?"

When Kish returned, he found Alex pacing up and down.

"We're going home."

"What, now? But it's right on dark."

"I have to see Merridy."

"What about?"

"It's about her brother. I can't tell you any more." He did not want to talk at all until he saw her, was with her.

"Then what about your windmill?" a good deal puzzled. "Isn't it going to be ready tomorrow?"

But Alex was already out of the door.

CHAPTER SEVEN

MERRIDY HAD A DANGEROUS drive home. Coming down Cerney Hill, her car hit a wallaby. Startled, she drove on. Around the next corner a possum stared at her, two bright pins of light, then scuttled onto the verge. It seemed that the road would never end.

She was in a tremendous state from more than one source and disturbed by her conversation with Tildy. She was ashamed to have been outed by someone with whom she had always felt safe. What she felt now was exhaustion and darkness – anger even – that she had had a drink and stirred it up in the first place. And overriding it all a feeling of dread, as if it had a force of its own and she was in its grasp.

It had happened long ago, but it was still there in her head. At the mention of Hector, she was overwhelmed by a resurgent grief. As she drove back to Moulting Lagoon Farm, she ached, she physically ached, for her brother.

On the dark, winding coast road she thought of her family's shack near Wynyard. She was standing on the deck, staring into the bush. It was morning, in late summer, and the large gums threw thick shadows. She could hear a wattlebird and the roar of the waves breaking on the stony shore. Her father was in the house, and her mother was saying something to him. She had no reason to think this, but she already knew that she was not going to see Hector again. She knew that the world for which her mother had a moment before been washing her face and grabbing the towel off the floor had altered, and that whatever now happened she was exiled from it.

Her headlights picked out the entrance and swept from the road. She drove through the gate, over the cattle-grid, into the drive. A little drunk, a little floaty, and enormously upset, she switched off the headlights. Her eyes scoured the sky. No stars, nothing but a yawning blankness. Only the white track beckoned, a pale arm that reached down out of that blankness and drew her in.

She followed the gravel drive up. The smell of horse and sheep manure rolled over the paddock. Grasping the wheel and staring at her thumbs, the moonlight on the polished nails, she was conscious of the trees reaching over the drive and animals watching. She shuddered, but she was not cold. Severed from its previous life, her heart had gone to ground. Tugged back into a hole that led to who knew where and was inhabited by God knows what.

Alex drove for five hours, stopping only in Epping Forest for petrol and a cup of bitter coffee and to ring Merridy.

Again, no answer. She had to be down at the oyster shed.

In his distress, he telephoned Tildy. He rehearsed what he would say: "Could you dash to my home? Please go out there and get Merridy before she reads it herself, or is told, or hears it on the radio." He did not want her to hear it on the radio. As he listened to the dialling tone, he thought: What about the *Mercury*? But he was confident that the *Mercury*, being a Hobart newspaper and concerned more with stories from the south, would not yet have reported the discovery.

It was Ray who answered. Rattled when he heard that

it was Alex. "No, I have no idea where she is and I'm too busy to go chasing around town . . ."

Alex crunched his paper cup and threw it away. He called over to Kish and they drove on.

Night fell as they came into Campbell Town and turned onto the Lake Leake Highway. The ute's headlights roamed through the bush. In some of the shacks – makeshift cabins set among the she-oaks – Alex could see sofas on the deck and corrugated water tanks. Every now and then a wallaby hopped across the road, stopping to peer at the lights that approached at such speed, and hopped away.

After an extremely long journey, they arrived back at the dark house shortly before ten o'clock. It looked a strange place under the full moon, the windows blacker than overcooked coffee and the light glinting on the ripple-iron roofs. But no sign of Merridy, no sign of her car.

"Well, I'm going to have to see if she's at the shed," he said to Kish. "I'll drop you here."

It crossed his mind to wonder how safe it was to leave Kish alone in the house. He always thought twice about leaving his Purdey around when Kish was at home and had taken to locking the shotgun in his office. But Kish showed little inclination to go inside. He stood on the drive, stretching himself and looking up at the moon.

Alex left him there and drove down the hill, fast, towards Moulting Lagoon.

Her eyes not yet adjusted to the night sky, Merridy parked on the lawn and switched off the engine. The moon had floated into the treetops. It shone with unnatural brightness on the roofs and on the grass, save for a dark patch where the fallen pine soured the land.

She made her way, tripping on the edge of the lawn,

towards the house. She could hear the telephone ringing as she opened the kitchen door, and then it stopped.

She undid the top button of her dress, not bothering to turn on the light. The night was hot and the kitchen still smelled of the simple red sauce that she had left on the table and the walnut cake that she had baked for the men's dinner. Relieved to have the house all to herself, she kicked off her shoes and tramped along the corridor. Through her rum eyes the place was alive; the samplers glowed; and the cockatoo looked bigger when she went into the living room where she had shut Rusty. She followed the puppy out of the room and fumbled open the door into her study. The moonlight fell across her Huon pine trunk. With a sigh she sank to her knees and unbolted the lid and plunged her hands inside. Throwing out the cotton sheets and lace curtains that she had never unpacked, now speckled with dead insects, the cassette that she had never watched, until, at the bottom, her fingers encountered the edges of a plastic bag.

She shook the objects onto the floor, and in the lozenge of moonlight picked through them: the orange feather; the photograph of Hector on the beach near Wynyard, taken the day before his seventh birthday and that she had never been able to stick in a book; the scrapbooks of cuttings from local papers; the messages relayed through Taffy; the scuffed Blundstone.

Merridy held the child's boot to her face, in quick breaths inhaling the smell of leather and rubber.

Something moved on the deck with the intimacy of an animal's footfall that had walked there for years. And she heard the dog addressed and the shoe-squeak and the twanging of the closed door.

"Hello," he said, speaking from inside.

Who was it? Not Alex – nor Kish. They were north.

She saw, then, it was Hector.

"Hector?" fluting, and stood. There was the sound of what she had held dropping to the floor. She brought her fingers together in the way people did when they were helping one another over fences.

In that narrow passage lined with admonitions and hopes, he came creaking towards her on the cedar floor.

"Hector . . ." She pronounced it to herself as though licking the bottom of a bowl. For she had never spoken his name, never. Apart from that once. He had survived somewhere in the catacombs.

His shadow blended with the samplers, a long dark blade shucking her.

She had become a little girl again. "Hector," she repeated, licking the last leaves so that she would not have to read a fortune. And felt her hunger and panic rising.

A smile crawled along his face.

"You look nice."

"Hector!" A name to shout through her palms. She could not stop herself. His eyes quivered as if he had heard shots. Never had they seemed so strange and round and listless. His hard, deep mouth like an initial engraved.

He came closer. He smelled of stars. She wanted to tell him how much she had missed him; her brother.

"I was just out looking at the moon," he said and smiled.

She heard her young girl's laugh. The *Advocate* was open on the floor. They were dancing around a newspaper. And over in the corner Mr Twelvetrees was playing the piano.

"You're back." In a voice that she used for another person from another world. And threw a hand over her eyes against any thought of the future. "Thank God, you're back," and ran forward in her drugged state to embrace him. Her shirt was unbuttoned; she was sailing towards him in the *Otago*, the gulls cawing, the spray nicking her face and the wind licking at the ice-cream mast and up between her legs. The whole planet was sailing on a wave across the floor towards him.

"Is something wrong?" he asked.

She plastered herself onto him. Longing enamelled her lips. She had bandaged him away inside herself, but all burst out when she touched him. She kissed his face, squeezed away the years, in the ferment of her passion unbuttoning his shirt, taking off his glasses.

"No, no, nothing's wrong." As sobbing she lost herself in his flesh.

He seemed grateful for her outpouring of affection. For a moment he gave in to her embrace.

But he was so unhappy, or sick. Or burning. His mouth made an ugly shape. "No," he said – like that. When she touched him.

Ungluing, she felt his eyes on her. His trapped look.

She looked at her sky-blue hands on his face. Her fingers like tubes squeezed out. Her capacity to touch had dried like paint.

"No," he simply said. And pushed her.

The illusion that it was Hector passed like a shadow down the corridor. Leaving behind Kish. "Pull yourself together."

"Kish . . . ?" She looked at him, incredulous. "I thought you were someone else." And heard her lunatic words fade away. As he ran from her.

A door slammed.

"Kish."

She flung open the door to his room and stood there, her head dishevelled. Nobody.

"Kish!" She was snivelling now. Suspended between her childhood and Kish.

One by one she flung open the doors along the passage. Until she came to her bedroom. No one there. But something had changed. She looked slowly around. Flicking her eyes back and forth. Before she saw what it was.

The wardrobe door – closed.

She started forward and hammered on it. "Kish . . . let me in." But the door was locked fast, from the inside.

Merridy stooped, peered through the keyhole. Filled with his damned piece of pine. She listened to his breathing. And moaned. "Kish! Let. Me. In."

In the kitchen, the telephone was ringing again.

The gate to Oblong Oysters was locked.

Alex returned along the lower road, stopping now and then to check the troughs. He parked next to the shearing shed and after satisfying himself that the bullocks in the paddock had sufficient feed decided that he was too tired to climb back into the ute. He left the vehicle where it was and walked towards the house through the farmyard.

The route took him past his old workshop. Out of habit he looked up at the window. Still no light on inside the house, but over on the lawn the bright moonlight reflected from the roof of Merridy's Toyota. Thank God, she's back, he thought. But how funny she hasn't turned on the lights. There must be a power cut. He was about to walk on when he heard the sound of someone talking in excited tones. He stepped across the flower bed and pressed his face to the glass. The door to Merridy's study was open.

He could make out Merridy in the corridor. She was standing sideways on, one hand up to her face. Instantly, he had the feeling that had seized him when he first saw her. And remembered her forthright laugh and how gamine she was. He was about to tap the window to get her attention, but something about her posture stayed his hand. Then her knees straightened and she ran towards a figure who stood framed in the kitchen doorway, flinging her arms about his neck and clinging to him.

And the man clinging to her.

The news that Alex had to give her bled away. He stumbled back, tripping over roots, heart thudding. He picked himself up.

A door slammed, then another, excluding him. Not knowing what he was doing, he forced his way through the shrubs and bottle-brushes, obedient to a blind force that dragged him around the house, over the flower bed that encircled it, until he stood outside their bedroom window.

He put his neck forward to the glass as if shaving himself. Merridy was in the room. So, evidently, was the man she had embraced, because she was calling to him in a voice haunting and low – the most entreating sound that Alex had ever heard.

"Kish! Let. Me. In."

Alex had no response, no defence for this situation. He remained where he was, absolutely stationary. A tiny bit surprised that Merridy did not see him as she flew out of the house a moment later.

He was rooted to the spot for as long as it took Merridy to scramble into her car and accelerate away down the drive.

This was too much. He did not want to talk to Kish. He did not know what he wanted. He was going to go away and think to himself what in God's name was he to do with his wife and this young man, who would have to get out of his house at first bloody light.

He blundered off, as on the morning when his parents

were killed, letting his body take him in the direction of the sea and the sanctuary of his lichen-spattered rock.

The moon shone white on fields where convicts had been flogged for speaking. Blasted with grief, he roamed the paddock that he had walked through ten minutes before, a different person then. His shadow snaked after him, blending with charred stumps. Startled cattle looked up at him as they might have looked at a spectre. And all the time the thumping in his chest.

He staggered towards his rock.

CHAPTER EIGHT

FROM ITS SHELF HIGH up on the Welsh dresser Kish seized the bottle with the *Otago* in it, and fled the appalling house. Across the drive, the clothes-line reared up. The silhouette of the Hill's Hoist against the moon sharper than any gallows.

He swerved onto the lawn and stood very still, panting. He saw that she had taken her car.

His breathlessness was slow to pass. He could not recall this fear before. Fear, though his legs were fast and his knife was sharp. He felt the wind on his torn fingers. Already he missed his room. The consoling smells of kitchen and puppy and log-fire, not to mention the sensation that came over him whenever his eyes looked into those bottles with their ships, shelf after shelf of them. It was so difficult, believing in an abstract. At Moulting Lagoon Farm he had come as close as he had known to belief. That household had offered him the prospect, if not of a lasting home, then a place he would like to have had as home for a little longer.

Warm memories buzzed in his head. Her car – without any headlights on – braking in a skid on the lawn. The way she had stumbled into the house like a sick animal. The windows he had watched, waiting for her to switch on a light. It had relieved him to be away from the farm all day: he had felt the stirrings of desire, but even if he thought Mrs Dove attractive he was not going to get involved there. When at last he had stood up to follow her inside, it was to see if she needed help. Not to be suffocated by her. Not to be mistaken for someone called Hector. Not to be . . .

So he stood by the tree stump, dazed and offended at the violence that she had disturbed in him. In his chaos, he thought: Ah, fuckit. What am I going to do when Mr Dove gets back? Towards Mr Dove he experienced a mingling of gratitude and respect and even a wish to learn from him. But now he had no idea what to do, where to go. He skirted the upended pine and ran and ran across the grass with the bottle burning his hands, until he could tolerate it no longer. At the bottom of the drive, he flung it into the darkness. But no sooner did he hear the scrape of glass on stone than he sank to his knees and scrambled on all fours searching for the bottle. He was convinced that he had lost or broken it, had given up hope, when in a glint of moon he saw the edge of the penny and the bottle still intact. He grabbed it and lay in the gravel and held it tight against his chest.

CHAPTER NINE

IN THE DEPLETED BAR, Ray lectured a truckie.

"A man is a single person, though he might have a second nature. A woman is twenty-three different people, none of whom can stand to be introduced to each other."

"Fair dinkum," the truckie said, stroking a wide black beard.

"Chap in Melbourne told me that," Ray said. Contentment had made him expansive.

"Mathematician, was he?"

"A businessman, more like." Ray smelled his wine and sipped, rolling it around his mouth before swallowing. "Tell you another thing about sheilas. As soon as they get you, they want to change you. They want to bring out the heavy rollers and the sandpaper and rub off the rough edges."

The truckie finished his glass of Boag's. The crowd had thinned and there was no one left to listen to Ray but him.

At his end of the counter, Ray had had another thought. "Why is it that women ask other women for advice about men? Surely they should ask men, since that's the area they want to know about. It's like asking a colonist about the Aborigines. It really is."

The truckie patted his beard philosophically. But did not dwell on Ray's wisdom. Perturbed still by the strange young man who had flagged him down an hour before. The truckie was coming round a tight corner north of Wellington Point when the man ran out at a crouch. His first thought: A large animal had skittered from the bush. Then in the middle of the road it stood up. Barely human, in the headlights.

With the face of a persecuted creature, scary too. Any faster – roadkill. He had slammed on his brakes with every foot he had, skidding across the road and jerking his log-truck to a stop with less than the length of his arm to spare. So had he sat recovering his breath in large gulps, his eyes taking in this creature who nursed to his chest what he saw now was a bottle. A fucking wino! Wearing spectacles and with a ring in his ear and glitter in his hair and on his jeans like he'd been to a party. Except that it wasn't glitter. You could see by the dashboard light when he opened the door and scuttled up into the cabin that it was little flecks of glass. Thousands and thousands of them. The wino had asked for a ride into Wellington Point. Too late to refuse him. He had sat for the next ten minutes, hugging that bottle of his, not speaking, until the truck hissed to a halt outside the hotel. "I'm gonna stop here and have a beer. Wanna beer, mate? Or you can have a gin if you like?" But he shook his head. Cheeks rigid in the street light. Eyes emptier than two cemetery jamjars. Then opened the door and leaped into the night, no word, not even a "Ta-ta, mate".

In ebullient mood, Ray ordered a glass of Merlot for his new friend and another for himself. "You, too, Belinda?"

He had bought a whole carton of it.

"He's celebrating," explained the lavender head.

"Oh," said the truckie, and turned to look at Ray. "Lotto?"

"Not quite."

The truckie nodded. "I was gonna say, because there's nothing in the whole wide world you look less like than a man who's won the lotto."

"But almost," said Ray, straightening a sleeve on which there gleamed a gold cufflink. "Almost."

*

383

It was in a different frame of mind that Ray had opened his door to Mr Talbot five hours earlier.

"Ah, Albert, please come in." In a grave voice tinged with surprise. Save at Keith Framley's funeral, he had not seen him so formal. The oversized blue suit brought home to Ray the gravity of his son's offence. As for his eyes! They stared at Ray with a distended look, as if set lengthwise in his face. "Do come in."

Mr Talbot had asked for this private meeting. His manner on the telephone furtive so that Ray immediately divined the reason behind the rendezous. Mr Talbot was going to discuss the problem of Zac, who waited in his bedroom to be summoned, forbidden to leave the house until he had delivered the apology over which father and son had spent time this afternoon rehearsing.

"You'll join me, I hope, in a glass of Craigie Knowe?"

"Don't open it on my account," Mr Talbot said.

"I was going to anyway," smiled Ray, whose terror it was that Mr Talbot would make an official report of Zac's small criminal misdemeanour to Sergeant Finter and so the news would inevitably reach Hobart and the columns of the *Mercury*.

Mr Talbot felt the sofa and sat down. He dragged his morbid gaze around the room, the posters of the pyramids and Sphinx, the shelves double-stacked with books, before his eyes came to rest on the coffee table where there was a tray with six glasses on it. "That's nice," he muttered unenthusiastically, tapping his fat fingers on the pewter surface and rattling the glasses.

"A wedding present."

"Mrs Grogan well?"

"Tildy's out," in a light voice. Ray had furthermore instructed Montana to absent herself. And Savannah. And take Cherokee with her. This was man's business.

"She'll be sad to miss you, but she's good," and pulled the cork.

Mr Talbot's eyes commenced a second circuit of the room. "Sorry to hear about your boat," he said.

"Yes, wasn't that sad? But she was fully insured. No damage to your garage, I hope?" At the same time tempted to hope that perhaps, after all, this might be the reason for Mr Talbot's visit.

"Oh, no, I don't think so."

Ray looked agitatedly at the wine label. He would speak first, he decided. "Mr Talbot . . ."

"I'll come to the point." The oversized suit wriggled.

"I'm sure we can reach some accommodation," Ray said.

"That remains to be seen."

"Before you say anything, try this. It's young, but suggestive, I think."

Mr Talbot gulped at the young Cabernet with an indefinable thirst. It was many a year since he had felt this need to drink.

Ray hovered, impatient for his reaction. "Well?"

"It reminds me," Mr Talbot said thickly, "of New Britain."

"I'm sorry?"

"Papua," Mr Talbot said. "Where I was in the war." Waiting for the rum-drop. The alcohol floating out of the bomb-bay in a chaff bag that rolled and rolled and rolled. Sometimes the chute tore and he had to go with a spade and dig the stuff out.

"*Ologeta nau*," he urged the native who stood before him.

Ray said nothing. He wondered if Mr Talbot was having a stroke.

"'All together now'," explained Mr Talbot, and took another gulp. "It's in pidgin."

"It must have been awful," said Ray.

Mr Talbot dipped his eyes to the tray, in which the elongated reflections of glasses seemed to hold some sort of fascination.

"They say you should have won the VC three times over. For what you did. That's what they say at the RSL."

Mr Talbot swallowed more wine. He said: "People think we won the war, but we sat on our arses most of the time. We could have been charged tourist rates. In fact, I wouldn't mind doing it again."

Even so, he did not look happy. Remembering line after line of waiting women, the dried grass sticking out from between their legs like a rooster's tail. The *meri* whom he had treated and sometimes comforted, his forbearance. And a woman and an evening that no quantity of Craigie Knowe could extinguish. Whether it was her sarong of blue-and-red silk, or the baby that she carried in a string bag or her stoicism towards her wound – the Japanese had damn near severed her arm – this young widow had pierced Albert's defences.

He cleared his pleated throat. "I have, as you know, no family."

"Then you are the lucky one," Ray smiled tartly.

But for mournfulness Mr Talbot outdid him. "You are looking, Ray, at the last Talbot. The last one," and slumped back. "It is a responsibility you cannot imagine, to be at the end of the line."

Ray studied the blanched sockets, suspecting them of sheltering a hidden menace. Not finding it, he was uncertain where to settle his anxiety.

"Mr Talbot . . ." he began pacifically, casting about for a line to take. "No one in Wellington Point understands better than I your wish to protect your property. No one."

"No, no, you cannot understand."

She smiled as she put down her *bilum*. In the bag, her baby slept. He remembered the shadow of the fibre mesh on the child's face, the discreet and graceful motion of her arm, the pool of parachute silk on the beaten earth floor.

"As I said, I am prepared to do anything to put this unfortunate business behind us."

"What?" he could just ask.

She stood naked. The skin on her flat stomach palpitating where her heart beat quicker. But not so quick as his heart. She was still smiling. A smile without conditions attached, or secrets.

"No women," his commander's final briefing reminded him.

But did he have the strength to restrain himself? He would never discover.

From outside, from beyond the chieftain's hut, there came – soul-destroyingly – the sound of steady typing.

Nothing would ever seem to him more separating than the vanishing of her smile as she recognised machine-gun fire, or the barbed wire of knotted string behind which a child woke.

He sat motionless. Watching her scrabble to cover her nakedness and gather up the baby with the arm that he had managed to mend, and run for her life. He tried to be more invisible than ever that night.

After an appropriate and respectful silence, Ray said: "Speak frankly. How much would satisfy you?"

"What were we talking about . . . ?" Albert shook his head. "This wine. It's making me forgetful."

"Another glass?"

He let Ray pour. His lips were rather dry.

It was after that night that they killed the members of a Japanese patrol. They watched them walk up the head of the valley and picked them off in the moonlight one by one as they crossed a river – their reflections on the water like a row of glasses on a pewter tray. One man had cried out all night. Albert went down in the morning to treat him and found his body on the riverbank. As he turned round, he became aware of the eyes of a Japanese soldier on him. He was propped against a rock and staring. Albert had raised his hands above his head before he saw that the soldier was dead, shot in the back by his own men. He began to weep then.

His eyes looked at Ray out of their hatched face. "I have decided to sell."

"Sell?" With extreme care, Ray put the bottle down. "What, the store?"

They were sitting side by side on the sofa.

"I want to know what you think it might be worth."

And after Ray had blurted a sum, so relieved that the visit was not about Zac – who would remain forgotten in his room for the rest of the evening, even after his mother arrived home and passed out on the sofa – Albert enquired what advantageous terms Ray might offer in the event that he would agree to act as agent, an agreement reached after a second bottle of Craigie Knowe stood empty on the round pewter tray, but not before Ray had jotted down a few particulars of the building, including its history – and, while he was about it, relieved a by-now tottering Albert of a spare set of keys.

"Give me a couple of days to sink about it."

"Take all the time in the word," said Ray.

"There is just one fibrillation," Mr Talbot slurred as Ray walked him home. "And I'm serious about this." A log-truck coming towards them had jogged his memory. He caught the flash of a drawn pale face and was reminded of another – an oriental woman with a baby, peering anxiously out of her crowded, chauffeur-driven car as she was motored ever so slowly down the main street, ostensibly looking for properties to buy.

"Yes?" – but Ray was not in a listening mood. Thrilled that Zac was off the hook. Thrilled at the prize of Talbot's. So that even as Albert told him very seriously about his one fibrillation, he did not quite grasp the subtext: "Oh, don't worry. That's easily arranged."

All in all, Ray was brimming. He was already thinking along the lines of the development of the bark-mill in Swansea. Perfectly adequate, but a bogan's shack compared to the potential of Mr Talbot's building. There was, in fact, no limit to what he envisaged for the Talbot emporium. His fellow councillors were sure to line up behind him. They were going to be as jealous as bright green cats. He was thinking marina, fish restaurant, bottle-shop, youth hostel, art gallery, a library even! In the morning he would speak to his contact in Melbourne. Pump her up. A once-in-a-lifetime opportunity to invest in the undisputed jewel of east-coast real estate.

"Well, thanks for that, mate," said the truckie. "I have to be in Triabunna." And stood up, leaving his wine untouched and Ray on his own.

CHAPTER TEN

MERRIDY DID NOT KNOW how long she drove around before deciding to head back to the hotel. The bar was deserted, so that now it became possible to forget her visit earlier in the evening; indeed, to believe that no time at all had passed since the first occasion she came into this room, kitted out in Keith Framley's flummery. Step by hesitant step she moved forward in the semi-darkness.

The television was still on. With his back to it, a beefy man sat solitary at the counter.

"Excuse me, but have you seen Tildy Grogan?"

So addressed, the figure rotated. Thickset with a cigar-coloured moustache. His mouth gilded in the television light.

"Why, Merridy!" His eyes seized her, growing wider and brighter.

"Ray . . ."

His scarlet skin was squalid, but it erupted, and she realised, on averting her eyes, that the Pope was being wheeled from the balcony – although not before one last upraised finger that mimicked an obscene gesture. Or a native pine teetering.

Her look said: Jesus bloody wept, but he patted a chair.

Hypnotised, she stood her ground. "I was looking for Tildy." She had driven here with no other plan, only to find her cousin and to ask if she might stay the night.

"Tildy?" and appeared bewildered. "Oh, Tildy."

The lavender-headed woman called over her shoulder:

"She was here about an hour ago." And pushed herself through the swing-door.

"There you go, she's not here," Ray said.

For a bad second, all Merridy heard was the grave low buzz of the commentator and tearful American voices. Her foot stepped back. She did not want to stay.

"Hey, don't leave. I've hardly spoken to you. I've hardly seen you."

Last time together in the same room as each other – at the funeral service of Tildy's father, but as per normal they had exchanged not a word. Otherwise, Ray saw her in snatched glimpses when she came out of Talbot's. Or every summer at the Cranbrook Fair, selling oysters. It was amazing, now that he came to think of it, how in seventeen years the two of them never once had occasion to meet on their own; how they had continued to avoid all meaningful contact, beyond: "Hi, Merridy, how ya doing?" "Hi, Ray, not too bad. Yourself?" But he had thought of her, oh yes. From the moment she left him in his bedroom staring down at what, then, was unrevivable.

The stool was hard. He parted his legs. "Like a glass of this? What we're drinking, Belinda and me, is box wine, chateau collapsible."

It had never happened again, his inability to perform.

"I think I won't."

She seemed upset, with a flayed, uneasy look. Her hair springing from her head in tufts. She might have seen a ghost, or been violated. In that dress.

The memory of her, shoes off, sitting on his bed made Ray wince.

"Here, I'll do it," seeing as Belinda had disappeared into the kitchen.

Still, she stood. Her thoughts slamming doors down the corridor of her skull. She was confused, but above all she was loathing his attention. This man who incarnated her own deficiency of character. Who had he been consorting with? That barwoman, she supposed. The hairdresser. A young Japanese businesswoman. And tensed herself to slap him, the complicated loathing like an ecstasy in her. At what he had done to Tildy. At what he might have done to her, had he only been capable. She shuddered. Even in her most unstable moments, she had not gone there.

"Come on," Ray said, in the soothing tone of an acupuncturist.

So that she was left poised between her feeling of repulsion and another feeling, in which all sorts of opportunities for shame rehearsed themselves. Numbly, her rage deserting her, she sat on the patted chair and accepted the glass that he had poured. His kindness was an attrition, but she had no contours, she could blur into anything.

Denting his cheek with a fist, Ray took a longer look at her. He wondered if he would find Merridy so beautiful were he first setting eyes on her. This evening she reminded him, in a way that he had never considered before, of Tildy. But still attractive.

"That's a nice dress," fingering the lapel as his wife had done and picking some fluff off the shoulder.

She rocked back. "I have to go to Melbourne."

"Oh?"

"My wholesaler. He's been pestering me to sign a contract."

He shifted on the hot stool, though it was not lust exactly that rose within him. Rather, the consciousness of a tenderer person who was obscured by this other Ray.

"Well, you've certainly made a name for yourself," giving her a smile. "With your oysters."

"Yes, they do seem popular," she mumbled. But his politeness did not deceive.

"Pity one can't get them locally. Pity you have to go all the way to Melbourne to eat them."

"You only have to call the shed. Jason could deliver. Or I could," reminding herself that he disgusted her.

"You would?" Looking into her eyes that swilled with Captain Morgan and tonic. That stared sightlessly ahead. At the photograph of the log-truck. At the bottles that flickered in the reflected light of an empty balcony in Rome.

In this watery light, a dreadful vista opened up behind her: of untaken roads, unopened doors, unkissed faces. So with a pang she remembered Kish and the absurdity of a passion that she could not now credit, or explain. And most of all the panic that suddenly had seized her in the bedroom. The knowledge that if Kish was home then so too was Alex, and she could not face him in this state.

Ray sat forward. It was important that he told her. It was more vital to him even – in that moment – than the once-in-a-lifetime chance to develop the Talbot emporium. A Mass had started and the music emphasised to him the solemnity of his emotion. He had aimed his passion at her and it had missed its mark, but he had kept Merridy upright in his head, unattainable as an angel.

"You know, Merridy, you always made me feel, somehow . . ." But it was out of reach, what he wanted to say.

"What?" Her tactic of not looking at Ray – as if he would thereby vanish – not working. "What are you saying?" And swivelled her head.

He wore a belt now around his wider waist, and gold cufflinks. Plus gold in a bangle on his wrist and in his ear and in a thin chain around his neck; anywhere visible, it seemed. Apart from the gold, he was older. More sinew about his neck and across his shoulder, and under his chin the adipose fin of a scar. But not so very much changed.

393

"I'm saying that you always made me feel good."

"Oh, Ray." In her eyes a glint of frost, because of her disdain. But her disgust was not collaborating with her desire.

Ray touched the convict brick on the counter. Matches were still arranged in its hollow for smokers to strike. He laid them out carefully side by side. They might have indicated dead men. Or his conquests.

"It's true," he said, emboldened by the organ music and her gaze. Never had he felt so serious. He wanted her to slice out the tender person encased within him. Whom he glimpsed whenever he tracked the sun as it toppled over Maria Island, or inhaled the wind across the bay; or fished for stripy trumpeter on the continental shelf.

He struck a match. It flared and shrank.

Smiling at the flame in rather a sad way, Ray thought again of how little he had seen of Merridy and of how very much, by contrast, she had consumed his thoughts. She served to remind him that his life was not more wonderful for his success. He would have left Wellington Point years ago if it had not been for Tildy and the children, like five spears through the feet. But also – a little bit – because of Merridy too.

He didn't even bother pretending to himself otherwise. He had dreamed of Merridy so deep on his wedding night, at a self-contained cottage in St Helen's, but all he retrieved from his dream was a sturdy erection that caused him to leap out of bed and race through the house shouting: "Tildy, Tildy," until she relieved him of it against the low bluestone wall of the rented kitchen, pressing her buttocks into his groin until she had rubbed and squeezed it away.

But it was Merridy he was thinking of. Impregnable as Talbot's. Whose image he had continued to summon to any number of creaking beds. Who sat less than a yard away, so close that if he wanted he could reach out and touch her face; who watched the flame eat its way along the matchstick, twisting it, blackening it.

He had such thin wrists, she saw.

Her eyes smarted.

It was Captain Morgan leading her astray. And Tildy's joint. And now the wine. Grape and grain don't mix, her father used to say. She wanted to leave this place and go back to what she knew. The samplers stitched by young girls for future husbands. The cockatoo and the sieve. But Kish was there. Sealed in the wardrobe behind his absurd pine key. What would she have done if he had desired it? If he had permitted? No, she could not go back. Not tonight. Not while she was so indistinct to herself.

He blew out the flame.

So they continued to sit there. Red wine has its own moroseness in a dark room with a television on. There were a number of people she could call on, but when she imagined greeting them at the door she lacked the energy to drag herself away.

While he tossed the dead match behind the counter and waited for her to expose his second nature, the good man she had discovered during a rain-soaked barbecue for his twenty-seventh birthday.

Then Ray, who had lined up his matchsticks like so many years of his life that separated him from that moment, leaned forward.

"You never liked me, Merridy."

"That's not true," studiously not looking at him.

"You saw what you saw and you made up your mind."

She touched her hair. "That's not true."

His lips drank the wine. "What did you want with Tildy, by the way?"

"Oh, nothing that can't wait." It did not seem appropriate, now, to tell Ray that she had hoped to spend the night under his roof.

Bending, he said: "You know, I'm worried about Tildy. I think she's not well. All those books. All she ever does is read."

If Merridy had expected Ray's view of his wife's reading to be contemptuous, his next words surprised her.

"It makes me jealous. It really does. I'd like to be able to understand, too." And thought of his bookish wife on the sofa, her thick legs under her, away in some realm where he could never expect to join her. "Thing is, Merridy, she prefers books to me . . ."

"Oh, come on," and kicked him.

"Aah!" said Ray. "Aaah!"

He rubbed his shin. His face crumpled. And now he longed for her. To win her without cheating. Without the intervention of his outward self, who – he could understand – repelled her.

The muscles softened round her eyes. With pleasurable dread she looked at him. His moustache so close to his mouth, like a mutton-bird gliding low over the water.

His intensity surprised him. He felt an old warmth spreading over him. He felt exalted.

"*King Lear*, wasn't it – what you read to me? I never forget a name. I tried to get hold of a copy afterwards. But it was different without your voice. It didn't make sense. I mean, why would a king want to give up his throne?"

"That was another Lear, Ray," in spite of herself. "Another species of Lear altogether."

He smiled back and his smile made his eyes small. She could see the gold fillings and the illusion of some bright luminosity.

"Then that explains it!" He was mightily relieved. "I remember there was a fella with a big nose and there was a light attached to it. Come on, how did it go?"

"I thought you knew."

"No, I never knew, I was just boasting," and took another pace unchallenged into the citadel.

His moustache was thicker with straws of grey, but he had not changed. She saw that in some circumstances he might be a comfort.

His mouth opened and all of a sudden the light burst incandescent on his grin and on his neck and wrists and sleeves. He was, in that moment, something holy. She wanted to be sated with that golden light. Her hunger for it had the sharpness of pain.

"And Alex?" he said. With all that that word implied, a weak and infertile Pom.

"In Woolnorth."

"You know," in a voice austere with emotion, "I still can't figure out why you married him."

"No, well, you wouldn't."

At this, the other Ray moved forward to protect Merridy, but the old one elbowed him aside. "All on your own, then?"

She felt her throat tighten.

"Go, Harvey, go, Harvey, go Harvey Norman." On screen the Mass had yielded to a commercial.

"You can turn that down, love," said Ray to the woman behind the bar.

She had come out of the kitchen, giggling and holding a plate at which her fingers pecked. "Hey, didn't I see you earlier?" to Merridy.

"This is Belinda," enlisting her. "I've been trying to persuade her to buy the tearoom. Belinda, my old friend Merridy."

"Sorry, folks, but I'm going to have to chuck you out. It's eleven o'clock." And, with a finger that she licked, began to snap off the lights one by one.

In the street he was all chivalry. "I'll see you to your car."

No Taj Mahal in this moonlight, she thought. He's afraid I will laugh at him. And under the influence of rum and wine felt a spasm of nostalgia for what might have been.

Mist was coming off the road. There was no sign of anyone. A bilious light in Harry Ford's window suggested the only life.

The houses drifted by. Ray held her arm. He was bigger than Alex. He towered over her, a minaret from a poster she remembered.

She bent forward a little, not in step with herself, and he caught her arm. She straightened her knees.

Then he kissed her. She neither thrust him away nor responded. She thought how his breath was strange and the smell of his skin. But his mouth was warm, not greedy. Her lips relaxed and spread into the kiss.

She was drunk. "You're drunk," she said, wiping and staring.

"No, no, I'm not."

This is not how I saw it, he realised. He continued to hold her, a wobbling minaret of indecision.

But his closeness was contagious. She wanted more of the light that the moon was already discovering in little gold flashes all over him. To have the desperation that was in her taken away.

"Listen, I think you'd better not drive home. You'd better come and stay," he said, as she held onto him.

"Your house is the last place."

So rather than escort Merridy back to his home he applied a pressure on her shoulders in the direction of the tearoom.

"Then you must sleep it off in here. I have the keys."

"No," she said. "I wouldn't want my mother to see."

"Your mother?" he said, not really asking a question but to keep her steady. It would not do to startle her. "What about Talbot's?" kissing the top of her head. He had Albert's keys in his pocket.

She thought of Rose-Maree and again shook her head.

But Ray had stopped, was gaping upwards. "Look, Merridy," speaking in a careful voice with words like kindling that would leap into flame at the smallest spark. "Look at the moon."

They looked at it together. The moon had sailed free of the Norfolk pines and shone with a penetrating glow on Talbot's. So that it became not a four-storey brick building – erected as a warehouse for wool and skins that were block-and-tackled to the second floor; then closed after the '29 depression and reopened only when Sergeant Talbot returned from the jungles of New Guinea – but a palace that mesmerised, with windows of honey-coloured marble and pillars inlaid with jasper and jade. A memorial to the gods of love whom Ray had invoked ever since he touched Rachael Ehrman on the cheek at the age of fourteen.

Ray had never seen anything like it.

"Merridy . . ."

Holding her hand. Who was thinking:

And at night by the light of the Mulberry moon
They danced to the flute of the Blue Baboon.

"Come with me."

Stroking it.

He looked around for a bench, a wall, somewhere to sit and watch the operation of this moon – its light also falling, he noticed with excitement, on the feldspar of the Freycinet Peninsula and giving to the highest peak the contour of a volcano, perhaps, in the Bay of Naples.

"What about that bus shelter?"

Then Ray squelched on something, disturbing up a smell. In the middle of the road, a dark smear of fur and bone and sleek entrails.

"What's that?" aghast. And stared down at what had been a large animal, but so disfigured that in that light he could not tell if the corpse was that of a dog or feral cat or quoll, or what it was.

All thought of a bench was extinguished, too.

They were opposite a place he recognised.

"I know where you can spend the night!" and walked in confident quick steps across the yard where as a small boy he had rolled marbles, patting his pocket for Tildy's spare key and encountering a condom. "I'll put you in the staffroom. And I'll wake you up tomorrow."

In the schoolroom, standing amid the sloping moonlit desks, the smell of textbooks and furniture wax and cooking oil, Merridy started weeping. Her tears came without warning and surprised herself as much as Ray, who really was about to go.

"Don't leave," she whispered. She needed his shoulder more than anything else.

He touched the top button of her dress.

Her tongue found his teeth and then his tongue. Then her clothes were being pulled inside out and she was following her dress and stockings to the wooden floor.

Ray collapsed on top of her, his hands – that once had all the answers written on them – on her thighs, her breasts. In his groping, a cup of crayons fell. He kneed apart her legs and buried himself between them.

So she ground her face into a hard metallic surface, gusts of pleasure rocking through her, slave to a fatal and lacerating hunger. Shaken by the lust – if that it was – he had outed.

In time, she became aware of Ray pinning her down; and her arms stretched back behind her head, grasping the cold iron legs, black-painted and intricate, of a classroom desk. Images came to her as they used to, sometimes, after prayer. Hector, pulling on a new shoe and looking down at his foot, how it fitted. Upside down, Kish's face staring at her through the window. And Alex, whom she suddenly wanted to run to and kiss, to tell him.

But no prayer.

She moved her leg, which hurt from a splinter when she had opened it wider. Where had Alex sat?

The Blue Baboon stirred in her. Now he was sighing. The gloom of a man who had winged an angel. He had not failed this time, but his lust remained and because of it he was still.

Then he rolled over, leaving his hand awkwardly in hers. He stared at the ceiling, his brown body covered in scrolls of greying hair, and thought of the boy out fishing on his father's boat, the tug on his line as certain as a handshake, and the shiny darkness of the tuna's eye, round and black – he had never seen anything so black, not before or since – a retina that had only ever focused on the deep and now was confronted by Ray. Whose life flapped from him in awe and fear.

She withdrew her hand. The stickiness drying on it.

And now she did in fact remember some words of a prayer.

Beside her on the splintery floor, Ray raised his hand that she had been holding and squinted at the freckled back of it, as if to examine answers to questions that he still, after forty-three years on this earth, did not understand the first thing about.

While she, looking at the same ceiling through the interrupted tears that were leaping back to her eyes, mouthed to herself: "*There is a mystery in every meeting, and that is God.*"

"What's that? Did you hear something?" said Ray, his neck alert. Staring at the window.

"No."

It was Ray who got up first. How his ankles were hairy she saw between the legs of the desk. He could not look at her. Her breasts white as eyeballs. Her glossy cheeks.

She began to pull her clothes towards her. She was awfully cold, though she felt so little for herself that any feeling was a comfort.

"I think that's yours," picking up a cufflink.

She stood on one leg like a stork and put her shoe on. It was untenable, she saw that now, to stay the night here.

Then they were outside and he was throwing something into a bin, muttering: "I'm not sure how safe that was."

The street looked at them. Harry's light had gone out and the world had dwindled to a pitch-dark stain on the road.

She waited for it to absolve her.

High in the sky, a hole – and in the hole a movement.

"What's that?" For she, too, had seen the face. Like the face on a coin.

Behind her, she heard a sound – a muffled explosion almost – in the playground, but she did not turn around.

402

Ray went on looking at the round fourth-storey window where Albert Talbot stood – the corrected proofs of his *Newsletter* in his hand – swaying slightly. "I'll see you to your car."

CHAPTER ELEVEN

SOMETHING CRUNCHED UNDER HIS Blundstones. Alex found the switch and turned on the light. Cowering under the table, Rusty; and everywhere broken glass.

His eyes moved to the dresser – the *Otago* was missing – to a strange dark redness on the wall.

The clock that had survived this tempest told fifteen minutes after midnight. He had been gone two hours.

"Kish!" he shouted. "Merridy!" and stumbled into the corridor, a channel of shattered glass in which there floated splinters of Huon pine and bits of fluff. He ran into his bedroom and cried out. As for the wardrobe. Both doors wrenched from their hinges and the oak struts gaping open and raw-coloured as if something had exploded with terrific force.

It was easy to follow Kish's path. He had destroyed the house to look like something he knew. He had slashed the sheets and then the samplers. He had next gone into the kitchen and flung the red sauce over the walls and the cappuccino-maker on the floor and the cake down the sink. His ankles trailing coloured strands of ancient wools and letters all jumbled up, he had marched down the corridor to her study and hurled the bottles to the floor. With the exception of the *Otago*, which Tildy would discover next morning in the middle of the school playground, he had trampled to pieces each and every model ship. In his fury, he had then ripped up the photograph of Hector on the beach. He had wrenched open the cassette of *Saucy Sally Sees it Through*. He had taken a bottle of ink and spilled it over the scrapbooks and mud-maps. He had seized Merridy's favourite fountain pen and screwed it into the pages of the novel she was rereading until the nib crossed. In the living room he had snatched the cockatoo from the wall and when Rusty barked at him hurled the lithograph into the fireplace. Only then did he run from the house.

How long Alex sat in the chair by the fire, stroking the puppy that had crawled quivering onto his lap, he had no idea. Kish had gone out of his way to obliterate everything that Alex held most dear, and he waited for his body to make a commensurate response. But – peculiarly – no anger came. Alex's instinct told him that he ought to be crushed by the devastation. Instead, he was overcome by what he could only name as a great inner relief. He was conscious of his chest rising and falling, of the distant boom of the waves, of a devil or a possum screeching on the lawn. He could taste the vanilla scent of some herb or plant – a wattle, perhaps – in the air. He breathed in, feeling not anger but on the contrary a deep and authentic peace, as if a barrier which had not, until that evening, been visible to him had been removed. Under his caressing hand, Rusty snored.

Sometime later, Alex returned to the kitchen and began to clean up. Among the glass shards was a piece of paper all scrunched up. He unfolded it, and was reading the words when the sound of a vehicle brought him to the window.

The car skewed to a halt at a distance from the house. He watched a figure climb out and the small dot growing taller and taller up the drive. Against the white gravel, the cornflower dress looked ashamed.

Merridy stepped into the cast of the bright neon light and tugged open the door and then the fly-screen.

"Alex," she greeted him.

He could see from her eye that something had changed. "Kish has gone."

"Kish?" She went red.

"He's disappeared." And waited for her to explain. He so much wanted to trust her. Maybe there was an explanation.

"What's that?" She did not seem so much interested in Kish. She did not seem to have taken in the destruction. Her eyes anchoring on the scrap of paper that he held in his hand.

"This? Oh, a note I once wrote you." The only message he had ever written her. In a hand that did not know the storm or Kish. For years now, he had stored it under the *Otago*, in the same bottle. Kish must have shaken it out.

"Oh, yes," she said. What was he talking about? She could not remember.

"I forgot that I tucked it inside," he said numbly. All the excitement he had felt on the journey, all the sensations of release, had dissolved into this hollow feeling.

She scratched the side of her leg. There was something hectic in her eye. "You're back early, aren't you? Weren't you staying tonight in Alexandria?"

"I was looking for you. I thought you might be in the shed." He folded the piece of paper and put it away in his hip pocket.

"No, I was in the hotel with Tildy. Oh, my God! What's this? What's happened, Alex?" in an altered voice.

Now he remembered. "Listen, there's something important I have to tell you. Or have you heard?" She looked like someone who had heard something pretty awful.

"My God. What's gone on?" absorbing the mess on the walls, the floor, where contents from her pan had congealed and stuck.

"They've discovered your brother's body."

He took it from his jacket and, after brushing away several bits of glass, laid it flat, a page from the *Advocate*.

"Read this," he said.

And Merridy, who thought she heard a cockatoo's cry, read that the high seas during the recent storm had crumbled a cliff west of Wynyard, exposing a cave that contained the bones of a young child.

She was leaning on the table.

"Hector," she said.

"It looks like it. I'm so sorry, love."

They had come together over the newspaper article.

"How do they know?"

There was the picture of a cliff and a cave. They were looking at it.

"They found a shoe. A Blundstone."

Often, when they argued, her face had a twisted look. But never this expression.

Unimaginable: in that cave, there all the time he was.

"I thought maybe he was alive still," she choked.

They were reading the article again.

"No," said Alex. He wanted to do or say something comforting. But he carried on reading. It had seemed so important that he tell her in person.

A considerable sensation has lately been produced in Wynyard by the discovery of a human skeleton under circumstances which leave no doubt that it is the bones of a child who has been missing for thirty-one years from that neighbourhood. A post-mortem will take place on Tuesday.

For some years it was believed that seven-year-old Hector Bowman was abducted or murdered. An investigation into all circumstances connected with the boy and with his habits of life followed. Dead men tell no tales.

It is often remarked that at some time or other every murder that is committed is certain to be brought to light. But it seems that this tragic death did not come about by murder. Rather, it was the result of a young and innocent lad following his nose and getting lost.

On the facing page a lawnmower had been stolen from a shed in North Motton.

She looked outside. The light from the kitchen blotted out the stars.

"I wonder where Kish is," she murmured absently.

The silence was broken by the telephone ringing.

At last, Alex crossed the room and answered. He listened, nodding. "Yeah, she's right here," and handed Merridy the receiver. "It's your Aunt Doss. She says she's been trying to get hold of you for the past two days."

PART V

Melbourne, April 2005;

Moulting Lagoon Farm,
April–May 2005

CHAPTER ONE

MERRIDY LABOURED UP THE front steps of the grand blue-stone house and pressed a bell near a little grate. She stepped back, catching her breath. There were scratch marks on the cinnamon-coloured door.

"Ashfield" lay ninety miles north-east of Melbourne. A white-haired man with some effort dragged a roller up and down the lawn, and beyond the high wrought-iron gate stretched bleak flat open fields with sheep and Friesians and young horses.

The door was opened by an oldish, angular woman. Large sunglasses, loose-fitting jeans, a man's pink shirt. She had on an apron and a little dot of something floury was caught in her nostril.

"Mrs Anselm?"

"Mrs Dove?"

Merridy registered the tentativeness with which each took hold of the other's hand.

"But where's your car?" looking over Merridy's shoulder.

"I told the taxi to come back at five. There's a train at twenty past."

"A taxi! That will cost you . . ."

There was a whimpering sound. A black labrador with a hairless patch on its throat that framed a visible scar squeezed past and investigated Merridy through nervous eyes.

Merridy left her coat in a hallway adjoining the stairs and followed Mrs Anselm and the dog through the living room. Tall-ceilinged with cane furniture and expensive-looking modern paintings. On an upright piano, their likenesses framed in tendrils of silver, were arranged photographs.

"That's him," said Mrs Anselm in a Teutonic accent. She picked up a silver frame and smiled at it. "That's Daniel."

Mrs Anselm was an Austrian who had come to Melbourne after the Second World War. She had worked in a shop, selling children's shoes, and as a freelance reader for a small publisher, and finally as a secretary for a psychologist, in whose clinic she had met her architect husband. He had been building a recital hall in St Kilda. He had invited her to visit the work in progress.

"He asked me to marry him three weeks later. Three weeks."

Merridy saw by the texture of her white skin that Mrs Anselm might have been quite beautiful.

"You must have loved him immediately."

"Oh no, not immediately."

"When did you know?" angling her head the better to study the murdered man's serious, intelligent face.

"I just did – eventually." Mrs Anselm repositioned the photograph.

She had arrived in Melbourne not speaking a word of English, only the words taught by her husband's friends who played such awful tricks on her so that once, when she went to church, she looked at the children in the front row and smiled tenderly at them and said: "Poor little bastards."

Mrs Anselm turned from the piano. "I think it's warm enough to sit outside, don't you?" unknotting her apron.

She led Merridy to a screened-in deck and urged her to choose any of the three chairs to sit in – "They were all designed by my husband" – while she fetched the tea-trolley.

Merridy creaked into a high-backed cane seat and watched the old man rolling the lawn. Shattered after all her activity in Melbourne, she suddenly felt really tired, but the events of the last two days had been intense and they replayed word for word in her mind.

Merridy had spent her first morning at a nursing home in Brighton East, her mother having been admitted soon after the discovery of Hector's remains. Mrs Bowman had been watching *McLeod's Daughters* with her sister when the policewoman called.

"Why don't you sit down, Mrs Bowman."

"Why, what's wrong?"

"Please sit down." Then: "It's about your son."

She collapsed when the news sunk in. By the time Aunt Doss managed to get through to Merridy it was two days later and the *Advocate* had printed the story.

The coroner's inquest was low-key and lasted twenty minutes. Dental records, combined with DNA samples that the doctor was able to take from Mrs Bowman, confirmed that the skeleton in the cliff-face near Wynyard was very likely Hector's. The policewoman had combed the Missing Persons files and discovered a record of what Hector had been wearing. His clothing had lost its colour, but was intact. There were two coins in the pocket of his shorts, minted in England in 1963 and 1957. And there was the discovery, in the same cave, of a left Blundstone boot. Contacted by the forensic anthropologist, a spokesman for the shoe company who examined the boot had no doubt that it was manufactured in the period of Hector's disappearance. From the DNA evidence alone, the chances of the skeleton not being Hector's were less than 1 in 76 million.

Merridy had sat beside her mother's bed in the Sanctuary, holding her hand, not speaking. Mrs Bowman was a husk. Once or twice Merridy began to talk, but her mother squeezed her hand to stop her doing that. Ever since attending the burial ceremony in Ulverstone she had crumpled without warning, like a coat from a hanger, but at the same time a peacefulness filled her to know that Hector's soul was finally at rest and that she had an angel in heaven to plead her case with the Lord. So for three hours they sat in their private grasp. The square of light on the bed growing rhomboid. A young doctor giggling in the corridor. A nurse wiping a Kleenex over Mrs Bowman's Bible on which some cranberry juice had spilled.

Only as Merridy stirred to leave did Mrs Bowman peer into her face: "Aren't you going to tell me?"

Merridy pulled back her hand. "Tell you what?"

Mrs Bowman looked irritated. "I know when you've something on your mind."

"Nothing, nothing."

But the telling was a relief.

Following her fit of candour, Merridy had spent the remainder of the afternoon in Country Road on Lygon Street and then at various boutiques in Chapel Street where she bought herself a yellow dress in a larger size than she was used to wearing, and a pair of expensive suede boots. And a navy-blue, crew-neck jersey for Alex.

Next day, in a busy restaurant not far from the fish market, she arrived early for the long-postponed meeting with her wholesaler. She recognised immediately the figure who advanced between the crowded tables: a huge, swaying, black-bearded Greek with a narrow green tie that did not quite reach his belt of snakeskin.

"Dmitri?"

"Mrs Dove," holding her hand and lingering the better, as he put it, "to put a face to Oblong Oysters".

Dmitri was all politeness over lunch. Merridy let flow over her whatever he was saying. Only towards the end of the meal did he become flirtatious again. "Your ears would go a funny colour if I told you what Les Gatenby said about you."

"Really?"

"They really would. This colour," and pointed at the remains of his crayfish.

"Good. Then Les will have warned you how impossible I am," and smoothed out the contract that Dmitri had been pressing her to sign ever since Christmas.

"As you will see, I have added some conditions."

"Oh, yes?"

"I will make our agreement exclusive only to this state. And, since I'm putting my reputation on the line, I want to see all documents relating to your food standards. And I want to know how you are going to label my oysters."

Dmitri nodded. He ordered a coffee and a grappa. In amongst his beard, his lips were shining. "Is that it?"

"Not quite. You mustn't mix mine with any other product."

Dmitri wiped his mouth with a napkin, first the top lip, then the bottom. "Go on."

"I want you to give me all the names of restaurants and food houses that are going to sell Oblong Oysters – so that I can ring at any stage and see if they're happy with the product and service, and if they're splitting them correctly."

Across the table, Dmitri had folded his arms.

"One more thing," she said.

"Yes?" and lifted his chin.

"You pay electronically fourteen days after receipt. I don't have time any more to go putting cheques into banks."

She signed, after which Dmitri enfolded her in his grappa-permeated arms and asked her to dinner at his favourite place, but she declined.

Upon returning to her hotel she had taken a nap, in the course of which she was visited by an idea so powerful to her that she woke up. She only caught the tail of it, but following a call to the Bilgola Mission, Merridy contacted directory enquiries and eventually was put through to "Ashfield".

This was her idea: if there was one person in the world to whom she must speak, it was this Mrs Anselm.

"How do you like your tea?"

The tea poured, the cake sliced, the two women would converse for a further half-hour before touching on the reason which had brought them together on this windless afternoon on a deck overlooking the Victorian country-side, the paddocks that stretched flatter than an aerodrome towards Broken River.

Anxious to keep her dialogue and mood above the surface, Merridy talked about mothers and shopping and the popularity of oysters, while the roller pressed the lawn into strips of light and dark green. Until the widow, at last, broached the subject.

"They haven't found him?"

"No. He's still at large. He may not have left Tasmania."

"He escaped from your house, you said."

Merridy nodded. She expected that he had gone by the beach. His tracks erased by the new tide. She saw in circling images, like wasps making figures-of-eight above Rusty's bowl: Alex driving away to tell Sergeant Finter; Harry Ford appearing at the door to pant his urgent message – "I have a contact at the *Herald* . . . your Kish is a murder suspect"; the policeman checking through the printout delivered by the telephone company to see who Kish might have contacted. But there was nothing.

"Every district is on alert," Sergeant Finter told them. "You guys don't need reminding – this place is second to none at swallowing murderers. If he gets in touch—"

"Oh, he won't," Merridy assured him. "Not with me. I can't speak for Alex." But the commotion in his eyes betrayed just how shaken Alex was. She could not remember when she had seen her husband so angry.

"You let this man stay with us, Pete, knowing what he'd done. How could you?" He looked haggard.

"But, Alex, he'd done nothing. Not officially."

"You believe that?"

"Of course, now it pokes out at everyone like dogs' balls, but not at the time, it didn't."

"You took his statement, for God's sake!"

"Yes, and he had no record – at least to speak of. That's what he kept saying. 'I have no record.' I told him I didn't come down in the last shower, I came down in the shower before – and he was a lying bastard. But what could I do?"

"Did Mrs Wellard tell you he was a murder suspect?"

"Listen, Alex. I understand why you're pissed off. But he wasn't *convicted* of anything. Otherwise, he wouldn't have been on board the *Buffalo*. They don't take people with a record. OK, he had had a number of minor convictions – but that's in Sydney. It's a tougher place. You'd expect him to be a petty criminal in Sydney, for fuck's sake. I'll spell it out again: none of those kids on that ship were involved in cases that had gone to trial."

"Then why was he late in joining the *Buffalo*?"

Sergeant Finter drew a long breath. "He went AWOL from the Bilgola Mission. A week later, an architect is murdered on a farm in Victoria. Kish is picked up as a suspect in Melbourne. There's no evidence. So they let him go. Two days later he's packed off on the *Buffalo* under Gangell's supervision. End of fucking story."

"Is that how the criminal justice system works?"

It was a jibe too much for Sergeant Finter. "Hell, and what do you know about the criminal justice system?" He laughed angrily. "I don't need this."

"Alex, Pete. Please," feeling giddy all of a sudden.

There was a creak. In the cane chair opposite, Mrs Anselm sipped her tea and her words seemed hotter. "When I try and go on a ship, I can't pay enough. How come these delinquents get to go – and for free? A nice way to see the country, isn't it? At taxpayers' and victims' expense. Why don't they pay to catch him?"

Merridy was surprised at the level of detail that Mrs Anselm had wanted to go into. She reminded her: "There was no weapon discovered – and you identified someone else."

He had been arrested in St Kilda market knotting balloons into inflated swords for children; his earring and short blond hair matching the description given by Mrs Anselm, who promptly failed to pick him out in the identity parade.

418

"Pah!" And Mrs Anselm looked helpless and angry out of her sunglasses. "As soon as I left the police station I knew which one it was. I was on the steps and I had to hold my daughter's arm. He was standing right next to the man I had chosen! I went back and told them I had made a mistake, I had accused the wrong person, but they weren't interested. They didn't want to listen."

"You're kidding."

"Exactly." She returned her saucer to the trolley. "Some more?"

"No, thanks."

Mrs Anselm looked with a troubled expression into the milky tea that Merridy had left untouched. "I don't understand. My husband wasn't a bad person. He was only trying to help. You see, I have no experience of such people." She uncrossed her legs and cupped her hands around her knees. "Tell me, Mrs Dove, this boy Kish, what was he like? I hardly saw him – well, a moment only. That's why in the line I didn't recognise him right away. They all looked the same . . ."

A hubbub of memories and longings blasted about Merridy's head. "He was strange. He seemed lost in another world."

"Lost?" sitting back.

"We felt sorry for him." It was not what Merridy intended to say. Nor what the older woman wished to hear.

Mrs Anselm raised her sunglasses. "What do you want with me, Mrs Dove?"

"I thought . . . since I knew your husband's killer, well, it might help . . . for us to talk . . ."

"Talk?" Mrs Anselm looked at her. And Merridy, meeting Mrs Anselm's receded, hurt eyes, was also at a loss. On the train from Melbourne, she had stared at the galahs arranged on the telegraph wires, sheet music for some inaudible melody that was drawing her in, and believed that she understood why she was making this impetuous journey to "Ashfield".

But now she wondered: Can this help either of us?

Less than five feet away, Mrs Anselm readjusted a pair of round dark lenses on the bridge of her nose. She pretended not to see as far as she did. But she had seen. Merridy's halo of anguish.

She picked up the pot.

"Let me tell you, Mrs Dove, what it means to lose the man you love."

"There were two of them. They were standing beside the fence, by that quince tree.

"The only thing he said while lying there: 'Who was it? Was it those boys?'

"They'd come to ask for work. They said they'd do anything – sweep leaves, even. I told them we had nothing for them to do. But Daniel was kinder. He remembered how it was to have no money.

"He said to me: 'Darling, they're still there. Let them sweep leaves.'

"'You speak to them, then.'

"He opened the door. Then the dog started growling – and suddenly I heard a shout and I saw someone lying on the grass – like that, two hands over his head. Daniel. Daphne raced up to him. She kneeled down and kissed her grandpa and came up with her face and golden hair full of blood.

"The boy had stabbed him. For no reason at all . . . My husband didn't lose his watch, they didn't take his wallet. Like they were just out to kill him, a man they didn't know . . ." Her words were crushed as the grass.

Seconds passed before Mrs Anselm spoke again. "I ran

on to the lawn and pulled off his shoes and tried to sit him up, which I should never have done. I screamed at the kids: 'Get back, everything's OK.' Then I held a cloth over him so he'd get a little shade over his head. His arms and legs were drawn up, and his wrist – hanging on a thread. Nine times chopped up. Well, I knew he would never play again. He had trained as a pianist and I prayed, squeezing his shoulder: 'Please, God, for his sake let him die, but for my sake let him live.'

"Of course, to him I said: 'It's OK, darling, everything is OK.'

"Then I ran back to the house and called for an ambulance. The kids were screaming when I came outside. They'd found Ruskin. Your Kish had slashed him, too."

Merridy felt sick. "How do you know it was Kish – not the other one?"

"Because I saw his knife . . ."

Mrs Anselm lifted the pot that she had clasped to her lap, and put it back on its stand. "I thought it would be quicker if we drove Daniel ourselves, so we got him into the car. His head was slit over his left eye. But he died that night. I'm glad they didn't see. He died in agony . . ." and patted away the labrador which had come up with a rubber bone in its mouth. "But *you're* OK now, aren't you, Ruskin?"

The labrador's tail was wagging. Catching sight of his mistress's face, the dog retreated and dropped the bone into Merridy's lap.

"He wants you to throw it." Mrs Anselm's voice sounded as though it was echoing off the plain outside.

Merridy picked up the toy bone that gleamed with slobber, and got to her feet. She studied the quince trees, the striped lawn where out of the blue Kish or whoever had launched his savage attack on a perfectly innocent stranger, and wondered where best to hurl the thing. It was – everything that she had heard – quite overwhelming.

Just at that moment the doorbell rang.

"It'll be the taxi," Merridy said, and put down the bone.

Mrs Anselm saw Merridy out. Not until they stood on the steps did she notice how Merridy's dress fell in uneasy lines across her body.

"Your first?"

"Yes. How can you tell?" quickly doing up her coat.

"You are starting late," and sighed. "I started too young."

"We've been trying for a long time."

"Your husband must be overjoyed."

"He doesn't know."

The driver was opening the door of the taxi.

"You're going to have to tell him soon," searching Merridy's face. She smelled of banana cake and fragility.

"When I get home."

Mrs Anselm relaxed. "There's nothing so wonderful as making a family."

CHAPTER TWO

COUNCIL ELECTIONS. There are a select few who reciprocate, contribute, extend respectability and bestow blessings on our town and its people. Then there are the takers, the ones Councillor Grogan refers to as "stakeholders". Their decisions are arrived at behind closed doors, quietly, secretly, with a select few muckety-mucks, the so-called ey-leet and the wanna-bees. They take objection to interference from we "the ordinary people", the "country bumpkins", the so-called "brain-dead" seniors or their supposedly ignorant siblings. I could have sworn we voted Mr Ray Grogan in as our councillor to help us fight for a sports complex. Was that a fantasy? Together let's dismantle our council in April. Ray-as-in-sunshine, ho, ho, ho. Ray-as-in-scorched-earth-policy more likely. (Mr Talbot, could you run this past a lawyer before you print it? Thanks, Abby.)
Abbygail Deverill.

Orange flames blazed in a circle on the lawn. Alex stood the far side of them and kicked a smouldering branch into the pyre of browned foliage. He was burning off the last of the Oyster Bay pine.

Merridy parked beside the ute and even before she had taken off her seat belt Alex was bounding across the grass, followed by Rusty, opening the car door, leaning down. She let him kiss her, but she could feel the whimper in his throat.

"How was Melbourne? I missed you," and kept kissing her face in search of what she was withholding. His kisses had the flavour of woodsmoke and kerosene.

"Hey, let me get my suitcase," extricating herself.

"No, I'll get it."

She waited by the car while he opened the trunk. The air unnaturally still. The twisted sheets of flame. She stood looking up at the pipe-cleaner of smoke rising vertical from the lawn, and followed him inside.

Across the safe distance of the kitchen table, she told Alex about her visit to her mother and her lunch with Dmitri.

"And I bought you a present," she smiled.

Later on, he came into her study wearing the blue jersey.

"Oh, but Alex, that's far too tight!"

"No, it's not," and stubbornly flexed the short arms.

"Really – I can send it back." She stood to help him take off the jersey, before he got it caught on a wire or covered in muck.

"What are you doing?" to deflect her.

Half out of her chair, she looked down at her desk. "I have just put in an order to Shellfish Culture in Bicheno for a hundred thousand seedlings."

"Do you want me to post it?"

It pained her heart, his eagerness to please.

"Only if you're going into town."

"I have to go to Swansea. I need to get a pipe fitting from the hardware."

"Then let me find an envelope."

"Anything else?"

She considered the jersey that hemmed him in. As if she had bought it for someone a good deal younger. "We've nothing for dinner. Maybe you could buy a chicken at Talbot's on the way? And Alex—"

He turned. On either side of him, the walls of the corridor were bare – ever since he had taken the frames to Hobart to be replaced.

She had to sit down. "I know this sounds odd, but I'd love you to get some more Coco Pops."

WELLINGTON POINT GOLF CLUB.
Talbot's Memorial Qualifying Round:
Competition results for Saturday.
Winner: N. Fujita (visitor) 56
Runner-up: R. Grogan 58
Junior: Z. Grogan 65
Due to lack of bookings the Golf Club Annual Dinner has been cancelled.

It was a stunning blue calm afternoon – smell of early autumn, dry pines – and whales splashing in the bay. Their spouting had drawn a small crowd to the railings above the beach.

Alex watched the pod of Southern Rights for a while. Then walked along the esplanade to Talbot's. Taped to the windows, black-and-yellow posters advertised Ray Grogan's forthcoming auction of the general store's contents: *The opportunity to acquire something unique, a part of history.*

At the checkout, Rose-Maree said: "You must be hot in that, Mr Dove."

"My wife gave it to me."

She squinted through knowing eyes at the cereal packet. "Hear you might be starting a family." And her incredulous expression that liked to displease added: After all these years!

"I'd be the last to know," Alex joked with a smile that believed it knew what she was talking about.

He left Talbot's and walked in stiff steps along the main street, past the newsagent, past the Op-Shop, not breathing in so as to avoid the fragrance of old clothes and to suppress the irritation that coiled through his head. You only had to nurse a thought and already Rose-Maree had heard it articulated from Chyna, who worked at the chemist's.

Alex had little doubt that if Merridy had bought a pregnancy test it was for Madasun, their frizzy-haired cleaner – she had probably missed her period yet again. And remembered his wife's exasperation the last time this had happened, after Madasun implored Merridy to visit the chemist's on her behalf.

"My boobies are hurting, Mrs Dove. The nipples are hard and I feel so good. I only had one glass of wine. I thought it was a safe time."

Madasun was in such a state of nerves that while she was peeing she dropped the stick in the loo and Merridy had to go back and buy another test.

"Oh, she annoys me so, that girl. And what's the betting it will turn out negative!"

"Why is she asking *you* to buy it?"

"Her parents are full-on Catholics. She lives in permanent fear that they'll find out she's not a virgin – at thirty-one, heaven help us."

So by the time he climbed the steps into the post office had Alex explained away Rose-Maree's remark.

Immediately she saw him come in, Mrs Grogan leaped out from the queue, tugging the small dark poodle at her feet, her trouser suit giving her the look of a tea cosy. She was dressed in her customary pink and clutched at Alex, one hand imitating the other, but she had not worked out what to say.

Perhaps she was ill; she was not, though. Her mouth ungummed itself. And smiled kindly though she was not by nature a kind person.

"I hear Merridy's having a baby."

In the queue some woman coughed and another copied her.

Meanwhile, Mrs Grogan was smiling so broadly that she might have owned the beach. "My father used to say: 'Barren ground can sometimes be what a seed needs.'"

Hostile eyes recognised Alex for what he was, a cuckolded Pom in a close-fitting jersey. White as a rinsed plate, he said: "It's early days," and added with as much dignity as he was able: "Anything might happen."

Mrs Grogan's face, which speech had animated, was turned wrinkly again. Her hands touched her mulberry frill, like that around her dog's mouth, and then fanned themselves out on Alex's constricted chest.

"If she's pregnant, you must come to tea."

Alex posted Merridy's envelope and walked back along the esplanade, avoiding the crowd, to the ute. The cabin had heated up and he tucked the plastic bag with the cereal and chicken under the seat.

The afternoon sun through the windscreen showed a middle-aged man in spectacles – forty-three years old, broader in the chest than when he met the two cousins by Ray Grogan's fence, and darker, with less hair – who switched on the engine and then switched it off and sat looking out.

Is it mine? It could be mine. Couldn't it? And remembered

427

a doctor saying: "Those who are infertile do sometimes remedy themselves."

The whales had swum close to shore. In an elegant and unhurried gesture, the largest of them raised its tail in the air. Alex expected the tail to slap down, but it remained vertical, a gigantic black hand that set the mood and tempo of the bay, and of all who watched, until it seemed to Alex that he was himself caught up in the whale's own slow, mysterious rhythm that was in defiance of gravity or time.

And felt an ache of uncertainty.

A crawl of fear moved in his chest. Where had his head been? He was not a stupid man. It wasn't as if he had not seen it coming: he knew. He had the evidence and had not confronted her, and now he had to deal with it.

The whale's tail was still poised in the air when he retrieved his sun hat from behind the steering wheel and put it on. He turned the key in the ignition and was about to drive away when – "Alex! Alex!"

Tildy, crossing the road.

He wound down the window. "Hey, congratulations. I hear you're on the town council."

"Did you vote for me?" lowering her head. That had never looked so bubbly.

He smiled. "As far as I remember, it was a secret ballot."

"Anyway, it's you who must be congratulated. Is Merridy with you?" peering into the ute.

"She's at the farm. She got back this morning."

"I haven't hugged you for the pure joy you must be feeling."

Before he could say anything, she thrust her arms through the window and held him in an awkward embrace.

"Tell me more," ever so slowly.

"Oh, come on, stop being British. We're so happy for

428

you, Ray and I. We're thrilled. It's a cousin for me. I'll be
Aunty Tildy. Uncle Ray. No, really, it's the best news."

*Anyone who has copies of my short stories could they
please contact me on: 62568583. Thank you, Agnes
Lettsom.*

From his porthole, Mr Talbot watched Alex's ute meander
out of town towards Swansea. He followed Mrs Grogan
following her inescapable poodle from the post office to
the bowls club, in time for the five p.m. Twilight Bowls
competition. He adjusted his binoculars north to the golf
course where Abbygail chatted with Jack Fysshe on the
apron of the seventh hole, having done everything she
decently could to put a spoke in Tildy's wheel at the recent
council election, assuming that Tildy was only standing
to further her vile husband's interests. To the lane behind
the school where Rose-Maree's son played catch-and-kiss
with Cherokee. And back to the main street to survey the
faces absorbed in the whales, although not before he
spotted Tildy going into Ray Grogan's office.

Mr Talbot put down his binoculars. He felt all tuck-
ered out. At all that he had seen. All that he had reported
back and typed out in his steady hand, or simply kept
intact in his head. The children whom he had witnessed
growing up, courting and marrying. The husbands slinking
like possums at dawn from the doors of other men's wives
– and sometimes of other husbands! The sausage sizzles,
the ANZAC parades, the golf tournaments and cricket
matches, the Safe'n'Sound car seats in good condition, the
visiting speakers and the funeral services . . .

He closed his eyes. For the first time since he had long,

long ago taken up position at this window, Mr Talbot looked forward to quitting his eyrie. Ray Grogan was agitating to show him around a retirement villa on a cliff south of Swansea that sounded congenial to his habits and purposes: it had a view only of the sea. He was tempted to take a look, despite not altogether trusting Ray. He said to himself: Funny how nervous he was that night. He thought I was going to nail him for his horrid little son. And while Ray readily agreed to his sole stipulation, Mr Talbot had kept an eye on the real-estate agent for too many years not to discuss the contract with his lawyer. "This is fine up until – and not a millimetre further than – this devious, untrustworthy person mentions any Nippon corporation. So if he comes to see you . . ." And instructed him to put in a clause to the effect that whoever bought or developed the store could not possibly be Japanese.

Up until that time, there would still be the *Newsletter* to compile, proofs to correct. He opened his eyes and stood at the third go and shuffled over to the table under the skylight.

WELLINGTON POINT RSLA. ANZAC DAY, April 25. 11 a.m. service at the Cenotaph – marchers to assemble at 10.40 a.m. opposite Talbot's Store. Wreaths will be laid out for pick-up at the Uniting Church.

Not until late afternoon did Alex return home. He checked the bonfire for embers and was walking towards the house when he almost trod on a tiny brown object.

Dead on the ground, a beautiful bird.

He picked it up. A young swift. He held it in his palm, but even as he ran his finger over the porcelain-white throat,

430

the minute legs and feet, the wings trembled and a drop of saliva oozed from its black bill.

With the utmost tenderness he placed the bird on its back on the flower bed, and opened the fly-screen and went inside.

Merridy had not left her desk. "I meant to ask you to get olive oil. But there's butter in the freezer. And, Alex, you didn't forget that cereal, did you?" still writing.

He stood behind her. His eyes on her sideways face, the exposed bra strap, the new yellow dress that was too large for her body. Almost seventeen years together and he did not recognise her. She was stranger to him – suddenly – than the young man who had wrecked all the ships in this room.

She felt the force of his glare and twisted in the swivel chair.

"Or did you?" She looked radiant.

He crossed his lead arms. "Are you pregnant?"

She blushed. "Now why would you ask that?"

He looked at her very closely and saw her eyes rocking with new colours. But her gaze did not meet his. Her face eloquent of something that she would rather not reveal, not yet.

"Are you? I was in the post office. Mrs Grogan suggested you were."

"A ridiculous idea." She occupied herself with screwing the top back on her pen. "What a bunch of stickybeaks people are." She did not quite believe it herself.

"Did you buy a pregnancy test?"

With a desperate smile, she said: "Everyone in Wellington Point seems to know what I've done."

"Yes," he said. "They do." But still he waited for her to mention Madasun. When she did not, he said with terrifying gentleness: "I also bumped into Tildy."

"You did? And?"

"I don't want to hear any more until you decide to tell me the truth."

She cooked the chicken for dinner. They were eating in silence when she pushed back her chair and rushed past him, prolonging her smile until she reached the bathroom and then vomited into the basin.

He came into the bedroom a few minutes later, holding a glass of water.

She sat on their bed and stared blankly ahead at the faded wall where the wardrobe had stood. "Perhaps I undercooked it," in a whisper. And watched Alex step in front of her, into the space where Kish had sought to shut himself away.

Alex had sold the wardrobe to an antique shop in Campbell Town. A broken piece of furniture with a promise attached. But Merridy had interpreted it as something mystical and unravelling. The room was bigger without it, both of them smaller.

In silence, she accepted the glass. She did not look at him as she drank.

"Are you?" he repeated, in his gentle voice.

His gentleness had the impact of a cudgel.

"I was going to tell you tonight," her head bowed, clasping the empty glass. The water had wiped the taste of vomit from her mouth.

"Is it mine?"

Her smile fluttered on her lips, then was inert.

"I'm not that stupid. Not a fool," and felt out of breath.

She lifted deadly, sad eyes. Alex's expression was terrible. His face not constructed to express his hurt.

"It's not mine, is it?" blinking against a blow he had yet to receive.

432

She had trouble getting the word out. "Alex . . ."

The noise of air sucked through a dry throat.

His mouth hung open a little. Around him the silence burned.

"Alex . . ."

But his gaze was crumpling under its load of sadness. As if the moment of illumination would snuff him out.

Now he would ask who was the father. She braced herself to tell him. And stopped. Was there not an outside chance it could be Alex – even after all this time?

But he did not have to ask. He knew. Had seen it with his own eyes.

It was curious. In the four months since Kish's disappearance, Alex's sleep had been largely untroubled, pacified by a not disagreeable sensation that everything was out of his control, and by the parallel conviction that Kish's destruction of his collection of ships had in a sort of way released him. But soon as he woke, before he could reassure himself that all was well: the despair.

Even after Sergeant Finter finished putting his questions to them, Alex did not ask Merridy about the events of that night. The image of her embrace with Kish had not penetrated. It remained suspended, so that a small part of Alex was able to persuade himself he had not seen it. Or rather that what he had seen was of a parcel, somehow, with the ghostly figure suggested by the Friesian cow beneath the macrocarpa, a product of humidity and moonlight, of fever and shadows. A mist-mirage. And so he blotted out that night as he had learned to blot out his parents' death. In the days that followed, he explained it away as something that could not be explained, and did not refer to it again. What else could he do? Kish had

433

gone, vanished off the map. As for Merridy, he could not interpret her face. Her thoughts lay unreadable, like letters on a jolted Scrabble board.

Since the discovery of her brother's remains, Merridy had been careful with Alex and attentive, which made him unhappy. He was reminded of the expression in her eyes at their first encounter, her childlike eyes that found it hard to settle on an adult surface in case they might be scalded. And he, in his turn, avoided looking at her in case he saw what he did not expect. Especially, he did not want to discover how infantile she might still be. Her life so firmly organised in response to her own childhood that she had failed to move beyond her childlike beliefs.

So they settled back into an uneasy truce.

More frequent than moments filled with the image of Merridy and Kish in their shocking embrace were those of immersion in the farm.

The windmill worked. Alex could not decide if he regretted or not that Mr Scantlebury, in the course of stripping it down, had scrubbed Merridy's name from the vane. The main thing was, it drew water to the feeding troughs – and in an uninterrupted flow that his father's cattle had never enjoyed. Alex would look at the spinning blades and see the widening ripples of a trout feeding on mayfly. "Good dog," he would call. As he rounded up sheep below Barn Hill. Driving slowly behind and giving the occasional toot to hurry them up and to make Rusty bark. Trees were in blossom and the mutton-birds were in. Out in the bay the sea was bluer than ever. Once, for no good reason he could think of, a snatch of a football song from Sedbergh came to his lips: *The sunshine is melting the snow on the Calf/And the Rawthey is loud in the dale.* Meaningless now. He went through the motions of living.

While at her desk, or down at the oyster shed, or out

in the bay on the *Zemmery Fidd*, Merridy glowed. She did not think of what her body had done on a splintery floor, or that she had betrayed her cousin or husband or herself. It had taken place in a dream, her atrocious outburst of lust or whatever it was, so that the dull fact of its having taken place was all she remembered, and not any history. But her eyes skipped away from the primary school whenever she had to go into Wellington Point.

Above all, she succeeded in driving from her head all thoughts of Hector. It was extraordinary, the degree to which her pregnancy had dissolved her brother's memory. She had discovered that she was pregnant two days after Minister Twelvetrees conducted the burial ceremony in which Hector's friends, all middle-aged and married now, stood with their puzzled children behind Mrs Bowman and Doss and tried to remember the seven-year-old boy and also to imagine him as an adult. From that moment on, it was as if Hector had soared up into the sky to disappear out of her life as emphatically as the young man whom Alex had rescued from the sea.

"Do you know what happened to Kish? Have you seen him? Does anyone know where he is?" she had asked Tildy, to whom she had grown close again.

"Not a thing."

But Alex did not have this consolation. To Alex, Kish was the reason. The awfulness. It was Kish who had made them enemies. Whose child swelled under his wife's yellow dress.

It was therefore a double assault for Alex to look back at the past four months in which he had accommodated and denied what he had seen.

Sudden as a fist jagged into his chest, winding him, and

with a lucidity that tore at his heart, he now understood the fury that had slashed his mother's collection of samplers and trampled his father's precious ships into smithereens. The tears trickled down his cheeks.

Merridy could not bear to look. He stood there like something painted on wood. A rattle of breath in a too-small jersey.

She got up from the bed. Her excluding voice saying something. Her mouth running after the words. Trying to sound adequate.

"He will be our child," she said. "We always wanted a child."

He reached to touch her stomach. Their barrenness so often had caused him pain. Yes, he had wanted a child, a better version of himself. Out of his love for Merridy, he had grown as impatient as she to put something into the future and not to have to look back.

Then stopped in the middle of the bedroom with his hand up, like something farewelled, not able to touch, not able to look. Aware that what Merridy was saying was a snakebite whose venom had yet to reach his heart, but was sluggishly and intently heading that way through his blood-stream, and he knew that he must not encourage it even by the smallest motion.

If only he could concentrate hard enough. He wished he was a boy again so that he could weep without embarrassment or scream his pain at the sea instead of bolting it behind an awkward smile. His hands colliding with a living creature, he stroked the dog.

Slowly, he sank onto the bed. But only for a moment.

He was trembling. He felt the chilled anguish in his soul, a choking. His voice sagging under the weight of what she had done to him, he mumbled stupidly, "I'm going to see if that bird's all right."

He lurched to his feet and manoeuvred past her and she saw, then, the abolished light in his eye.

Her stomach rumbled.

"Alex!" She had never been good at shouting. "Alex, where are you going?" as if they were her last words to him. He walked on. Into the bare corridor. Through the kitchen. Vigorously outside. He was going to the unrevived swift; he had always been at ease with dead things.

When he kneeled to recover the bird, it was gone.

CHAPTER THREE

HE STUMBLED DOWN THE drive. The windmill called after him, and the young dog that he had shut behind the fly-screen, but he pressed on, his feet slipping on the gravel that he scattered, rolled downhill faster by the impetus of the seething in his chest. And did not stop when he reached his boundary fence.

He walked on for two miles, along the Avoca road – gorse hedgerows and a red track bounded by low rolling hills with clumps of dark green eucalypts. Another farm, also empty: the bark of locked-up dogs and horses under blankets.

He heard the sound of a car and hurried on. He pushed his way through the bush. Touching the branches for company; the wire barbs.

The swifts that were spending their night in the sky saw him tracking west beside a river. The gums smoky green, the trunks covered in a tight plumage of ivy. Between the trees, he made out horizons of forest like the coat on Mrs Grogan's poodle. Wads of cloud appeared high up. There was a shower and then the rain stopped.

In a clearing, he passed a white fibro shack. A dog yammered at him and stood still and shivered. More dogs followed, trotting over the ground with their tails up and the dying day in their eyes glinting red from the darkening pools. It rained again, harder this time, and the rain swept across him until he was a figure that had been rubbed out. The lead dog licked a raindrop from its snout and turned back.

At the top of the hill, he heard a thuck thuck thuck and

438

turned to see a figure below, chopping wood. The damp crunch of firewood after rain carried the sound of someone axing their own flesh.

An hour later, the shape of the skyline that he had left behind stood black and solid against the grey sky. His boots were soaked through and he felt blisters on his heels. He did not know where he was, didn't care.

Bathed in the light of dead stars he staggered on through the moist undergrowth, a creature in his shambles. Smell of wet rock and Kish's child beneath her freakish yellow dress. Branches snapping and the reek of mould.

In the darkness of the woods, with the fronds scoring his face and his sore feet and a devil growling not far off, he was the Piers of his childhood.

Merridy.

He stopped moving only when fatigue overpowered him. He lay where he had tripped, his cheek resting on a bed of damp leaves. Once, hearing a voice, he looked up. But it was himself gabbling. His words spinning off in a senseless stream, his blubbering orphans, their fading cries inarticulate.

He slid back into sleep.

Waking, he saw that he had slept beneath a pine tree. He blundered through the next day and into the night. He did not stop to differentiate, where he had been, what he had done, and mouthfuls of brackish water and hours on hard ground. Pink tentacles bunched with unripe berries plucked at him. He tore off the berries and crammed them into his mouth. The juice tasted marshy, rancid almost. His scratched hands toned in with the strips of bark and the smell of deserted barns came off his clothes. He remembered the wind blunting the young maize, the sneeze of a gun, a curtain across a room and on the stove a saucepan from which an old woman was about to feed her cat. And all the time the soft pad of wings in his chest.

439

He imagined his chest sawn open. Merridy had scooped up the swift and freed the terrified bird into his darkness and the scars had healed and this tiny thing flapped and squeaked and tormented its beak on his sides.

Sometimes in the stillness of wind he heard a cockatoo laughing at him, cackling out the word: Kish, Kish, Kish, Kish – Kish.

On the third evening, he climbed a hill and peered into a deserted cottage with a high-pitched shingle roof and small panes, where he slept. The noise of rats in the walls was someone eating crisps in a cinema. In his jealousy, he summoned the unexplained chuckles, her mouth red and contented.

At first light, he stepped from the shack and saw the Midlands Highway below and the metal roofs of Ross. Out of habit, a bruised hand patted his trousers to check that he still had his wallet. He pulled it out and a piece of damp paper fell to the ground. He read the words written in blurred ink. *Without you I am so unhappy, I am.*

In Ross, he sat in a café with a busload of raucous, fat tourists, the windows fogging up and a westerly coming through.

The tour guide called out: "Do we have any New Zealanders with us? No? Oh, I'm going to have a great day today."

The group hollered dutifully and tucked into their scallop pies, paying no attention to Alex. He looked down at the jersey that Merridy had given him and saw how burrs had stuck to it, how wire had ripped it, how filthy it was. Stenchy with the bitter smell of mud, he waited for his coffee.

Night had fallen when he entered Green Ponds and saw the red lights of the Old Ship Inn. Because of his father, he avoided pubs. Now he dragged himself towards the neon blare.

He pushed open the door and stood blinking in the dowdier light. Then bent his back and crossed the floor to the U-shaped bar.

Sitting over their six-ounce beers, three beards tracked his advance from the far side of the polished counter.

Separate from them at the end of the same counter, a clean-shaven man in a green jacket sat eating a sausage off a paper plate. He, too, studied Alex: his bristly cheeks, his bloodshot eyes, his hair all over the place like slashed wool, the tired swing of his arms as he came up to the bar.

"What can I get you, mate?" asked a pleasant Aboriginal face.

Alex looked at the bottles all hanging upside down, all full. As he remembered them on his father's shelves. And waved at one.

"Shot of that. No, make it a double."

So he drank his father's favourite gin. Smiling back at the uncaring beards. His thoughts with their children's masks on them as if he could disguise his hurt with false cheer.

It was almost the first thing that he had noticed on his return to Tasmania, twelve years after the death of his parents: the sight of so many massive beards. There came into his mind, nudged by the gin, the unkempt face of the man who visited Moulting Lagoon Farm six months after Alex had taken up residence again. Alex had mistaken him for an itinerant Jehovah's Witness: Harry Ford had warned that they were operating in the area.

"Are you Mr Dove?" bunching his hat.

"That depends," Alex said. "Are you seeking contributions?"

"No," said the beard, hopping from one foot to another. In the paddock, the horses lifted their heads and went back to tearing the grass. His eyes kept looking out of their corners at Alex. "I need to know. Are you Piers Dove?"

"That used to be my name, but people generally call me Alex."

The beard braced himself. "I'm George Bird." And when Alex did not react explained that he was the driver of the log-truck that had ended his parents' life and sent them into the next one.

Alex sucked in. Hearing his father in red braces talking about boats; smelling his mother's sherry-scented breath. He came up for air. The only sound his heart, and the grass being torn.

"Do you want to come in?"

"No, I just want to let you know that not a day has passed when I didn't wish it was me in that car."

He swallowed the rest of the gin.

"Go on, Whizz, get your arse moving!"

Over by the pool table, two players in their shirts of wife-beater's tartan cheered the television set. A mouth missing several teeth yelled: "Get on with it, Whizz!"

"One more," thumping his empty glass on the counter. In the trapped warmth of the lounge room. Its brutal cordiality.

He drank. He looked around. The television, with its horse race going on. A counter, scattered with slips and the paraphernalia of betting. And flashing up on screen, the Keno numbers.

At the end of the bar, the man in the green tweed jacket removed something from his eye. He stood up and looked at Alex and went outside.

The cheers had become jeers. Two disappointed faces turned away. A cue was chalked and the thump resumed of ivory against ivory.

"I'm going," Alex said after a while to no one in particular.

The beards at the bar simmered approval.

At the pool table, they were making bets on roadkill. How many dead animals could they notch up on their way home?

"Winner in Swansea! Winner in Swansea!"

Alex walked outside into the car park and pissed between two utes. Out of the ground-floor window another peal of undenticulated laughter.

He was zipping up when he became conscious of someone observing him through the windscreen of a stationary Pajero. The red lights picked out a South Australian number plate.

Alex left the car park and set off along the road, the jeers reverberating through his head, and the shrill announcement of a lucky lottery winner.

Behind, an engine started up. The vehicle turned onto the road and followed Alex at a slow pace until it was alongside. The driver leaned across and the window whirred down.

"How ya doing?"

"Going well, mate."

"Need a lift?"

Alex stopped and looked at the face framed in the open window. He took in a man more or less his own age, fleshy lips and chin, sparse hair, drooping, slightly bulging eyes.

"Why would you do a thing like that?"

"We might be heading in the same direction."

"Where you heading?"

"Orford."

"Which way?"

He considered this. "Lake Leake," after a pause.

Alex stared at the ground. "Could you drop me off near Wellington Point?"

"No trouble."

The man opened the door and Alex climbed in and they drove out of Green Ponds and onto the Midlands Highway.

"I've never been in that pub before," the man said after an interval.

Alex eyed the cloth on the arms that held the steering wheel and was conscious of his torn blue jersey, stiff with dried earth. His eyes moved up the arm to the driver's face. His own face by contrast was covered by an unchecked stubble and he smelled of ditches. "Me neither," he said.

The man picked his teeth. "I don't reckon I'll stop there again. But the ferry into Devonport was two hours late and I was famished. I could have eaten the crotch out of a low-flying duck."

"Do you live in Orford?" Alex said.

"I live in Adelaide, but my family have a house on Spring Beach."

He was down here visiting his parents; normally they came to him because they liked to get into better weather.

"What about yours?" he asked Alex.

"I'd like to get into better weather."

"I mean, what about your folks? Are they still around?"

"No, no, they died a long time ago now."

"Oh. Sorry."

Alex looked out at the side of the highway. As if half-expecting to see himself shuffling into the headlights. He had walked beside this road for the best part of the afternoon. "A log-truck."

The man frowned at the road ahead. "Forgive me for asking, but you're not Piers Dove, are you?"

Alex looked around. "I might have been."

"I thought so," nodding to himself.

"How did you work that out?"

"We were at school together."

Alex took stock of the driver's silhouette in the darkness. His double chin, his kind protruding eyes, his sparse hair rumpled like a judge who has removed his wig.

"I remember that accident," the man went on in a deferential tone. "We were pretty cut up for you. But you'd left town before we had a chance to pay our respects to you and your family." He paused and cleared his throat awkwardly. "You – that is."

Still, Alex could not decipher the boy in the double chin. In the adult voice with the mainlander's vowels.

"Were we in the same class?"

"I sat behind you," and turned and smiled in a sad way.

Headlights from an oncoming vehicle fell on the man's cheek and nose.

"Jack Cheele . . . ?"

"That's right."

They regarded each other. Thirty-two years disappeared and the lines on the face, and all at once Alex discerned the features of the new boy whom Miss Pritchard was introducing to the class.

"Jack Cheele," he repeated in a voice just as strained.

"You remember my name," chuckling.

A car flashed by.

Alex shook his head. That they should meet in a pub in the middle of nowhere.

"Miss Pritchard told us you'd gone to England. It wasn't till I heard you speak that I knew I was right."

Alex twisted to face him. "Jack, I've thought about you so often."

"Well, here I am."

"No, no, you don't realise," in an urgent voice. "I really have thought about you an awful lot."

"You have?"

"That day in the school yard—"

445

"When you kicked me in the balls?"

"I'd made up my mind to come and see you, to apologise, and then . . . then it was too late." Everything erased by the accident.

"Well, that's decent of you to tell me."

"I tried to find you."

"We moved to South Australia."

"I bet you haven't forgotten."

Cheele gave another chuckle. "Jesus, no. I haven't. But it didn't do too much damage. Four children later. Anyway, it wasn't your fault."

"What do you mean?"

"Ray Grogan set you up, didn't he?"

"You heard that?"

"He told me so himself. I think what surprised him was that you'd gone along with it." He squinted out at the road. "Hey, don't say this is Campbell Town already."

The headlights picked out Federation houses on either side, an antique shop, and an orange telephone kiosk with a light on. Cheele slowed down. "Sorry, but I've got to just drive. The coppers are brutal here. Last time, I got a ticket for doing seventy."

He put on his indicator and moved into the middle of the road and turned right and did not accelerate again until they had left Campbell Town behind them.

"We should make Wellington Point in an hour," he said. "All right with you?"

"That's fine."

Cheele did not speak for a while. They had passed Lake Leake when he cleared his throat again: "I wouldn't want you to take this in the wrong spirit, but when I saw you tonight in the pub I thought: I recognise that fella. That's Piers Dove. But then I said to myself: You've been driving all day, Jack, you're seeing things. Piers Dove wouldn't be in a place like this any more than you would be – not in the normal course of events. Although, as my wife would say: What is normal these days?" He laughed and when Alex said nothing he looked over at him: "I hope, Piers, you're not offended by what I just said."

Alex wondered if he should let it go. It was a comfort that he had not expected, to be called Piers again.

"No, no, far from it, I'm not offended."

"That's good."

So he sat in silence, content to be Piers for just a small while longer, until he saw the streaks of burned rubber and sat up. "You can drop me here."

"Hey, let me take you to your door," Cheele said. He peered out at the road: the blind corner, the tyre marks still black after four months. "Looks like you've had visitors," he murmured, looking for a turning. "Or else someone's been dodging a kangaroo."

"I mean it," Alex said. "Please drop me here. I'd prefer it."

Cheele parked on the grass. He glanced over again at Alex. "You OK, Piers? You don't look so good. I hope you're not still worrying about that incident. It's history. Forget it."

"Yeah, OK, I will," and opened the door and climbed out.

CHAPTER FOUR

MERRIDY WAS NOT AT home.

Alex drank three glasses of water, one after the other, then opened the fridge and made himself an omelette. Out of habit, he looked around for the dog's bowl. Not seeing it, he called out: "Rusty!" – and when nothing moved realised that she must have taken him with her. Afterwards, he ran a bath and lay in it until the water was cold. It unsettled him to stretch out alone in their bed, but sleep quickly overtook him.

He got up earlier than usual and shaved. He pulled out a clean blue shirt and pair of brown corduroy trousers from the chest of drawers, and dressed. Then he went into the kitchen and made a pot of tea and three pieces of toast, and spread Vegemite and marmalade and butter on them. It was not yet seven when he finished his breakfast and grabbed his hat off the dresser and went out to milk the cows, their udders fit to bursting, and to feed the animals that he had neglected.

For the rest of the morning, he rode over the farm. He was keen to make up the four lost days. The barley was showing signs of sooty mould from a big rain. Along the edge of Moulting Lagoon, the black swans had come in for grain and fouled it up a bit. In the afternoon, he sprayed the barley and moved sheep between paddocks. And as it grew dark fired a gas-gun to scare off the swans.

When the telephone rang in the kitchen that night,

448

he dug out a half-bottle of gin that he kept for guests and poured a tumbler.

Half an hour later the telephone rang again. This time he picked it up.

"Alex?"

He sat back. "Merridy."

"Thank God. I was so worried."

"I'm OK."

"Where were you?" She had driven up and down the Avoca road, hoping to find him. At one point she had urged Rusty out of the car. "Go look for Alex," in a fraught and rather hysterical tone so that the dog had barked at her.

"I had to clear my head," he said.

"I tried ringing, you've no idea how many times . . . I couldn't think where you might be."

Her husband did not have many close friends. She had telephoned his agent, Agnes, Jack Fysshe, the Macdonalds. She had even – in her despair – contacted Harry Ford. "What's that? No, no, he's not here."

So when Jason enquired – they were drifting in the *Zemmery Fidd* above the oyster lines – "Has Alex run away?" she had no clear answer.

"I'm not sure," replied Merridy, for whom the tangle of ropes, of small knots that fastened the lanterns was suddenly too much. "I haven't seen him since Monday."

Alex took another swallow of gin. "I'm sorry for leaving like that," he said. "I didn't know where I was going myself."

"I'm the one who is sorry. I'm so sorry, Alex. I should have told you before."

"Like I said, I wanted to clear my head."

"I was milking the cows when suddenly I got this idea that you might have been waiting for me to leave. I thought you'd be happier if I wasn't there."

449

"Probably."

"Alex," she said.

"You've got Rusty?"

"I'll bring him back if you like."

"No, keep him. I bought him for you."

"Alex?"

"Where are you ringing from, anyway?"

"Aunt Doss."

He nodded. "I suppose you'll be there a while?"

"Alex . . ."

"What about Kish? Any news?"

"It's you I love."

"Don't!" and slammed the tumbler on the table, though it was the receiver that he meant to crash down. "I'm sorry, Merridy—" and stood up.

She asked him to hear her out. "Even if you never want to see me again, please listen."

He had spilled gin on the table and it was dripping to the floor. He squeezed the receiver between cheek and shoulder, looking around for a cloth.

"You told me this would happen," her voice was saying, quite hoarse, "and, Alex, it has. Alex, are you there?"

"Yes, I'm here." But he could not see straight. He was thinking: Could it be the gin that's given me this quick fuse? Beefeater had been his father's drink, and he was a novice.

"I've had time to think everything over. I love you, Alex."

"Where do you keep dishcloths?"

"When you first understand something you've not been able to understand for ages – how it all fits together – suddenly everything is obvious . . . What?"

"A dishcloth, where would I get a dishcloth?"

"Third drawer on the left. Alex, did you hear what I just said? You were right. It's happened – as you promised." She sounded elated.

"I've found them. Listen, I'm going to have to go."

When the telephone rang again he did not answer. He mopped up the pool of gin and poured himself another glass and sipped, but did not answer.

He expected her to call again the following night. Before turning in, he picked up the receiver in the kitchen, and then checked the receiver in the living room. Nor did she ring the next night, nor the night after that. He walked up and down. He had forgotten how to live on his own. The house without Merridy, without a dog, without the bottled ships and the wardrobe, with nothing on the walls – no paintings, drawings, samplers – was a place far emptier than the house to which he had returned from England as a young man.

He had his hair cut. He started to read again. He took his rod to the river mouth and fished for flat-head, cooking it with a tin of tomatoes that he found in the larder. But he was lonely for Merridy. He dried his face with her towel and, assaulted by a trace of her perfume, tried in vain to summon her laughter.

FOR SALE: TALBOT'S NEWSLETTER
As a complete operation – including computer, printer, Mita photocopier, Risograph high-speed printer. An ideal occupation for retired or community-concerned persons. Please contact me to discuss what is involved – not much really. Albert Talbot.

One cold evening, he was cleaning his father's shotgun in the laundry room when he heard a car pull up and then yapping.

"Alex?"

They came into the kitchen at the same time.

"Tildy."

He had been back an hour, after an exhausting day's tractoring, plus a quick walk over the pastures for a hare for his supper, and was pleased to see her. He switched off the radio that had become his only company.

"I won't stay long," she said, and he supposed that she needed his vote for something or was going to put pressure on him to stand for the council.

He turned on the tap. "Merridy's not here," soaping the oil from his hands.

"I know. She called me."

"Tildy," she had said, "I have a favour to ask. Could you scout out the ground and go and see Alex? I do worry about him."

"He's the father of your child. Why don't you go?"

"I have to be here. Please. Just go and hug him for me."

So on this wintry night Tildy had driven out to the farm and now stood in her grey coat beside the blackwood table.

She sent her eyes down the corridor. "Hey, is something different?" She had not been for several months. "I know what it is, you've had a clean-out. That's good. They were a bit too old-fashioned for me, those tapestries."

She picked up a glass on the table, sniffed, put it down.

"Did Merridy tell you? I'm starting a book club. I want you both to be members." She started bandying the titles of books.

"Tildy . . ."

"Oh, it doesn't matter. You aren't going to have the time anyway."

His face had closed a little. He felt quite lonely. Was she trying to smoke something out of him? She sounded unnaturally concerned. How you must miss your wife, her face implied. At this special time. But not to worry, Merridy will be back soon from Ulverstone. In the meantime, don't forget to water the garden.

She looked away, at the Welsh dresser. "Did you hear Mr Talbot is selling the store?" for something to say.

"So I saw in the *Newsletter*."

"Everyone's quite upset. My mother-in-law is talking about the end of an era."

"I don't mind who owns the place so long as they look after it."

"Ray's been given the sale."

Alex nodded.

She said: "Knowing Ray, he'll probably want to sub-divide it into mansions or convert it into a Melbourne pensioners' parade."

"Has he got a buyer in mind?" filling the kettle.

"He won't say, but it wouldn't be Ray not to have a developer already lined up."

"She's not Japanese, by any chance?"

Tildy stiffened. "Now why do you think that?"

"I saw him escorting a Japanese woman around Jack Fysshe's property. I thought: Hello, he's trying to sell her farms. That was some months ago."

She crossed her arms. "You don't like my husband, do you? I don't like him much myself."

"No, I don't like Ray a lot. But more than that – and I never quite got over this – he really let this farm go to rack and ruin when it was his to look after."

"Alex, I never knew that!"

"It's not something I like to talk about. I never told Merridy. I'm just hoping to God that Jack doesn't put his fine acres into Ray's hands, that's all."

He switched the kettle on.

She was thinking about what he had said. "But you've

made such a success of it, haven't you? And you have Merridy. And now you're going to have a baby." It might have been Tildy who was having the baby, such a burst of unexpected goodwill did she feel in that moment. Towards him, towards her cousin. All thought of Ray dismissed as she remembered: "Merridy wanted me to hug you for her. I don't mind telling you, Alex, I've often thought of hugging you for myself."

Then, arms outstretched, she was advancing towards him: "Talk to me, Alex, don't go into one of your long silences . . . No, I don't want tea. I want you to talk to me and tell me how happy you are."

And while he had uttered not a word – not one word! – she was moved by his response.

Because what he experienced was an ungovernable wish to put his arms around her and press his cheek against her plump cheek and kiss, out of some tremendous gratitude, the top of her head where she had gathered back her hair to expose a lined, freckled face. Not speaking, just standing in the middle of the kitchen, holding her.

Hair, table, light – all trembled.

Then the fly-screen was squeaking and the door opening with a rush of cold wind and Tildy was leaving.

She wound down the car window and shouted: "I'll tell her you are lovely, Alex. The happiest man in the world, too. Is that what I'll tell her? Get down, Midge, you bastard. You'll scratch the seat."

Merridy ran deep for four days and then on the fifth she called. He was reading beside the fire in the living room when the telephone rang on the little glass-topped table. He picked it up.

"It's me," said her voice. Calm but guarded.

"Yes."

He enquired after Aunt Doss, who had had her hair dyed and looked foxier. He asked Merridy how she was feeling and she replied that she had stopped being sick and added that she was going the following day for an ultrasound scan.

"Tell me how it goes." There was nothing else he could think of to say. He did not really want to hear how it went.

But the following evening he sought her reassurance that the baby was all right. He listened as Merridy told him how Aunt Doss had accompanied her to Dr James. They had sat before a monitor and watched the image of the child.

Dr James had guided Merridy through the body parts: "Nice arch of foot. Spine there is really healthy. Legs look good. That's the ventricle. The cerebellum at the back of the brain is the normal dumb-bell shape. Lips. That black circle there is the stomach." Next to the circle, the heart was beating in flashes. "A very nuclear heart," Dr James said approvingly.

"What did it look like to you?" Alex asked.

The baby – moving within its skirt shape – provoked a stream of disconnected images in Merridy: corn on the cob, frogs' legs, Churchill, a crab, the black-and-white footage of Nagasaki.

"Do you want to know the sex?" she said.

"Not particularly."

"Well, if you change your mind . . ."

"What is it?"

A pause.

"Merridy, tell me."

Another pause. "Boy." She coughed. "A boy." And explained how the midwife had given the game away. "I asked her if you could tell the sex at this stage and she

455

said: 'Oh, yes,' and pointed: 'There's his little penis sticking out.'"

"I thought of him as a boy for some reason," Alex said, unscrewing the cap on the bottle. "What did he look like again?"

"He looked like an old man on his back with a large bald head and his chin tucked in. And, Alex, do you know what his first gesture was? He put his right hand up to his forehead."

Alex could not help but smile. "That's what you do in your sleep."

"Just imagine, Alex. My baby is going to have a very nuclear heart. What do you suppose that means?"

He ran his finger around the lip of the bottle. "I've been thinking," he said.

"Yes?"

He clammed up. But it was not a hostile silence and they both knew it.

So was established a pattern that continued over the days that followed. He only drank gin when they had these telephone calls; the Geneva talks, as he came to think of them. He had bought himself a new bottle and when the telephone rang he poured a tumbler and sat in the living room and sipped. As the gin went down, the warmth rose, but it was not an alcoholic heat. It was something else.

They talked in a way that they had not talked in years, maybe never talked. Merridy started to uncover in him an intimacy, and Alex to renew an old pleasure and sense of possibility. And not really having spoken on the telephone in his life, he now talked himself into closeness. Their nightly conversations were a little shell that both crawled into. Together with Merridy he returned in shy, but increasingly jubilant, steps to their first encounter in the lane behind the school; their honeymoon on Flinders, digging for Killiecrankie diamonds, the film that he had taken her to see in Whitemark, and the low-flying peacock that cracked the windscreen of their hired car. With recovered optimism, they went over and celebrated the work, time, energy that each had invested in the house, the farm, Oblong Oysters. They remembered the rapacity of their bodies.

Distance protected them. He was spared the sight of her belly; it would have been a reality too harsh to see his wife's stomach growing with a baby not his own. On the other hand, when the baby began to kick or had hiccups or Merridy had to go to Dr James for the amniocentesis, he surprised himself with his anxiety.

One evening, getting ready for her call, he was drawing the curtains in the living room when he caught sight of his reflection in the window and teased himself. He had never considered what a dignified cuckold might look like, but now he knew.

Her line was engaged that night. When they spoke the following evening she told him of an emotional conversation with her mother. "I'm trying to make sense of it. She wants to leave the Sanctuary."

"What, and live with Doss?"

"Don't laugh. She plans to move in with an old boyfriend – the man she was engaged to before she met Dad." Randal Twelvetrees had been constrained to get in touch with Mrs Bowman after his father alerted him to the discovery of Hector's remains. The Minister's son explained – in the letter that he wrote from Albany and which was forwarded on by Doss – how he had nursed his wife through a long illness and was now a widower. After speaking with her mother for three hours, Merridy could not tell if she was acting out of a late-flowering need for companionship or out of a long-held guilt, or whether she wanted to repent for Merridy. "All I know is that Randal went to see Mum in the Sanctuary and made this offer. He has a property – she won't tell me where it is, except that it's 'somewhere in Tasmania, somewhere a long way away'. She's already making arrangements to have her stuff moved down there."

It was not long afterwards that Alex reached his decision about Merridy's child. "I'd like to raise him as my own," he told her, and when she started to speak: "I'm not going to ask any questions. I don't want to know. But as far as I'm concerned, this is my child."

Two topics they avoided. The first was the question of her return to Moulting Lagoon Farm. She had left Jason in charge of operations while she stayed with her aunt in Ulverstone. But the oysters were ready to harvest and she had signed a contract.

What Alex did not tell Merridy was that he had taken to going down to the shed. He asked for Jason's discretion: "Let's keep this between ourselves, but I reckon you could do with some assistance."

Wary at first, Jason was grateful to have an extra pair of hands. He taught Alex how to cut out the mesh and repair the lanterns and to tie the special knot that would never let anything go – a knot that Alex knew of old, but he said nothing. While Jason was busy handling and loading the stock, Alex mended buoys. He emptied the lanterns and tipped the oysters into the rotary grader and scrubbed down the keels and deck. And one afternoon, leaning against his ute, paper and pencil in hand, was moved to sketch the *Zemmery Fidd*.

"Why don't you come home?" he said to Merridy one night.

"What?"

He repeated it twice.

"When?"

"What about next week? I've got to go to Launceston for a lamb sale. Come down during that."

"Next week would be good."

"Or is that too soon?"

"No, no, it's not too soon."

"Merridy?"

"Yes."

"I've started preparing," incapable of containing his excitement. In the Talbot's closing-down sale, he had bought a small child's wheelbarrow.

"But, Alex," laughing, then tentative, "you do realise he won't be able to use that for another five years!"

He felt his face grow warm. But he didn't care. It was worth more than he could have anticipated to hear the responsive echo of Merridy's laughter. He treasured it so much that he decided not to tell her about his other surprise, on which he had been working night and day in time for her return.

So Merridy agreed to drive back to Moulting Lagoon Farm the following Tuesday. She felt quite positive. She had passed through the Stations of her Cross. It might not be his child, but Alex would come to love it as his own. Alex loved her and the child in her was the best part of her. And she knew, now, that she loved him. She was certain.

The other topic that was not discussed was Kish.

Merridy, because away from his presence it became easy to forget him. It was almost a convenience to her that Kish had disappeared: she would not have to tell Alex.

Alex, because he needed to forget.

CHAPTER FIVE

HE JUMPED DOWN FROM the cabin and ran off along the main street. Opposite the school was a small wooden bus shelter with a bench. He would catch a couple of hours' sleep, then hitch a ride before the town was up, when the log-trucks started rolling through.

He crawled into the corner and lay on his back, revolving Alex's bottle, turning it slowly in his torn fingers. He brought the glass close to his face, but its contents remained dark to him. Too dark at any rate to divine what it obsessed him to see, though he did not understand why. Frustrated, he tucked the bottle under his head and was falling asleep when he heard a woman's voice.

Instantly alert, he slid from the bench and looked out. Across the road, a man unlocked the door to the school. Standing beside him was Mrs Dove.

A little while later he sat crouched beneath the window. He could hear them on the schoolroom floor. They were not piecing together jigsaws or trying out the alphabet or singing "We are the Vegemites". They were playing doctors and nurses.

Alarmed by the racket, he at one point rose from his hiding place between the rubbish bins and looked down through the glass, down the slope of a desk. The sight snatched his breath. Below him, upside down, Mrs Dove. Her closed eyes running together to form a smile, her breasts whiter than eggs, her mouth a fluttering eye.

And sank noiselessly back.

He had put Alex's bottle on the ground beside him and

he stared into it. He rested his elbows on his knees and sat there staring, until Merridy and the man had finished their ruckus and shut the door behind them and left.

The man, lifting the lid to throw something in, did not notice him squeezed up against the bin.

For a few moments more he remained squatting there, his head drowned in his hands and swollen with brackish thoughts. Then holding the bottle by its neck he struck it with one hard blow on the gravel.

There was the tink of imploding glass and the ship sailed onto the playground.

He gripped the broken bottle. The way he brought its jagged jaw to his face, he might have been about to lacerate his forehead to release his pain and to stab at the blowflies or red-eyed moths or whatever it was that kept swishing about in his skull. Then with a conscious effort he let the bottle drop and looked around for the *Otago*.

The hull adhered to a segment of glass on a strip of withered blue plasticine. He flicked open his knife and fell upon the delicate assemblage – varnished pine, triangles of stiffened cotton, ice-cream sticks – and with the tip of the blade gently levered the penny from its deck.

He had never been able, not properly, to make out the face on the coin, but now he held it up to the moon. A severe young woman glared back at him.

Once he had the penny in his hand, his whole being fastened around it. In the front seat of log-trucks he zigzagged his way south to the Huon and spent a fortnight repairing nets for cherry trees on a farm outside Franklin. He made himself useful: dressed in Mr Dove's jeans and shirt, and wearing Alex's spare pair of spectacles, he cleared the paths of duck crap and took the garbage to the tip and watered the horses

as he had watched Mrs Dove do. At night, he slept in a
room, its walls papered with embossed flax. And for
companionship caught flies. Bluebottles that he attracted
with duck crap into a plastic bag, which he knotted. In his
hand, the bag buzzed like a toy running down and then
stilled to a splutter. He would sit on his mattress and hold
the bag to his ear while he checked his pocket for the coin
that he sometimes produced and stared at through Mr Dove's
glasses, and at other times was content to pinch through
his trouser leg. As if the sound of the flies was telling him
where to go and the penny was courage in his pocket.

In the meantime, while he thought about what he was
going to do, he needed to earn a different currency. Money
that would enable him to lie low until an opportunity came
to leave this freaky island.

In Franklin, he read a notice handwritten in black felt
pen and pinned to a board outside a boatbuilder's yard:
"MAN WITH VAN NEEDS ANOTHER MAN". The
man was a talkative Englishman: fiftyish, small, with a
gold propelling pencil clipped to his T-shirt at the throat.
He had longish thinning hair and a crease about the eyes.
Left some money by his father, he had decided to start a
removals business. That was his explanation.

His van was a white U-haul. In the front, there was a
potted-plant arrangement-tray filled with geraniums that
he watered first thing in the morning. His living accommodation was a bunk-bed in the back, where he slept,
more often than not while listening to the radio,
surrounded by flippers and goggles and oxygen cylinders.
The paraphernalia of a skin-diver.

Next to the bed was an old-fashioned Elsan and a basin
where he washed.

"You can sleep in the bottom bunk," he said to Kish,
who disliked the van immensely.

Eager to get back outside, Kish stepped onto the tow-bar and jumped down.

But something intrigued him about the polished metal ball. "Do you have a caravan?" he asked.

"A caravan? Honestly!" Insulted. "That's for my boat."

Which, he went on to explain, required a complete overhaul. He had put her into the boat yard in Franklin while he earned the money to pay for this.

For ten weeks, Kish lifted bookshelves and refrigerators and once a piano into the van and drove from one corner of the state to another, unloading, sleeping in the back, listening to the man, who was called Joseph Silkleigh, prattle on about the North African coast, where he had spent time frog-diving; or his father who had blamed his mother for everything, like a bad maid; or the girl he had met on a beach south of Perth who had jilted him, after he had parked his van outside her house once too often. Joseph claimed still to be bruised by the rejection. "She's that rare thing" – he said it wistfully – "a woman with a sense of humour."

Joseph's past was a country that he had fled, he suggested, in tatters. "I was the last man out, old soul." But no experience was ever wasted. All would go into his book. The story of Joseph's life. An astonishing story. That he had begun and abandoned countless times, and always for the same reason: he did not have the right title. "But now I do. Now I do." He turned to Kish with an expression of innocent triumph: "I'm going to call it *The Making of Me*."

Kish frowned and then at his lap. "I don't read much," he said.

"You don't talk much either, Knish, if you don't mind my saying."

"It's Kish."

463

Joseph nodded as if he did not believe him. "I'm a sod for names. Jewish, are you?"

"No."

"A *knish* is a dumpling with chopped liver."

"I didn't know."

"I'm telling you it is." Then: "Not Canadian, are you?"

"No." He was worse than the blowflies.

"I know, I know. When you are down, even dogs don't come near you. But just how *did* you get down here, old soul, if you don't mind my asking?"

"A sailing ship."

"A sailing ship, eh? Then you're a man after my own heart, Knish. I *love* ships. Spent most of my life on them, wouldn't be surprised. Yawls, yachts, gin palaces, smacks, hermaphrodite-brigantines, you name it." He rubbed his nose. "Only ship I've yet to sail in is a relationship," and gave a sad laugh, but a laugh nonetheless.

They drove through Geeveston.

"What about you, Knish, do you have a girl?"

They were heading south with a van-load of second-hand books.

"Yes."

"A nice girl, is she?"

"She is nice."

"Musical?"

"I don't think so."

"Well, as long as you're happy, old soul," said Joseph. "Are you happy?"

Kish said nothing. He eyed the object that he had dug out of his hip pocket and said nothing.

"What is it with you, Knish? If you're not fiddling with that ruddy knife of yours, you're flipping old coins. Not gold, is it? Here, let me see. I used to be a bit of a numismatist."

He plucked the coin from Kish's hand and framed it against the steering wheel and studied it.

"Victorian Bun Penny. 1841. Cheapest type of copper. I found one of these once. Worthless, like yours. Found it at the bottom of the sea. You might get eleven dollars for it. Ten, more likely." And handed it back. "Now if it was 1843 you'd be in the money. 1843, then you'd be talking, Knish," and chuckled. "Or maybe, if it was you, you wouldn't."

Kish grabbed at it. "You bastard." His eyes blazed with darkness and he jerked out his hand. In which a knife flashed.

For a millisecond there was an offer of violence to Joseph, who with one hand took the knife off him and said in a fantastically calm way: "We're working together, don't fuck about. It means nothing to me whether you kill me. It's quite late on in my life. But while we're here, wake up. I don't give a bugger why you're on the run. Nonetheless, I quite like you. And while I don't mind sharing the back of the van with you, I don't need to share your criminal and emotional baggage."

He slowed down to let two girls in bikinis with dripping hair cross the road. "I say," he murmured, "they rather appeal to my aqueous humour."

He watched the girls pick their way barefoot along the gravel towards a shack and then turned to Kish.

"There you are, there's your knife. And it wouldn't be the worst thing if you took it and found a sheep that we could cut up and cook."

He put the van into gear and drove on, concentrating on the road.

They had been driving in this way for a while when he threw Kish another look. "You all right, old dumpling? You look like the proverbial grave in which something's been spinning."

465

"I'm OK."

Joseph nodded. "I wonder if—" His sentence broke off, like a pencil pressed too hard. Once more his eyes roved down over Kish's spiky hair, his earring, his spectacles, his oversized white shirt, to the hand that fretted with the coin. "I don't want you to swallow this the wrong way, Knish. But it's struck me on a sudden that we've been sitting here nattering contentedly for the best part of ten weeks, and yet all I know about you is that you're a total orphan who has no idea who his father was or his mother. Absolutely no idea. And that you came to Tasmania under full sail. Oh, and that you have a girl who's not especially musical." Joseph looked back at the road ahead and stared at it in a hurt way. "Now, old soul, I hope you will agree that's not much. I mean, that's not much to show for ten weeks of sharing the same precious space, day in, day out. Not when I've told you all about my life. Know what I'm saying?"

"Why do you have to know anything?" It was almost a hiss.

"Why do I have to know anything?" Joseph repeated slowly. He shook his head. Whatever Kish was, he was not a day at the beach. "Because I'm interested, you oaf. Because it passes the time. Because it's polite. Because I'm a bit of a *uomo universale,* you might say. I mean, what are your interests? I've got my goggles and flippers. Just as you've got your knife and penny. But what do you like doing? That's what I can't work out. What floats your boat, eh?"

Kish leaned back. He slipped the coin into his jeans alongside his knife and glowered. "Don't worry about it."

"Then tell you what. Let's play a game. What do you hate? What sickens you?"

"Fuckwits asking questions."

"Come on. Don't be like that. That's not the point.

What are your favourite words? Mine are elbow, biltong, claret."

"What's biltong?" asked Kish.

"Biltong? You don't know what biltong is?"

"No, I don't know what biltong is."

Joseph smiled. "I'll say one thing, old dumpling. You keep your cards pretty close to that chest of yours. Jeepers, I can't tell if you're happy, if you're angry, if you're out of your fucking ugly tree, or what you are."

At any rate, Kish must have thought about what Joseph had said because all of a sudden he flung out his hand over the tray of geraniums and pointed at a green flag that dangled from the driving mirror.

"What's that?"

"Irish. Everyone loves the Irish."

"You don't sound Irish."

"I didn't want to draw attention to a colonial bastard. But, hey, you're getting the point. You don't get anywhere without asking questions. I mean, nowhere."

Then: "What does it mean, The Long Haul?"

"*What does it mean?*" incredulous. "What a question! What. A. Question." But once Joseph had stopped shaking his head, he confessed in a voice more solemn: "Actually, I'm toying with the idea of a name change. And maybe, Knish, you're the one to help. There are myriads of possibilities, as well you may imagine, but after a lot of aggro – a lot of aggro – I've boiled them down to two."

He paused. Now the moment had arrived to reveal his choices, he seemed strangely vulnerable. "Either DELIVERANCE" – he turned to gauge the reaction – "or BUT IT MOVES." And when Kish still looked blank, explained: "*E pur si muove*. Attributed to Galileo after his recantation, although generally conceded to be apocryphal. So which one takes your fancy, eh?"

They were passing a refrigeration plant on the Huon. Kish looked out of the window at two sailing boats and touched his earring and mumbled something. Whatever it was did not reach Joseph.

"Hey, blabbermouth, don't keep it from Silkleigh. Not when your words are such gold."

Kish turned. He said in a hard voice: "I have so much anger that sometimes it can near kill people."

"Is that so, old soul? Is that so?" And picked his nose. He seemed relieved that the subject had moved on. "I used to be angry like that until I realised it was just frustration coming out the wrong way. Ah, here we are. Dover. Now where do you suppose this bookshop is? I'll just park on the dirt and ask that nice old lady."

For four months, Kish busted his gut doing manual labour. Punishing, healing, galvanising himself. The whole time flipping the severe young woman into the air and catching her and trying to outstare her. Waiting for her to give him some sort of direction. More direction anyway than BRITANNIA REG FID DEF, whoever that was when she was at home.

A conviction took hold that the letters contained a message that would tell him what to do. He tried patiently to work it out, this loop of meaning, but all he felt was desolation. Like when he was going clean for the first time after using heavily. The effort hardly seemed worth it, it was so hard; and what was to be gained? Such a small plus in the middle of such a big mess.

Once or twice he came close to asking Joseph, but always at the last moment he pulled back. This was something that only he and the woman could settle.

There were moments when he hated her long sharp

nose. The ringlets of hair tucked over her ear and gathered into a bun. Sometimes he had the feeling that, like him, the penny was really bad. Most of the time he felt that it was a compass, leading him round in circles, leading him all over the island in his quest for reparation. He still did not know what he ought to do, but he never lost faith that the stern face might one day rouse itself from its coma and fix him in the eye and tell him.

One autumn morning, they were in Gladstone – a tin-mining town in the north-east – to deliver a widow's furniture. He opened the back of the van, waking late after their mutton barbecue, and saw Joseph, legs up on a bench, outside the store in the street where they had parked for the night. He was talking to a bald, red-faced man in wire-framed specs who nervously rolled his gaze over the top of Joseph's knees to Kish.

"Hey, Knish," said Joseph. "This is Mr Beeley."

"Hi."

"I was saying to him I bet this place has a lot of kink."

Mr Beeley gave a frightened laugh.

"I've also been telling him about my book. *The Making of Me*."

Mr Beeley had three large mosquito bites above his brow and his moustache was frosted with ice cream. "Sounds most intriguing," he said charily, and smiled at Kish. "Talking of books," looking from one to the other, "I had a visitor this morning."

"Really?" said Joseph, suddenly not very interested. He tucked his propelling pencil back into his T-shirt and picked up Mr Beeley's newspaper. "What kind of visitor would that be, pray?" as he scanned the front page headline: *EAST COAST SALE SCUPPERED. Plans to develop*

Talbot's General Store at Wellington Point mysteriously fell through yesterday when owner 84-year-old Albert Talbot took the property off the market . . .

"I was just cutting the front lawn when she opened the gate. A nice lady, she'd wanna be on her way to sixty. I thought: Oh dear, oh dear. I said to her, 'Last week, I know I was busy and put you off. But I'm very, very busy today.'"

The sound of rushing air made Joseph raise his eyes. "So who was she?" distracted. He had forgotten to water his geraniums.

"I don't know her name. She lives with Mr Twelvetrees," said Mr Beeley. "But I reckon she's a Jehovah's Witness is what she is."

"How extraordinary," watching the flock of birds move at great speed over the roof of the van.

Kish followed his gaze.

Mr Beeley was not to be distracted.

"Anyhow, she gave me a big thick Bible and said: 'I can help you,' and I said: 'Leave it there.' She said: 'To make sure you know the full gist of what's going on, turn your Bible to Peter, Chapter 1 and you go to Verse 23 here, and that tells you for sure. *Being born again, not of corruptible seed, but of incorruptible, by the word of God, which liveth and abideth for ever.*' Well, I looks at her and I say: 'When you go to the Bible, it's all right up to a point,' and she said: 'What do you mean?' I said: 'Jesus was nailed on the cross and so forth, but if you think it's right to bring Him back, it can't be done.' She said: 'Oh, yes, it can. Where do you think we go when we die?' I said: 'Under the ground.' She said: 'No. God will tell Jesus. He'll instruct him and they'll bring you back to life.' I thought: Oh dear, oh dear. She said: 'If you want to, you can give a donation,' and I said: 'No. You might get a donation next time. But there's a lovely pair of gentlemen over the road. They

470

only arrived last night and I'm sure they'll spare you something. Would you like to see them?'"

"You didn't," murmured Joseph.

"I did, too." Mr Beeley lifted his spectacles and rubbed
an eye and giggled. "I'm surprised she hasn't been 'long
already."

"When was this?" stirring.

"Round twenty minutes ago."

Joseph's eyes scouted the road both ways. "Time we got
going," tossing the newspaper aside and standing up. He
consulted his notebook. "Knish and I have a delivery to
make," he apologised to Mr Beeley. "Hey, Knish! Let's go
and find this Mrs Bowman and give her her furniture."

But Kish was watching the birds. They flew in squab-
bling circles above the roof of the van and settled on it
repeatedly as if the van exerted some sort of pull. He
wiped his cheek with his shirtsleeve and his eyes followed
their short glides, one flat curved wing beating faster than
the other, and the sound of the wind rushing through their
feathers, until they rose from the van and this time circled
upwards into the sky in high-pitched screeches.

"Wonder what they are . . ." Joseph said half to himself.

Until the specks were too tiny to see.

Kish dropped the hand that shielded his eyes. He rucked
up his trousers. Then he went and closed the back of the
U-haul and bolted it. He knew now. He did not know why
he wanted to do it, but he wanted to do it. For the solvency
of his conscience, he had to go back.

CHAPTER SIX

TALBOT'S NEWSLETTER. EDITORIAL
I think I have an old man and a soldier's right to say that
whereas we listen to a great deal of codswallop about the
peaceable intentions of our powerful northern neighbours,
you can take it from me that the nation that laid waste
the New Guinea archipelago, that visited a regime of
terrible brutality upon the genuinely peace-loving natives
of New Britain – well, I saw it all with my own eyes, so
I can say it and to hell with your political correctness – I
would just like to put a marker down for the next gener-
ation. Don't fall asleep, my friends and fellow citizens.
That dragon may rise again. A.T.

On the eve of Merridy's return, Alex walked one last time
through the house and checked that there was nothing
he might have overlooked. He made a bouquet of her
favourite flowers and arranged them in a vase beside the bed:
white hammer-headed stylidium gathered from beneath their
window, red rugosa from down by the beach, pink tubular
correa. He rehung the samplers, back from the framer's and
repaired by a seamstress in Sandy Bay, as well as the cockatoo and her pencil drawing. He stocked the fridge with
meats from the Wursthaus Kitchen in Hobart. And in the
waning light went into the room that he had prepared for
the child.

His eyes passed over the cot, the black felt Tasmanian
devil on the pillow, the red wheelbarrow, the sieve.

472

The room was cold and he noticed that Madasun had left the window open. Beyond Moulting Lagoon, the sea crashed down with a personal note. He stood listening to the waves before he fastened the latch. Then he turned out the light. The luminous paint had dried on the ceiling that he had retouched that morning, and before he closed the door he waited for the lemony stars to begin competing with the darkness gathering outside.

He waited until last to go into Merridy's study.

For more than a week he had taken to coming in here, shutting himself away once he had finished speaking to her, working without pause, at times until daybreak, hunched over an empty gin bottle. Now his work was finished.

Years had passed since Alex had attempted such a project. And yet something troubled him. He suspected that for all the pains he had taken with this particular ship his wife would be disappointed.

He picked up the bottle from her desk and took it into the living room.

Alex added a log to the fire and sat down under the goose-neck reading light.

He was still inspecting his model of the *Zemmery Fidd* when he heard a noise and saw that the door had opened.

A shadow stretched into the room. As if it had detached itself from one of the frames in the corridor: white shirt, his very own jeans, a rustic satchel and a gold earring.

The room lurched and all sorts of emotional somersaults went through Alex's head when he saw the father of his child. This was the one thing that he had not factored into his resolution to look after Merridy's baby. It never had occurred to him, not once. Kish was a wanderer, a blow-in who had blown out. He had gone and was probably on the mainland. He certainly was not going to come back to Moulting Lagoon Farm.

"Kish?" He rubbed his eyes with his knuckles. "Kish?" and put down the bottle. "Is it you? You've changed."

"Mr Dove, you look a little different, too. How are you, Mr Dove?"

"I'm fine. Where have you been?"

"I've been in the north, in the south, all over the island. I've been with Mr Silkleigh."

"You look all bushed," preparing to get up. "You'd better come and have a cup of tea."

"I don't think so."

"Don't worry, I've had the place cleaned."

"And Mrs Dove, how is Mrs Dove?" unfastening his satchel.

Alex sat back. "Mrs Dove is coming back tomorrow. Mrs Dove is going to have a baby."

"A baby? That's wonderful news."

"Do you think so, Kish? I'm happy to hear you say that. Because I very much hope that you didn't come back to claim this baby. It's taken me a long time, but I've made up my mind to adopt the boy and bring him up as my own."

Kish laughed in disbelief. "You've made a mistake there, Mr Dove. I haven't come back to see your wife."

"Then what are you doing here? What do you want?"

Kish walked across the room and opened his satchel and took something very reverently out of it, wrapped in cotton wool, that he laid on the glass-topped table at Alex's elbow.

"What's this?"

As soon as he let it go, Kish felt a rush of lightness to his head. He sat down opposite Alex and crossed his legs and smiled. "Mr Dove, the only reason I came back is to give you this."

Alex looked from Kish to the cotton wool and picked it up. Inside, a tarnished Queen Victoria, the colour of shoe-leather.

He examined the young monarch's face without taking it in. Then returned his gaze to Kish, who was acting as if he had been a good boy. Pleased that he had done what he had to do and now was waiting to be thanked.

Kish said: "I'm here, too, to tell you that I'm very, very sorry for what I did."

Alex stared at this boy whose life he had saved. Who still wore his – Alex's – clothes, for Christ's sake! Who had done everything to destroy his marriage. Who was suspected of murder.

"You come in as if you own the place," he said slowly, "you sit in my wife's chair . . ."

He should have left him to drown.

And remembered when they brought him in, his pheasant flesh all blue and plucked. His guts expelling an awful, bad breath. He had been so touching in his helplessness.

"I suppose you want a reward for returning my own property?"

"A reward? Mr Dove, I'm not after no reward." His brow crinkled at Alex's misjudgement.

Alex looked again at the copper penny. Competing in his head, treacherous thoughts about Kish – and also a bewildered delight at this tribute or penance. In a very extraordinary way, he was grateful to see Kish. His re-appearance rounded the whole thing out.

He put down the coin and it rolled off the edge of the table, onto the possum rug.

Kish stared at it with dismay; Alex impassively, without seeing it.

"I thought you'd be missing it," muttered Kish.

"I don't give a damn about the penny," in a cracked voice. "The penny I care about is in my wife's belly."

Kish frowned.

"That's right," Alex said. "Which you put there."

"Me?" his mouth falling open.

There was a trace even of sadness in Kish's eyes, carried up by the reflected firelight to a dark and private place from which he looked back at Alex. As if he did not know what Alex meant at all.

When Alex noticed his baffled expression, he thought: God help us, will our child be as half-witted?

"Kish, I saw you," and brought his chin forward. "I saw you kiss her," harping on it. "Snogging like rabbits in the house that night we came back."

Kish stiffened at the injustice of the accusation. "Look, Mr Dove . . ."

Alex held the bottle tighter. He thought: It has taken me this long, but I have got over my qualms, and now I know I can live with the idea it's going to be all right.

But he could not help it. He felt his resentment unloading. He looked across at Kish who was, before he set another child in train, in a funny way the child that Alex and Merridy had never had. "And why smash all my ships, for God's sake? My father's ships."

Kish uncrossed his legs and leaned back, emptying a pocket. "I guess I've done a lot of things that I shouldn't have done, Mr Dove, but I'm hoping this makes up for it."

All at once, seeing the wad of dollars, a fierce anger developed in Alex. "I don't want your money, Kish. You'd be better backing your future rather than mine. On the other hand, I would like to know why you rampaged through my house destroying everything."

"I was scared," Kish said, and his eyes jittered. He was

476

agitated now. By Mr Dove's behaviour. By the memory of what had happened in the corridor. He had never been scared like that, not even as the *Buffalo* broke up around him. "Mrs Dove, she upset me. She was like a ghost or something."

"Pah! You were the ghost."

Kish stood up and placed the money on the table. "Look here, Mr Dove, I came to say I'm sorry for what I did. If you won't take this, then I'm not sure what I can do. But I'm off."

"No, you're not." Alex leaped from his chair – and the bottle that was in his lap.

He caught up with Kish at the door. Skinny in the over-sized trousers and the firelight dancing on the buttons of his shirt. What was it about such a man that he did not have?

"I save you from the sea. I take you in, dress you, feed you. And you fuck my wife." He shoved him against the wall. He sounded pathetic to himself, so self-pitying.

Kish squirmed out of his grasp. A ruthless look dulled his face and his right arm flexed back. "Don't, Mr Dove."

Be careful, Alex! warned the cockatoo above the fire-place, speaking in Merridy's voice.

As soon as his eyes saw the knife, Alex knew that his next step would determine the rest of his life. He knew this with a clarity that he had not felt since coming face to face with Merridy behind the school.

A log slithered in the grate and untrapped flames glinted on oiled steel. Here, in this room where he remembered two Scrabble players pondering their next word, Alex was on his own. He had outlived both his parents. But over the past few days the prospect of a happiness that they were denied had begun to stretch ahead of him in a precarious but tantalising vista. Blocked suddenly by Kish.

Who started to laugh. His laughter was blended with pity, and the sharp teeth of it prowled closer. "I didn't want to tell you" – his hand sawed back and forth, he could have been carving an ice-cream stick for a brigantine – "I didn't want to tell you, Mr Dove." What he had heard. What he had seen. They were as close to him as . . . as that bird over there, and he looked out of those isolated eyes in which he saw her lying on the classroom floor, the man on top, her legs around his back, two animals.

"I could have had her. I might have done . . ."

Don't listen to him, Alex, the bird entreated. It's you I love. Not Kish, not anyone else. You – Piers Alexander Dove.

Alex must have taken a step forward because he tripped over the bottle, but recovered his balance. He could hear a child's voice and Merridy speaking. She was standing in her garden that she had sculpted from the dunes, and by her side there was a boy. She brushed a leaf against his uptilted face, and Alex saw that the boy looked like him at that age. "Lemon balm," she was explaining. "It gladdens the heart and makes a beautiful tea. Here, give me your hand." She broke off a frond of bracken and cracked it open and rubbed the creamy stem on his wrist – "to protect you against jack-jumper ants". She bent down and nipped a stalk that she had spied in the rhubarb. "Spurge. Now you wash your hands after touching that. There's a white sap under the leaves. Get it in your eye, you end up going blind." And taking him by the wrist led the way deeper into her garden.

A different voice said threateningly: "I warn you, one more step . . ."

Alex hesitated. She had disappeared behind the dune – it was where they had made love – but he could hear her talking, in a voice of such kindness that he was willing to sacrifice his last breath in order to catch what she was saying. "With tomatoes, you give them a big scare. You put them in bad soil and they think they'll have to seed or die, and then you pamper them like anything."

Fingers tightened on the silver handle. "Don't!"

At the sight of the blade, a rage balled up inside Alex to think of everything that he risked losing.

He rammed his knee into Kish's groin.

Kish screamed, dropping the knife.

Alex snatched it up. And kneed him again, putting into his savage kick all the strength that he had saved up since childhood.

A table fell, and a glass and lamp – that stayed on, but spilling light elsewhere.

Smell of gin and burning peppermint gum and fire-light flickering on Kish's excruciated face. He was on his knees, burrowing and gasping for breath, his speech blurred like a prayer that he mumbled. "Why did you have to do that? Why?" In a bright red voice, he said: "I brought you your coin back. I thought you'd be pleased."

Alex pressed the blade to his throat and sharply tugged back his head in the position of a wether selected for a mutton roast. If hate had permitted, he would have gouged out those eyes that stared back at him through his own spectacles.

"Listen carefully. Before you went away very suddenly that night, I had made up my mind that I wanted you to be here for a long time, that you could stay here, that you could live with us and we could adopt you, and perhaps give you a home you'd never had before. Don't interrupt – because what I have to say to you is very tough. I want you to go now. And I don't want you ever to come back, because Mrs Dove is returning tomorrow and it would upset her to see you. And now what's happened has happened, it upsets me to see you here. I will repeat this one last time. It did take a while for me to accept, but I have decided to bring this baby up as my own. Have you got that, Kish? My own. Or is there something you wish to say?"

There was. And he was all set to say it, too, once he had got his breath back. He sucked in another quart of air and opened his mouth to speak.

And felt a coppery finger on his lips, shushing him.

He stared back at Alex with a glassy concentrated eye in which all the sea in the bay seemed suddenly to have collected. Because he was not seeing Alex. Vivid images flared inside his head. Birds flying. Oysters spawning. Dunes of sand. A sudden wind was streaming them one into the other, and he had the sensation that he himself was melting into the mix, part of an infinite and dazzling whiteness. The tinnitus buzzing and twittering died away and there was a great silence at his core. A fathering silence in which it dawned on Kish that it was not only the penny that he had to give back to Alex.

Those words that haloed the woman. He thought, then, that he understood. She was whispering it into his head.

So instead of saying, as he had been about to: "Your child is nothing to do with me, there's no way in the world it could have been mine," and revealing what he had witnessed through the schoolroom window, he stifled the denial that had been forming in his throat and stood awkwardly up.

"You know what, Mr Dove, the man who dropped me off here called me Blabbermouth. Actually, he's going to collect me at 10 p.m. He had to do something and he dropped me and we're going on. But before I go, I would

480

like to say this. Whatever you saw, it's not what you think. Nothing happened between me and Mrs Dove. Absolutely nothing. It's you she loves. It's yours, the baby. Whoever else's could it be? It is yours."

CHAPTER SEVEN

IN THE GOLDEN HOUR of dawn, when sails come out of the horizon, Alex launched the *Zemmery Fidd* into the river.

The young oysters that he had fed into the rotary grader were repacked and loaded, ready to be returned to the sea, and though, strictly speaking, another person ought to have been on board to assist, Jason's girlfriend had arrived the previous afternoon and Alex saw no reason to disturb them.

There was a man sitting at the end of the jetty, fishing. He watched Alex start up the engines and bring the boat alongside. He had longish thinning hair and a white T-shirt.

Alex tied up, stepped onto the jetty.

"Wonderful to see so many oysters," said the man, as if he had been waiting for him.

"They're my wife's," recognising an English accent. He looked back at the lanterns on deck, each tray bulging with small shocked oysters, and felt a renewed pride in Merridy's achievement. "She's the oyster-grower."

The man wrote something down in a lined notebook. Beside him, a fish flapped in a bucket.

"Guess how I caught that. Go on. Guess."

The fish was flat and grey, with orange spots.

"I don't know," said Alex. He saw that the jetty was marked around like the fish with circles of orange lichen.

The man pointed his pencil at a large Pacific gull standing on the jetty. The gull was staring into the sun.

"That bird dropped it, so I took it off him. I think it's a flounder. It was too big for him."

Alarmed at the man's propelling pencil, the gull shook open its wings and flew off low over the shore, where a white van was parked.

"Catch you later," said Alex, straightening, and went to drive the tractor up from the water's edge to the shed.

When he came back, the man was stripping in his line, preparing to leave.

"I've left some mussels in the water if you want live bait."

"Thanks, mate," Alex said, casting off the rope. "I'm not fishing today."

CHAPTER EIGHT

IN THE EARLY AFTERNOON, Merridy's red Toyota scrunched to a halt at the top of the drive.

The door on the driver's side opened and Rusty jumped out and scampered onto the lawn to pee.

Alex watched his wife push herself from the car. He breathed out "Whoa!" at the size of her belly. She looked round, almost comical, and his heart swelled. It pressed with a sharp pain against his ribs, the fullness of his love for her and his tremendous need to protect their child, whatever it took.

She turned and saw him at the kitchen window and gave a small nervous wave. He lifted his hand, as when he had dropped the coin overboard, and then the knife, and observed them spinning towards the ocean floor, the darkness of seaweed and sand and shifting tides, and felt his anger purged. He remembered the lanterns like bodies floating. And how the sea that had delivered him to them, began to roughen, to whiten and toss like something alive.

He opened the fly-screen and ran to embrace her.

ACKNOWLEDGEMENTS

THIS IS A WORK of fiction and none of the characters are drawn from anyone in life. The town of Wellington Point does not exist any more than does Moulting Lagoon Farm or the Bilgola Mission. Nonetheless, I would like to thank the Melrose family, in particular Ian and Cass, for their unflagging goodwill and patience in educating me about oysters; John and Jo Fenn-Smith and Margaret Ann Oldmeadow, for details of farming life on Tasmania's east coast; Murray Bail for his memories of Methodist dances; Jane Devenish-Meares for her forensic expertise; Michael Stutchbury, Adrian Caesar and Rachael Rose for comments on the text. I am grateful to the late Alan Gow for sharing his experiences as a coast-watcher in New Britain. I would like also to thank Niko Hansen, Jenni Burdon, David Scarborough, David Vigar, Dominic Turner, Jon Johnson and, as always, Gillian Johnson; and lastly my editor, Christopher MacLehose, for two decades of friendship, encouragement and support.

The stanza by A. D. Hope is from "Ascent into Hell", written in 1943–44 and published in *The Wandering Islands* (Edwards and Shaw, 1955), reproduced by arrangement with the licensor, The Estate of AD Hope c/- Curtis Brown (Aust) Pty Ltd.

The lines about black swans are taken from Chapter VI of *My Home in Tasmania*, by Louisa Meredith (reprinted by Sullivan's Cove, Hobart, 1979).

The poem "What do you see, nurse?" is adapted from "A Crabby Old Woman", by an anonymous Scottish woman, that first appeared in the Christmas edition of the *News Magazine of the North Ireland Association for Mental Health*.

The lines of Kenneth Slessor's poem "Beach Burial" are taken from *Kenneth Slessor: poetry, essays, war despatches, journalism, autobiographical material and letters*, edited by D. Haskell (University of Queensland Press, St Lucia, 1991), reproduced courtesy of Paul Slessor.

I would also like to pay tribute to *A Farm at the World's End*, by Thomas Dunbabin (Hobart, 1954) and *The East Coasters*, by Lois Nyman (Launceston, 1990).